To Heather and Andy,
who've only just begun the journey
toward your happily-ever-after.
May you always travel it side by side and hand in hand.

Praise for *Gaining Visibility*

"Cross *How Stella Got Her Groove Back* with *Under the Tuscan Sun,* and you've got *Gaining Visibility,* a novel that is at times beautiful, at times heartbreaking, and ultimately uplifting. Pour a Chianti and savor the story of how Julia found her place in the sun."

—Wendy Webb

"*Gaining Visibility* is a moving tale of reawakening, as Julia transcends the traumas from her past to embrace the exciting possibilities life has laid before her."

—Barbara Longley, bestselling author of the Love from the Heartland series

"A beautiful story, eloquently written and full of heart. Pamela's best book yet."

—Kimberly Lang

"Pamela Hearon brings a new and powerful voice to women's fiction with her poignant story of rebuilding life after breast cancer and divorce. From page one, the reader is drawn into a passionate journey that doesn't let up until the emotionally satisfying final page. Hearon's ability to blend substance and texture with moments of humor makes this one delicious read."

—Cynthia D'Alba

Gaining
Visibility

Pamela Hearon

KENSINGTON BOOKS
www.kensingtonbooks.com

KENSINGTON BOOKS are published by

Kensington Publishing Corp.
119 West 40th Street
New York, NY 10018

All Kensington titles, imprints, and distributed lines are available at special quantity discounts for bulk purchases for sales promotion, premiums, fund-raising, educational, or institutional use.

Special book excerpts or customized printings can also be created to fit specific needs. For details, write or phone the office of the Kensington Sales Manager: Kensington Publishing Corp., 119 West 40th Street, New York, NY 10018. Attn. Sales Department. Phone: 1-800-221-2647.

Kensington and the K logo Reg. U.S. Pat. & TM Off.

eISBN-13: 978-1-4967-0429-0
eISBN-10: 1-4967-0429-0
First Kensington Electronic Edition: October 2016

ISBN-13: 978-1-4967-0428-3
ISBN-10: 1-4967-0428-2
First Kensington Trade Paperback Printing: October 2016

10 9 8 7 6 5 4 3 2 1

Printed in the United States of America

ACKNOWLEDGMENTS

Although writing this book has been an extremely personal journey for me, there have been far too many companions along the way for me to ever feel alone. I'd like to recognize a few.

First and foremost, the Pink Warriors—those who have fought the battle against breast cancer, those who are currently fighting, and those who have been touched by the disease through someone they care for. Be strong. Stay courageous. Keep the faith, and never give up hope. A cure is out there.

My fabulous agent, Jennifer Weltz of the Jean V. Naggar Literary Agency, whose keen vision recognized the potential for this book, even in its earliest stages. Thanks for making me stretch on tiptoe until I could see it, too.

My amazing editor, Esi Sogah, who knew exactly what the story needed and set me on the correct path to find it. I couldn't have found my way without your guidance.

Kensington Publishing, a publishing house that feels like family. Thanks for the warm welcome and the wonderful support.

My longtime critique partner and friend, Kimberly Lang, who has seen this book through more rewrites than she could've ever imagined—and somehow loved them all.

My critique partners at WriteRomance: Sandra Jones, Angela Campbell, and Maggie Van Well. You all have extraordinary, yet different, critiquing skills—and I get the benefit of them all.

My precious, loving, and supportive husband, Dick, who stood valiantly beside me through every second of the battle . . . and who never makes me feel invisible.

CHAPTER 1

She was invisible.

She'd first noticed that she was fading from view four years ago, about the same time she'd noticed the first gray hairs. The signs were subtle. No heads turning as she walked through the gym. No catcalls or whistles at construction sites. No compliments from then-husband Frank when they got gussied up for some formal affair. Alarms should probably have gone off more frantically in her head, but the changes were so gradual they remained inconspicuous and certainly nonthreatening.

And the gray was easily covered.

But the phenomenon had increased exponentially in an equation of Einsteinian proportion two years ago. $E = mc^2$ plus total loss of breasts equaled total loss of visibility.

Scientific equations could prove how the laws of nature literally make the world go round; no equation could show why her world had been thrown into a tailspin she was still trying to gain control of.

Looking back, it seemed more like a combination of science and magic than science alone. Five hours of surgery and—poof! She'd vanished . . . at least to the male half of the world's population.

Which is why it came as no surprise to Julia Berkwith that, at that exact moment, it wasn't one of the male doctors working on her but rather a female nurse who asked the question.

"You doing okay?"

"Fine," Julia answered, although she wasn't. The next item on her self-improvement list was to quit saying she was fine when she wasn't.

Lying flat on her back with her arms stretched out as wide as possible gave the doctors behind the white curtain of sheets plenty of room to work, but they seemed to have forgotten there was a beating heart and strained muscles below the mounds of silicone sacs.

During preparation, when they'd asked if she wanted her arms restrained, she'd promised she could keep them still without the bands. That had been over an hour ago when the surgery was ahead of her and exciting. Now, retaliating because of their awkward position, both arms were snoozing but sending telepathic messages to the muscles in her back and shoulders, demanding they redouble their efforts to bring pain in memory of their sleeping comrades. Adding to her discomfort, the temperature in the OR had been set to *morgue,* which worried her more than a little.

A white sheet draped from the overhead rod fell to below her chin, blocking off her view and allowing her no audience participation to her own procedure. The sheet started to sag, and now folds gathered in her mouth and nose region. In a normal setting, she would push them out of the way with a flick of the fingers, but she'd promised not to move her arms, so she blew puffs of air at them when suffocation seemed imminent.

An angel of mercy appeared at her head and gave the sheet a quick flick, sending the material away. The ensuing gust of cold air filled Julia's nostrils with the antiseptic scent she'd grown used to over the past two years.

"They look great." The young woman's smile was reassuring, even viewed upside down. "How long since your mastectomy?"

"Two years." The buzzing started again along with the odd vibration that seemed detached, though Julia knew it was occurring to her body. "Are they tattooing again?"

The nurse nodded. "They're finishing the second areola. It won't be too much longer."

The conversation diverted Julia's attention from her phantom arms and the frosty operating room. "I never realized how much design work went into building breasts," she said. "First-stage saline sacs. Injecting solution every two weeks to stretch the skin. Implant surgery. And now this. I could've had a house built in this length of time."

Her companion pulled up a stool and perched beside Julia's head. "Can you talk about it? The cancer, I mean. I know some people don't like to."

Julia shook her head as much as she dared, unwilling to risk jiggling anything that might make the doctors miss and result in a third areola. "I don't mind. I've been told talking about it is therapeutic. Is there something you'd like to know?"

The strange vantage point gave her a clear view of the woman's neck muscles, and Julia watched them tighten.

Talking about cancer wasn't a mission she would've chosen, nor was it one she totally accepted. But the subject was frightening to women, so guilt gnawed at her if she didn't answer questions when they asked.

"Did you have chemo?"

There it was—the nearly imperceptible cringe on the last word. Julia had learned to watch for it. Fear of chemo was greater than fear of cancer for many.

"No, I'm one of the fortunate ones." The badge of guilt she wore pricked her. She'd gotten off easy when others suffered so much. "We caught it early, so no chemo or radiation, and no hair loss. I only lost my breasts." She never added *and my husband,* though she always thought it, and ignored the tendril of pain that accompanied the silent admission.

"Well, the reconstruction looks fantastic." The nurse gave a tug on the cloth shower cap working its way down past Julia's eyebrows. "How do they feel?"

Julia stifled the shrug that would've moved her arms. "Honestly? Like two aliens have taken up residence in my chest." Her companion grinned. "I have no sensation on the outside. No feeling because of the nerves they cut. Today's procedure could've been done without the numbing shots, I think." The buzzing stopped, and Julia noted pressure like she was being wiped down. A stronger medicinal scent invaded the area between her and the sheet.

"Sometimes nerves regenerate, though, so don't give up on that yet."

Two years and not even a twinge. Regeneration wasn't going to happen. But nobody touched them anyway, so fretting about it seemed silly.

The nurse started to get up, then hesitated. "I have a biopsy scheduled for Friday." Her bottom lip, which had curved up earlier, now had teeth dug into it, which still couldn't control the tremble.

If her arms had been free, Julia would've pulled the new member of the sisterhood into a hug. As it was, she could only embrace her with words. "You're doing the right thing, staying on top of it. Early detection's the key. We didn't even know it was in my left breast, too, until the post-op report came back."

The young woman's eyes widened. "You were brave, going with the bilateral when you didn't know for sure."

"No, honey, I was terrified, so don't try to make me into a hero. I just didn't want to live in fear the rest of my life."

The woman's chest rose and fell with what Julia hoped was a steadier breath as she tilted her head toward the sheet. "Sounds like they're getting finished. You've done great." She patted Julia's cheek before sliding off the stool and scurrying away to take care of some post-op business.

Finished. Fabulous word, that.

Julia's fingers curled into triumphant fists. She couldn't clap her hands, but she hadn't promised not to move her feet. Gleefully, she smacked her big toes together in applause.

As the doctors completed their work, she turned up the volume on the *Fond Memories* playlist in her mind. Listening to the music had become so habitual, she no longer needed a device—simply switched it on and off at will.

She pressed the rewind button until she was once again in the backseat of her parents' powder blue convertible, racing down the highway on a summer night. A hot wind slapped her cheeks while a gazillion stars danced in her view, and her voice blended with her mom's and dad's and The Crew-Cuts on the cassette player in a rousing rendition of "Sh-Boom."

Three repeat plays and the doctors were done.

An hour later, she stepped into the sunlight with the playlist *Survivor* running through her head along with a new mantra:

Invisible maybe, but not dying.

For the first time since being diagnosed, after five million tears, four panic attacks, three surgeries, two years, and one divorce, Julia left the hospital with her designer breasts and her head held high . . . in that order.

"Hold on a second, sweetie. Mosquitoes are eating me alive."

Julia lit the citronella candle, hoping it would keep away the pests long enough to finish the telephone conversation with Melissa without having to move inside. The temperature on the deck was balmy and perfect, but the pesky insects seemed more plentiful than usual for western Kentucky in late May.

"You ought to see them up here, Mom. They're like the size of bats."

"I've heard Alaska grows them big, but that's sort of an advantage, isn't it?" Julia pulled the phone away from her ear long enough to smash one of the creatures who'd chosen her right pinkie for his dining option. "They can't sneak up on you." Wondering if perhaps the mosquitoes were coming up through the cracks between the wooden slats of the decking, she set the candle down by her feet. "Anyway . . . where was I?"

"Your tats, which, I might add, is totally weird for me to say."

That brought a chuckle. "I'll bet." Julia waved her hand to direct the smoke from the candle toward her legs. "So, no, like I was saying, the tattooing didn't hurt at all. I could feel vibration but no pain."

Her daughter's snort was draped in sarcasm. "Wish I could say that. The one on my lower back wasn't too bad—"

"You mean the freedom banner you rushed out to get the day after your dad and I left you at college?"

"Yeah, that one." A little sheepishness accompanied the tone, but Julia could still hear the smile that hung on the fringes. "It wasn't bad at all, but the one on my ankle—*ghah!* Halfway through, I seriously considered stopping him. But I figured it would look stupid to have a charm bracelet that only went part of the way around."

"Well, it is pretty." Julia admitted that only grudgingly. "But two's enough, don't you think?"

"Yes, Mom. Two's enough. Or it was until today." The laugh that came over the line was throaty and mature, reminding Julia that her precious daughter was an adult now—all grown up and living three time zones away. "Since you have two, I may have to get another one. Can't be bested on tats by my mom."

"To the world, you'll always be ahead by two because nobody but me will ever see mine."

"You don't know that." Before Julia could wonder if her child was making commentary about her nonexistent sex life, Melissa added, "The doctor might want to use photos of you on his Web site. You know . . . to show how good he is."

"I can't see that happening." Julia cringed at the thought of her scars bared to the world. Frank's reaction to them still haunted her.

"Well, you never know."

A long, uncharacteristic pause ensued, and Julia kept quiet . . . waiting. Conversation came easily between them, so pauses were signals. Whatever was on her daughter's tongue right then bore some weight.

A sigh. Julia braced herself.

"Dad came for a visit last week."

The apologetic tone took a swipe at Julia's gut. She and Frank worked hard to keep their daughter from feeling that she had to take sides. Julia forced a smile onto her lips, hoping it would give a lift to her voice—or, at least, take the bite out of it. "Was it a surprise? I didn't know he was planning a visit."

"We'd talked about *him* coming, but, yeah, there was a surprise." Another weighty pause. "He brought Dawn with him."

"Oh." Julia swallowed the retort that appeared on her tongue—the one that would confirm Frank's insensitivity. It left a bitter trail going down. "Was that . . . okay . . . with you, I mean?"

"It was okay." Julia sensed the shrug that accompanied the answer. "He looked good. Brown as a biscuit. And I could tell he's been working out."

"Good for him." A shallow answer, but it would suffice.

Another pause and then Melissa changed the subject, obviously not wanting to discuss her dad and his young girlfriend, which was fine with Julia. Preferable, even. "I went ahead and accepted that three-year offer, by the way."

Julia's breath left her in a rush. *Three years.* She tilted the phone up so Melissa wouldn't hear the shocked gasp. "You did? That . . . that was quick. You were still just considering it the last time we talked."

"Yeah, I know. But Michael's got some cool stuff in the works, and Dad thought it sounded like a good deal, so I decided to grab it before somebody else did."

The excitement in her daughter's voice caused a tug-of-war in Julia's conscience. She wanted Melissa to be happy—wanted her to be confident in her decision making—hoped the impetuous decision to follow Michael into the wild was the right one.

But committing to three years?

The nagging fear she was too far away to care for her daughter's broken heart should the relationship go south never completely went away.

The remainder of their time was taken up with Melissa's ongoing saga of life in Alaska with Michael, and Julia's recently added details about her upcoming trip to Italy in July.

By the time the conversation ended and Julia sat alone with only the mosquitoes for company, the Far North seemed more familiar and real to her than ever . . . and farther from Paducah, Kentucky, than she could've ever imagined.

CHAPTER 2

The following day, Julia sauntered into Room 187 at the Manor Hill Convalescent Center bearing a bouquet of sunflowers in one hand and a box of Godiva chocolates in the other. "I have nipples!" she announced.

At eighty-three, Hettie Berkwith still cut a fetching image in her pink silk gown with her silver braid of hair lying sleekly over one shoulder. "So do I," she countered. "And I'd show them to you, but at present, they're tucked snugly between my knees." The stroke, which paralyzed the left side of Hettie's body, might've made her grin one-sided, but it hadn't slowed the speed of her one-liners.

Julia laughed and gave her mother-in-law's cheek a peck before presenting her with the chocolates and arranging the flowers in the vase that always awaited them on Thursday.

"So, do I get to see them?" Hettie already had the cellophane off the box and sat poised to pounce on the foil-wrapped dark chocolate medallion.

Julia set the flowers on the bedside table and eased into the La-Z-Boy. "Not today. The bandages don't come off for a few days, and then I have to keep them protected for a couple of weeks."

Hettie cocked an eyebrow. "So that would mean no heavy sucking."

"Not even if there were someone who wanted to." Julia returned the look with a cocked brow of her own.

Hettie drew a long, dramatic breath. "Man, that just sucks." She popped the medallion into her mouth and replaced the lid on the box. "So, what other news you got? Heard anything from my son, the prick?"

Julia had grown so used to Hettie's "term of endearment" for Frank, it no longer fazed her. "Sort of." She pulled the handle to raise the footrest a notch and tilted the recliner back a bit. "I talked to Melissa last night. She said he and his new friend Dawn flew up to see her for a few days. Apparently he looked tanned and fit." Julia noted that whereas talking about Frank used to stir her anger, now it mostly made her tired. She stifled a yawn.

"Tan and fit, eh? I'd like to tan him. Guess that's what Hawaii does for you."

This was a day for celebration, not one to dwell on her ex, so Julia eased the conversation in a different direction. "Melissa and Alaska seem to be a good fit. She took that three-year offer they gave her." She'd advised Melissa against the move—losing her "little girl" to adulthood, a man, and Alaska in one fell swoop was enough to make any mother retaliate. But talking to Melissa last night had loosened the hounds of contrition, and they were nipping at her heart. "I was wrong, trying to talk her out of going," she admitted, more to herself than to Hettie. "But thank heavens she knew her own mind and didn't listen to me. Following Michael to Alaska was the right choice for her."

If she repeated it often enough, maybe it would stick.

"Doesn't anybody want to stay at home anymore?" Hettie grunted as she started to work on the box lid again. Julia watched the struggle but knew better than to offer help. If Hettie needed it, which she seldom did, she'd ask. "My son, the prick, in Hawaii. My granddaughter up in the Alaskan wilderness. You traipsing off to Italy." She shook her head and drowned her disgust in a caramel cream.

"That's still two months away, and I'll only be gone three weeks. Then I'll be back home to stay." They'd been over this all before, but this was the first time Hettie had acted the least bit upset about the Italy trip. Her mother-in-law was out of sorts about something.

She wagged her finger in Julia's direction. "Just be sure to stock me up on chocolates before you go."

"I will even splurge on the large box of truffles if that's what it takes to keep you happy while I'm—"

"Good afternoon. Mrs. Berkwith, is it?"

A man Julia had never seen before strolled into the room like he owned the place. Hand extended, he stepped closer to her mother-in-law's bed as Julia brought the recliner to the upright position, quickly taking note of the salt-and-pepper hair framing dark eyebrows and eyes that looked like drops from the Caribbean had found their way to Kentucky. She did a quick check of his hand. No ring.

"I'm Joe Proctor, the new administrator." His voice was like a toasted marshmallow—warm crust surrounding a tender center— and Julia's mouth watered at the sound. "I'm making my way around, trying to meet everyone this afternoon." His eyes bounced from Hettie to her, then back to Hettie without so much as a pause. *Invisibility at work.* She sighed mentally and again eased the recliner back.

"Nice to meet you, Joe." Hettie gestured toward Julia. "This is Julia, my daughter by marriage."

"Glad to meet you." He glanced and nodded cordially, but immediately shifted his eyes back to Hettie. "Mrs. Berkwith, if there's ever anything I can do—"

"She was married to my son, who's a prick." Hettie continued her introduction. "But they're divorced now."

Joe Proctor's eyes widened ever so slightly at what must have been surprising language coming from one of the residents, but he recouped quickly and smiled. "Well, I'm sorry to hear that. But if there's ever anything—"

"She got new nipples yesterday. So, are you married, Joe?"

Maybe invisibility wasn't as bad as she originally thought, Julia decided as she looked around for a hole to slither into. With any luck this guy would totally forget what she looked like three minutes after he left this room. Which happened quickly.

A shake of his head and a rapid "Congratulations" shot in Julia's direction, then Joe Proctor beat it out of Hettie's room as fast as his long legs could carry him.

Julia lolled her head against the corduroy back of the chair and groaned. "Hettie, why would you say that?"

"Because I can get by with it." Hettie set the box of chocolates off her lap. "Life's too short to mince words."

An odd, gravelly texture to the ancient voice made Julia sit up again. "What's up with you today?" She pushed out of the recliner, mindful of her stitches, and cleared a spot to sit on the side of the bed.

Hettie's tone flattened like a deflated balloon. "Thelma from across the hall passed away during the night."

"Oh, Hettie." Julia's throat tightened around the words. "I'm so sorry. I know how fond you were of her. You were good company for each other." She laid her hand on top of Hettie's cold one in a futile attempt to transfer some life and emotion into a soul being weathered away by loss.

But her mother-in-law's eyes were clear, and no tears clouded either them or her voice when she spoke. "Yeah, well, life goes on. People pass in and out and through our lives. It's the ones who stay and visit who leave their mark." She squeezed Julia's hand with a strength that belied her age.

Julia wished with all her heart she could get Hettie out of this place and take her home to live. But her own home—the one she and Frank had shared—had too many levels and no full bath downstairs. And Hettie's house was built before handicap accessibility was even a term. Not a single door was wide enough for a wheelchair to pass through. Realizing that going home was never going to be an option, Hettie had sold all of the big pieces of furniture. The old, stately home with the shady corner lot now sat shuttered and empty.

Julia rarely drove by anymore. The good memories were too overshadowed by the sad.

"Tell you what." Julia patted Hettie's hand, trying to conjure enough enthusiasm to raise both their spirits. "It's a gorgeous day, and the peonies have started to bloom. Whatcha say we go for a walk?"

Hettie's eyes flashed with appreciation, and she started kicking the covers off using her good leg. "I can't go strutting my stuff in my gowntail. We'll have half the men here chasing after me." She eased her right leg off the edge of the bed and reached over to grab under the knee of her left one.

"Be careful." Julia took a small step back to give her room but stayed close enough to help.

"Quit hovering," Hettie snapped, and pointed toward the closet. "Grab my turquoise housedress, will you?"

Julia found the duster that buttoned up the front while her mother-in-law struggled to a sitting position on the side of the bed, panting from the exertion. She didn't protest when Julia took over the job of getting her out of her nightclothes and fully dressed. They'd moved her from the bed to the wheelchair and back often enough to know what worked and what didn't.

"Got this down to a science, don't we?" Hettie gave a loud grunt as she settled into the seat.

Julia lifted her foot and set it on the footrest. "That we do." She shot her a grin as she unlatched the brake. "Ready?"

"More than you'll ever know."

The trip to the front door took a while since everybody they passed wanted to stop and talk. They all knew Julia, treating her as something special because she chose to take care of her mother-in-law when Frank bailed. But, like with the cancer, Julia assured them she deserved no medals when the subject came up, which it rarely did these days.

She loved Hettie as much as she loved her own mother. When her parents were killed while she was in college, her soon-to-be mother-in-law became *mom* to her in every way except name.

Jim Overby was parked in his usual spot in front of the TV in the lobby. When he saw them coming, he used his good leg to propel his wheelchair toward the front door to intercept them.

"Morning, Hettie. Hi, Julia."

"Good morning, Jim."

Jim always spoke to her and Julia always answered, but he seldom looked her way, and when he did, it was merely a quick glance. It was fine to be invisible to Jim. When Hettie was around, the whole world was invisible to Jim. The old man had eyes only for her mother-in-law, and it had been that way since the day Hettie moved in.

"My daughter sent me a new Celtic Woman CD. I'm going to listen to it this afternoon if you'd like to stop by." The hope in his voice was unmistakable.

Hettie gave a one-shoulder shrug. "We're going for a walk, but I will if I'm not too tired."

Jim nodded. "Okay."

To Julia's delight, he actually winked at Hettie before he pushed back. She held her giggle until they got outside in the sunshine. "Oh my goodness, Hettie. He was flirting with you."

"The doofus." Hettie chuckled. "He got that CD last week, and we've listened to it at least five times."

They had a good laugh together as they made their way into the garden at the side of the building.

"Know what you should do?" Hettie tilted her head back to make eye contact. "Find yourself a man in Italy. A good man."

Julia rolled her eyes. "I'm going to Italy to hike—not to find a man."

"Three weeks should give plenty of time for both." Hettie pointed to where the hummingbirds darted around a feeder in aerial combat. "That damn rubythroat thinks he's king of the realm. Runs all the rest of them away. Did I ever tell you I fell in love in Italy?"

The lack of segue caught Julia off guard. "You did not," she challenged.

"Yes, I did." Hettie's eyes twinkled as she looked back again, and her cheeks took on a rosy hue that wasn't only from the heat of the sun. "It was before I met Lon. I was there with my aunt. His name was Carlo Panicci, and he was the most handsome man I'd ever laid eyes on."

Julia couldn't believe she'd never heard mention of this man's name from Hettie's tell-all mouth. "Well, what happened? You can't start a story like that and leave me hanging." She pushed the wheelchair over by a bench and took a seat. This story needed face time.

Hettie shrugged. "I came back home and met Lon. I stopped answering the letters, and eventually they stopped coming." She smiled slyly. "But those Italian guys are amazing in the sack."

"Hettie!" Julia had always assumed her mother-in-law had only been with Frank's father, so this shift in the paradigm hit her from out of the blue.

"Does that shock you?" The glimmer in Hettie's eyes dared her to deny it.

"Yes."

"Do you think less of me?"

"No." Julia touched her forehead to her mother-in-law's. "It gives you more . . . dimension."

"Helps you see me in a new light, eh?"

"Definitely."

"Good." Hettie held up her right hand and extended her little finger. "Now pinkie swear the story will never go any further than us."

"Agreed."

They hooked pinkies and swore their oath, but when it came time to pull apart, Julia held on. "By the way . . ."

"What?" Hettie's eyes narrowed to wary, thin slits.

"You remember the last time we pinkie swore?"

"Yep." The silver head bobbed curtly. "My eightieth birthday."

Julia kept her face straight, not giving in to the smile that tugged at her lips. "And do you remember *what* we swore?"

Another nod. "Yep, to get tattoos before we died."

Julia gave a triumphant chuckle. "Ha! My dear Hettie, my re-constructed breasts now sport two of them, so it's your turn."

Hettie's eyes took on an impish gleam, and she crooked her finger tighter. "Okay, so I want to modify the oath a tad. The new agreement is to not only get a tattoo, but to bed a sexy Italian before we die."

Julia protested. "But you just told me you've already done that."

Hettie squeezed the pinkies together and then gave them a quick jerk apart to seal the bargain. "And you just told me you already have a tattoo, so we're halfway there and even steven."

CHAPTER 3

Julia slouched down low enough in her desk chair to rest her head on the back. She ran her fingers into her hair, grasping the roots for a quick squeeze. "How did people travel to foreign countries before the Internet? If I hadn't read the comment on that blog, I wouldn't have considered taking a bus from La Spezia to Lerici. It's a lot cheaper than a taxi and runs every twenty minutes."

Her business partner, Camille, glanced up from the catalog she was ordering from. "Will a bus take you to the hotel, though?"

"No." Julia rolled her head from side to side to loosen the tight bands of muscles in her neck. "But I checked that out, too. It's only a short walk."

"Two miles is short to you." Camille jotted something on the paper in front of her. "Remember, you'll have luggage."

"I'm packing light." Julia sat up and stretched her arms over her head. "The heaviest item will be my hiking boots."

"You're sure your boobs are ready? It's only been six weeks. What's going to keep the friction from rubbing those new nipples completely off?" Camille flipped the pencil she was holding and rubbed the eraser roughly across the paper. Then she lifted it to her lips and blew away the debris. "Like that."

"Thanks for that visual." Julia shook her head as she covered her eyes. "Only you would come up with that comparison. The doctor says I'm already good to go, and the trip is still two weeks away. Trust me, the girls are ready." Grasping a breast in each hand, she bounced in her chair. "And so am I."

Camille's chin buckled, putting her face in serious mode. "I worry about you. Going by yourself. Hiking alone in a foreign country. Nobody to take care of you."

Camille could be such a mother hen, despite being sixteen years younger. "I don't need anyone to take care of me. You know that." Julia used a firm tone, hoping to put this subject to rest for good. "You know I've done my research and checked everything out." She held up the brochure she'd been looking through yesterday. "The hiking trails around Lerici are popular, so there'll be plenty of other people on them." She dropped that one and picked up another. "And the Cinque Terre trails will be filled. I'll probably have to step over the slow ones who get knocked down in the stampede."

That brought a giggle from her friend. "I'm sure you'll lead the pack." She turned her attention back to the catalog.

Julia stared at the photo of the village of Monterosso gracing the front of the pamphlet. The Cinque Terre was in her grasp. In two-and-a-half weeks, she would be living the dream she'd first conceptualized nine months ago. Her "baby's" due date was almost here.

Her hand and the brochure it held trembled with excitement.

She'd worked hard for this—going from couch potato to someone who could walk twenty or more miles a day.

But she would be all alone.

Was she ready?

Her hand trembled again. She laid down the brochure and pressed the hand to the middle of her chest. Cancer-free, reconstructed breasts. Perky, new nipples, completely healed. What had once been her broken heart, now beating wildly at the mere thought of this adventure.

Oh yeah. She was ready.

* * *

Hettie squinted her good eye and peered at the paper Julia had given her containing the trip itinerary. "I've never heard of any of these places until you get to Florence. You're sure they exist?"

"Oh, they're popular destinations." Julia considered it for a couple of seconds and then shrugged. "But maybe not so much for the first-time visitor to Italy." She grabbed her tote and rummaged through it but didn't find the map she thought she'd put in there. That's right, she'd decided she wouldn't need it until she got to the hotel, so she'd put it in her duffel instead. "Let me grab an atlas." She left Hettie at the table and hustled over to the reference books on the shelf of the nursing home's limited library, returning with the thick world atlas. She sat down and flipped to the page containing the map of Italy. Spying the magnifying glass on another table, she jumped up again and grabbed it, then settled on the edge of her seat.

Hettie gave her a lopsided grin. "You're as feisty as spit on a skillet this morning."

"I am, aren't I," Julia agreed. "I can't believe the day's finally here, and I'm on my way." She positioned the magnifying glass over the northwest area of the map and pointed. "See. Here's Lerici." She glided her finger across the small body of water and tapped the five villages. "And these are the five little towns that make up the Cinque Terre."

Hettie's good hand clasped around Julia's finger and tapped it against the map again. "And see right there? It's the sexy Italian you're going to meet. He's waiting right there."

The pull of her mother-in-law's hand had brought the finger over the Ligurian Sea area of the Mediterranean. "If he's waiting right there, I hope he's on a boat . . . or a good swimmer."

"Fisherman." Hettie's hand lost its grip and dropped to the table. "They make the best lovers because they've learned to be patient."

Frank's dad had loved to fish, so Julia couldn't keep from smiling at the subtle but unmistakable innuendo. "That so?"

"If I'm lying, I'm dying." Hettie winked and made a cross over her heart.

"Well, patience is something I've been in short supply of lately." Julia laid down the magnifying glass and slid back in the chair. "Camille was talking about how antsy I've been just yesterday."

"Now don't start belittling yourself. You've got loads of patience. Too much when it comes to some things." Hettie didn't say what, but Julia suspected she was referring to Frank . . . or herself. "I like seeing you restless and excited."

"That pretty well sums me up right now."

Hettie plucked another truffle from the new box Julia had brought this morning and nibbled on it. "Not sure where I failed with you. I can't imagine wasting fabulous vacation time with exercise—at least, not the kind you're planning on—much less getting excited about it."

Chocolate dribbled down Hettie's chin and Julia dug in her tote for a tissue to wipe it with. "Then you'll probably disown me for admitting this." She dabbed away the sweet spot. "But honestly? I'm looking forward to the business part almost as much as the hiking. Getting to be the procurer? Mmmm! I *love* the treasure hunt." She lobbed the tissue toward a nearby trashcan and drummed the table when it went in. Then she clasped her hands together, determined to quiet her exuberance. "Camille is way better than I am with the customers."

"Don't sell yourself short." Hettie laid a cold hand on her arm, but it warmed Julia's heart. "You're the one with the eye."

Julia glanced down at her watch as she patted her mother-in-law's hand. Time was running out here much too fast.

"You need to go on. I don't want you rushing." Hettie's words and tone were pure *mother*. Julia had said the same things to Melissa countless times in exactly the same manner.

She really should be going, but she couldn't bring herself to leave just yet. The trip was only for three weeks, but she'd never left Hettie that long, and the separation was one of the things that had her so jittery. "Do you want me to push you back to your room?"

"No, the book club will be starting here in about ten minutes."

Julia had shifted to the edge of her seat, but now she settled back again. "What was this month's book?"

"*Pride and Prejudice.*" Hettie grunted and fitted the lid back onto the candy box. "Poor Lizzie. Blinded by her pride." She gave her head a sad little shake. "Seven times I've read the dang book, always thinking one of these times she'll drop those blinders earlier and go for it."

Austen was a favorite, so Hettie's comment piqued Julia's interest. "Hey, if Darcy had let his prejudice slip and quit being Mr. Snootypants sooner, she would've come around. And I didn't know you were reading that one. We could've read it together."

"No, thanks. Seven times is enough. Lizzie and Darcy will just have to go on learning the hard way." Hettie raised an eyebrow. "But don't be thinking you'll find a Darcy where you're going. Those hot-blooded Italian guys? They're anything but stuffy. Not a Mr. Snootypants in the bunch."

The gentle reminder had Julia glancing at her watch again. She really should be on her way, but . . .

"Julia."

She raised her eyes to meet her mother-in-law's firm yet tender gaze.

"It's time, sweetheart. Get out of here before you get caught by the book club. Those old women will be all over you wanting to talk."

Julia's eyes blurred with tears. She was being silly and overly emotional, but she couldn't help it. She scooted close enough to give Hettie a long hug. "I'll miss you."

"Love you, sweetheart." Hettie let go and pushed her firmly away. "Now shoo. Don't worry about me. I'll be fine."

Julia stood. "Can I do anything for you before I leave?"

"Yes." Hettie nodded toward the candy. "Stick that in the chair pocket, would you? I don't want to have to share."

Julia did as she was told and then rested her cheek for a quick moment to the top of the lovely white head.

She paused at the door for one last wave.

Hettie threw her a kiss in return.

During the three-hour drive from Paducah to the airport in St. Louis, Julia sang loudly with each song that came on the radio—no need of her playlist to make her happy this day. And later, tethered to the airplane by a seat belt, she still felt like a kite set free, literally soaring above the earth, on her way to a new place, ready for a new experience.

Anything was possible.

The two-hour weather delay in Chicago didn't dampen her spirit either, even when she struggled to get her carry-on into the overhead storage compartment.

"Here, let me get that for you."

Played against the surrounding drone of muffled murmurs, the vibrancy in the voice caught her off guard. Her body stirred at the brush of the hand that grasped her case and the male body that leaned in to her to give it a shove.

She turned to find herself staring at the pocket of a dress shirt and had to lean back slightly to make eye contact with the speaker, a payoff well worth the effort.

Fringes of dark blond surrounded jade-green irises in a pair of eyes that crinkled at the sides when he smiled. In fact, his whole face crinkled when he smiled. Deep dimples creased the jawline at the sides of his mouth, and a cleft staked its claim in the middle of his chin.

The whole effect was engaging and warm and, Julia couldn't keep from noticing, directed entirely at her.

He *saw* her.

She flashed him a smile of gratitude. "Chivalry's alive after all. Thanks so much." She edged past the first two seats to the window seat she'd been assigned, and her heart launched into a three-two beat when he settled into the middle seat beside her.

She didn't even try to hold back the smile that sprang onto her lips. The next eight hours might prove to be very interesting.

"I'm Lancelot, by the way."

Lancelot? Julia choked on the laugh that bubbled in her throat. *Poor guy.* "Do people call you Lance?"

"No, they call me Howard." A twinkle in the jade irises hinted she was being toyed with.

She ran her thoughts back to her chivalry comment. "Well, my real name is Guinevere, but my friends call me Julia."

"Then Julia it is." His face broke once again into a pleasant mass of dimples and grin wrinkles that somehow enhanced his features rather than detracted from them.

Men were so lucky. People would be chasing her down armed with Botox guns if her face wrinkled like that, yet on him it looked charming.

He slid the book he was carrying into the pocket of the seat in front of him. "And you're obviously on your way from Camelot to Italy."

Julia nodded, getting her travel necessities out of her bag before shoving it under the seat in front of her.

"Business or pleasure?"

He punctuated the word *pleasure* with a flash of dimples that sent a tingle into places she'd all but forgotten.

"Both." She buckled her seat belt, enjoying the feel of tightening it around a stomach thirty pounds lighter and much firmer than it had been a year ago. "I'm in interior decorating, so I'll be on the lookout for unique pieces for my clients. But before I get to the work part, I'll be hiking the area around Lerici and the Cinque Terre."

Howard's eyes squinted. "What's the Cinque Terre?" He seemed genuinely interested, or else he just wanted to talk to her. She liked either option.

"There are these five villages in Liguria that are connected by a trail overlooking the sea. They're called the Cinque Terre, and people hike from one to the next. That usually only takes five or six hours, but then there are extra trails running from the villages up into the hills. I plan to hike most all of them."

Howard let out a low whistle and those jade irises did her a quick once-over. "You must be in great shape."

Julia's face grew a tad warm, in what she hoped was a becoming blush. "I've been training for a while, but it's not that bad really. Five to seven miles a day. And the terrain isn't too rugged."

"Well, I'm impressed. Training for a while for the *fun* part of a vacation? I admire that conviction."

Admire? What a great word. She hadn't been admired in years. This guy was totally flirting with her and it felt marvelous—like someone had popped the cork on a champagne bottle inside her.

How long had it been since she'd had a fun, flirty conversation with a man? She was forty-eight, had married when she was twenty-three. Twenty-five years? No wonder it seemed so foreign. She'd forgotten how exhilarating it could be.

The flight attendants encouraged the passengers standing in the aisles to find their places quickly with reminders that the flight was already late.

Julia settled back into her seat for the ride. Howard propped his arm on the armrest between them, and when the tight setting brought their arms into contact, the temperature in the plane vaulted several degrees. Julia readjusted the vent above her head so the air streamed directly onto her face.

"So tell me more about these hikes you'll be taking." Howard shifted his posture toward her as much as possible with his long legs scrunched against the seat in front of him.

"Well, I have a couple of short hikes in the area around Lerici planned for the first two days. After that I'll be playing it by . . ."

A willowy brunette with smooth, olive skin plopped into the aisle seat. Her black tank top clung to a pair of breasts that had no need of a bra to support their ample size. Denim short shorts showed off perfectly shaped, tanned legs that must've started at her shoulders.

"*Scusi,*" she murmured in a soft Italian accent.

Howard's attention diverted so fast, Julia wondered if he would suffer whiplash. "Well, hello there."

". . . ear." Julia finished her sentence, speaking to the back of the chair in front of her.

Howard extended his hand and introduced himself to the new seatmate. The fact she was native Italian must have fascinated him as he immediately started to bombard her with questions about her country, none of which mentioned hiking, his all-consuming interest three minutes before.

And with the appearance of Miss Italy, Julia once again vanished before her own eyes.

She told herself to ignore the slight. She should be used to it by now. But she wasn't. Something short-circuited inside her every time it happened. More than once she'd noticed how the streak of gray hair running from her left temple looked ominously like burned wires. How long would it be before her motherboard burned out completely? Before she was just a gray box of dead, worn-out wires and fuses?

She reached inside to pinpoint the emotion churning there. It wasn't jealousy precisely. Watching people fascinated her, and nothing was more intriguing than two beautiful people coming together for the first time. The magic. The spark. She saw that with Melissa and Michael and prayed every day it would continue for them and that the years wouldn't extinguish it the way it had for her and Frank.

But at that moment, it was the obvious twenty-year age difference—at the very least—between the two people beside her that disgusted her. Men who'd reached the age of Howard and Frank should be interested in more than a woman's physical makeup. Shouldn't they have developed an "inner eye"? One preferably located somewhere other than their penis?

Her clenched jaws couldn't exactly be chalked up to envy either. She didn't want Howard, didn't want what anyone else had, except in a general way.

If she had to put a name to it, it would simply be . . . longing. She so longed to feel full again—full of love and desire and life.

Of all the things she resented Frank for—his weakness, his abandonment of her when she needed him, his self-absorption—she shed the most tears over the loss of the life she used to know. The loss of who she used to be.

Now she was a white sneaker in a world of stilettos.

Howard's right shoulder cocked far enough forward to give her a spectacular view of his shoulder and the nape of his neck. He chatted easily with the brunette, who soon discovered the book he'd placed in the seat pocket in front of him was "the most amazing book" she'd read in a long time. And it sounded infinitely more appealing described in a sultry, Italian accent.

Armed with her new copy of *Interesting Interiors,* Julia prepared for what was shaping up to be a very long flight.

In the seats next to her, the book club met throughout the take-off, the climb to cruising altitude, the meal, and the start of the movie, which was one she'd seen recently. Although it wasn't entertaining enough to sit through again, she watched it anyway, hoping it would put her to sleep.

It didn't.

She donned her blindfold and her ear buds, willing the music on her *Sleepytime* playlist to drown out the sounds of the growing acquaintance.

The blow-up travel pillow wasn't nearly as comfortable as the woman on the box, smiling in her perfectly restful sleep, implied. But Julia tuned her music to the series of Strauss waltzes and imagined herself as the woman on the box. She smiled dreamily and coaxed her mind into a restful frame for all of seven minutes, at which time she woke with a start to the mortifying realization she had drooled down the front of her blanket.

Fretting her seatmates might've noticed or that her fidgeting might bother them seemed needless, though. Howard's left-hand lady had him so absorbed, three-year-old ADHD twins could've been sitting in the window seat and he wouldn't have noticed.

With that comforting thought, Julia relaxed and enjoyed almost two full hours of sleep before the crew started waking everyone for breakfast.

Howard did acknowledge her presence once more when he passed a cup of coffee to her. His eyes took her in with a quick once-over. "Rough night, huh?"

She looked at him closely. Lancelot's irises had changed. They were actually more jaded than jade. She took the coffee without comment, sipping it as Milan appeared on the horizon.

When the plane landed, Howard and Venus de Milo scurried off together, his hand casually pressed against the small of her back. Julia managed to get her carry-on out of the overhead compartment by herself.

After a two-hour layover, a second flight took her from Milan to Genoa. A taxi ride to the train station and a short train ride from Genoa got her to La Spezia. From there, the crowded bus took her to Lerici.

Her hair was frizzed, her attitude frazzled, and her nerves frayed.

One look, however, at the small jewel of a town snuggling around its breathtaking azure bay, and she was renewed.

Time seemed to have slipped into slow motion somewhere between La Spezia and this place.

Gone were the bustle and the noise of the city, replaced by a palpable tranquility. Maybe it was the warm breeze that slowed people's walks to a stroll or the tangy, salty air that filled their lungs and quieted their speech to a pleasant hum. Whatever it was, the magic cast a spell around her instantly and pulled her under its power.

"The Lord Byron Hotel?" she asked an elderly woman waiting in line at a gelato stand.

"*Sì.*" The woman expelled an additional line of something that hadn't been on the Italian language CDs, but she pointed to a conspicuously orange building set high up on the hillside—and the walking path that led to it.

Julia eyed the steep incline, noting the weight of her carry-on and her duffel. Both pieces of luggage had wheels . . . and in a few days, she'd be conquering the Cinque Terre.

Determined, she took on the hill, schlepping her bags behind her.

Dragging the extra forty pounds up what felt like eighty degrees of cobblestone incline for two hundred yards left her questioning her fitness *and* her sanity, however. She stopped at intervals, filling her lungs with huge gulps of air that apparently held no oxygen as she felt little to no recoup in her body. The bags threatened to pull her arms from their sockets, and her fingers gripped the handles with terror, knowing that any slip backward meant having to retrace her excruciatingly painful progress.

By the time she reached the turnoff onto the hotel's walkway, the twenty-two hours of travel since leaving Paducah hit her like a Mac truck. The warm fuzzies she'd started up the hill with had been abandoned along the way, replaced by hot pricklies that caused her blouse to stick to her chest and back and underarms, making the areas alternate from itch to burn.

She stomped along a walkway built on yet another incline, albeit gradual, up to the sign that indicated the office. In front of the door, two men blocked the path, discussing something that apparently had to do with the swimming pool. From their wild gesticulations and heated tones, one of them had released piranhas into the water.

If you stop, you drop, Julia reminded herself. But it was the sight in front of her more than her mantra that inched her closer.

Adonis—or whatever the Roman mythology equivalent was—had come to life. Stripped to the waist, his torso was an ocean of waves and ripples that made her mouth so dry she longed for a taste. Long legs defined with muscles bulging from the shorts he wore pivoted him gracefully toward the pool and back to the other man whom he towered over.

Julia drew close enough to appreciate the sunlight glistening on the perspiration that poured from the black curly hair onto the wide, sculpted shoulders and chest. Despite the angry undertones, his deep voice had a smoothness that glided across his tongue like caramel gelato.

This was the man, rather than Howard, who should've been hooking up with Miss Italy. At thirtyish, he was the perfect age— the perfect everything—and Julia released the breath she'd been holding with a sigh.

"Um . . . excuse me. I need to get through here."

Adonis swung toward her, pinning her with a sullen gaze from eyes as dark and rich as mahogany. "*Mi dispiace,* signora. I did not see you."

Julia drew another sigh and shrugged. "That doesn't surprise me."

His dark eyes filled with confusion. "You expect the surprise? A package perhaps?"

Her sarcasm had obviously gotten lost in translation. Julia brushed her fingers through the top of her hair to get the sweaty strands out of her face. "No—never mind. You'll have to excuse me. It's the jet lag talking."

"*Americana*." Adonis pinpointed the accent, and Julia nodded. "But . . . the jeta-lag, she is the . . . ? He twirled his hand as if it could wind out the word he was groping for.

Julia would've filled in the blank if she'd known what he was going for. But the fogginess in her brain wouldn't allow the foggiest notion to penetrate the surface layer.

He finally gave up. "English." He spat the word. "She is the confused language." His sullen manner pinned all the blame for that on Julia.

The shorter man finally lost the exasperated glare he'd been using on Adonis and turned his attention to her. "You wish to check in, signora?"

Julia nodded. "I'm Julia Berkwith.

"I am Signor Moretti, the owner." His tone slid into smooth hospitality as he opened the door to the office and held it for her.

Adonis's disgruntled frown said he hadn't finished the conversation with Signor Moretti that she'd interrupted, but he directed a pointed look to the hotel owner before stomping off.

Julia breathed a relieved sigh when she stepped into the cool office—out of the heat of the day and away from the heat of their argument, not to mention the heat Adonis generated simply by his presence.

Thank heavens, everything was in order and check-in was easy. She could tell her brain had started to misfire as she signed her name the last time and left out the *k*.

"You will check out on Sunday, just ahead of the crowd." Signor Moretti's English was much better than Adonis's. "That is when all of Italy come to Lerici."

"I read that this is a prime vacation spot for Italians. In fact, it's the main reason I chose this place," Julia admitted. "If you want the best restaurant, you ask a local. I assumed it would be the same for vacation spots."

"*Sì,* signora." Signor Moretti beamed at the compliment. "Leave your luggage. I bring it to you."

"I'll get it," she assured him, though not sharing the reason why. She couldn't bear the thought of having to wait even an extra ten minutes to take a shower. "Thank you, though."

"As you wish."

He gave her the directions to the room and held the door open for her again.

Before she made the left out of the office, she was treated to one more quick view of Adonis's perfectly sculpted backside.

Melissa would describe him as a *total hottie,* and for once, Julia thoroughly understood the term.

* * *

By the time Julia dragged her bags all the way to her room, she was nearly delirious with exhaustion.

She showered, hoping it would revive her, but the warmth made her almost catatonic, so she lay down for a short nap and awoke to different lighting.

Her foggy brain took a minute to explain the discrepancy. She'd gone to sleep with streaks of afternoon sun casting long shadows in her room. She awoke to darkness . . . and hunger. The clock on her bedside table told her it was barely after eight in the evening.

She slipped into one of the new knit dresses she'd bought for the trip and smiled at the bit of cleavage showing in the scoop neck—certainly nothing that would draw attention, but enough to make her marvel at how normal she looked . . . as long as she kept her clothes on.

The scrumptious scent surrounding the hotel led her to its restaurant. She stopped in the doorway, taking in the white linen tablecloths and candlelight—much more romantic than her single status called for. She started to turn away but got caught by the maître d's greeting.

"*Buona sera,* signora."

He asked her something in Italian, which she didn't understand, but she held up a hesitant finger. "Uno?"

"But, of course," he answered in English, and his unruffled

elegance eased her discomfort a notch. He led her to a table for two but made quick work of dismantling the extra place setting and directing a server her way.

As she waited for her glass of wine, a twinge caught between her shoulder blades—that distinct feeling of being watched, though no one around her seemed to be paying her the slightest bit of attention. She was about to chalk it up to a mild case of woman-traveling-alone paranoia, when her eyes wandered to a dark corner and met with a brooding stare.

Adonis. Showered and changed into different clothes . . . sipping a glass of wine . . . no doubt waiting for a hot date.

Julia glanced away, discomfited by the impression he was looking through her rather than at her. She took a sip of wine, trying to carry off a nonchalance she didn't feel. She scanned the room, letting her eyes drift toward the dark corner again. Yep, still staring.

Maybe it was some kind of game with him. A form of "Who'll blink first?" She wasn't about to be drawn in by something so childish. She fished her phone from her small clutch and absorbed herself with checking for nonexistent texts, calls, and e-mails while the gentle rhythm of the Beatles' "Across the Universe" played in the background of her mind.

Her salad arrived, giving her reason to look up again. She glanced to the back of the room, relieved to see Adonis had pulled out a pad and seemed to be sketching. But the forkful of luscious spring greens clogged her throat when he glanced at her and back to his sketch.

Was he sketching her? Oh, surely not. He was probably day-dreaming about the woman who was on her way to meet him.

An elderly gentleman, elegantly dressed in a full suit, entered the restaurant. The maître d' nodded in recognition, but a hand gesture told him not to bother with a menu.

The gentleman's eyes scoured the room, landing on her and staying a fraction too long to be appropriate. A quick exchange with the maître d' and then he headed in her direction. She absorbed herself in her salad and her phone again.

He stopped beside her table. "*Buona sera,* signora."

Julia looked up with feigned surprise. "*Buona sera.*"

His head cocked in question. "You are English, yes?"

"American," she corrected him.

He gestured to the empty seat next to him. "I see you dine alone."

His English was almost perfect. "Would you enjoy company?"

Was this a pickup? It had been so long since anyone had tried, she wasn't sure how it was done these days. Even with the nap, jet lag had left her enervated and not in the mood for forced interaction. "No," she replied, then felt a little ashamed of her curt reply. "But thanks for the offer," she added.

He shrugged. "As you wish." He turned in Adonis's direction.

The younger man was watching their brief interaction with a look of keen interest. He quickly closed the sketch pad and pulled out the chair beside him, gesturing its availability to his elderly friend, but not before spearing Julia with a disapproving look.

She arched an eyebrow and shot the look right back as the two men greeted each other amiably. They spoke low and, of course, in Italian, so she wouldn't have understood them anyway. But the telltale glances in her direction raised her suspicion she was the topic of a terse conversation.

Men like Adonis and Frank and Howard from the plane—and ninety-nine percent of their species—viewed the world as open season on women . . . thought at her age she should welcome *any* attention. Well, the welts of still-angry scar tissue that closed the tear where Frank ripped her heart out, as well as the ones that ran like vines across her breasts, were made of tougher fiber than the original and were pleasantly numb. They'd convinced her to come to Italy alone . . . to hike alone . . . she certainly could survive eating alone. She'd done it often. And while she didn't particularly enjoy it—a part of her longed for companionship and conversation at the table—it by no means targeted her as easy prey.

Anyone who thought differently could go piss up a rope.

She swallowed another forkful of salad and washed it down with the wine.

The waiter arrived with her grilled fish entrée, and she welcomed the distraction although the conversation in the corner had moved on, and she no longer sensed the looks directed her way.

Her sea bass was half eaten when the two men got up and left after having only a glass of wine. Neither looked her way, which was no surprise.

The surprise came, though, when she asked for her check and the waiter informed her that it had already been paid "by the gentleman in the corner."

She didn't have to ask which gentleman. Adonis would never pay for a dinner without expecting something in return.

CHAPTER 4

Julia woke to the cheery brightness of morning in Italy. Well, morning, yes—but barely. The clock read 11:37—a far cry from her usual 6:30. These two days in Lerici were for preparation. A short three-mile hike today, and a bit longer seven-mile tomorrow... nothing like the long all-day walks she would be doing later. But these early ones would leave plenty of time for sightseeing and pool time. With a no-guilt attitude, she stretched languidly, embracing the air with her arms and the place with her heart, thankful to be alive and here.

The next ten days, hers alone. She would hike and eat and rest at her own pace, and day by day, she would win back the vitality stolen from her over the past two years.

Tap, tap, tap. The sound drifted up from the ground through the open door of her balcony.

Curious, she roused herself from the bed.

Adonis was back at work. As she watched, he hoisted a huge stone and carried it effortlessly to an unfinished area of stone paving that surrounded a sculpture near the pool. The sight of his backside once again proved as perfect as the front without the intimidating, piercing eyes.

Instead of dropping the stone with a thud as she expected, he carefully placed it on the ground and stepped back to study it.

Ah! A stonemason, then. A fitting job since he appeared to be made of the same matter.

So what did that imply about her work with antiques? She pushed the thought away.

He knelt and chiseled delicately around the edge of the rock, shaping it to snuggle tightly against the one it would rest beside.

Julia brewed a cup of coffee and decided to sit on her balcony, enjoying it along with the view. Invisibility had its advantages and watching Adonis unobserved was one of them. Today he wore a T-shirt, which pulled taut across his chest even when he wasn't in motion. Drenched in morning sunlight, he was the epitome of raw masculinity with the heat shimmering off him like it did on the sea below.

The sculpture he was paving around drew her interest. An iridescent ball rested within what appeared to be a clamshell or a sunburst folded in half. The effect was that the ball could be a pearl or an eye or even the moon. She would check it out more closely if she found a time when the stonemason wasn't around.

His dark eyes unnerved her yesterday with their piercing stare. They hummed with the same power she could see coiled in his movements now as he worked the hammer, the same power that resonated in his voice.

She wouldn't want to get in this man's way.

As if he'd heard her thoughts, he stood abruptly and threw his hammer in disgust. It thudded against the wall behind him. Picking up the stone he'd just placed, he hurled it and some colorful phrases in the direction his hammer had taken.

Julia chuckled at his temperamental actions. A stone that didn't fit exactly the way he wanted? Big deal. *Suck it up, pretty boy. If that's the worst thing life throws at you, count your lucky stars.*

He stalked off, and she redirected her attention to the view of the countryside.

Surrounding the hotel property, houses clung like plants to the hillside, a spring garden in pastel hues, drawing water and life from the jewel of sea below. Not a single cloud marred the infinite blue stretch of sea and sky. Heat was already evident, even in the shade of her balcony, but it wasn't a stifling heat. It was a warm bath set to the perfect temperature.

She drew a dreamy breath. Her planning and training and hard work paid off. The interior decorating company she'd started five years ago had shown a fine profit for three years despite her personal setbacks. She'd even been able to expand and take on a partner. And soon, she would begin her conquest of the Cinque Terre. She would conquer this ruggedly handsome terrain just like she conquered the cancer and the depression and the weight gain.

Voices below the balcony caught her attention. One she thought she recognized from yesterday as the stonemason's. She stood up, catching sight of two figures lingering in the shade beneath the balcony next to hers. Sure enough, Adonis and a young man sipped dark liquid from espresso cups, deep in conversation.

As they talked, a well-endowed blonde sunbathing by the pool stood up to adjust her nearly nonexistent bikini. The young man gave a low whistle, making a motion as if squeezing a proffered breast.

Adonis's snort held a derisive edge. "*Americana,*" he muttered. He leaned over and picked up a large, round rock and squeezed it, giving an exaggerated grunt. His companion laughed as Adonis tossed the rock away.

Julia felt her face heat as Frank's remark that she now came equipped with jawbreakers surged to the front of her mind. He'd been trying to cover his revulsion at her appearance . . . had sought to make light of the horror he tried to hide.

She blinked away the tears. If he'd stuck around, he would've been surprised by how supple her fake breasts had become over time, almost lifelike really.

But he *hadn't* stuck around.

She'd been fading in Frank's visibility for years. The cancer caused him to lose sight of her completely.

She stepped back into her room and closed the door on the conversation below. Let them think whatever they wanted, these perfect young men surrounded by their perfect women in their perfect world.

Age would give them a different perspective.

And if it didn't, God help them.

Julia's heart jumped with delight at the sight of the trailhead at Piazza Garibaldi. Everything she'd read led her to believe that hiking in Liguria was *the* way to see the countryside, but until that very moment, she'd been afraid to trust the information completely. She needn't have worried. The trail was well marked and obviously very well used.

A group of a dozen or so people dressed exactly like she was— armed with backpacks, hiking boots, walking sticks, and small GPS devices attached to their belts—stood listening to a young man speaking in German with an easy smile.

She hurried to get ahead of them. Although the assurance that she wasn't alone on a trail in a foreign country calmed the first-time jitters, she didn't want to share her premiere celebratory adventure with anyone—especially not strangers.

She headed up the shady trail, which was quite steep at the beginning, but eventually was broken by level areas that wound through tall stands of trees. She didn't recognize them, although the leaf shape indicated some type of oak and closer inspection revealed acorns with hairy caps.

Determined to stay ahead of the German group, she pushed upward until the trees gave way to a meadow and a spectacular, unbroken view of the *Golfo dei Poeti*—the "Gulf of Poets." There she paused to munch on the granola bar and water she'd brought along. Looking across the breathtaking vista, she fully understood why Dante and Petrarch felt inspired to write about its beauty, why the Romantics, Byron and Shelley, chose to live here. A fleeting memory of Shelley's *Adonaïs* came to mind, which conjured an image of the stonemason this morning. The scenery at this place could apparently make a poet of anyone.

Or a romantic. This beauty was meant to be shared with someone special.

An unexpected stab of loneliness hit her hard enough to make the scenery blur. She swiped away the tears and tucked the remainder of the granola bar into her pocket, no longer hungry.

I'm here, she reminded herself. *Alive and healthy. And alone is preferable to being with someone who can't stand the sight of who I've become.*

Across the gulf lay Porto Venere and beyond that, the tiny villages of the Cinque Terre waited for her.

But first, she had Lerici to explore.

And if she wanted the pool time this afternoon that she'd promised herself, she had to get a move on.

The olive grove ahead—and the sound of chatter from the first of the German hikers—spurred her to start moving again.

She tuned the playlist in her head to the one that offered the quickest pace—*Dance Like Nobody's Watching.*

She used that one often because, of course, nobody was.

One hour at the pool lengthened to almost two.

Julia slathered on another huge dollop of sunscreen, paying careful attention to her chest area. The modest cut of the one-piece she'd bought for the trip showed only a bit of cleavage and kept all the scars covered, so she was relatively comfortable. Except for the fact that sitting next to the overly endowed *americana* the young men had spoken about that morning made her wonder exactly what fantasy her mind had been in when she'd also purchased the two-piece hidden in the bottom of her luggage. But the sun and the warm water felt so perfect, she couldn't bring herself to leave the pool yet. She'd denied herself this pleasure far too long—too self-conscious of her body in a swimsuit to go near a pool or a beach.

Another thing that pinned her to the seat was the spectacular scenery—Adonis, still hard at work. Still hard everywhere. She'd given up trying to make sense of the article in the magazine on her lap, although she kept it there as a prop to thumb through. The man was too great a distraction. Hidden behind her large sunglasses and floppy hat, she'd been enjoying the view for quite some time.

He dropped a stone into place, and suddenly, his head snapped her way as if her stare had called him. A "caught ya" smile played across his handsome, dark features.

Julia went rigid with embarrassment, quickly thumbing another page to prove the arrogant playboy wrong, but a hot flash of seismic proportions sent her scurrying to jump in the pool and wash away the telltale sweat.

As she swam a couple of laps, Adonis took a break, moving to the shade to down a bottle of water. Out of the corner of her eye, she saw him pick up his pad and start to sketch, as he'd done the night before. She went back to her chair and toweled off just as the *americana* bombshell stood and stretched and readjusted the back of her Brazilian bikini, eyes glued on the stonemason.

In the perfect position to see and hear all, Julia put her invisibility to work. She donned her hat and sunglasses, and opened her magazine as the blonde strutted her stuff in Adonis's direction.

He flipped the sketch pad closed when he saw the woman approaching.

"You don't have to be shy." She came to a stop—more of a pose, really—with hands hugging the back of her hips and breasts thrust far enough forward to look dangerous. "I've noticed you watching me all afternoon, and then I saw you sketching me. I thought I'd come over and introduce myself."

So that's how the visible crowd did it these days. Even if she were visible and the young woman's age, Julia never could've been that bold. But it was intriguing to watch.

"*Mi dispiace.*" Adonis's deep voice carried easily.

The blonde waved her hand in front of her chest and let her fingers play lightly at the base of her throat, drawing attention to her breasts as if they might somehow be overlooked. "You don't have to apologize. I wanted to let you know I wouldn't mind posing for you . . . like in a more *private* setting? We could meet later for drinks and talk about it if you'd like."

And have sex, of course. Sheesh.

"*Sì.*" He shrugged. "My friend Romano meet me for the drinks in the bar." He indicated the door to the bar with a nod. "You join us?"

"That sounds fun." The blonde's tongue glided along her upper lip in a provocative manner. "What time do you *want* me?" She flashed a smile. "To meet you, I mean?"

Seriously? Shouldn't a body like that exempt you from having to be coy?

"*Le diciannove.*"

Blondie giggled. "What's that mean?"

"The nineteen hours."

"So that would be . . . ?"

Adonis held up seven fingers.

"All right, then. I'll see you at seven in the bar." Blondie gave a tiny wave and strutted back to her seat.

As Adonis downed a second bottle of water, Julia gathered up her things and headed for her room. The last three minutes had added at least a decade to her age.

Adonis had worked moving rocks all day in the hot sun, yet was primed and ready for sex.

She, on the other hand, had relaxed for a good part of the day—and was ready for a nap.

From her corner table in the restaurant where she relaxed un-noticed, Julia watched the three young people in the bar, playing out the scenario she had overheard being planned.

The ubiquitous stonemason and his friend had scored . . . or were well on their way.

Blondie had indeed met them for drinks. Although Adonis had been anxious to accept her offer this afternoon, now his friend seemed more aggressive in the pursuit. Adonis appeared a bit more aloof, to the point of being standoffish, actually.

Julia swallowed her last sip of wine. No doubt, one of them was going to get lucky tonight. Maybe both.

Waiting it out with another glass of wine to see who left with whom was tempting. The subtle—and sometimes not so subtle—interaction was fascinating. When the blonde turned her attention to the stonemason, he would do something every time to divert her attention back to the friend, who was handsome and sexy . . . but he was no Adonis.

Even fully dressed—if the low-cut, backless minidress could be considered fully dressed—Blondie was pretty, but a little hard around the edges. "Rode hard and put away wet" was the descriptive Kentucky term.

The stonemason could have his pick and was probably waiting for better fare.

A third glass of wine just to assuage her nosiness seemed silly when a walk down to the village would be beautiful tonight, not to mention better for the tummy Julia was fighting to keep flat. She also wanted to get to bed early because she'd decided to do tomorrow's hike first thing in the morning. That way, she'd have the rest of the day for sightseeing—her last chance to explore Lerici . . . at least, for this trip.

While she contemplated her choices, Adonis excused himself, making up her mind for her. With him gone, the tableau wouldn't be nearly so interesting.

She signed her check and left the finale of the interlude to her imagination.

CHAPTER 5

By ten the next morning, Julia had already hiked seven miles, showered, traded her shorts for a skirt and her hiking boots for flip-flops, and was enjoying a continental breakfast on the patio of the hotel, which once again gave her a full view of the pool and Adonis at work.

She noticed yesterday how he worked from a hodgepodge of large stones sometimes piled two feet high, sifting among them to find the one that worked best. He would eye both the spot and the rock carefully, then chisel the edge for the fit he wanted. And sometimes, after all that work, he'd fume and throw the stone away, and search for another. He certainly was picky about which stone went where. Perhaps color also influenced his choice? As a designer, she could appreciate that.

And she could appreciate the man . . . from a distance. She certainly didn't want to get within his radar and risk the embarrassment of getting caught watching him again. He was used to it, though, she could tell from the self-assured way he carried himself. She couldn't help but notice the number of looks he garnered from the women in the area.

If he lived to be a hundred, this guy would never know what it meant to be invisible.

As she sipped the last of her *caffe latte,* he disappeared around the edge of the building. When he didn't return for at least ten minutes, she decided maybe the coast was clear for a while. Today was her last day in Lerici, so if she was going to get a closer look at the sculpture she'd studied from afar, it had to be now, and preferably while the temperamental stonemason was away. She signed her check and moseyed over toward the clamshell.

The closer she got, the more intriguing the object became. Overlaid with polished mother-of-pearl, the part housed inside the shell—the ball or moon or pearl or whatever it was meant to be—begged to be touched, so she obliged. The smooth orb had already caught the sun, was warm under her palm. A delicate stroke sent it rolling to one end where the concave form sent it back the other direction. She stood mesmerized, rolling the orb from one end to the other, watching the ever-changing display of colors as it moved along the path. It reminded her of the kaleidoscopes she'd enjoyed as a kid, making her feel like a magician wielding great magic with the turn of her wrist or the flick of her finger.

"You like?"

Julia spun around to find the stonemason and the same dark eyes she'd encountered before, but today they weren't so brooding—and they were much closer. So close they stopped her breath for a couple of seconds. "It's . . . it's beautiful," she finally managed. "I've never seen anything like it. I was trying to decide if it was a pearl or an iris or the moon passing in front of the sun."

"Iris?" The eyes squinted in the same questioning way as they had the day she arrived, but today they lacked the fire that lit them from behind, replaced instead by a pleasant warmth.

She made a little circle with her finger in front of her eye. "The colored part of the eye. The iris."

"*Capisco.*" He studied her eyes for a few seconds. "You have the beautiful . . . iris. Like the sea in winter."

Oh my. She'd heard about the legendary charm of the Italian men, but she hadn't prepared to deal with it—or her resulting momentary lack of brain function—firsthand. His gaze continued to scrutinize her eyes in a disconcerting manner, and she suddenly felt sorry for all those amoebas in high school biology classes. "Thank you. That's very nice." She turned back to the sculpture, finding her escape by rolling it once again to the end and back.

"I must work now. I finish today."

The comment drew her back around to face him. He had one of those smiles that melted a woman's insides. Perfect teeth gripped a lusciously full lower lip. She felt a twinge of disappointment she wouldn't enjoy him with her coffee tomorrow. "Please, go ahead and work." She gave a dismissive wave. "Don't mind me."

He didn't move, just continued to stand close, shifting his weight.

"It's been nice talking with you." She gave a little wave.

He still stood there, then his smile broke into a low chuckle that vibrated in and out and around her. "I am Vitale. I work here." He pointed to the exact spot where she was standing.

Her eyes flitted across the way to the area where he'd been working earlier, only now noticing it was finished. "Oh, of course. Sorry!" Embarrassed she'd been gawking too much to pick up on his hint, and more than a little flustered, she moved to get out of his way, a stack of nearby stones forgotten.

The side of her knee connected with the precarious pile. She stumbled, trying to miss them, but lost her balance in the process. *Oh God, I'm going to fall.* She fought to keep her skirt from bunching around her hips, trying to preserve some scrap of dignity on her way down. Just when she thought all was lost, two strong hands gripped her arms and kept her upright.

Too bad he didn't have four hands, for while he managed to save *her* from falling, he couldn't do the same for the stones. They toppled every which way with the largest one choosing her foot to break its fall. The corner of the huge rock lunged at her toe and bore into it.

Her knees buckled with pain, but his hands continued to keep her vertical.

"*Aieeee! Ow, ow, ow, ow, ow!*" She pushed the sounds out through clenched teeth, similar to the Lamaze techniques she'd learned when she was pregnant with Melissa.

They hadn't helped much then either.

With a swift leverage movement using his own foot, Vitale sent the errant stone tumbling, and once the weight was gone, Julia's pain eased a little. But a pulsing throb continued up through the middle of her foot. She leaned away from the comfort of the male body that surrounded her and sneaked a look. The foot was red, darker near the toes, but otherwise appeared fairly normal.

"*Non muova.*" He held her tightly as she regained her balance. "Are you injured?"

Julia caught her breath. "I don't think so."

He let go, and she shifted her weight to the foot. *Ghah!* A knife stabbed through her middle toe and cut its way through the top of her foot. "Shhh—" She cut off the expletive. "I need to sit down."

Vitale's arm snaked around her waist, all but lifting her off the ground. The pleasant sensation of being held so tightly took her mind off her toe for a split second until her foot made contact with the ground again. Then the pain tore through her foot, more intense this time.

Leaning heavily against his solid body, she hobbled to the nearest chaise and eased down, dreading to look again. The way the pain was increasing, if her toe looked half as bad as it felt, it was going to be ugly.

He stooped down in front of her and took her ankle gently in his hand, raising her foot. The warmth of his touch and the gentleness of his manner gave her courage. She looked—and immediately wished she hadn't.

The toe was already turning a peculiar shade of blue with a black tinge creeping in. She tried to curl it, but it didn't cooperate, and the movement hurt too much to force it. A sinking feeling in her stomach confirmed what her brain didn't want to admit.

"I think my toe's broken."

"*Sì,* signora. I think you are right."

Julia's mind whirled with the ramifications. Would she be able to wear a hiking boot? Or even a shoe? Her heart bounded into a thudding rhythm. "Help me up." It was more of a command than she meant it to be, but this was no time to be courteous. Besides, if this peabrain hadn't left his stones piled so high, it wouldn't have happened. He took her extended hands and pulled her to her feet.

Instinctively her weight shifted onto her left foot, avoiding the inevitable. She put the right one down on the warm paving stone, rolling it from the outside in. A little pain, but bearable. Her heart slowed a notch. She took a step. As soon as her weight shifted from her heel in the direction of her toe, the intensity of the throb increased from mild to excruciating.

"Damn!"

"You should not walk on it."

"I know that," she snapped. Frank had broken his toe a few years back. After five hours in the emergency room and a seven hundred dollar x-ray, the doctor had taped his toe to the one next to it and sent him home telling him to ice it and take ibuprofen.

She also knew she wouldn't be hiking the Cinque Terre tomorrow.

Disappointment and anger festered in her like a boil ready to pop. "I can't believe this happened." She swung her fists into the imaginary punching bag in front of her. "What in the hell does this world have against me?"

The question was rhetorical, but Vitale evidently felt she wanted an answer. He shifted his weight, staying well out of reach of her flailing arms, and scratched the back of his head. "I do not know, signora."

"Stop calling me that." She punched a fist in his general direction, catching herself before she stomped her foot. "My name is Julia." She was acting childish—shrewish even, but she didn't care. She needed to unload, and Vitale was the nearest dumping station. With all those muscles, he should damn well be able to take it. "Months of training. A year of planning, and hoping, and dreaming. And it all came down to this? A jet-lagged night and two measly hikes? I can't hike the Cinque Terre with this!"

"You come to hike the Cinque Terre?"

She nodded, not trusting her voice since the sympathy in his made her want to collapse in tears.

"I am sorry."

The old gentleman Vitale fetched to her room had to be a hundred if he was a day, but he had a charm about him that enchanted Julia. She wished she could introduce him to Hettie. They would make a great pair.

She sat on the bed with the ancient doctor kneeling in front of her. He held her calf firmly, occasionally giving it a light squeeze, his eyes focusing on her toe, running slowly up to her knee, then back down to her toe.

He made a gesture and said something in Italian that appeared to have three parts. She looked to Vitale for the interpretation.

He gave a sheepish grin. "He says you have pretty legs . . . nice ankles . . . and the broken toe."

Great. The old guy thinks I'm hot.

Julia tapped her finger to Matchbox Twenty's song "Overjoyed" and tried not to grimace when he started taping her toe to the one beside it. She also tried not to think about how Vitale's presence in her room seemed to be using up the oxygen her brain needed to put together a rational thought.

"You cannot hike the Cinque Terre now." Vitale hit on the point again, as he'd done several times since her accident.

She cocked her head and gave her best imitation of an Italian gesture of impatience. "I get it. I won't be hiking the Cinque Terre. You don't have to keep repeating it."

Her irritated tone didn't seem to faze him. "You will need to change the plans. Where were you to stay?"

"I have reservations in Monterosso. I'll go there and spend time on the beach." Not a great plan, but the best she could come up with since she'd already paid a deposit.

"That will not be enjoyable. Monterosso, she is very small. Two days, you wish you were not there."

"You have a better idea?"

"You stay here. Much to do in Lerici. Monterosso, not so much."

She knew he was right. From what she'd read, Monterosso was tiny, and lying on the beach for ten days wasn't her idea of the dream vacation. "But I have reservations, and they'll charge me if I cancel at this late date."

Vitale's bottom lip protruded in a sensuous pout, heavy eyebrows drawn together. He pinned her with that brooding stare she'd encountered at their first meeting. "You have the number for the telephone?"

The small journal lay on her nightstand. She pointed to it, and he handed it to her. She flipped to the page with the hotel information. "I cancel the reservation for you. I do not let them make you pay."

Julia's stomach did a quick tap dance. She'd never had a man take charge of things for her. Frank was more of a sit-back-and-let-her-do-it type, and that included everything from paying the bills to making love. But Vitale was waiting for an answer. If he could get her out of the reservation in Monterosso, maybe she could go on to Florence or Pisa or Genoa. Or maybe she would stay here in Lerici for a few more days. "Okay. If you think you can."

Vitale rested the receiver under his chin as he held the book with one hand and punched the numbers with the other. He started talking as soon as someone answered on the other end. His tone wasn't angry, just no-nonsense. It wasn't long before he turned to her. "What is your name?"

"Julia."

He nodded. "Julietta what?"

Julietta? She started to correct him, but it sounded so nice the way the word rolled off his tongue. "Um, Berkwith."

"*Che?*"

She didn't know the word, but she caught the meaning from the question in his eyes. "Berkwith. B-e-r-k-w-i-t-h."

He held out the journal and a pen, and she wrote it down for him.

A pat on her leg surprised her. Doctor Old-But-Still-Interested had finished taping up her toe, and she hadn't even felt it, she was so caught up in Vitale's conversation. Or in the man, if she dared admit that.

She reached for her purse, but the doctor waved it away and said something she didn't understand. In her head she translated it as, "No, no. You are such a ripe and luscious woman, it was my pleasure to tape your toe merely to have the opportunity to fondle your shapely legs."

Vitale's voice vacillated between stern and forceful to mellow and cajoling, and if hand gestures meant the same as in the States, he told the person on the other end to let his fingers do the walking through a tornado. Twice.

The doctor pointed to her and to the single crutch he'd brought with him. She made a couple of laps around the tiny room to satisfy him. The crutch bore the bulk of the weight on that foot, but she could still touch it down, so she didn't lose her balance. This was going to be okay. She should be able to do plenty of sightseeing, and the whole vacation wasn't going to be a bust after all.

"*Grazie, grazie mille.*" She shook the doctor's hand warmly.

"*Prego.*" He patted her hand and responded with something that probably meant, "When you decide you want to bed that Italian Hettie talked about, give me a call."

At least she wasn't invisible to him, though, and for that she was grateful. She wasn't invisible to Vitale either, but it wasn't lost on her that Vitale was taking care of her the same way she took care of Hettie.

The congenial doctor said his "*Arrivederci*" and headed out as the hotel manager flitted in again, bringing two more ice cubes for her toe. Ice must be a precious commodity, and she gave them a once-over to see if they were being recycled from left-over drinks from the bar. The faint telltale lemon scent had her worried.

"Mr. Moretti." She wanted to catch him before he made another round to the bar. "I'd like to stay here a few more days. Would it be possible to keep this room? Or I can move to another if this one is booked?"

He looked at her like she'd asked for the impossible—like more ice. "*Aaiee,* signora, the room, she is reserved. All the rooms, they are reserved for two week."

"All of them? You have no rooms available?"

"No, signora. The tour arrive tomorrow."

"Tour?"

"*Sì.* The tour come each July."

"So, I can't stay here." That would put Monterosso back in the plans. *Oh crap!* "Vitale!"

But he was already hanging up the phone, and the smug smile on his face said it all. "You have no reservation, Julietta, and you pay no money."

"Well, you got that right." She inwardly cringed when his smile broadened. *Gotta quit using sarcasm around this guy.* No way was she going to ask him to call and try to get the reservation again. She tossed the crutch on the bed and plopped down beside it.

"Julietta, you are not happy?" Vitale moved over in front of her, looking down at her with soulful eyes. Damn gorgeous soulful eyes.

This guy could never lie and get away with it. He gave everything away with his face. She thought briefly of Frank's poker face but shoved it out of her mind.

"Vitale, I appreciate everything you've done. Really." She leaned her weight against one arm and ran the other hand through the hair at the top of her head. "But Mr. Moretti says I can't stay here, and we just canceled my reservation in Monterosso, and my toe is broken so I can't hike the Cinque Terre, so I'm thinking I need to cut my losses and go on to Pisa or someplace where I can work."

Vitale swung his gaze around to Mr. Moretti, and Julia watched it harden.

"Is this true?" he demanded.

"*Sì,* Vitale."

And then came a flurry of words such as she'd never heard before. She wouldn't call it an exchange—one didn't wait for the other to finish. Instead, they talked at the same time, spoke over each other, gestured wildly. Faces reddened, voices rose, and Julia watched . . . fascinated.

It ended when Mr. Moretti stormed out of the room, still talking.

She stood up and limped awkwardly toward Vitale with no idea who had won . . . but he didn't look happy. She reached out to pat his arm in a friendly gesture, but he caught her hand, and she caught her breath.

"No rooms." He squeezed her hand gently, and she had to force herself to quit watching his mouth and listen to his words. "But I find you the place to stay."

"No, you don't need to do that." She jerked her hand away, feeling silly at the excitement his touch roused in her. "I know I blamed you earlier, but I was just upset. It wasn't your fault. I should have been watching where I was going."

"I want to do."

"Why? You don't even know me." She squared her shoulders, preparing to take the blow when he said she reminded him of his mother—or worse.

"Because you work hard." His fingers skimmed lightly down her arm, causing her to reach across and clutch the crutch with both hands for grounding. "You come to Italy. To Lerici. You cannot hike, but you can enjoy. You want to be here. It make you happy."

"Happy?" Sarcasm crept back into her tone. "My whole vacation has fallen apart, and you think I'm happy?"

"You are happy. The body, she say happy."

"How in heaven's name do you get 'happy' out of my limping around the room on a crutch?" She threw the words out like a challenge.

"The finger . . . sometime the toe." He nodded to her hand resting on her hip. "She dance to the music inside you. On the table when you eat. On the chair by the pool when you rest." He pointed to the imprint in the comforter where she'd been sitting. "On the bed."

His answer stunned her. To battle the depression after her cancer diagnosis and the ensuing divorce, her therapist encouraged her to use music as therapy—make playlists of songs that made her happy—to keep her mind occupied with something other than fear. She'd never realized she tapped the rhythm unconsciously.

But Vitale noticed?

That was actually kind of nice. "But . . ." It still didn't make sense for a perfect stranger to go to this much trouble, dancing finger notwithstanding.

"No but."

He touched his finger to her lip, and she fought the sudden urge to draw it into her mouth and suck on it. Her brain shouted at her to stop that line of thinking, but other parts of her body seemed to have a mind of their own.

"I want to do it, so I do it. I leave now to finish the work. But I find you the place to stay. I come tomorrow morning to take you there."

"Well, here." She grabbed her journal from the table. "The hotels where I have reservations in Florence and Rome are here." She copied the listings from the first two pages and handed him the paper. "Maybe one of them will have a room available, and I'll just spend more time there."

He looked as though he was about to comment, but then he stuffed the paper into his pocket and walked out, head held high, reminding her of stories of demigods in Roman mythology.

Poor mortal women. Never stood a chance.

Julia needed fresh air.

She needed to check in with Camille, and she needed to check on Hettie. Most of all, she needed to keep her libido in check. Reacting foolishly to Vitale the way she had put her in the same league with Frank and Howard, a thought that made her skin crawl.

"Get hold of yourself, Julietta," she muttered, but the pleasant shiver that fluttered down her spine when she imagined Vitale mispronouncing her name mocked her attempts to follow her own advice. She grabbed her bag and the crutch, determined to let the salty breeze cleanse the overcharged synapses in her brain.

Passing through the hotel lobby, she spotted a brochure advertising a boat excursion around the area. There would be just enough time to grab a bite and make it to the three o'clock tour.

The walk down the incline went fairly well with the crutch, though a bit slower than she was used to. She hadn't ventured very far before she found a lovely bistro with alfresco dining. After ordering a panini and a pinot grigio, feeling smugly decadent for drinking wine at lunch, she dialed the business number.

"Panache. This is Camille."

"So the business hasn't folded in my absence."

"Julia! How are you?"

She drew out a long, dramatic sigh. "Well, my toe got broken this morning when Jupiter became angry that I was gawking at one of his gods, so I won't be hiking the Cinque Terre after all."

"Oh no." Camille groaned the utterance in such a way that adequate sympathy and a hug were both conveyed over the distance.

"And I lost my hotel reservation, so I don't have anyplace to stay, but said-god is looking for a place, and he noticed my dancing finger, so all in all, I'd say things aren't *too* terrible."

"I'm not even sure I followed all of that, but it sounds like you've met a man, so I'm impressed." Impressing Camille wasn't difficult if romance was involved . . . even the fantasy kind.

"I've met a man named Vitale, who's gorgeous, but he's only about thirty, so hardly in legal range for me. The good part is that he's taking care of me like he would his mother—so you got your wish—and he's very helpful."

"His mother, huh? Better wait and see what he wants for his trouble before you continue down that line of thinking." Camille's philosophy came out chewed around the edges. She must be eating breakfast. "And how'd the broken toe happen?"

Julia opted for the dramaless version. "Vitale was laying a pathway, and he had this pile of stones. One fell off and landed on my foot."

"Are you in pain?"

Julia thought about that before she spoke. "No, not really."

"But you can't hike." More crunching ensued. "That's terrible."

"Could be worse. Of all the great places in the world to get laid up, the Italian Riviera's got to be at the top of the list. How's business?"

"Nora Travis called this morning." An eye roll was evident in Camille's voice. "She's ready to do her library and got all excited when I told her you were in Italy looking for new lines."

Julia answered with an eye roll of her own. "Glad you're there to take care of the pretentious little twit. You were so good with her last time."

"As long as she's willing to pay the price, I don't mind wearing my boots and carrying my shovel." Julia heard the familiar door chime in the background. "Anne Hutchens. How are you? Hey, Julia, somebody just came in, so I've got to go. Call and let me know where you are and how you're managing, 'kay?"

"I will. Go make us some money."

"And you find us some great stuff. Love you!"

As the warm sun beat down on her back, Julia was surprised at how relaxed she felt considering the circumstances. She should be upset . . . in a foreign country virtually homeless. But Vitale's manner had been so assuring, she really wasn't worried. He would find her a place to stay.

Allowing someone else to take care of things this once was rather nice, actually. But she wouldn't want to make a habit of it.

She sipped the crisp white wine, which tasted of sunshine and air and sea—Liguria in a bottle—and soon her server sat the grilled sandwich in front of her, bits of roasted red peppers and eggplant oozing out the side along with the cheese.

Julia's mouth watered at the sight.

"You meet Vitale?"

Julia's surprise must've shown on her face.

"I hear you say 'Vitale.'" The girl pointed to the cell phone.

"Oh." Julia pointed to her toe. "I broke my toe this morning, so I'm having to change my plans. Vitale helped me do that."

"Vitale, he is nice." The girl took a dreamy breath. "And beautiful. Do you love him?"

Ah! Just as she'd suspected—no woman was impervious to the man's charms. Julia chuckled and shook her head. "No, I don't love him. He's much too young for me." She estimated the girl to be around seventeen. "And much too old for you, I think."

The girl flashed her a sheepish smile. "All the women love Vitale. *Mia nonna, mia madre, mia sorella . . .* me. All love Vitale." She pursed her lips and gave a knowing nod, looking wise for her years, and shook her finger meaningfully. "And Vitale, he love all the women."

"So look, but no touch, eh?" Julia tried to match the girl's wise and somber look.

"*Sì.* Plenty of look, though." The sweet face dissolved into a moony smile before she walked back inside.

"Done more than my share of looking already," Julia murmured, then washed away the admission on a sip of wine.

One bite of the panini, and she was sure she could live here forever. Gorgeous men, great wines, luscious foods—all works of art. What was there not to love about this place?

The young server sat a plate on the next table over with four perfectly formed chocolate truffles. They reminded Julia of Hettie. She dialed the number that would ring directly into her mother-in-law's room.

Hettie answered on the fourth ring, which was a feat for her.

As soon as she heard Julia's *"Buon giorno,"* she opened with, "Gotten laid yet? Remember, it's got to be by an Italian. Americans you meet on planes don't count."

"The American I met on the plane was a jerk. And the only Italians I've met would be better suited for Melissa or you."

"Go for one of the young ones," Hettie said. "If you caused one of the old guys to have a heart attack, it could get ugly."

Julia tucked that away under *needless advice* and shifted the subject to the news about her toe and her change in plans. Hettie was sympathetic, but not sappy. "That stone didn't just fall on your toe. Fate pushed it there, so be ready."

"Ready's my middle name."

Hettie snorted and launched into a tale about Mable Tarrington's foray into the game room that morning wearing only a smile.

The time neared for her excursion, so Julia said her good-byes and asked for her check. The girl brought her change along with a small bag.

"For Vitale. From Rosa."

Julia hesitated. "I won't see him until tomorrow."

"Pasticceria. They keep."

Julia tucked the package into her tote and went to meet the boat.

CHAPTER 6

The tour headed south to Tellaro first, giving Julia a different perspective on the town than she'd gotten yesterday from the hike in the hills above, though just as tranquil. The picturesque pink and orange houses set against the vibrant green backdrop made it difficult to imagine anything but perfect harmony behind those walls. No cancer. No infidelity. Nothing but blissfully happy couples living out their days in peaceful perfection. However, the quick stop the captain made at the spot where Percy Bysshe Shelley's boat went down, which led to the poet's drowning, served as a sad reminder of her parents' death in a boating accident on Kentucky Lake.

"Every life has stormy seas," the captain said.

The poignancy of his statement stung Julia's eyes, and her throat burned with the bitterness of all she'd lost.

Across the gulf to the small islands of Tino and Isola, up to La Spezia, and back down to Lerici, the afternoon flew by as quickly as the Italian coastline. Fingers of the Mediterranean grasped the land deeply in places, holding it still as the world revolved around it. Quaint fishing villages rose and fell like the tide, winking into and out of view. Fishing boats with wizened old men smoking pipes. Yachts with bikini-clad beauties—mostly topless. Blue sky and azure water coming together at some indistinct point Julia wasn't sure even existed. She felt like any moment they would be riding one of the waves into the air, and she wouldn't be surprised in the least.

When the boat returned to shore, she realized it had been hours since she'd thought about her toe—or her life. Out on the sea, Frank, cancer, Melissa's move, Hettie's stroke—everything, at last, dissolved into a blue oblivion.

Relaxed and exhausted from the shiatsu massage of the wind, she returned to her room and fell asleep on a chaise on the balcony, awaking sometime in the middle of the night with a vague worry about where she would be the next night but sure Vitale's word would be good.

She dragged herself to the bed, not waking again until a loud knock startled her. She scurried to the door as fast as her toe would allow.

Vitale.

His eyes raked down her, and he gave a cocky grin. *"Buon giorno,* Julietta.*"*

Her eyes dropped to see her designer nipples protruding through the thick camisole she'd slept in. Of course, Vitale thought they were greeting him personally. *"Buon giorno,* Vitale.*"* Although she didn't think her scars would be visible to his casual glance, she stepped self-consciously behind the door and peered around it.

"I have the place for you to stay. Are you ready to go?"

She looked at her watch, astounded to note that it was past ten thirty. What about Italy caused her to sleep so late? She'd been living out of her suitcase since she'd arrived, so there wasn't much to pack. "I can be ready in twenty minutes. Is the place you found far?"

He shook his head and she shut the door, wondering if he was going to continue standing there, but pretty sure there was no way she could breathe enough to move if she asked him in.

She took the quickest shower she'd ever taken, brushed her hair and teeth, and slapped on a minimum of makeup. Moving from one hotel to another didn't require dressing up, so she slipped into a short skirt, tank top, open blouse, and the flip-flops that would unfortunately have to be standard footwear this trip.

As she suspected, when she opened her door twenty-three minutes after answering it the first time, Vitale was still standing there.

He grabbed her suitcases, obviously not even considering using the wheels. "I talk to Mario. He do not charge for your stay here because of the injury."

"Oh, I don't want him to do that," Julia protested.

"It is the correct thing to do, and I borrow his car, so we must hurry. It is the Sunday."

A bright yellow Smart car waited on the road at the front of her hotel. Julia put on her seat belt while Vitale filled the back with her two pieces of luggage.

He got in, taking off so quickly she lost the ability to speak for a minute, able only to clutch the sides of her seat and take in quick breaths through clenched teeth. But when Vitale took the road that led away from town, the threat of impending doom gave her voice back. "I thought you said it wasn't far! Where *is* the room you found?"

He gave a wolfish smile and threw a sidelong glance her way. "*Casa mia.* You will stay with me."

Chapter 7

"Oh no, you don't." Julia flung her arm out the window and held on to the door as Vitale swept around a curve. "I am *not* staying with you. Take me back to the hotel. Now."

Vitale kept his eyes on the road and shrugged. "I cannot do that. We to be late."

A curve in the opposite direction careened her back to the middle of the car. She came up hard against Vitale's arm. "Late for what?"

"*Il pranzo con la mia famiglia.*"

The words were some from the CDs she'd practiced with, so they were familiar. She just hadn't heard them put together this way. It took a few seconds to translate. "Lunch? With your family?"

He nodded, seeming pleased that she understood. "*Sì.*"

Realizing he wasn't likely a serial killer if he was taking her to Sunday lunch with his family, her heart rate shifted from *panic mode* to *unexpected guest*. "Oh no. I can't impose like that."

"You like."

Julia looked down at the skirt riding up on her thighs. "I'm not saying I wouldn't enjoy it. I'm sure they're lovely people, and it's very kind of you, but I'm not dressed for Sunday dinner with anybody's family." It crossed her mind that her clothes were only an arm's length away. Was there something she could change into? She loosened her grip on the door handle, intending to unzip her luggage and have a look, but a fast curve made her rethink that action. "Is there someplace we can stop and let me change clothes?"

"No, no to change."

"But . . ." A protest was on her tongue.

"You look beautiful."

Beautiful? Of course, the word was merely part of his woman-appeal jargon, but it hung pleasantly in her ear. She sat back and thought the situation over again. Sunday lunch in the home of an Italian family might be fun. The food would probably be amazing, and it would be a great way to practice her Italian. She'd never see these people again, so what difference did it make what she was wearing? She nodded. "Okay. Why not? That is, if you think it will be all right with your family."

"It will be all right with the family."

"Then thank you for inviting me. I'm sure I'll enjoy it very much. But after lunch you'll take me back to town, and we'll make calls until I find a room."

He ignored her comment, but his reaction didn't make her feel ignored. His smug smile said he knew she was there. This was simply a man used to getting his own way. Julia mentally rolled her eyes.

They came around another hairpin curve too fast, and Vitale slammed on the brakes to keep from hitting a car at the back of a long line of stopped ones.

Julia braced a hand against the dashboard and gritted her teeth while the car jostled to a stop. "Where in the hell did you learn—and I use that term loosely—to drive?"

The line started to move, he threw the car back into gear, and Julia latched on to the door for another wild takeoff.

"I do not learn. I just to drive."

"Well, that explains it." She could do a better job, but her toe wouldn't let her press on the gas pedal at all. She wished Vitale had a hurt toe that would keep him from pressing it so hard.

He gunned it, and they roared ahead a few more yards. She

clenched her jaws and held on, foregoing conversation until they were a safe distance from the car in front of them.

At last, the obstacle, a minivan with a flat tire, managed to pull far enough off the narrow road to allow others by, and traffic picked up to breakneck speed again.

They were headed into the hills. *The hills I should be hiking today.* Patches of purple and yellow wildflowers whipped past her vision. She closed her eyes to keep from getting carsick. *Instead, I'm in the passenger seat with a madman at the wheel, going who-knows-where, up and down hills, around blind curves, with no hope of finding my way back to where I started.*

A metaphor for the past couple of years of her life.

Conversation didn't seem like the safest option, but a safe option didn't jump out at her right at the moment, and it might keep her mind off Vitale's driving skills. Or lack thereof. "I don't usually dine at someone's house without taking something. Should we stop and let me pick up a bottle of wine?" *And find a nice, safe donkey to ride back to town.*

"No, they have the wine. You are the guest."

"How many people will be there? Do you have a large family?"

Vitale shook his head. "Not large. Mama, Papà, Maria, Giovanni, Rachele, Paolo, Adrianna, Antonio, Giada, Michele, Celeste, Piero, Lia, Enrico, Orabella, Cesare, Chiara, Elia."

"Oh, for heaven's sakes. You don't consider that large? I mean, you're talking to an only child who was married to an only child and produced an only child. How many siblings do you have?"

His brows drew together in confusion. "Ceilings? In the house? I never count them. One for each room."

Julia tried to suppress a giggle. "Not ceilings. Siblings. Brothers and sisters."

"Seeblings." He tried out the new word. "Five see-blings. No brothers. Five sisters."

Aha. That explained a few things. The only boy and five sisters. No wonder he was used to getting his own way. Articles she'd read about Italian culture painted Italian men as quite spoiled by their families. It would be interesting to see if that was actually true in Vitale's case. "Are your sisters older than you? Younger?"

"Three older. Maria, Giada, Celeste. Adrianna and Orabella younger."

"They are married?"

"*Sì.*"

"All of them?"

"*Sì.*"

"I assume you're not married?"

"No."

"Girlfriend?"

"No girlfriend."

So, unless his family gets the wrong idea, I won't have some hotheaded Italian mistress putting out a contract on me.

"Oh, that reminds me." Julia pulled the small parcel from her tote. "This is from Rosa at the café in the village. She tells me all the women love Vitale."

Vitale laughed, and Julia realized it was the first time she'd heard him really laugh. The sound originated from somewhere deep, and it made her feel like she was sharing something intimate with him, warming her from the inside out.

"Rosa, she talk too much, and she think all the world is like Rosa." He chuckled again and shook his head. "But *sua nonna,* she make biscotto *deliziosa.*"

He started to tear open the parchment package, but that required him to let go of the steering wheel. Julia grabbed the parcel out of his hands. "Here. Let me do that."

Inside the paper were four pastry pinwheels.

"Eat," Vitale insisted. "You understand." He slowed the car and reached over to hold one up to her mouth. She bit into it and the buttery crust seemed to dissolve away, leaving a tangy concoction of apricot and chopped chestnuts.

"Mmmm. Yum." She closed her eyes and savored the taste. When she opened them, Vitale was watching her with a look that made her feel like *she* was being devoured. She smiled and he laughed again.

"You like biscotto, yes?"

She nodded.

"Eat." He pushed it toward her mouth. She took another bite and caught the pastry in her hands as it started buckling under the assault.

A crumb hung on her bottom lip, and she slipped her tongue out to catch it just as Vitale's thumb brushed it away. When her tongue grazed him, she quickly sucked it back into her mouth, drawing another smile from him. He responded by stroking his thumb slowly across her lip.

Her breath caught in her throat.

Then he helped himself to a biscotto, shifted in his seat, and lay down on the accelerator again.

They drove in silence for a while, seeming to understand any conversation while eating such a treasure would amount to sacrilege.

Julia's stomach adapted to the lurching of the car, though she concentrated on keeping her eyes glued to the road to aid her backseat driving—on anything that would shift her focus from the flirtation this man inspired. "Your English is good, Vitale." She broke the silence. "How did you learn?"

She saw his shrug in her peripheral vision.

"I do not learn. I just do."

"Is that your answer for everything?"

She cast a quick glance his way and caught the hint of a smile.

"Most important thing, person just know."

They rode again in silence a few minutes.

"Vitale." She decided to broach the subject again. "I don't want to seem ungrateful. I really do appreciate all you've done for me and your hospitality . . . offering me a place to stay. But I don't think it's a good idea. I mean, for all I know, you could be a serial killer." She flinched as a tree branch missed her window by mere inches.

"I do not eat the cereal, but I do not kill it. I will get you the cereal if that is what you eat for the breakfast. I am the good host."

Even his offended look couldn't keep her from smiling at the thought of Vitale plunging a knife into a box of Special K. "I'm not worried about breakfast, and I'm sure you're a very good host."

He took a long, exasperated breath. "Julietta, there is no room. I try to find, call many places. The tour, she take everything. Do you worry because I am a man?"

"Of course not." She waved away the absurdity. "I mean, I'm not afraid that anything will happen. But it doesn't look right. It's not proper to stay with a man I hardly know."

"We will not have the sex. Unless you want it," he added.

His tone was matter-of-fact, but the mention of the word hurled Julia way over the edge of her comfort zone. "Have sex?" she sputtered. "Who said anything about having sex?"

"Vitale say it."

"I know who said it . . ."

"But you ask who say it," he replied flatly.

"It's just an expression. I meant that it hadn't even occurred to me to have sex with you," she lied, trying not to let her face show that she actually had envisioned it pretty graphically numerous times since first seeing him. "You're too young. How old are you?"

His quick laugh inferred her fears were inconsequential. "Thirty-four. I am a man. You are a woman. And the breasts say—"

"You can't believe my breasts," she countered, still reeling from the realization that a thirty-four-year-old had obviously thought about having sex with her. "They lie."

"Breasts no lie. The woman lie." He brought the car to a grinding halt in front of a house and shot her a triumphant smile.

She opened her mouth to protest again but dropped her next comment, choosing to use the time to gather her wits about her so Vitale's family wouldn't think she'd been thinking about having sex with him.

The quintessential two-story Italian farmhouse surrounded by olive and cedar trees remained tranquil for all of two seconds before someone inside must have noticed their arrival. Then it became a beehive of activity with men, women, and children flying out from every direction shouting, "Vitale! Vitale!"

A young boy of eight or so bolted up first and jerked open the door on Julia's side, brown eyes wide with wonder. His expression faded to exasperation when her toe and the crutch kept her from vacating the area as quickly as he wanted. But once she cleared the path, he dove into the seat, giddy with excitement.

She stepped back out of the way as more and more family members joined the throng, buzzing like bees swarming around their gigantic yellow and black queen.

They talked excitedly, running their hands across the smooth leather interior and sleek exterior curves.

"*Non, non. Non ho comprato l'automobile,*" Vitale protested in response to the rapid-fire questions aimed his way. At last, he quieted the group long enough to point toward Julia.

Seventeen pairs of eyes turned toward her in unison, seeming to see her for the first time. "Julietta, *la mia famiglia.*" He smiled warmly as he came around the car to stand by her, placing a hand at the small of her back. She was sure it wouldn't have happened otherwise, but the touch coming so fast on the heels of his comments about having sex gave her a shameful tingle of excitement. She tried to stop the smile that popped onto her lips. *Oh, this is ridiculous.* Maybe the family would perceive her expression as excitement about sharing lunch with them.

With his customary gesturing, Vitale introduced each person, then apparently proceeded to explain about her toe and the crutch because all the eyes shifted down at the same time, and the surprised expressions softened to sympathy. Or maybe they felt sorry for her obvious fashion faux pas since they were all dressed up.

She tugged on the skirt, trying to cover more leg as her eyes scanned the gorgeous array of people surrounding her. Vitale's sisters were as beautiful as he was handsome—all of them tall and lean, like their father, Piero. Their mother, Angelina, while shorter and stockier, still had a manner about her that let everyone know she ruled the hive. The queen bee personified.

The family members kept their distance until Angelina graciously took Julia's arm. "*Benvenuta,* Julietta," she said, and gestured toward the house. Then the hive became frenzied again, welcoming the newcomer in English that ranged from stuttered to flawless, but always accompanied by handshakes and hugs.

After the preliminaries, Julia waved as Vitale and the men disappeared around the side of the house.

* * *

Angelina walked her slowly up the uneven sidewalk, which was paved with ancient stones that matched the ones on the house. "You *americana?*" she asked.

"That's right. I'm from Kentucky." Julia watched the woman's eyes narrow in question. Vitale had done the same thing when she mentioned the state to him. "It's sort of in the middle of the country," she explained. "I wish I had dressed more appropriately. I didn't know we were coming here for lunch. I thought I was switching hotels . . ." She remembered where Vitale actually intended for her to stay and quickly dropped that line of conversation. "But thank you for having me."

Angelina's eyes stayed narrowed while she shrugged. "My English not good."

A flowering vine with small, poppy red flowers blanketed portions of the house's façade, and huge bushes flanked either side of the stone stoop. Their scent was familiar, and Julia took another sniff as they passed. Rosemary. Gigantic versions of the small pot she grew on the deck at home.

A deluge of mouthwatering aromas assaulted her nose and taste buds as she stepped through the doorway. One whole side of the house was a gigantic kitchen/dining room combination. A massive table, already set and surrounded by an eclectic mixture of chairs, dominated the room.

Angelina directed Julia to a caned chair against the wall. "Sit now."

Julia sat helplessly to the side as the women scurried around placing platters of food on the huge, marble-topped buffet. One of them—Giada perhaps?—quickly set one more place and rearranged the chairs to allow for the addition of another.

"Can I help?" Julia offered.

Angelina answered with *phtt, phtt, phtt* and an impatient gesture Julia translated as "No, and stay out of the way."

Two little girls sidled up, eyeing Julia warily. When she smiled, the oldest one attached firmly against her thigh while the smaller child held out her arms. Julia gathered the child onto her lap. Tiny arms encircled her neck and a warm cheek nestled against hers.

Precious memories of Melissa at that age brought a lump to her throat. God, she missed her.

Both of the children chattered away, asking Julia question after question, obviously perplexed with her pat answer, "*Non capisco.*"

Through the great French doors at the back of the house, Julia could see what had stolen the men away so quickly—a bocce ball court and what already appeared to be a heated competition.

With movie director precision, Angelina choreographed the position of each dish until, at last, two large terrines of soup were placed, one at each end of the table. She seemed satisfied that all was ready.

A gentle command was directed to the little girl leaning against Julia's leg. She ran out the back door, but soon returned, leading her grandpa, Piero, by the finger. Vitale and the other men followed.

Everyone gathered around the table, moving so quickly Julia had to assume seating was assigned and set for life. Vitale took her hand and led her to the seat beside him at his father's end of the table. He continued to hold her hand, which made her heartbeat speed up to its third-cup-of-coffee level. What would his family think of them? Holding hands like a couple of teenagers! When Celeste took her other hand, Julia understood, feeling a bit foolish as Piero intoned a beautiful blessing for the food.

He finished and Vitale pulled her chair out for her and pushed it in after she was seated. All the men and boys did the same for the women and girls sitting near them.

Angelina and Piero ladled the orange-colored soup into bowls and passed them down the sides of the table amid lots of banter that Julia could only grapple single words from. She understood "automobile" and "Mario Moretti," so she inferred Vitale was explaining whom he'd borrowed the car from.

Proud of her accomplishment, and already exhausted by the effort of trying to understand the foreign language, she rewarded herself with a spoonful of the soup, which had been placed in front of her. The delicious sweetness of butternut squash surrounded her tongue, chased by a hint of nutmeg. Another flavor teased her senses, and she concentrated to name it. Sage maybe? She was so caught up in the mulled flavors, she didn't think anything of Celeste's sharp but whispered utterance, "Vitale . . ."

It was the jerky movement of his arm against hers that drew her attention.

"*Merda!*" He swore under his breath and scooted his chair back. His napkin landed hard in his empty seat, thrown down like a gauntlet.

"What's wrong?"

But he was already making his way to the front door.

She glanced around the silent table.

All the eyes were focused out the large front window. She followed their gazes to the small black sedan parked behind the yellow Smart car.

As she watched, a petite brunette with hair to her waist ran up the walk toward Vitale and launched herself into his arms, smothering his face with kisses.

CHAPTER 8

Julia watched the dramatic pantomime taking place in the front yard, trying to piece together what was happening.

After the initial shock, it seemed everyone at the table began talking at once. Most of the tones were angry, though whether they were directed at the young woman, Vitale, or someone else entirely she couldn't tell.

She watched Vitale extricate himself from the woman's embrace and send her away. The chatter at the table increased as the woman threw up her hands and took a step toward him, but Vitale held his palms up in a "stop" gesture and motioned toward her car. This brought on a collective whispered gasp from inside the house. The woman wheeled around and started toward her car, only to stop and turn back to Vitale. This time she was obviously crying, and the talk at the table rose to a crescendo as the woman held out her arms, pleading. Vitale turned back toward the house. The woman shouted something and made a hand gesture that must have meant something obscene based on the sharp tones of the audience surrounding Julia.

She felt like she was watching an opera, trying to keep up with the story without any subtitles.

Before she had time to piece it all together, which mostly meant deciding who was the protagonist and who was the villain, Vitale stormed back into the house, slamming the door behind him. The talking came to an abrupt stop, though a telltale silence hung over the group. Everyone, even the children, seemed fascinated by the ingredients of the smooth concoction in their bowls.

Vitale's chiseled jaw was set in stone, and the brooding darkness had returned to his eyes when he sat down and placed his napkin back in his lap. He addressed the group with a quick "*mi dispiace*" and resumed eating his soup.

No one made eye contact with anyone—especially not the stranger in their midst. *Oh dear!* Did they think she had something to do with the scene outside?

She needed to show his family she and Vitale weren't lovers, if they'd jumped to that ridiculous conclusion. Which they surely hadn't, considering the age difference. A lover would be upset by what just happened, so she would show them how not-upset-in-the-least she was.

She smiled broadly toward Vitale's mother, whose frown was set as hard as Vitale's. "*Angelina, la minestra è magnifico.*"

She watched the transformation as the woman absorbed the compliment. The tense muscles around her mouth and eyes went slack before she returned the smile, but a hint of worry clouded her eyes. "*Grazie,* Julietta."

She added something else, but Julia only understood "Thank you." She looked to Vitale for translation.

His brown eyes locked with hers, and his mouth twitched at the corners. "She did not know you speak Italian."

Julia turned back to Angelina with a sheepish grin. "I don't speak Italian. Only a few words."

A laugh with a definite feeling of relief swept over the group. Whether it was relief she hadn't understood their conversation during the confrontation outside or relief that she and Vitale weren't lovers, she couldn't be sure.

Maybe both.

But the tension remained broken and normal family conversation returned to the table along with plenty of laughter. This was obviously a close-knit group.

Throughout the remaining courses—delicate fettucine with peas and prosciutto, roasted chicken, a variety of cheeses, and dessert—Vitale worked hard at translating and keeping Julia involved in the conversations near them.

Occasionally, someone would ask her something directly in English and then it was such a relief to relax and talk about things she knew. Giada, whose English was perfect because she'd been an exchange student in Chicago, asked about her business in the States. Adrianna wanted to know all about how she trained for the long hikes. When Celeste asked about her family, Angelina became all ears, especially intrigued to hear about Melissa.

"Bring her to Italy. We marry her to Vitale. Is time he have the children." Angelina's tone didn't sound like she was kidding despite the snicker that moved through the group.

Well, obviously his *mother* didn't think they were lovers. In spite of its smooth texture, the bite of *panna cotta* she'd just swallowed wedged in Julia's throat. She forced a laugh around it and shifted uncomfortably in her chair, tugging again on the skirt. And, of course, there was no reason Angelina *would* have thought that. They *weren't* lovers, and they weren't *going to be* lovers—no matter what Vitale said in the car.

The custard certainly took its time, wiggling its way past the constricted muscles in her throat.

"Mama." Vitale's voice held a don't-go-there warning, which Angelina ignored. She dove into a lecture filled with motherly tones that Julia understood despite the language barrier. And the way she kept pointing out the window made Julia think the young woman who'd shown up might've been Angelina's choice of daughter-in-law.

Piero jumped in, appearing to take his son's side, and then it seemed like everyone at the table had an opinion about whatever-it-was, and they all voiced them at the same time.

Although Vitale made no move to translate any of it, the name Francesca seemed to be repeated by everyone, so Julia assumed it to be the young woman's name.

This put a new wrinkle in the where-was-she-going-to-stay mystery. Vitale said he didn't have a girlfriend, but they could just be on a break. Julia sighed, remembering the angry breakups when she and Frank were going out and the makeup sex.

She finished her *panna cotta* in silence.

Vitale stayed mostly quiet also, occasionally giving a sarcastic snort accompanied by a gesture, but the rest of the table was anything but quiet. The volume continued to rise until, at last, Vitale stood up abruptly, his chair grating backward again across the worn floorboards.

The room grew silent.

His steps were slow and deliberate as he made his way to Angelina's end of the table. He stood for a moment, towering over his mother, whose chin rose defiantly. "Mama." He stooped down beside her and took one of her hands, pressing it to his lips. "*Ti voglio bene.*"

Angelina's anger visibly melted. "Ah, Vitale." She took his face in her hands and kissed him on the forehead, and a collective feminine "Aw" lapped the table.

Julia smiled at the sweet scene, but she let the words from Rosa, the young server from yesterday, serve as a warning.

"*All the women love Vitale.*"

The kitchen didn't take long to clean and straighten with so many hands working. Julia convinced her reluctant hostess she was capable of washing dishes, happy to repay their warm hospitality at least in part.

Afterward, Giada took her for a short tour of the olive grove, walking slowly so as not to tax Julia's foot as she pointed out some ancient trees that had been growing on the spot for over a hundred years.

A beautiful, ornately carved wooden bench sat nestled in a shady corner. Giada indicated for Julia to sit and settled herself at the opposite end. "You are disappointed you cannot make the hike, yes?"

"Yeah." The wine at lunch and the warm breeze brushing her

cheeks lulled Julia into a tranquil mood and loosened her tongue. "It's not so much the hike that disappoints me as what it meant to me."

Giada cocked her head. "The hike had special significance?"

"I had breast cancer two years ago." Sharing something so personal with a virtual stranger felt odd, and the second she said the words, she wished she hadn't. They hung heavy for a few seconds before they pierced the air, and she felt the serenity flow out and away.

Giada's eyes grew wide—maybe it was a good sign her vitality had returned enough for people to be surprised. "I'm fine now." Julia hurried to get to the good part. "But the hike was like my victory symbol. The ultimate sign to me that I'd regained my health."

Giada nodded, but Julia watched as the redness of unshed tears bloomed around the young woman's eyes.

She'd obviously scraped a raw nerve. Cancer? Some other disease? Vitale's sister looked like the picture of health.

A few beats of awkward silence passed before Giada spoke. "Adrianna has a lump in her breast, but she will not go to the doctor. She is afraid. She made me promise not to tell Mama."

Julia's stomach twisted with empathy at the terror the young woman was going through. She'd been in that exact spot once. But the danger of Adrianna ignoring the lump spurred her to speak out even though it was none of her business. "She *has* to have it examined. You have to convince her to go to the doctor."

"I have tried. She does not listen to me." Giada's face shifted from sad to imploring. "Would you speak to her? Maybe she will listen to you because you have been through it." She chewed her bottom lip, then added, "But she cannot know I told you."

"I'm not sure how I could do that. I mean, she's going to know you told me." The weight of the information she was now privy to hung in Julia's belly. This was touchy. Trying to talk with someone she didn't know and who didn't want to hear, about an awkward subject, with a language barrier thrown in to boot?

Her conscience poked its head in the ring. What if Adrianna lost a breast or died because she was too chicken to speak out?

Potentially saving a life would be worth the discomfort in her toe when she kicked herself later. Besides, she reminded herself again, she was never going to see these people again anyway.

And Giada's eyes, wide with fear and hope, would haunt her forever if she said no.

"I suppose I could *try* to talk to her," she offered. "But we'll have to be sneaky." An idea started to take shape in her mind. "We'll go back to the house, and you'll casually bring up my hike again like you just did, and I'll mention my cancer, and we'll let it go from there."

"That is perfect." Giada nodded. "Thank you."

They followed the path back the direction they'd come. Sounds of laughter and spirited conversation drew them around to the side of the house where they found the rest of the women enjoying the shade from a pergola that overlooked the bocce ball court, while the children chased each other around the yard.

On the court, it was Vitale's turn, and the tension cording the muscles in his arms and back implied the world championship was at stake. Her imagination ran amok, and for a split second, she was running her tongue along those deep grooves.

Her breath stopped as he stepped softly, with the fluid grace of an Olympian, and tossed the ball, which landed with a *thud* and then proceeded to roll right into the space that separated two others.

A cacophony of joyful and mournful howls split the air, leaving no doubt as to who were the victors and who the vanquished.

Amid the pats on the back, Vitale threw a glance toward the house. When his gaze found Julia's and locked on to her appreciative stare, he kissed two fingers and turned them her way.

She returned the motion, and his eyebrows shot up in surprise.

Ack! Had she just propositioned him here in front of God and his family?

A mischievous grin spread from ear to ear, and he sprinted to her side.

"How is the toe, Julietta? Do we need to leave?"

The thoughtful question was innocent enough, but the idea of being alone with him coupled with the thoughts that had been racing through her mind were anything but innocent. And Giada cast her a pleading glance.

"My toe's fine. I'm in no hurry to leave. Go. Play." She motioned him away and out of her space so she could breathe again.

One of the men called his name, and he headed back to the court, throwing a wink over his shoulder in parting.

Julia turned her focus to the group of women she approached, not daring to glance his way again for fear of drooling. Hettie certainly knew what she was talking about when it came to the sex appeal of Italian men!

Orabella scooted over to make room for her on the wicker couch. "Your foot. She hurts, Julietta?"

Before Julia could answer, Giada moved into place with her practiced cue. "Not if you walk slowly, though, yes? But what a disappointment to come all this way and not be able to hike the Cinque Terre."

"Yeah." Julia gave a disappointed sigh that held no pretense. "I was supposed to begin those hikes today. I'd worked out for months, training for them. It meant a lot to me."

"The hikes held some special significance to you?" Giada's act was Academy worthy. She fed lines to Julia as though reading from a script.

"Well, I planned it as a victory hike to show myself I had completely regained my health after my bout with breast cancer."

The women all stopped what they were doing in unison and looked at her. It grew so quiet, even the men threw questioning looks their way.

"*Che?*" Angelina leaned forward.

"I lost my breasts to cancer two years ago." Julia aimed for a perky tone. "But I'm fine now. I'm healthy, and I feel wonderful. Well, except for this broken toe."

"But you . . ." Maria's gesture toward Julia's chest wasn't quite a point, but it conveyed her question adequately.

"Have breasts?" Julia smiled and nodded. "Yes, I had reconstruction done. The doctors built me new ones."

The crease between Angelina's brows deepened, and Giada translated what Julia said. The woman eyed Julia's chest with wonder, and she returned Julia's smile with a gentle one of her own.

"You had cancer." It was Adrianna who spoke this time. She swiveled her chair around to face Julia. "Were you afraid?"

"Oh yeah." The perky façade faded, replaced by serious truth. "I was very afraid. Every woman is afraid." The sidelong glances they cast toward their own and each other's breasts confirmed the perceptions in her mind.

"We caught mine with a routine mammogram very early—stage 0, actually."

Adrianna's worried frown deepened. "I did not think they remove the entire breast for only the small place."

"Mine wasn't in only one place. There was no lump. The cancer was very tiny, but it was scattered in several places. To remove all the cancer would've meant losing at least a third of my breast anyway." She paused as Giada translated for Angelina. "So, I chose to have the complete breast removed. That way, I didn't have to go through radiation or chemotherapy. I had both breasts removed, in fact."

"Why?" An astonished gasp accompanied Adrianna's question.

Julia met her gaze head-on. "I was afraid, and I didn't want to worry the rest of my life about whether I was going to get cancer in my other breast." Adrianna's nod confirmed that she understood where Julia was coming from on the matter. "And, as it turned out," Julia added, "there *was* cancer in my other breast, too—just too small to be picked up yet on the mammogram. Six months later, I would've had to go through it all again."

Adrianna sat back, but it was Orabella's eyes that now shone with curiosity. "The new breasts. How did the surgeons . . . ?"

"That's the best part of the story." Julia smiled and felt the atmosphere grow lighter. "The plastic surgeon—the one who built the new breasts—was in the operating room. When the first doctor finished, he stepped in and inserted sacs, um . . . like . . . balloons?" She wished her Italian was better when Orabella giggled at her word choice, but the young woman nodded that she got the idea and pantomimed blowing up a balloon to her mother.

Angelina's eyes rounded as her hands formed an imaginary balloon growing. She finished the imagery with a *pop* that made everyone laugh.

"Not quite," Julia assured them. "But close. Every two weeks, I went back to the doctor and he pumped saline solution . . . um, saltwater into the sacs to stretch the skin slowly." She used her own hand motions to indicate her breasts getting larger. "When he got them to this size, he removed the saline sacs and replaced them with silicone implants, and *voilà!*"

"How long did the process take?" Giada obviously wanted Adrianna to have all the information.

"Two years total." Julia looked at Giada, then innocently slid her eyes to Adrianna. "I had nipples built two months ago. That was my last surgery." She opened her blouse enough to show the results poking through her camisole. "The only problem is that they stay erect all the time."

A titter of laughter passed among the woman again before Angelina's eyebrow rose in a knowing gesture and she said something.

Julia didn't understand the question spoken in Italian, but when Giada translated it, her voice grew quiet. "Mama asks the cost—not in money, the emotional toll."

Julia had answered everything with candor until then, and the irony came like a punch to her gut. The whole Frank/divorce thing—the aspect she most needed to talk about—was the part she never spoke of. Except with the therapist she'd gone to those first few months . . . and Hettie and Camille, though not often to them.

She couldn't share with these strangers how Frank had been repulsed by her scars, couldn't bring himself to touch her, had turned to other women. Admitting that still dredged up too much hurt and anger. Hurt that the person she'd trusted with her heart found it worth so little. Anger because she wasn't strong enough to move beyond it all, even with the reconstruction. She skirted Angelina's question with a shrug. "My body healed quickly. My head—and heart—took a little longer."

Angelina nodded and, for the first time during the conversation, didn't ask for a translation.

Several hours later, as the shadow of the olive grove crept within inches of the house, Vitale announced it was time to leave.

A flutter of panic scampered across the nape of her neck when she thought about what that meant. Caught up in her enjoyment of Vitale's family, she'd allowed the day to pass without finding a room anywhere else. Had that been done subconsciously?

Now the two of them would be alone for the rest of the night.

And while she no longer considered that he might be a serial killer, she worried about that other danger he exuded. The delicious one.

Among the affectionate hugs and warm good-byes, something must have clued Angelina in to their clandestine arrangement. Mother's intuition? Maybe the woman had felt a flutter of her own at Vitale's words.

Earlier in the afternoon, after the cancer discussion, Angelina had asked about where she was staying, and Julia had truthfully answered "Lerici" and, not entirely truthfully, but not exactly lying either, had gone on to praise the accommodations at the Lord Byron Hotel.

Now, as they got to the car and Julia was about to escape with her Good-Woman-and-Mother image intact, Angelina took her hand. "I come to Lerici this week. We eat. What room you stay at hotel?"

"Julietta does not stay at hotel," Vitale answered without picking up on Julia's warning look. "She stay with me."

Angelina dropped Julia's hand like she'd been holding a snake. And from the withering look she received, Julia was pretty sure that's exactly how the woman now viewed her.

"I can't continue to stay at the hotel. It's full. And . . . and the others were, too, and I lost my reservation at the other place I was supposed to stay, so Vitale offered . . ." Julia closed her mouth, convinced that her forked tongue was digging her into a deeper hole.

No explanation was going to change Angelina's perception of what was going on.

Vitale rested her crutch atop the luggage in the back and helped Julia into the car. Julia waved good-bye, and everyone waved back.

Everyone except Angelina, whose down-turned, silent mouth spoke volumes.

CHAPTER 9

Vitale still drove very fast, but the urgency of the previous ride was gone, along with the lurching and braking.

Julia didn't mind the speed this time, and she wasn't sure why. Maybe it was the incredible red streaks of sunlight blazing across a now-purple sky, or the perfect blend of fragrant cedar and fresh air, or even the hum of the engine as it revved. It all came together into a perfect singularity she felt blessed to be moving toward. At whatever speed.

Being part of an Italian family for a few hours had given her insights into the culture she'd never be able to get from books. Vitale was obviously special to his family. From the dynamics she'd observed, it was an earned place in their hearts and not simply given to him as the privilege of being the only son. Everyone turned to him for advice, and he treated everyone with tenderness and love from the children to his parents.

He was a remarkable young man—and she found herself wishing he'd been born a decade earlier.

"Today was wonderful, Vitale," she said in an effort to dispel the frivolous thoughts running through her mind. "I had such a marvelous time with your family. It's one of those days I'll remember forever. Thank you."

He slid her a sidelong glance, and his face relaxed into an easy smile. "They like you."

Julia gave a self-conscious laugh. "I think most of them liked me. Your mom I'm not so sure about. Did you see her face when you said I'd be staying with you? *Reowr!*" She pawed the air with one hand.

The sound and gesture brought a laugh and a shrug from Vitale. "She is Mama," he answered simply.

"So, if I stay with you for a couple of days, should I expect a visit from Angelina?"

"No, Mama will not visit."

Something about the way he said it conjured tension into the space between them. The sensation surrounded Julia and prickled on her skin. "What about the young woman? Francesca? Will she be coming after me?"

His mouth slid into a deep frown and a crease burrowed between his eyebrows. "*Sì,* her name is Francesca, and I think she will not come."

"You didn't know she was going to show up today, did you?"

"She come the three time. I hope she not to come again." He sounded sincere. Disgusted even.

"Can't blame a gal for trying." Vitale's expression indicated this was a sore subject, so Julia kept her tone light. She was curious, though. "When did y'all break up? Quit being together."

"Six, seven month."

"And she's still trying to reconcile? Get you back?" The young woman must be very much in love if she was willing to make a scene three times in front of his family. And six months after the breakup? Sheesh!

"She try to make me forgive." His face clouded as the brooding look fell into place. "She do the very bad thing."

He didn't elaborate, and Julia didn't pry. She dropped the subject, telling herself it was none of her business.

Still, she couldn't keep from wondering what Vitale would consider to be "the very bad thing."

* * *

They followed the road they'd taken that morning, which wound its way down through the hills and skirted the edge of Lerici before climbing back up into the hills on the other side.

As they passed the village, it seemed to Julia the population had doubled. No doubt the tours had brought in the mother lode Signor Moretti had been expecting.

Vitale pointed out the hot spots for the tourists—the flashy signs and overdressed waiters were dead giveaways for the places to avoid—and the ones for the locals.

"I show before you leave," he promised.

Julia cleared her throat, determined to sound authoritative. "About that, I'll try to be out of your hair in a couple of days."

Vitale's eyebrows buckled in question and his fingers pushed through his hair just before the spark lit his eyes, leaving no doubt where her comment had taken his thoughts. This guy was used to women literally being in his hair.

"I really have to stop using so many idioms in my speech." She laughed. "I mean that I hope to find somewhere else to stay maybe by Tuesday."

Vitale brought the car to an abrupt halt on the side of the road and put it in park. He leaned across the console until his face was only inches from hers.

His breath brushed her face and, although hers was coming much faster, no air seemed to be reaching her lungs. Her head pressed hard against the back of the seat

"Julietta, you have the choice to make. You stay with Vitale." He paused dramatically and brushed his knuckles lightly down her arm. Goose bumps popped up in the wake of his touch. "Or, you stay with Angelina." The side of his mouth twisted up into a triumphant smirk.

Unwilling to let him win that easily, Julia cocked her head and pretended to think it over. "Well, she *is* a good cook."

"Vitale is the good cook also. And many other things." He leaned closer, and his lips touched hers softly.

Julia's brain immediately demanded she pull away, extricate herself from this surreal fantasy she'd fallen into. But her lips whined that these were the first lips they'd touched in two years and the only ones other than Frank's they'd experienced in soooo long, and his felt soooo good, so full, so warm and inviting. . . .

She closed her eyes and leaned closer, allowing the warmth to radiate down her throat and into her lungs and from there to every oxygen-infused cell of her body.

His lips were slightly parted. She kept hers the same. No movement. No tongues involved. Just a tender moment of coming together that lit a candle inside her and ended with a gentle sound of release.

She tried to take a deep breath to feed the fire with oxygen, but her breath hitched in her chest.

"So, I think you choose Vitale, yes?" He nodded in answer to his own question and pulled the car back onto the road.

Julia shook off the lovely warm glow that had started to infuse her and reluctantly shrugged into her cold, battle-worn armor of prudence. This situation had already gone entirely too far. She'd allowed it to get out of hand. "Vitale, my staying with you isn't going to work."

Vitale released the steering wheel and reached out to cup his hand lightly across her mouth. "Julietta, I tell you no sex unless you want. I am honest. I tell the truth, yes?"

She pushed his hand down and nodded firmly. "Yes, okay. I understand you're leaving it up to me." She pointed a finger in his direction. "But there *will* be no sex. Understand?"

"Yes." He mimicked her curt nod and pointed his finger in her direction. "But the kiss, she is my choice."

He *wanted* to kiss her? Julia's mind reeled. "Why did you kiss me? I mean, what in heaven's name made you *want* to kiss me? I'm a lot older than you, and you can't find me very attractive. I saw Francesca—the type of woman you're used to being with. I'm nothing like that."

Luckily traffic had thinned because, this time, he didn't bother to pull over to the side of the road. He just stopped the car and put it in park. With one arm leaned on the console and the other draped across the steering wheel, he seemed oblivious to the cars going around them. "You are nice. You make me laugh." His hand reached out and turned her face to his. "I do not see the age. I see only the beautiful woman." He lowered his voice to a whisper. "I want to kiss you again."

The way his fingers slid beneath her ear and into her hair sent Julia's body into alert, every nerve ending prickling with anticipation.

His mouth captured hers delicately but firmly, and the hand pressing the back of her head gave no chance of easy escape. With a sigh, she relaxed into him, parting her lips, luxuriating in the feel of his tongue fluttering against them, not demanding entrance, but merely taunting with a promise of what could be. How could such a gentle touch create such an ache inside her?

She kept her eyes closed as he pulled away and the car started to move again. She couldn't contain the smile that broke across her lips when she felt his finger graze over them.

She opened her eyes and studied his strong profile. This wasn't a man who would be easy to say no to.

And he damn well knew that.

But she would have to say no. Sex was out of the question, and in the quiet of the Italian countryside, she finally realized the why of it. It wasn't his age. It was *the perfection* of his age.

At thirty-four, he was perfect. In his prime. Used to perfect women in their prime. Like Francesca.

During the conversation she'd overheard below her balcony, he'd made clear his disdain for fake breasts. And from the afternoon's conversation with the women in his family, it was evident he'd never been exposed to breast cancer or breasts with ugly scars slicing across the middle. Nipples designed from gathered and stitched skin. Tattooed areolas with no sensation whatsoever.

Her new breasts looked amazing covered by clothing.

Bared was another matter altogether.

She squeezed her eyes closed, trying to block out the memory of the repugnance in Frank's eyes. He'd been with her during the early stages and had surely prepared himself somewhat.

How would the sight affect someone who was totally unprepared?

Yeah, hot kisses notwithstanding . . .

Sex was most definitely out of the question.

* * *

Vitale turned the car onto a narrow lane, which wound back through a wooded area and dead-ended at a house sitting by itself near the base of a hill. He stopped the car, came around, and opened her door with a bow. "*Benvenuta a casa Vitale de Luca.*"

"*De Luca,*" she repeated, realizing it was the first time she'd heard his whole name. "Nice."

"*Sì.*" He chuckled with that low vibrato that trickled down between her shoulder blades. "Much nicer than the Berk-a-weeth."

"Finally!" She took his hand to ease out of the car. "We agree on something."

Vitale's house was beautiful in an interesting sort of way. The structure had a distinct masculine feel with sections of massive stones exposed through terra-cotta. Four columns carved from wood surrounded a flagstone entrance that led the way to a pair of ornate, carved doors. Large, paned windows on either side of the entrance lightened the heavy effect.

The yard, the flower beds, the bushes trimmed into interesting shaped topiaries—all of it spoke of pride of ownership.

"What a lovely home, Vitale." Julia pivoted slowly on the crutch, taking it all in. "This is the perfect setting for this house."

"Yes? You like?" Vitale beamed. "I make."

"You built it yourself?" Julia ran an appreciative hand over a lustrous column.

"*Sì.* I build all of it. I lay the stone. I make the columns and the walls from the trees that grow here."

Julia looked closely at the intricate vine-like carving on the post. "You carved these?"

Vitale nodded. "*Sì.*"

"My goodness, you're an artist!"

"*Sì.*" He opened the door to reveal a white marble floor that ran throughout the house as far as she could see, wringing a gasp of delight from her.

"I buy the not perfect from a church they destroy." Vitale stooped to point out cracks and deep depressions from years of traffic. "And I do the much work."

The entryway was a foyer, flanked on the left by a living room

and on the right by a dining room. Furniture was sparse but taste-
ful, all in leather or wood.

He walked her around the entire house, built as a rectangle with
an open courtyard in the middle.

The only bedroom took up a back quarter of the house and was
designed with a stone fireplace tucked into a corner. A leather love
seat was placed close enough to catch the heat, though, with the
things Julia could imagine taking place on the love seat, a fire was
probably unnecessary. A massive bed sat in the middle of the room
facing a wall of French doors, which opened onto a flagstone patio.
The bedposts were carved with an elaborate design, reminiscent of
the columns out front.

"Did you build the bed?" She tried to jerk her mind out of its
musings that all centered around why he needed a bed that looked
like it couldn't be jarred by an eruption of Vesuvius. She could
almost feel the heat . . . from the lava.

"*Sì*. All of the wood, I build."

"Everything is so beautiful. You're very talented."

He scratched the back of his neck and shifted uncomfortably.
"*Grazie*. Papà, he teach me when I am very young."

Julia thought back to the beautiful wooden table they'd dined
on at lunch. Probably built by Piero. These men were masters of
their art. She started to comment but decided it would sound like
gushing, and she didn't want to embarrass him further.

The patio stretched across the back of the house and additional
French doors led into the kitchen and dining area. While an area
inside had been furnished with a larger dining set that would
accommodate several guests, a wrought-iron table with two chairs
provided a romantic area for alfresco dining on the patio.

It was obvious Vitale had built the house with two in mind . . .
and only two.

The iconic bachelor pad.

The stonemason/carpenter certainly had impeccable taste, too.
Sprinkled around each room were art objects in various sizes ranging from a six-foot mahogany palm tree with fronds of hammered
copper sheeting to a delicate pair of shell wings that looked like
they might have been left behind by a fairy.

And each room they passed through had a different scent. She noticed rosemary in the kitchen, lemon balm in the living room, lavender in the bedroom. Each room had a door across the narrow hallway that opened to the courtyard with small knot gardens of herbs. The ones strategically planted near the doors caught the breeze, allowing their fragrances to suffuse the nearest area inside.

At the center of the garden was a fountain that gained Julia's immediate attention. It was a match to the sculpture she'd admired so much at the hotel, but the iris of this one floated leisurely back and forth on a stream of water that alternated from each side before cascading down into a marble trough.

"This is like the one at the hotel, except smaller," she remarked, once again amazed with the beauty of the piece.

"*Sì,* I make this one first. Mario, he like. He want one for the hotel."

Julia turned to him. Had she understood him correctly? "You made this? And the one at the hotel?"

"*Sì.*"

"You're an artist!"

"*Sì.* You say before. I tell you yes."

"But I just thought you did the stonework really well. These pieces"—she waved her hand toward the house—"all these fascinating pieces I see throughout the house, they're yours?"

"*Sì.* I make. I, um, how you say? Sculpt? Many different materials." He seemed as proud of the word he'd used as he was of his incredible artistic ability.

The house contained pieces created in vastly different mediums. Bronze, wood, marble, clay—and to think that this man had created them all boggled the mind. When he told her he was very good with his hands, she'd thought he was just flirting. She didn't know the half of it.

Her own hands shook with excitement as she picked up a bronze abstract of a female figure. "Vitale, I came to Italy to find some sources for home decorating. I can sell some of your pieces. I'm sure I can. In fact, I think I could sell quite a lot of it."

His demeanor grew somber. "I hope I sell already. I write the letter to the gallery in Firenze. They show the interest, so I send the photographs. If they buy, I make the much money and I spend the time creating rather than breaking the stone to walk on. I hear from them very soon, I think."

He became more animated as he spoke. Clearly this was his chosen profession. The stonework was a means of making a living. Sculpting was his passion. "I have the studio in the garden." He flipped a thumb toward the back door.

Julia remembered a nondescript shed at the base of the property. A humble beginning for work with such panache.

"I show you, but I think we eat first." His gaze dropped to her hand, which still held the bronze piece. "This one, she is very special." He traced its form delicately with a fingertip. "She is the favorite of my wife."

Julia's eyes widened involuntarily with shock, and she jerked them up to meet his as the figure trembled beneath his touch. He placed his hands around hers and held firmly, obviously to keep her from dropping the piece.

"Your wife?" Her vocal cords strained at the words.

"*Sì.* My wife. Luciana." He closed his eyes in a long blink.

"But you told me you weren't married. Oh my God! I let you kiss me." Accusation etched Julia's tone like acid on glass.

"I do not marry for the ten years," he explained. "Luciana, she die."

A widower! She'd have never guessed. Another shocked tremble ran through her arm and gave him reason to ease the bronze piece from her grasp. He placed it back on the table while she gathered her wits.

"I'm sorry, Vitale." She laid a hand on his warm arm, her touch drawing his eyes back to her. "It's just that . . . I mean . . . you're still so young. It's hard to imagine you lost your wife. And at twenty-four?"

"Luciana, she is twenty-two. She has the *aneurisma.* The . . . blood in the brain." He bunched his fingers at his forehead and spread them quickly, adding an explosion sound effect.

Julia nodded her understanding. "Aneurysm. Such a tragedy. You obviously loved her very much."

"Yes, very much." He gave her a sad smile, suddenly looking much older than five minutes ago. "It is nice to speak about my Luciana. Most people do not speak of her to me." He paused, and Julia remained quiet, encouraging him to go on, which he did. "The name Luciana, she mean 'the light,' and she bring the light into my life. After she die, I live in the darkness for the many years. I do not see the friends. Only *la famiglia*. I build the house and do the sculpt." He waved his arm at their surroundings. "I work and work, and, at last, the darkness, she break, and I return to the world of the life."

Julia's eyes dropped to the bronze once more. Luciana's favorite—a piece cherished and guarded by him. She took a deep breath and squeezed his arm, patted it lightly before she removed her hand.

When she looked back up at him, something had changed. The superficial veil she'd been looking at him through had dropped away, and she saw him no longer as Adonis, the demigod, but as Vitale de Luca, a man with a soul as deep as his laugh and a heart that could be broken.

"We eat now?"

She smiled and gave a quick nod; then she swiveled on her crutch and gave an awkward little hop to turn. His gaze dropped to her arm thrown over the crutch. He reached out and traced a red welt where the rubber top had chafed her skin, causing her to flinch. "She is no good. She hurt you."

Before she could protest, he slipped the crutch from beneath her arm and slid into its place, arm around her, pulling her firmly against his side, forcing her to weave her arm around his waist.

He took a step and almost lifted her completely off her feet.

"Whoa." She laughed. "Maybe, if I held your arm."

He gave her a sheepish grin and let his arm slide back around so she could grasp it. They took a few hesitant steps.

"This *is* easier than the crutch," she admitted. "If I keep my weight back on my heel and point my toe up, the pain's not too bad."

He laid his hand on top of hers and gave it a squeeze. "You no need the crutch. You need the Vitale."

She snorted. "That's sort of trading one crutch for another."

* * *

Vitale de Luca was a man full of surprises.

And the gorgeous hunk had told the truth—he could cook!

Fifteen minutes after he started preparing a light supper, they were nibbling on Pecorino cheese and various sweet pickled rinds, a zesty salad of fresh baby greens from his garden tossed with cannellini beans, tuna, and a balsamic dressing, and washing it all down with a crisp pinot grigio.

They shared stories about growing up and realized that, despite their age and nationality differences, they really were quite alike. Both had grown up in middle-class families, had doting grandparents, and voted vacations spent on the beach as their favorite. They had similar tastes in artwork, though Vitale was a human storehouse of information on Italian artists she'd never heard of.

Julia found herself talking a lot about Melissa. Being with a family had kept her daughter on her mind today, and like Vitale's Luciana, Melissa was the light in Julia's life. It was nice to be able to brag about her to a stranger, although Vitale no longer seemed like one. He was funny and charming and kept up his end of a spirited conversation about the state of the world economy. And he loved "*calcio*" and enjoyed watching it and playing it, but work left him little time.

Julia noticed when she tried to draw him into telling about his stonework or his woodwork he became dispassionate and changed the subject.

"What do you want to do?" she asked.

"Do?" His eyebrows shot up. "What do I want to do tonight?" His mouth twisted up at one end in insinuation.

"Not that—and get it out of your head. It's not gonna happen." Julia sipped her wine, eyeing him over the top of her glass. "What do you want to do for the rest of your life? Will you continue to build and do stonework or what?"

Vitale swirled the wine in his glass and stared into it as if he could read the future there. "I work with Papà until I am twenty-eight. He want me to work with him forever, but I cannot. The houses and the furniture, they are fine, but they are not the life. I want the statue, the figure, the thing I see in my head and make with my hand."

"Your creations. You want to make your living as a sculptor."

"*Sì*. Papà, he do not like. He say no money. But I sell and make the money. For three years, I"—he waved his hand toward the house—"a . . . a group of things."

"A collection? You gathered a collection of your work?"

"*Sì*, the collection." His eyes were on her, but they seemed to be seeing something else. "Luciana, she love the work. She very proud. But Mama and Papà. They not proud. I do not become the man they want. I think if I sell, Mama and Papà will be proud like Luciana."

Julia could hear the pain in his voice. "I think you're too hard on yourself. Your parents seem *very* proud of you. In fact, your whole family adores you."

He wagged his finger in the air. "Mama, she no like that I do not marry again and have the children."

"Well, it's not like you're over the—um, I mean, you're still young. There's plenty of time."

He shrugged. "But the future, she is blind, yes?"

"You got that right." Julia nodded. "We never know what's out there ahead of us."

Vitale cocked his head slightly, studying her. "What about you, Julietta? Do you become the woman your parents want?"

"I hope so." She ran her finger around the rim of her wineglass, gathering her thoughts. No one had asked about her parents in a long time. "My parents died in a boating accident when I was in college. A drunk guy in a speedboat ran over my father's fishing boat."

"Ah, *mi dispiace.*"

"No, it's okay. It's nice to talk about them . . . like for you with Luciana." It *did* feel good—fitting. They would've liked this place. Would've liked this man who held his family close to his heart. "I still miss them terribly, but I feel so fortunate to have had them as parents. I decided a long time ago to be glad for the time I had with them, not to dwell on what I missed."

"*Bellissimo.*" His gaze held hers for a moment before he raised his glass in a toast. "Mama and Papà."

She raised her glass in answer. "Mom and Dad."

Quietness gathered around them for a while. Not an awkward quiet—a relaxed quiet. Julia thought back over the day. "Vitale, I can't remember the last time I had such a perfect day." She yawned, which drew a chuckle from him.

"I think we wait until tomorrow to show the work, yes?"

She wanted to be able to take her time and give a thorough inspection to his sculptures. And she was much too mellow to look at anything with a critical eye at the moment. "That would probably be better. What time do you get up?"

"I must return the automobile to Mario very early. But please, do not get up then. Sleep. Enjoy your holiday."

They continued their easy conversation as they started clearing the table, but when it became evident bedtime was fast approaching, Julia's insides jerked into a knot. She stacked his plate on top of hers along with the silverware, but when she picked them up, her hands shook and the knives and forks clattered around as though there'd been an earthquake.

Vitale gave her a knowing smile and set the wineglasses back down on the table. He took the plates from her, placed them on the table, and took her hands in his.

"Julietta, you sleep in the bed."

Her mouth flew open in protest, but he laid a finger on her lips to silence her. "You are the guest. You sleep in the bed, and I sleep on the couch."

"But . . ."

"No, no. No but. I say it." He raised her hands to his mouth and pressed a kiss on them.

Julia had never experienced a more romantic moment. Were she the woman she was before the cancer, she would've ignored the voice of reason and had sex with him right there in the moonlight on the patio.

No, she wouldn't have. The woman she was before the cancer would still be married to Frank and holding faithfully to that union.

But she wasn't that woman any longer either.

Maybe this trip was about finding out who she had become.

She gave his fingers a squeeze. "Thanks."

"And thank you for this." He let go of her hands to cup her face gently. His mouth connected to hers in a kiss that flooded her with enough heat to melt her insides and burn away the logical cells in her brain, leaving only one thought in her mind—would it be possible to have sex and keep her shirt on?

When he straightened, his hands dropped to her shoulders to hold her steady, so he was obviously aware of the effect his kiss had. One look in his dark eyes confirmed it.

"You need to stop doing that." She lowered her eyes to camouflage the conflict she felt inside.

He lifted her chin with his finger and waited until she looked him in the eye. "I do not do because I need. I do because I want."

She locked her knees to keep them from buckling.

Warm morning sunshine streaming through the French doors woke Julia. Apparently, curtains were superfluous when the nearest neighbor lived a quarter of a mile away. That morning had broken was proof last night's kiss hadn't stopped the earth from spinning. It was only a kiss after all, even though she still felt the heat from it these hours later.

Dishes rattling in the kitchen caused her to check her watch. 8:33. She hadn't expected Vitale to be back so soon from his errand. He must be a very early riser.

She smiled to herself. Two days ago, she'd awakened to the sound of Vitale's hammer knocking on stones. Yesterday, she'd awakened to him knocking on the door. Today, he was knocking around the kitchen. There were worse things than being awakened by a gorgeous Italian man. She found herself looking forward to tomorrow.

She limped to the bathroom for teeth and hair brushing, determined to fix him a Southern-style breakfast if he hadn't eaten yet. He'd been so sweet about seeing to her needs. It was time to show him she wasn't helpless. She'd spotted pancetta in the fridge last night along with some eggs. She could whip up some of her special biscuits. And there really wasn't much difference between grits and polenta.

The boxers she slept in were fine for lounging. She grabbed yesterday's blouse and slipped it over her camisole as footsteps moved down the hall toward the room.

Her hand was on the doorknob ready to swing it open when a sneeze outside the door brought her to a standstill.

That most definitely was *not* Vitale outside her door.

The sneeze came from a woman.

CHAPTER 10

Angelina? One of Vitale's sisters? Francesca?

Julia paused, wondering if this called for some kind of entrance strategy?

She had nothing to be ashamed of. Nothing to hide from any of them. She could be her normal, invisible self.

She opened the door to find a tiny wisp of an elderly woman armed with a dust mop in one hand and an aerosol can in the other. Julia smiled with relief.

Other than a quick tightening of her bottom lip, the woman's expression didn't register any surprise to see a woman coming out of Vitale's bedroom. "*Buon giorno*"—she paused, letting her eyes scan Julia from top to bottom and back before adding—"signora."

Julia thought she heard a tiny note of judgment in the word, but she couldn't be sure. She gave a mental shrug. *I guess I should be flattered she . . . or anyone else . . . even sees my sleeping with Vitale as a possibility.* "*Buon giorno,*" Julia answered. "Vitale?"

The woman brandished the can a few times, punctuating a string of words, none of which Julia understood.

Julia nodded politely and limped into the kitchen. Her crutch was nowhere in sight. No matter. Getting around was easier without it anyway if she kept her weight on the back of her heel or the side of her foot.

The kitchen sparkled, no sign anywhere Vitale had eaten breakfast yet.

Thinking he might be in his studio, she moseyed out onto the patio. A vase of vibrant sunflowers sat on the table with a note placed beside them. *Julietta, I return soon with the breakfast.*

It took only a second for it to register with her—how different this man was from Frank, who moved through life with an air of cool detachment, only touching people when it served *his* purpose or met *his* need. Flowers had never been part of her ex's modus operandi. He claimed they were a waste of money because they wilted too quickly. Hugs were limited to good-byes. Or foreplay.

So now, her insides went all soft at Vitale's thoughtfulness. She'd always figured guys who looked like Vitale did generally had no thought for anyone but themselves. But he wasn't like that. Not with her. Not with his family. She'd seen the way he hugged his sisters and parents, cuddled his nieces and nephews. He wasn't the average "pretty boy."

Remembering his kisses reminded her that nothing about him was average.

She ran her fingers over the bold, fluid script before tucking the paper in her pocket.

Having coffee waiting when he got back was the least she could do, so she returned to the kitchen.

The pungent aroma of freshly ground coffee permeated the kitchen, however, and made Julia's mouth water. She inhaled deeply and gave an appreciative sigh. The cleaning lady had beaten her to the task.

The woman gave her a sidelong glance as she added the last scoop to the French press pot. "*Caffe latte,* eh?"

"*Sì.*" Julia gave an enthusiastic nod, which finally brought a smile from the woman.

"*Presto.*"

Julia chuckled. Knowing the word meant "soon" didn't keep her from imagining a cup of coffee appearing out of nowhere. She decided to try a bit of conversation to ease the awkward silence. "*Sono Julia, um, Julietta Berkwith. Sono americana.*"

The woman pointed to herself. "*Loredana.*"

"*Loredana,*" Julia repeated, letting the "r" roll from her tongue. "*Che bello.*" She wasn't sure, but she hoped she had told the woman the name was beautiful.

"*Grazie.*" Loredana beamed as she poured the boiling water from the kettle over the coffee grounds.

The scented steam wafted Julia's way, and her stomach rumbled in appreciation. "*Ho fame.*" She patted her middle.

Loredana's eyebrows shot up. "*Ah,* signora. *Mi dispiace. Un momento.*" She hurried to the refrigerator and started filling her arms with fruit, eggs, cheeses, milk.

"No, no!" Julia protested. "Um, Vitale, uh, bring . . . *colazione.*"

"*Ah, capisco.*" Loredana nodded and put the items back in the refrigerator.

There was another round of awkward silence while Julia willed the coffee grounds to give up their essence a little faster. "*Ho una frattura.*" She tried again, pointing to her toe.

"*Sì. Lo so.*" Loredana walked a few steps in a circle, mimicking Julia's limp perfectly.

A comedian! Julia laughed and applauded the performance. *I'm in the company of an Italian Hettie.* Though Loredana was probably ten years younger, she had a knowing smile and a twinkle in her eye very much like Hettie that made Julia think she, too, viewed the world with a playful perspective.

Julia remembered she didn't speak with Hettie yesterday. She'd have to allot some extra time today to fill her in on the new developments. Hettie would love, love, love that she was staying with Vitale. And she wouldn't let it go until Julia admitted she was loving it, too.

Loredana repeated her pantomime and laughed with Julia, a bright, tinkly sound that made Julia think of fairies, or maybe brownies since she was cleaning house. The tinkly sound grew louder, becoming a cackle that would have been scary in different circumstances.

All at once, a hand snaked around Julia's waist from behind, startling her as a kiss landed on her cheek.

"*Buon giorno,* Julietta." Vitale's voice was a sexy growl, and Julia's breath hitched at the sound of it. He placed a paper bag on the table in front of her. "You meet Loredana." He strode over to the older woman and kissed each of her cheeks. "*Buon giorno.*"

Loredana's tender smile gave away her fondness for the man. She gave his shoulder a pat, then busied herself with plunging and pouring the coffee while he got plates and silverware.

Julia wasn't sure she needed to eat—she could fill up on the sight of Vitale. Army green cargo shorts sat low on his hips and a camouflage tee clung to every ridge, ironically hiding nothing. The man didn't have an ounce of fat on him. Every inch was sinew and muscle from his head to his sandaled feet.

As he started back toward the table, she tore her eyes away from him and opened the bag. If she drooled, she could blame it on the buttery croissants and rolls. And maybe her accelerated heartbeat could be chalked up to the extra bold scent of the coffee.

"I forget to tell you Loredana here this morning." He set a cup of coffee and a plate in front of her and leaned down to brush his lips across hers.

The tiniest of kisses, but her stomach responded with a gargantuan flutter. She fought to keep from stammering over the simplest of sentences. "No problem." She took a settling breath as he moved into the opposite seat. "She's a sweetheart. In fact, she reminds me of my mother-in-law, Hettie."

"Mother-in-law?" His face clouded.

"Ex-mother-in-law. My ex-husband's mother," she explained, pleased to have the conversation on familiar territory, which would keep her thoughts away from the feel of his lips and what they did to her. "She's like a mother to me. When Frank and I divorced, I got to keep Hettie."

That brought a smile, and he bit into his croissant with fervor.

A flake clung to his lower lip, reminding her of how he'd brushed the crumb from hers yesterday. And those kisses . . . the thought of them made her brain stall. She took a drink of coffee and let the strong brew lubricate her mouth back into action.

She rattled on about Hettie through most of their breakfast. "I visit or call her every day. I didn't yesterday, so I'll need to today. She'll be worried."

"I do not have the phone." Vitale's tone was apologetic. "But I think we go to Lerici. You call from there."

"I have my cell phone." Julia licked the last bit of tangy marmalade from her lips, and a jolt shot through her when his gaze dropped to her mouth and lingered. "But how is it you don't have a phone?" she finished, determined not to let him read her single-minded thoughts this morning.

"I do not like the stop and the answer when I work." His eyes moved back to hers, and he shrugged.

No phone. She'd pinpointed one of his idiosyncrasies. "Couldn't you simply turn the phone off while you're working? How do people get in touch with you?"

"I have the computer and the Internet. Much better. I work the early morning to the late night. The e-mail I read when I come from the studio."

"Which you promised to show me this morning," Julia reminded him.

"Yes, we do now, I think. How is the toe?"

She stood and began cleaning off the table. "Better. See?" She demonstrated how she could keep the weight off her toes. "In fact, I was going to fix your breakfast this morning, but you were already gone."

"Feex?"

"Prepare. Make ready." She listed synonyms as she placed the dishes in the sink.

She hadn't heard him get up from his chair, but his hands settled on her hips, causing her breath to intake sharply. "*Domani,* you feex," he said.

Man, he was laying it on thick this morning. "Okay, tomorrow." She tried to sound light, wanted him to see how his well-honed powers of seduction weren't going to work on her. But the way he was pressed against her . . . did he feel that involuntary quake that just shook her?

In answer, he nibbled her ear playfully, causing her knees to buckle. She gripped the edge of the sink, determined not to be silly enough to turn around.

His hands slid around to cover hers. "You hold this, so you no hold Vitale, I think. You let go soon, *bella mia*." He kissed the top of her head before he walked away, leaving her hanging by her elbows.

But hang on she did . . . and would continue to do—trying not to imagine how soft the landing would be if she fell into his bed.

Vitale was waiting outside the studio.

Through the patio door, Julia watched him tack something to the studio wall outside, and as she got closer, she could see they were sketches. Her feet came to an abrupt stop when she recognized the subject.

They were of her!

"When did you do these?" Her astonishment bubbled out on a note of disbelief, bringing a pleased smile to Vitale's face.

He pointed to the first one. "This one I begin at the restaurant the night you arrive."

She punched his chest playfully with her finger. "I had a feeling you were sketching me, but I thought I was crazy. Why were you sketching me?"

"You have the beautiful eyes. They interest me."

She felt the blush creep up her neck, so she turned back to the sketches. "And this one?" She leaned to peer closer at the one he had added some color to the eyes and lips and hair. "When did you do it?"

"While you relax by the pool. Sometime you take off the hat and the sunglasses, but not often." He nudged her with an elbow. "Behind the sunglasses, you watch me. I watch you also."

The heat deepened, spreading to her back and the nape of her neck. "You knew I was watching you?'

"*Sì.* The other woman, Bettina, she think I watch her."

"I saw you and her at the bar that night." She made it sound like she glimpsed him, staying just shy of admitting she was watching them.

"I see you also. I think to speak to you, but you leave."

Yeah, sure he did. He had a line ready for everything, and she couldn't resist calling him on this one. She tilted her head back to look him in the eye. "Really? Why did you want to talk to me?"

His return gaze remained steady. "To see the eyes to finish sketch."

"Oh." He made it sound so logical, so honest. So well practiced. She rolled her eyes. "Oh, come on, Vitale. Be honest. You know as well as I do you wouldn't have left a date like Bettina to talk to *me*."

"I do not tell the lie, Julietta." A flash of irritation darkened his eyes. "I want to see the color of Julietta's eye." He made a little circle with his fingertip right in front of her eye. "The iris, yes? And I do not have the date with Bettina. She want the sex, so she leave with Romano."

The refreshing honesty made her grin, but she changed the subject to something else she'd been curious about. She pointed to the first sketch. "That first night at the restaurant, who was the elderly man you sat with?"

His petulant mouth tightened with thought, then relaxed, telling her the exact moment when the memory came to him. "He is Aldo, a friend. His wife die also three month past. Aldo, he is very lonely. We have the drink together often."

Guilt tapped Julia on the shoulder. "Oh, now I feel bad I turned down his company. I thought he was trying to pick me up."

"Pick Julietta up?"

Okay, she understood how confusing that idiom might be. "Have sex." Her bluntness caused her to cringe, but Vitale nodded.

"*Sì.* Aldo want the sex with you, Julietta."

Instantly, her attitude shifted from sad for Aldo to appalled at him, and she blew out a disgusted, "Geez. Is that all you guys think about?"

The air shook with the deep vibrato of Vitale's laugh. "All the people want the sex, Julietta. The men and the women."

She quirked an eyebrow. "And according to Rosa, Vitale loves all the women."

"It is true." He opened the door to the studio. "Vitale love all the women . . . but he like only the few."

* * *

Soft music met Julia's ears when she entered the dark studio. Opera. "You work with music on in the background?"

"Yes, the music, she help me to work better—push the thought away and leave the hand to do."

Julia closed her eyes and listened for a moment. She didn't know opera and had no idea what the song was, but it was beautiful... in a sad sort of way. Quite different from her happy tunes.

The quick pat to her shoulder blade held a note of impatience. She opened her eyes and allowed Vitale's hand on her back to guide her a couple of steps deeper where he flipped on the bright overhead lights.

After a second of blindness while her eyes adjusted, the sight before her wrenched a gasp from her lungs. She was prepared for the high-caliber work she'd already seen evidence of in the house. She wasn't prepared for the volume of it. Sculptures—marble, granite, metals, stone, clay—filled the building. Bronze appeared to be the preferred.

"Oh. My. Gosh." Awe at the vastness of his collection reverberated her voice as she turned to take it all in. "Where do the ideas for all of these come from?"

"I find the inspiration—she is the word, yes?"

Julia nodded.

"I find the inspiration in the many things." Patting the front pocket of his shorts, he added, "I have the camera with me at all the times."

Julia moved from piece to piece, extolling his skill as she examined each thoroughly. Some were ultra-modern with the feel of a Picasso painting rendered in 3-D. Curved tubing with sheets of colored metal welded on at interesting angles. "You said you contacted the gallery in Florence." She followed the curve of copper tubing first with her eyes and then with a finger. The piece begged to be touched. She visualized it in the foyer of the new Langley home she'd been hired to decorate. It would be stunning. "But do you ever sell anything on your own? You have so many pieces, it doesn't seem possible you could've ever gotten rid of anything."

"*Sì*. I sell the many pieces. The small one. Gena, the owner of the gallery in Lerici? She is the friend. I take her the few thing this morning and every week. She sell many, most to the tourist, and she make the first contact for me with the large gallery in Firenze. Her gallery, she is small and cannot display the many big piece." He pointed to a grouping of large furniture items. "But I take the bigger piece in the automobile today. She fill up the little space. Sometime I borrow the truck of my papà."

Wooden dressers and tables with marble tops looked as though they'd been in a vault since the Belle Époque period. Julia ran her hands over the polished curves, admiring the detailed workmanship . . . and the man who created it all. Her business acumen kicked into gear, filling her head with ideas for a catalog or a Web site showcasing his work. "You could make a fortune with your creations."

"I hope the gallery in Firenze think as Julietta."

While most of the granite pieces had a distinct Art Deco flavor, the bronze items ran the gamut from classic human figures to whimsical conversation pieces. One portrayed a hand straining to push its way out of a box. The lines were so lifelike, it seemed only a thin membrane kept the hand from popping through.

She regarded it silently for a while, and when she looked up, found Vitale studying her just as intently. His gaze caused her breath to lodge in her throat.

"We—Julietta and Vitale and all the people—must break free of something, yes?"

A flash of panic zipped through her. Was he referring to her cancer? He had no way of knowing about it . . . unless he'd spoken with his sister this morning. With no phone, that seemed unlikely. Besides, he was still flirtatious—seductive, even. She nodded mutely in answer to his question.

"Come." He held out his hand and she took it. "I show you the something. She is the secret."

He led her to a corner occupied with a piece covered by a tarpaulin, slim, and about three feet tall.

When he pulled the tarp off, her breath came out in a rush. "Oh, it's Rachele!" There could be no mistaking that. It was indeed

Maria's oldest child, lifelike in every way, except that she was frozen in bronze. Her chin tilted up so she looked Julia in the eye, her face captured with a look of sweet mischief. Her arms were behind her back. Julia took a peek behind and saw the chubby little hands held a flower.

The exquisite beauty of the piece loosened an emotion that slammed into Julia's stomach and knocked her guard off its axis. The child's innocence. Vitale's understanding of it. His tender portrayal. This man was capable of reaching in and touching a person's essence . . . her soul.

No, he didn't simply touch it. He wrapped his artist's hands around it and pulled it to the surface for everyone to see.

She blinked back the tears suddenly looming in her eyes, but one escaped and slid down her cheek.

"Julietta, what is wrong?" His finger caught the tear at her chin and followed its path upward.

"It's . . . beautiful. So perfect." She sniffed and wiped her face with her hands.

"That is the good thing, yes?"

"It-it's . . ." her breath stuttered, ". . . a won-derful thing."

He chuckled and pulled her into a hug.

With her forehead and nose pressed against him, she breathed in his warm, masculine scent. His fingers splayed across her back, sending tantalizing signals to the nerve endings they touched and tingles to those farther down.

As his hand crept up the back of her neck, into her hair, her defenses fled like a gun-shy hound. He was going to kiss her again, and this time she would kiss him back and let whatever happened happen.

His understanding and appreciation of the human spirit; her need to be understood and appreciated . . . just being here with him opened up her mind in ways she never imagined. Maybe it was time to take a chance she'd never imagined as well.

He pressed against her awkwardly, reaching past her to retrieve something from the shelf behind her.

She opened her eyes to find him holding a photo. Heat rushed to her face at her foolish fantasy, but if he noticed her discomfort, he gave no indication. Her frustration dissipated, however, with one look at the photo. It was Rachele, striking the pose Vitale had captured for perpetuity.

"I feex for Maria," he was saying when she shifted her focus back to him. She smiled at his use of his new word. "I feex the one of the each child. Rachele, she is the first. She is the oldest."

Julia imagined how it would feel to receive such a gift of Melissa. "It's magnificent, Vitale. A . . . a treasure." She searched her vocabulary for a word that would be worthy. "It'll be the most wonderful thing Maria—any of them—will ever receive." She continued to move her eyes from the photo to the statue, enchanted by the likeness. "How long did it take you?"

"The few month. I work only when I have the time away from the other work." He sounded apologetic, and hurriedly added, "But I work very fast when I have the time." He let go of her and threw the tarp back over Rachele. "You have seen all the work. We go to Lerici now if you like."

When he released his hold, Julia used the time to step away and put some distance between her and this young man who was affecting her way too much. She meandered around a dresser and a lavatory, breathing deeply and clearing her head of the ridiculous thought that had been there a minute ago. "I'd love to go to Lerici," she answered, "but I need to change clothes first. And I have to call Hettie and Camille, my business partner."

She couldn't wait to talk to them both. Hettie would chide her good-naturedly for not taking advantage of the situation handed to her, but Camille would be thrilled she might've found a new line from an up-and-coming new artist.

Julia already had an image of the online catalog that would present Vitale's work to the world: Villa de Luca.

CHAPTER 11

"Lerici feels like a different town than the one I wandered around Saturday." Julia tried not to sound too negative as the crowd pressed around them on all sides. Having to stay on constant guard to protect her toe from being crushed under some stranger's heel was making her irritable. The consolation was, of course, that Vitale seemed to be on guard also. He kept her hand firmly rooted to the crook of his elbow and held her close to his side.

All in all, not a bad trade-off.

Vitale nodded at her observation. "*Sì.* The noise and the tourist, she make me feel like the pillow is on my face." He gave her hand a squeeze. "But with no crowd, Julietta would not stay with Vitale, eh?"

Well, there was that. A sheepish grin accompanied her shrug. "That's true."

"Of course, is true. I say it."

Being taken as a man of his word was a high priority for the Italian. She'd heard those words, or similar ones, often from him over the last forty-eight hours.

He opened the door of the gallery, which was teeming with people, but took the time to whisper in her ear before they entered. "I prefer the afternoon with Julietta, but I tell Gena I return to the gallery, so I must."

Julia's irritation melted away at his words.

Vitale waved at an older woman standing in the middle of the room, and she hurried toward them. "Julietta, Gena." He kept the introduction to a minimum.

The gallery owner's welcome was gracious and hospitable, and Julia suspected Vitale had already filled her in about the broken toe when her gaze dropped to Julia's foot. "Julietta." She pointed in the direction of the storerooms in the back. "You would prefer to sit. Yes?"

Vitale's quick squeeze to Julia's hand felt like a warning. No doubt, the woman was planning to bombard her with questions as soon as she got her alone in the back. "Thank you for the offer," Julia answered. "But I prefer to stand for a while."

With a little huff, Gena made her way over to the cash register to give the young woman who worked there some instruction.

After only a few minutes, it became evident many people were looking, but few were buying, so Julia decided to stir things up a bit. She picked up one of Vitale's sculptures and gushed in a loud voice, "And you're the artist?"

The place came alive then, with Vitale the center of attention. People pressed around him, interested in his sculptures and wanting to talk to him about them.

Some of the women didn't seem to care what they talked about as long as they got to flirt with the hot Italian artist for a while. One Brit was so bold as to flutter her fingertips down his arm as she pointedly asked him about his "techniques."

Julia rolled her eyes at that one.

Vitale answered the woman by going into great detail with his limited English about glazing techniques. The lesson was even more effective than Julia could've imagined as the woman's eyes did actually appear to glaze over before he finished.

When he flashed Julia a disarming smile, she understood that he knew precisely what he was doing. She also realized that shouldn't surprise her.

When it came to women, Vitale always knew exactly what he was doing. The thought, which started as a warning, ended with a tingle in her lower belly.

Julia could feel his eyes on her as he talked with the customers, and she wandered around, snapping pictures. Eventually, she moved to a safe uncrowded corner, where Vitale sought her out.

"Julietta, I want you to leave."

Aha! So he wanted rid of her after all? *Must be cramping his style.* Her prior irritation bloomed again until he added, "I worry the person step on the toe."

His genuine concern threw a hearty bitch slap to her unfair assumption, and she nodded. "I want to see some more of the town, so I'll meet you at the tables down by the water in, say, three hours? Is that long enough?"

"*Sì.* She will be the too long." He gave her a quick kiss, and she left him then. And while she was glad to be rid of the worry about her toe, she was surprised by the twinge of disappointment that she wouldn't be able to watch him talk with people about the art he held such passion for.

The day was certainly shaping up to be an interesting one, Julia mused as she put down her spoon.

It wasn't until they got ready to leave the house around noon that she'd actually realized—with more than a little shock and dismay—that the man's only mode of transportation was a motorcycle.

She'd never even *sat* on a motorcycle before. But once she got over her initial fear, she'd found it undeniably invigorating. Sitting straddled on the seat ... pressed against Vitale with her arms around him ... skirt hiked up around her thighs, the wind in her hair. Whew! That memory would play in her fantasies for years to come.

All the touching and kissing and even the sweet kiss he'd given her at the gallery had ignited all sorts of not-so-sweet thoughts. So for the last three hours she'd been trying to find *anything* that would redirect her invisible-but-apparently-not-indefatigable libido, but to no avail. She kept asking herself why, if she wasn't looking for romance, she'd picked the most romantic place on earth for her stay?

Shelley and Byron had warned her in their writings, but she'd been smug that her invisibility would have her watching from the sidelines, impervious to the allure. Instead, everything—the pleasantly sweet gelato on her tongue, the fresh scent of the sea, the heat of the sun, couples in various stages of embrace everywhere she looked, all set against a playlist whose backbeat was the thrum of life itself—blended into a sensory-loaded, sensual maelstrom she was incapable of avoiding. . . .

And maybe unwilling to bypass without a sample.

Even her wanderings, which had taken her off the beaten paths to the quiet back streets, had led to heart-pounding adventure when she'd happened on an art alley. Although the studios lining the shady lane showcased mostly wall art, some delightfully whimsical triptychs made her laugh out loud while other floor-to-ceiling photographs from inside caves at sunset held her spellbound. She filled her clutch with business cards and her hands with postcards and brochures—so many, in fact, she had to make a trip to Vitale's motorcycle to drop them into the storage unit.

With only a half hour left before she was to meet Vitale, she'd finally sought out a shady table near the edge of the water, in sight of the gallery. At that point, she'd made a call to Camille to warn her of all the money they were going to spend and to describe the feeding frenzy surrounding Vitale.

Her friend only exacerbated her delicate condition when she said, "Do whatever it takes—bribes, hot sex, whatever. Just get Vitale's line for us." Fortunately, Camille hadn't picked up on the nervous laugh given in response.

As she waited for Vitale to meet her, Julia caught herself drumming on the table. Restlessness—*that* was her problem. Maybe her body wasn't craving sex as much as it was craving physical activity of *any* kind. For so long she'd been in workout mode, preparing for ten days of hiking tough terrain. Walking, running, weightlifting, aerobics. She needed something that would exhaust her, make her sweat and groan—*grunt! Not groan!* She shoved the dish of gelato out of her reach as a woman with hair cut in a chic, angular bob walked by.

Since I can't hike, maybe a new look to celebrate my health?

She pulled her ponytail holder loose and ran a hand through her nondescript, shoulder-length, lackluster brown locks. It would be fun to go home with a major change. If anyone noticed, she could say, "*My hair? I had it cut while I was in Italy.*"

Snap. Snap.

The nearby sound caught her attention, and she turned her head to find Vitale with his camera aimed at her. *Snap.* He took another couple of shots before he tucked the camera into his pocket and pulled up a chair beside her. "You look sexy when you put the fingers through the hair."

"And you don't ever miss a chance, do you?" The question in his eyes asked what that meant, but she didn't want to have to get into that discussion now. "Actually, I was thinking it might be fun to have my hair cut while I'm here."

His bottom lip drew into a sensuous pucker. "But why? She is beautiful as she is."

"I've had it this way a long time." She ran her fingers through the top of her hair and lifted it. "Change would be nice."

"My sister Adrianna, she cut the hair. Is very good." He picked up a strand of her hair and curled it around one of his fingers.

Julia's toes on her good foot curled dangerously in response.

As soon as he released it, she tucked the strand behind her ear and stood up. "Oooo, that would be fun. Do you think she would fix mine?"

"Feex? Prepare? Make ready?" He repeated her words from earlier, tilting his head in obvious confusion.

She snorted and shook her head. "Sorry. Used this way, it means 'repair,' make better. Like you would fix a car that has something wrong with it."

"Your hair, she has the nothing wrong with it. She does not need to feex."

"But it'll be fun to do something different. 'When in Rome, do as the Romans,' you know?"

"The town, she is Lerici. Not the Roma."

"Then, when in Lerici, do as the . . . Lerici-ans?" He laughed at her word, and she could tell he was softening. "Please, Vitale? Will you call her?" She handed him her phone. "And I want to hear about your afternoon, so can we walk for a while? I need some more exercise."

He arched one eyebrow. "We do not have to walk for the exercise, Julietta."

When it came to one-liner sexual innuendos, this guy sat on dead-ready. She batted her eyelashes and exaggerated her Southern drawl. "Well, that seems to be the best option on this crowded street with all these people around." As soon as the words left her mouth, she regretted them. Her present state of mind and body vetoed *any* sexual banter. She gave him a brotherly arm punch and pushed her chair in.

Vitale looked perplexed at her sudden burst of energy, but he stood up and offered her his arm, dialing the phone with his other hand.

Julia could hear the enthusiasm in Adrianna's voice when Vitale asked the favor.

"*Domani?*" Vitale swiveled the phone away from his mouth. "She can tomorrow the morning, but not tomorrow the afternoon." Julia nodded and he went back to his conversation. A few seconds later, he turned to Julia again. "She want to know if you want the color. I tell her no, you already have the pretty color."

Julia squeezed his arm. "Yes, color would be great. Anything she wants to do."

He rolled his eyes and reported back to Adrianna, giving a couple of kissing sounds before hanging up. "Tomorrow the morning she come to my house. Not early. After the breakfast."

"Yay!" Julia waved her phone in the air before dropping it back into her purse. "Thank you so much. Now, tell me all about what happened at the gallery." She nodded toward the docks and the old fort in the distance, a place she still wanted to explore.

"We sell all the pieces! Gena want more." The exuberance in Vitale's voice was palpable. "You start the sell when you say I am the artist. Then people, people, people . . ."

His hand closed around hers as he talked, an innocent gesture that today felt uncommonly intimate.

She tried to shift her thoughts to follow what he was saying but found she was more preoccupied than ever with wondering why she was letting such a golden opportunity pass her by.

Gena had paid Vitale before he left, evidently a handsome sum, and he insisted on taking Julia for a celebratory meal at his favorite trattoria. He seemed to know everyone there, and everyone knew him.

Julia's head whirled at the number of names thrown at her, the array of foods she ate, and the volume of alcohol she drank. Most of all, Vitale's rapt attention made for a heady experience.

His arm hugged the back of her chair when he made introductions, and though she received little attention from those who sat and chatted, it scarcely mattered. She had *his* attention, and knowing that made all the difference.

He held her hand and kissed her fingers after they drank to his success with the premeal *aperitivo*. He fed her bites of spicy sausages and cheese off the antipasti tray, tracing his thumb across her lips in a way that echoed the pressure of that touch down below. His warm hand feathered up and down her arm as they talked over gnocchi de pesto. The scrumptious mixture of pine nuts and fresh basil exploded in her mouth, and a champagne-like effervescence flowed through her veins, heating her from head to toe.

Sharing the main course of succulent steamed mussels, they often touched foreheads or brushed noses when they laughed together. Every contact continued to suck Julia into the sensual vortex that hurled her forward through her insecurities and inhibitions.

By the time he ordered the *limoncello* for *digestivo* after dessert, last night's reticence filled her with regret. She really should've taken him right there on the table.

Luckily, by all appearances, she was going to get the rare opportunity of a second chance.

Not exactly *ignoring* her sense of propriety, but finally simply choosing to throw caution to the wind one time in her life, she excused herself to the ladies' room, removed her panties, and wadded them into her small clutch.

As if he sensed the final demise of her resolve—and probably congratulating himself for cracking a tough case—Vitale had already paid the bill by the time she returned. Swiftly, yet cautious of her limp, he led her through the crowd toward the door.

Once they reached the open air, he stopped and caught her under her chin, raising her mouth to meet his. She parted her lips, and his tongue made a quick and delicate sweep of her mouth. When he broke away, she leaned back and smiled up at him. He grabbed her hand and made straight for his Benelli parked around the next corner.

"Vitale! Don't forget my toe. Slow down." She protested his long strides, and he laughed and slowed his gait, though not by much.

They reached the bike, stopping to catch their breath before they got on. Adrenaline pumping through Julia's veins made her bold, and she lifted her mouth to only inches from his. "Kiss me." What she intended as a suggestion came out as a demand.

Vitale didn't seem to mind. He gathered her to him and kissed her with a ferocity that surpassed any fantasy she'd ever had. The fullness of his lips cushioned their fervent press as his mouth devoured hers from ever-changing angles, sweeping her into sensual oblivion of anything but the tip of his fevered tongue against the roof of her mouth. Their heated breath mingled, sending flames into the deepest recesses of her body. He didn't just kiss—he possessed. Their tongues sparred and tangled while their mouths met, parted, fused, danced.

Still pressing his lips and holding the front of his shirt for balance, Julia threw her leg over the seat. When her bare bottom connected with the cool leather, she stifled her surprised giggle and sucked his tongue with more vigor. He responded with a lusty grunt of approval.

At last, he pulled his mouth away slowly, but returned for three or four tiny kisses before he settled in front of her.

She molded her body against him, noting the seat beneath her was already warm and slightly damp. Clutching him around the middle, she whispered, "Hurry! I'm ready to let go."

He gave it the gas.

CHAPTER 1 2

Tightening her thighs against Vitale's hips allowed Julia to loosen her arms from around his waist, and she began a sensual bushwhack on his body, pulling his shirt from his waistband, employing her hands on his front, her lips, tongue, teeth on his back.

His muscles responded, rippling beneath her fingertips. She nibbled, nipped, scratched, licked, kissed—taunted him every possible way from her position on the seat behind him. All prior inhibitions were gone under the cover of darkness, but she continued her relentless assault even when the headlights of occasional on-coming automobiles placed the two of them in the spotlight.

She kept her hand above his waistband until he turned into the driveway; then she tiptoed her fingers past the barrier of his waistband to grasp him and tantalize him with a few strokes and caresses.

He revved the motor, making the plunge through the wooden columns, stopping a few feet from the door. In the sudden stillness, she could hear his hard breathing. She was breathing harder still.

When he rolled his head back to capture a kiss, she took the opportunity to nibble on the top of his ear. He sucked in his breath, making a hissing sound as his hands stroked her outer thighs.

"Julietta, you make me die," he groaned.

It took a second to figure out what he meant. She giggled, fluttering her breath against his neck. "You mean I'm killing you."

"*Sì.*"

Starting below his ear, she made a row of kisses around the back of his neck to the other ear. He grew more rigid in her hand, and her two-year fuse burned close to the powder keg. She released her hold on him and slowly eased off the seat.

When he stood up, she moved in quickly to unsnap and unzip the waistband of his cargo shorts. As they fell and he stepped out of them, her eyes were treated to the sight of a raging erection springing free, unencumbered by boxers or briefs.

She gasped, more in wonder than surprise. Until this very moment, she hadn't been sure she would ever again see a naked male in the flesh. To have that uncertainty quashed to such a degree was momentarily overwhelming. Swallowing the lump of emotion in her throat, she moved back just out of his reach and, after taking a fortifying breath, unzipped her skirt, letting it fall to gather around her ankles.

His eyes registered surprise at her panty-less state, then shifted up to hold hers in their heat.

When he held out his arms, she stepped out of her skirt and into his embrace with no misgivings. His mouth swept down on hers and the world spun as his tongue took possession of her mouth.

Oh God, it had been way too long. Her every nerve was at heightened awareness. Wanting to touch him. Wanting to be touched. She ran her hands under his shirt, gathering it up to expose as much bare skin as possible.

His hands were everywhere, working separately to inflame two places at once—gliding into her hair, squeezing her behind, smoothing down her arms, slipping under her top to smooth across her back.

She was so close now. Didn't want him to stop. Didn't want to have to think. But the niggle in her brain warned that she couldn't let his perfect touch come into contact with her hideous imperfection. So, in an act of frantic desperation, she tore her mouth from his and latched on to his nipple, pushing his T-shirt under his armpits to an annoying position . . . hopefully.

The diversion worked.

When he let go of her to wrench the shirt over his head, she dropped to her knees. She hadn't been with many men, but it was a technique she trusted.

Vitale expelled a groan of pleasure and then protested, first low in English, then louder in Italian. She ignored him until his fists tightened in her hair and she recognized the sign—the helpless state when a man's thought processes came only from his lower brain.

Vitale wouldn't be interested in her breasts now.

A trick, but necessary, and she was unapologetic. No way would she allow her imperfections to screw up this perfect night.

She broke loose from him again, backing away until she leaned against one of the wooden columns. "I want you here." Her breath came in ragged spurts. "Standing up." Moving into the house would be too dangerous. Like his, her own control was almost gone.

Vitale panted, a feral and deliciously dangerous look in his eyes. His body, covered in a thin layer of perspiration, glistened in the moonlight, made him one of his own works of art, polished to perfection. "We go in. I have the protection in the bedroom."

He held his hand out, but Julia shook her head. "We don't need protection. I can't get pregnant. It's been over two years, Vitale. I can't wait any longer. Here. Now. Please." The last word trailed off to a whimper.

He leaned in and kissed her long and deep. When his hands urged the light sweater off her shoulders, she caught it at the bend of her elbows. Locking her gaze onto his, she took his hand and guided it where she needed it most.

A moan exploded from her lips at his first touch. He braced his weight with his other arm on the wooden post and caught the next one with his mouth as his fingertip became a tool of sweet torture.

She arched against him, mewling like a kitten, scratching like a cougar, relinquishing control at last. He teased, making her scream with no breath to carry the sound beyond her captured mouth.

Teetering on the very brink she'd pushed him to a few moments ago, she was vaguely aware when he grasped behind her knee and pulled her thigh up tight against him. He slid his length into her, filled her to the point of bursting. She cried out in relief.

Two years of release.

He kissed her and murmured lovely, unintelligible things into her hair as his thrusts became more powerful. She met his rhythm, yelping in pleasure with each contact, grinding against him harder as her circuitry started to overload.

A scream tore from her mouth as the encapsulating current coursed through her body. The involuntary pulse of her muscles surrounded his last strokes. She felt his rush, heard his labored breathing through clenched teeth.

It was all she could do to cling to him as surge after surge sapped her strength, and he held her steady, pressed against her until her breathing returned to normal, then finally lowered her leg to the ground.

"*O Dio,* Julietta." He rested his forehead against hers.

"Oh, Vitale." His name was a whisper on her lips. "I expected it to be great. Wonderful. But never in my wildest dreams did I expe—"

He cut her off with a kiss, then another, and another as his hands massaged her back, stroked her hair. "We go to the bed now, yes?" He cupped the sides of her face gently and covered it with tiny kisses. "I sleep with you?"

"Yes, as long as you let me sleep." She laughed as a huge yawn gripped her. "I'm tired." She meant it, too. She was exhausted, too tired to worry how she could stay covered next time.

If there was a next time, she would have to figure out something then.

Julia woke early with Vitale's soft, steady breathing against her hair, his arm heavy across her middle. She hadn't slept so well in years.

After they'd gone in last night, she'd pleaded for some privacy in the bathroom and had used the time to slip into one of his T-shirts. And nothing else.

When he awoke in a sleepy but amorous mood in the middle of the night—as she suspected he might . . . and hoped he would even while she fretted about it—she pretended to be too cold to remove the shirt. The draping of the huge shirt coupled with the darkness gave her enough cover to allow his hands and mouth a physical, if not visual, exploration of her breasts.

Not being able to feel his touch brought her other senses to heightened awareness.

Imagining the feel of his kneading hands, the heat of his tongue as it laved across her nipples, kept her brain engaged in sensuous thought and the rest of her body responding as if the sensations actually existed.

As the time grew right, she'd lain on her side and snuggled her backside against him, guiding him into her from behind. Their orgasms had been explosively in unison.

And neither of them had moved since.

But she sighed now, all too aware she couldn't keep up with this façade much longer, all too aware it probably wouldn't fool him even one more time.

If she stayed here, she couldn't keep from wanting him—he'd make sure of that. She wanted him this instant, in fact, which probably made her some kind of insatiable Mrs. Robinson. Having sex certainly hadn't given her the extended relief she was looking for. It had only complicated things.

Her insides twisted at that sobering thought.

She could simply tell him the truth and show him the scars. Maybe he wouldn't find them repugnant. Maybe he wouldn't make her feel like a modern Frankenstein.

The memory of Frank's face when her bandages came off swam to the surface of her mind, bringing with it the haunting burn of rejection. She couldn't bear seeing such a look on Vitale's face . . . couldn't bear to *ever* see such a look again—from anyone.

She shuddered as the battle raged inside her—warring factions both deflecting and accepting what she had to—and the tightening of Vitale's arm around her was almost imperceptible, but it was there. He would wake soon.

She had to find another place to stay. Today. There had to be a room somewhere. Maybe Adrianna could help.

Thoughts of Adrianna and the upcoming hair event propelled

her out of bed. She'd promised Vitale a home-cooked breakfast. It was the least she could do to show her gratitude. For everything. And after breakfast, she'd explain that she had to leave.

"No, Julietta. Do not go yet." His words were slurred with sleep, but their poignancy pierced her heart.

She leaned down and brushed her fingers through his hair, kissing him lightly. "Don't get up. I'll wake you when breakfast is ready."

His eyes never opened, though he nodded.

She studied him as she slipped into her clothes, finding it difficult to tear her eyes away, knowing she'd never have this chance again. She was looking at perfection personified. The sable hair against the stark whiteness of the sheets. The perfect lines of his body. Bronze skin stretched over muscles defined even in total relaxation. And all the pretty packaging surrounded a soul that was thoughtful and kind and loving . . . but also petulant, arrogant, and demanding.

Human, after all.

This Adonis would make some mortal woman very lucky someday.

Her phone was still in her skirt pocket, but if she took a picture she'd probably wake him. Instead, she closed her eyes and drew in a deep breath through her nose, trying to inhale a small part of the essence that was Vitale. Something that would mingle with her, become a part of her. Stay with her forever.

She went into the kitchen and put the kettle on the stove to boil water for coffee. She'd have to watch it to keep the whistle from waking him. As she scooped the dark grounds into the French press pot, her thoughts wandered back to the night before, and she tried to relive it moment by moment.

Sex with Frank had always been the way she thought sex *was,* whereas sex with Vitale had been sex the way she'd always dreamed it *could be.* With Frank, toward the end, she'd felt somebody else in bed with them, knew that he was fantasizing she was someone else. She'd accepted it because she thought that's what happened when women started getting older. That their partners dreamed of them as younger women.

But Vitale seemed to be in the moment with *her*. She would always have that.

The pressure in the kettle caused the lid to jiggle. She poured the water over the grounds, then carried the pot and a cup out to the backyard.

The sun's warmth had already brought out the scent of the flowers that surrounded her, and normally the smells would have been calming. Today, they made her melancholy. She walked around, glumly examining the festive blooms with no enthusiasm.

She went back to the table and pushed the plunger down through the water and coffee grounds. The liquid swirled into a black brew, and she poured a cup, hoping the strong elixir would cleanse the negativity from her thoughts. Instead, one sip brought reality thudding into her brain. She'd had her one night of a lifetime, the fantasy every woman dreamed of.

And what scared her most was that she would probably never experience anything even remotely close to it again.

Guilt mingled with the taste of the coffee, intensifying the bitterness.

Yes, she'd had her night of fantasy. No one could take that away. For a forty-eight-year-old to have experienced that kind of sex.... She should be thanking her lucky stars instead of being greedy for more.

She turned to find Vitale watching her from the doorway, shirtless, wearing the shorts from the day before. "Hold it." She pulled her phone from her pocket and snapped a picture before he strolled toward her, a half smile tugging at his lips.

"I hope you do not need the photograph to remember the last night."

"No." She forced a smile. "Last night was pretty memorable without a photograph. But it'll be nice to have."

He kissed her softly. But when he moved in closer, she leaned back and pulled her mouth away, unwilling to let herself get more stirred up than she already was. "I, um, I haven't brushed my teeth yet."

His eyes narrowed at the lame excuse.

She nodded toward the sunflowers on the table to get his eyes off her. "Those are beautiful, by the way. I forgot to say anything yesterday."

He pointed to the flower beds that surrounded the yard with vibrant clumps of color. "Orabella, she plant. I do not have the time to care for, but she enjoy."

Julia took the opportunity to move around the yard, away from the man who had her heart racing again. The flower beds formed an arc around the yard, and each bed had its own color theme. Pink. Blue. Orange. Yellow. Red. "It's like standing in the middle of a rainbow," she observed. "So she has your artistic talent as well. Her medium of choice happens to be flowers."

"Yes, I think so." Vitale sidled against her. He didn't try to kiss her on the mouth again, choosing instead to plant a kiss on her knuckles.

Her hand shook, and she pulled it away.

"You do not wash the hand either?" Raised eyebrows punctuated his sarcastic tone.

"I'm still just a little shaky from last night." The truth relaxed her, and she gave him a weak, but genuine smile. "It had been a long time."

The eyebrows dropped to their normal position, softening his face. "*Capisco.* But you remember what to do very well, I think." He reached to stroke her face, but seemed to think better of it, and then he waved toward the studio. "I must choose the pieces for the gallery this morning, and I have something that will take the hour, so do not hurry to make the breakfast."

"Perfect. That'll give me time for a shower first." She turned and hurried toward the house before he could suggest joining her.

CHAPTER 13

Each bite of breakfast was torture. A massive wad of dread filled Julia's throat and refused to allow anything but the smallest particles by. Nonetheless, her stomach felt full, twisted into the tight knot such as it was.

While she was cooking, she'd convinced herself that a one-night stand was something Vitale was used to, being the well-known cad he was, and he would think nothing of her decision to leave. Would, in fact, probably be glad to see her go.

But his "something to do" in the studio turned out to be a project made specifically for her, and when she called him in for breakfast, he'd presented her with a beautiful cane he'd fashioned out of a thin table leg. He'd attached a carved handle that fit her hand perfectly and had painted the entire thing a lovely shade of cotton-candy pink with a delicate green vine twisting around it.

The surprise and his thoughtfulness had her fumbling throughout breakfast for conversation until a more appropriate time for her announcement presented itself.

Vitale had never eaten Southern-style biscuits and gravy, so watching his first bite and the accompanying dreamy eye roll was worth all the trouble. The polenta didn't taste exactly like grits, but with enough butter, salt, and pepper, served as a suitable substitute. The scrambled eggs and pan-fried pancetta had been a cinch.

Despite her best efforts to enjoy the food and these last moments together, the pressure built to the point where she was going to spew something. Be it words or food, something had to give.

She set her fork down and flattened her palms on the table for stability. "Vitale, I'm going to find another place to stay. Today."

He placed his coffee cup on the table too delicately, as if holding himself in check. His eyes grew dark, speaking the words before they left his lips. "Why, Julietta?"

"The sex . . . it complicates things. I know we're adults, and it shouldn't matter, but it does. At least for me it does." That sounded old-fashioned, but maybe that was a good thing. He might view her as a prude, although after last night's performance, that hardly seemed likely. "I just think it would be better if I didn't stay here." She caught her bottom lip between her teeth to keep it from trembling.

He didn't say anything, but his look spoke volumes. She averted her eyes and focused on a blemish in the marble flooring. "Last night, I thought it was what I wanted, but I was wrong." Surely, he read the lie in her voice, which sounded obvious to her own ears. Last night was exactly what she wanted . . . way too much.

He gave a derisive snort. "You thought you desire me, but you are mistaken? I am sorry to be not what you want."

"No." She made fleeting contact with his penetrating eyes. Hurt. Anger. Disbelief. Probably a myriad of other emotions she didn't want to see. She gazed at the sunflowers swaying in the breeze outside the door. "It's not you. It's me. I thought I was ready for this, but I'm not."

"You have the man in the Keen-tuck-kee, yes?"

His words drew her back in. God love him, he was trying so hard to understand. He brushed his fingers down the back of his hair, exasperation etched in the lines on his face.

"No, there's no one in my life, but I still have to go."

Too late, she realized she should've said yes. Being rejected for another man might not happen to him often, but that song was probably at least in his repertoire. To be rejected for no good reason would be as foreign to him as invisibility.

"There is no other place." He pronounced each word carefully as if he feared she wouldn't understand him. "I tell you this and tell you this. You do not believe." He set off on a long tirade in Italian, well aware, she was sure, that she couldn't understand a word of any of it. But anger gave his voice a jagged edge and turned the volume up a notch, causing her own emotion to breach the wall.

"Don't go being all temperamental with me!" The magnitude of her voice startled her. Why was she yelling? That wasn't like her. Except, right then, it damn well *felt* like her. She pushed her decibel level higher. "*You* started all this seduction stuff with your 'I kees when I want.' So, okay, you did, and I let you, and you got what you wanted." She poked her herself in the chest. "And so did I! Let's leave it at that."

He stood up and leaned across the table, meeting her loudness and raising it. "I do not have you to stay with me only to have the sex with you."

His phrasing, the stress on the word *only,* shook the ground beneath her, throwing her off balance. "I—um." She cleared her throat, but the frustration she'd opened herself up to stayed lodged between her heart and her mouth. She lowered her voice to almost an undertone. "Whatever. I only know that I can't stay here. Can't sleep with you anymore."

"You stay here." He lowered his voice, too, but his words rang out sharp and distinct, like he had shaped them with his chisel in a granite tablet. "I do not touch you again."

A movement outside the open door caught Julia's eye. To her horror, Adrianna stood there slack-jawed with her arms—and no doubt her ears—filled to brimming.

Vitale stormed out the door and past his sister without a word. A few seconds later, the sound of his Benelli faded away.

"I am sorry." Adrianna drew her shoulders toward her ears as she stepped hesitantly into the kitchen. "I did not know—"

"It's okay. Don't worry about it." The flush ran through Julia's ribcage into her face, but the heat did nothing to loosen the knotted muscles. "Come on in. Let me just go to the bathroom."

She went into the bedroom and closed the door, needing a few minutes alone.

Could that have gone any worse? she asked her reflection as she splashed cold water on her face. The redness in her cheeks abated, but sadness that her time with Vitale had ended like this and anger at herself for ever letting it begin scraped her insides raw.

She wished she could leave that very instant, but she would have to find a place to go to, and then she'd have to pack. And Vitale's sister was waiting.

By the time she talked herself into going back out and facing Adrianna, the young woman had everything assembled and laid out on the table on the patio.

"Do you have a color chosen?" Adrianna asked, steering conversation clear of the obvious.

Julia's enthusiasm for the project had drained away, but Adrianna had gone to so much trouble for her, she didn't want to back out. "I'll put my head in your hands, and go with whatever you think is best." She so hoped that choice wouldn't include any pinks or blues.

"I like this one." Adrianna showed her a box that pictured a woman with chestnut-colored hair. "I think it would be very nice with the skin. And maybe add the highlights, yes?"

"Different," Julia answered dully. "All I care about is that it's different."

Adrianna mixed the solutions and began applying the ammonia-infused concoction to Julia's hair. "Vitale did not look very happy when he left," she said at last.

She'd offered an opening, and Julia drew a hesitant breath, debating how much to share. If she was going to approach Adrianna for help with finding a new place to stay, it made sense to be up-front about the reason why. "No, he wasn't. He's angry because I told him I need to find somewhere else to stay. It's just not working, my staying here."

"He tell you of Luciana?"

"Yes," Julia answered. "She sounds like a lovely person," she added, not wanting Adrianna to think there was a jealousy problem with Vitale's wife going on here.

"After Luciana die, Vitale try very hard to not allow the hurt to touch the people he care for. I think because he cannot stop the hurt of Luciana."

"He's a fixer, all right." Julia had witnessed that firsthand.

"*Che?*"

"He fixes. Tries to make everything right. Make everything perfect."

"*Sì.* Too much he do this. Life is not the perfect. This is why he love the art. He feex it as he *see* the perfect."

Adrianna was a very insightful young woman. But the insight into Vitale's character only made Julia more sure than ever she needed to leave. One look at her breasts, and she'd become one of the artist's projects. "So . . . do you have any ideas where I might find a room?"

"That will be difficult. The tours are in Lerici for the two weeks." The young woman's lips pursed exactly the way Vitale's did when he concentrated.

Julia dropped her eyes, trying not to think about his lips or remember how they felt on hers . . . and everywhere else. "That's what he keeps telling me, so maybe I'll need to move to another town. I'll start looking when we finish here."

"Oh." Adrianna's tone flattened.

In the few days she'd been in Italy, Julia had learned all conversation was animated, and the lack of inflection in Adrianna's voice twanged a "mother chord" in her heart. She saw tears brimming in her eyes. "What's wrong, sweetheart?" She used the exact words and voice she would've used with Melissa.

A couple of tears ran down Adrianna's cheeks, and she sniffed. "I have the lump in my breast."

Julia opened her eyes in feigned surprise. "You do?"

"Yes." Adrianna nodded and covered Julia's head with a plastic shower cap. Methodically, she peeled off the plastic gloves. "After hearing of your cancer, I call the doctor yesterday. He want to see me today."

Julia reached out and took the trembling hand in both of hers. "You did the right thing."

"Yes, but I want to not worry anyone, so I did not tell Antonio or Mama or my sister."

Julia grasped the request, though it hadn't been delivered. "Would you like for me to go with you to the doctor?" Thinking about Adrianna all alone and receiving what might be bad news was unnerving. They were hardly more than strangers, but even a stranger would be better than no one.

Adrianna sat down hard in the other chair, tears flowing freely now. "Would you do that?" Her hold on Julia's hand tightened. "I would be so grateful. I know now that I am afraid to go alone in case . . . in case . . ."

She didn't have to finish. Julia felt the weight of the unspoken words on her shoulders and in the pit of her stomach. She patted the hand that clutched hers. "In case you need someone to celebrate with afterward."

Adrianna brushed the tears away with her free hand. "Yes, in case of that." She gave a weak smile.

"I'd be glad to go with you, Adrianna." Maybe celebrating her recovery wasn't her only purpose on this trip. Though she didn't share the idea with her young companion.

The doctor's office turned out to be on the same block as a travel agent. When Adrianna's turn was called, Julia gave her a hug and hustled out of the office to ask about any vacant rooms in the area. The beautiful cane from Vitale made it easier to get around than the day before when she roamed around alone.

But Vitale's arm worked better than any cane. The thought squeezed her stomach, and she squeezed the handle.

Determined not to think about never touching him again, she stopped to give Hettie a call. The window boxes on the storefronts were filled with flowers in vibrant hues, and despite the dreariness she felt, she tried to match their cheer with her voice as she dialed the number.

"Hello?" The voice sounded so old and tired, an alarm went off in Julia's head.

"Hettie? It's Julia. Are you okay?"

"I'm fine. But a good, steamy story about an Italian stud-muffin would make me better."

That was more like it. Julia switched her brain out of alarm mode. "Stud-muffin?" She laughed. "Wherever did you learn such a word?"

"That's how a couple of the nurses refer to the new administrator. Joe Proctor. You remember him?" The taunt in Hettie's voice hinted that she remembered well their introduction.

"I remember." Julia massaged the bridge of her nose between two fingers, still embarrassed by the memory. "You didn't really introduce us, though. You only wanted to introduce him to my nipples, if I recall."

"So you finally did it with the Italian, didn't you?"

Hettie's mercurial changes in topic always kept Julia on her toes. She suspected it was to catch her off guard. "A true Southern lady would never kiss and tell. You know that." *And I sure as hell don't want to talk about it now.*

"Which means you did because, if you didn't, there wouldn't be anything to tell after the kissing, so spill it, sister. Give an old woman something that will help her get her rocks off."

"Hettie! What have you been reading? Or watching?"

"Don't change the subject. Damn it! I played penny ante poker last night for two hours. That should count as physical therapy for today."

"Wha—?"

Muffled voices in the background. Okay, so the last part of Hettie's dialogue had been directed at someone—probably the physical therapist—who'd come into her room. Then she was back. "Make it quick, Julia. Make an old woman happy before they take her away."

"Nope, I'll just let you use that runaway imagination of yours."

Hettie's sardonic chuckle drifted over the line. "Eh, it's probably better that way anyway. I'll bet it was a quickie."

Geez, she knows me too well.

Voices were saying to Hettie that she had to hang up. Julia gave an exasperated sigh. "Good-bye, Hettie. I'll talk to you later."

"Yeah, yeah."

Click. The call ended so abruptly, the alarm in Julia's head sounded again. Her finger poised over the redial button. The last time Hettie sounded that way, one of her friends had died. That was most likely the case, but it was odd she didn't mention anything.

Julia tucked the phone back into her pocket and walked down to the travel agency she'd spied. She smiled at the woman lurking behind the door, then cringed with embarrassment when she realized a mirror hung there, and she was looking at her own reflection.

The change was remarkable. The chestnut hue drew out her natural peachiness while the highlights softened the area around her eyes. The angular cut with wispy sides and mussy top took years off of her face. So how was it that at the moment she was feeling every bit of her forty-eight years?

The American travel agent's chin buckled at Julia's request, but she typed a few strokes on her computer. "There's a room available in Tellaro for two nights. Do you have a car?"

"No. Well . . . maybe. I have a friend who has a car."

"It's only a fifteen-minute bus ride from here, but the buses are really crowded when the tourists are in. Taxis book hours in advance. Early morning would be your best chance."

Julia slumped against the counter. She hated to ask Adrianna to take her all the way back to Vitale's and then drive her all the way to Tellaro and then make the return trip home. It wasn't far, but that still seemed a lot of trouble to ask of someone she hardly knew. And she couldn't ask Adrianna at all if the news this afternoon happened to be bad. Two nights didn't help much either. But even one night at Vitale's now seemed out of the question. Things were too awkward. He probably wouldn't even speak to her. "Maybe there's something here in town? Anything? Even a tiny room would be fine."

The woman regarded her over the top of her bifocals. "Everything, and I do mean everything, books solid this time of year. If it's an emergency, I could find you a car for hire, but you'll pay an exorbitant price for it."

"No, it's not that urgent." Julia could almost hear her breasts snorting as her heart sank past them.

"So, do you want me to book the room for you tonight?"

"Let me talk to my friend with the car first, then I'll get back with you. It shouldn't take but a few minutes."

"Don't wait too long." The agent handed Julia her card. "It'll be gone."

Julia walked back to the doctor's office, frustrated and wondering what to do now. Approach Adrianna about hiring her to chauffeur her around for the next couple of hours? Certainly that was a possibility . . . if her news was good.

That flicker of hope flared a few minutes later when Adrianna came out of the examination room. Her cheeks were tear streaked, but the smile that dimpled them shouted joy and relief.

She hugged Julia, and whispered, "It was the cyst. He removed the fluid with the needle."

Julia felt her own hot tears of joy and sent up a prayer of thanks. She held Adrianna until the young woman's grip began to loosen, a secret rule she'd used since Melissa was a toddler. Let the person who initiates the hug be the one to let go first.

A male voice startled her, and she turned to find the ancient doctor who had examined her toe. She hadn't expected to see him again, but then, he was probably the only doctor in the village.

He smiled broadly when he recognized her, making an approving motion toward her hair. She couldn't understand what he was saying, although she picked up the gist of it when he pointed to her foot, raised his eyebrows, and nodded.

She showed him the cane Vitale made for her and demonstrated how well she could walk with it.

He chuckled and applauded her performance. Then his face went serious. His speech sped up so much she couldn't pick up even one familiar word, and his gestures gave her no hint of what he was talking about. He kept motioning as if he were pointing to the sky; then he would shake his head and point some more. He finished with a sad sigh and a shake of his head.

"He said he was thinking of you an hour ago when he got called back to the hotel where you were staying. It hardly ever happens, yet he's been called there twice this week. For you Saturday and then again today," Adrianna translated. "One of the tourists staying at the hotel had a heart attack, and they had to send him to the hospital in Genoa. He did everything he could, but he hasn't heard yet if the man survived."

"Oh, *mi dispiace.*" Julia patted his hand.

He squeezed her hand lightly, then kissed it. The gleam in his eye made her think the guy who had the heart attack might no longer be on the doctor's mind.

"We will go now." Adrianna looped her arm through Julia's and gave a tug that broke the doctor's hold. She thanked him the whole time they made their way to the door. When they got outside, she giggled. "I think he wanted to examine you next."

Julia laughed in agreement. "It must be the hair."

When the bright orange of the Lord Byron Hotel caught her eye, the doctor's story *cha-chinged* in Julia's brain. The heart attack victim was sent to Genoa. "Adrianna"—she grabbed the other woman's arm and motioned up the hill—"if they took the heart attack victim to Genoa, maybe Mr. Moretti has a vacancy."

Adrianna held back, chewing her bottom lip as she thought. Finally, she gave a resigned shrug. "Vitale won't like it, but Mama will be pleased."

Julia wheeled her luggage into the kitchen, anxious to get away as quickly as possible—and without a scene.

Damn!

Vitale stood with his arms crossed, leaning against the doorway to the backyard.

The house was quiet, except for the pulse pounding through Julia's veins. She saw no sign of his sister. "Where's Adrianna?" She glanced out to the courtyard but didn't see her there either.

"She leave." He lowered his arms and hooked his thumbs in his front pocket. "I tell her to leave. We need to talk. Alone."

Frustration simmered in the pit of her stomach. Adrianna was her means of transportation, and Julia so wanted this departure to be quick and easy. Tell Vitale she appreciated everything he'd done for her—emphasis on *everything*. Kiss on each cheek. *Arrivederci.*

"Vitale, we don't need to talk—"

He sauntered toward her. "I think we need to talk. After we talk, you call her back if you want. But first, we talk."

CHAPTER 14

Vitale stopped about four feet from her and moved his hands to his back pockets, shirt stretched taut across his chest.

Julia chose to stare at his pecs rather than make eye contact. His sharp eyes missed nothing and would slice through her tough outer layers and peel them back without so much as a blink. She continued to stand in the middle of the kitchen clutching the handle of her luggage, hoping for a quick and friendly departure, though her sweaty palms didn't seem to buy into that scenario.

"I have much gratitude for your kindness to Adrianna today." His soft, liquid tone washed away some of the grit from the more tender areas.

Julia glanced around the room, focusing nowhere in particular. "It was nothing really. I was glad to do it."

"She is the something. She is the much something. Adrianna say she very afraid, but you talk to her, and you go with her to the doctor. *Mille grazie.*"

Emotion weighed in his voice and drew her eyes to meet his.

"*Prego,*" she answered.

His lips pressed together as his chest heaved in a deep breath. "If she did not allow Antonio to know this, she should allow me to take her when she is afraid. Not you. I am the brother."

So, hurt for being left out of the loop fueled part of his anger. Julia's talk with Adrianna about Vitale had made some things clearer. "There was nothing you could've done any different from what I did."

"Yes, I hold the hand." He slapped the backs of his fingers across his other palm. "*Mi preparo.* Make ready to hear what the doctor say. I feex."

"Some things you can't fix, Vitale."

"She is correct for me to make the try, yes?"

Telling him he'd just drive himself crazy in the process wouldn't make any difference, so she swallowed her advice and gave him a shrug.

"Adrianna also say you have the cancer of the breast."

Noooo. Julia caught her top lip between her teeth to stop the groan from escaping. Vitale's eyes reflected concern too genuine to ignore. "I *had* cancer." She dragged the verb out to emphasize its tense. "I don't have it anymore. It's all gone. Completely."

He took a step closer, and her stomach tightened.

"*Capisco.* Giada, she say I do not make the words good. But I know you have the cancer in the past. Adrianna, she say you come to hike the Cinque Terre to congratulate yourself."

Julia nodded and gave him a weak smile. "That's right. And that's a lovely way to say it." Her smile faded as she swallowed.

"Julietta." He inched toward her as if she were a wild animal about to bolt. "I think the cancer, she is gone here." He brushed the back of his finger across her breast. "But not here." He grazed her temple with his knuckles, and she felt the pressure of tears building at the back of her eyes.

Raising her palm, she stopped him from touching her again. "You're wrong." She shook her head and fastened her eyes on his chest again. "I'm okay. I'm healthy and whole and thankful to be alive. And my head is fine. It used to not be. But it is now. It's fine." Even *she* knew she was protesting too much. She blinked, fighting the tears, determined not to get all emotional about this. "I'm not a survivor. That term implies I faced death, but I never did. I had a disease once. I'm over it. I broke my arm once. I'm over it. I don't need you to have sex with me out of pity. I don't need you to fix me."

Anger flashed across his face and then it was gone, replaced by a tenderness that was harder to bear. He rested his hands on her shoulders, then smoothed his palms down her arms to her elbows and back up. "Last night, you say, 'I am ready to let go.' But you do not let go. Fast. Let go." He released her arms long enough to "weigh" the terms in his hands, showing evidence of the imbalance. "They do not mean the same." He returned his hands to her shoulders.

So she hadn't fooled him at all. Tension corded the sides of her neck where she held her emotion in check. She wanted to apologize for using him in her self-centered game of "Make Me Whole Again," but her chin quivered, and if she spoke, her voice would do the same. She brushed the tear trying to squeeze from the edge of her eye.

"You keep the breasts covered when we have the sex." Vitale's voice was soft like his touch, and just as compelling. "If everything is fine, do not need the feex as you say, why do you do this?"

Why indeed?

Because beneath her glib exterior beat the heart of a coward. "I . . . couldn't let . . . you see." Her voice broke on the words, and with it, the tight rein she held on her composure.

Be careful what you ask for—the old adage had come back to bite her in the ass.

She'd wanted someone to see her.

Well, Vitale didn't only *see* her, he saw *through* her.

The statue of Rachele had warned her, shown her what he was capable of. But she'd plunged ahead, recklessly ignoring her instincts, and now here he was, reaching into her soul with his tenderness, pulling the real Julia to the surface—the scared one—exposing the truth that her bravado was as false as her breasts.

Anguish knifed through her.

Despite her best effort, the tear escaped. And then another and another, coming so quickly she couldn't keep up with wiping them away and finally gave up trying.

He knew, so pretense was no longer an option.

"I know what you think about American women and their fake breasts." His head tilted in question at her comment. "I heard you and that guy talking below my balcony at the hotel." A shadow of guilt passed over his face, and she spoke quickly to quell it. "You have a right to your opinion, and you spoke it honestly. I'm the one who hasn't been truthful. I don't really have breasts. Mine are as fake as they come." The words took up more space in her chest than the implants hanging there. Everything felt crowded, making it difficult to breathe.

Vitale removed his hands and placed them in his back pockets. Withdrawal—precisely the reaction she'd expected. But she had, after all, lived through it before.

She gained control of her breathing with a shuddering sigh and went on, determined to give him the details. "The surgeons removed everything inside so they could get all the cancer." She chose words simple enough for him to understand. "They left only the skin, and they filled the empty space with bags of fluid."

He reached out with a tentative hand and gingerly cupped it over her breast, then did the same with his other hand. His touch raised a sob that caught in her throat. She chewed her bottom lip as he spoke. "But she is beautiful. Soft and round. And the nipples . . ." He looked her in the eyes, but his thumbs circled the protruding folds of skin.

"Aren't real." She finished the sentence for him. "They're just nubs made of skin with tattoos around them. They have no feeling, no sensitivity . . . and they're permanently erect, so they don't tell you anything about how I'm feeling."

"But why do you not allow me to see?"

Her spine stiffened in preparation for when he pulled his hands away again, and the movement put some added strength in her voice. "Because you made fun of even the pretty ones, and mine are far from pretty. They're ugly. I've had three operations, so there are scars. Ugly scars right across the middle that you can't see until I'm undressed. But they're there, and they can't be fixed, and if I'd allowed you to see them, you wouldn't have wanted to touch me again."

His hands left her breasts, but only long enough to cup the sides of her face. He bent until his eyes were even with hers. "How do you know what I do?"

"I. Just. Know," she whispered.

"I think the large, the not real breast, she is foolish. This is true. But she is not you." He straightened. "And I am not *him*, Julietta. You do *not* know."

She raised her chin and met his steady gaze with her own. "You think you're always so honest about everything? Let's see how honest you've been with yourself." Her fingers flew to unbutton her blouse. It fell open, and she shrugged it off her shoulders until it slid down her arms to the floor. Then she slipped her fingers under the straps of her camisole.

A moment of panic gripped her chest, strangling any words that hung in her throat, but she'd come too far to stop now. Exchanging the fear of cancer for fear of rejection was still surrender, and she'd already lost too much to this damn disease. She wouldn't let it eat away another tiny bit of her.

What she'd said a minute ago? A lie. She *was* a survivor, and a minute from now, her heart would still be beating.

She kept her eyes locked on his, determined to face this with dignity, and not fall apart like she had with Frank. Her fingers tightened around the straps of her cami, and she tugged the material down, and down still farther, and down until it circled her waist.

Vitale's face didn't flinch. No long blink to cover emotion. No recoil in horror. No reaction. None.

Her brain barely had time to register his reaction before, with one stride forward—not away—he was at her. "You fight the battle with the cancer. You have the scar from the battle. The scar, she is not ugly. She is the proof of the courage." With gentle sweeps of his fingertips, he traced the scars, back and forth, back and forth, and his eyes burned with something she'd never expected.

Interest.

Julia felt nothing beyond pressure, but watching him touch her breasts and kiss across the scars—not under the cover of darkness, but here in the stark light of day—struck her as extremely erotic. His thumbs circled her nipples, and a flame flickered to life at her core.

The tip of his tongue replaced his thumbs, while his hands

moved behind her to make sensuous feather strokes down her naked back. "Do you feel this, *bella mia?*"

"Yes." She gripped his head, letting her own roll back languidly as she closed her eyes.

His mouth left a line of wet kisses in the valley between her breasts as he moved to the other side. His hand found its way under her skirt. "And this. You feel this, yes?"

She opened her eyes and nodded, his smoldering look taking away her ability to speak.

His hand started a sensuous creep up her stomach. "The breast, she is the thing of beauty." He smoothed a palm slowly across each of them, then up to her neck and into her hair. "But the body, she has the many places of the pleasure, yes?"

He caught her smile on his lips.

Desire for him coursed through her body, flooding her with the need to allow his exploration of her "many places of the pleasure."

"I do not see you naked last night. I would like to now." He flicked his tongue across her shoulder while his hands were busy unzipping her skirt. One deft push sent it fluttering to the floor along with her panties. He held her hand as she stepped out of them and continued to hold it as his eyes roamed slowly from her head to her feet and back.

Naked in front of a man.

Her breath stilled in her lungs.

The dramatic moment of revelation was over. His curiosity about her breasts was sated, and now, the light of day might bring a new dawning to him as well. One that would shed a better light on the difference in their ages.

His eyes climbed steadily until they met hers and came to rest. "Julietta." His tone was serious as he pulled her hand to his lips and brushed her knuckles across them. "I tell you to call Adrianna if you want this after we talk." The side of his mouth twitched. "I think we finish the talk, yes? Do you call her?"

Julia laughed softly, but a couple of renegade tears made warm tracks down her cheeks as she shook her head no.

"Good." Without warning, he scooped her up in his arms and

strode toward the bedroom. "Because I would like the hours to learn very much about your beautiful, naked body."

At first, she thought he must be exaggerating about the "hours" part, but he laid her on the bed and began exploring each inch of her skin, one at a time. Her mouth. Her earlobe. Her jawline. Her neck . . . his movements slow and enticingly deliberate. Whatever he explored at the moment received his thorough attention. A finger would trace an outline, or a hand would smooth or knead. His tongue tasted. His teeth nibbled. His mouth caressed.

She followed his lead, thrilling at the way she could make his body dance with her hands or her mouth. His whispered exclamations and endearments needed no translation. They encouraged an exhilarating boldness and soon, any inhibitions, imaginary or real, dropped away. He made her forget her breasts were anything more than merely breasts.

Julia imagined herself a sensuous butterfly, emerging from the protection of her carefully constructed cocoon.

She tried her wings and found she could fly.

Her quivers of excitement eventually gave way to prolonged euphoria. Like clay in the artist's hands, he molded and sculpted her into positions that yielded maximum results, each climax more consuming than the last.

After a long while, when he at last positioned himself over her, she wept at the intensity of the full release.

He kissed her tears away, and whispered, "Now, *bella mia,* you should let go."

And she did.

Then, and again a couple of hours later.

CHAPTER 15

Julia hadn't opened her eyes yet, though she could tell from the sounds it was morning, and much later than she usually slept.

Last night, she and Vitale made love for hours, choosing to skip the evening meal to stay in bed. And though she was hungry, she was also warm and comfortable and relaxed, curled against Vitale, and that made her reluctant to move yet.

As if in protest to her thoughts, her stomach rumbled against his arm, which was casually thrown across her.

She felt the vibration of his chuckle, confirming he was awake.

"Vitale did not fill you up?" he joked.

She gave a dreamy sigh and rolled over to face him. "I think Vitale made me insatiable."

"Een-sa-she-bull?" He repeated the unfamiliar word.

"Um, unable to be satisfied."

"You are not satisfied, *bella mia?*"

"You satisfied me completely last night." She kissed his bottom lip, his chin, his neck. "But I'll need another fix soon."

"Feex? *Preparare? Riparare?*"

"Geez, I never realized I used that word so often—and so many different ways." When she got home, she was going to check it out in the dictionary. "The way I used it this time means a drug I could get addicted to. I could get addicted to sex with you."

He sighed. "The English, she has the too many words."

"It's difficult, I know." She traced the sensuous shape of his mouth with a fingertip. "But you do a great job with it. I haven't had any trouble communicating with you."

"The word, she is not always of need, yes?" He eased his fingers into her hair at the temple and drew them slowly all the way to the tip. "The hair, she is . . ." He made a suggestive sound, a growl that drew a delighted tremor from her.

"I see what you mean." She snuggled closer and closed her eyes, serene and comfortable and content to lie like this until hunger demanded movement. Vitale rolled away from her, and she thought he was simply changing positions, but then he rolled back.

Paper rustled.

She opened one eye to see him holding his sketchpad. "What are you doing?"

"The camera, she is too far away." He pointed to his shorts that lay across the room where he'd kicked them last night. "I sketch. Only the few minutes. Go back to the sleep."

She closed her eye, and it seemed like no time at all before she heard him set the pad aside and he pulled her against him. They snuggled for a while, her head pillowed on his arm, her cheek resting against his side. Stretched full-length against him, she slid her foot languidly up and down his calf.

"Julietta, is it very soon now?"

Her yes came as a delighted squeal when he rolled on top of her, and unlike last night, this morning's lovemaking was fast and playful, fueled by hunger and need.

While they fixed breakfast together, she remembered the room she'd booked at the hotel. He used her phone to cancel it, but she was still out the money for one night. Having the memory of last night was worth whatever it cost her.

"Are you happy you stay, Julietta?" He slid his arms around her from behind as she put her phone back in her bag.

"I'm very happy," she said.

He took her shoulders and swiveled her around to face him.

"Then I think we do the something today that also make you very happy."

"Oh, yeah?" She clamped her hands onto his rear and leaned back to look him in the eye.

"Not the sex." He laughed. "That we do later. Today, she is the Julietta Berk-a-weeth Day." His broad gesture implied a banner stretched across the room. "We do only the thing you want to do."

Julia didn't have to even think about it—what she most wanted to do . . . what she'd planned on for a year. "I would love to go to the Cinque Terre. Maybe hike a little bit of it?"

A smile of surprise and approval lit Vitale's dark eyes. "Yes, we do this! We take the train to the town, and we walk the trail a small way if she is not too difficult for you, yes?"

"Do you think my toe can take it?"

"We walk as far as the toe allow; then we go back to the train."

She could hardly believe it. Hiking the Cinque Terre—at least a portion of it—was still possible! Flinging her arms around Vitale's neck, she rewarded him with a giant hug. "Oh, *grazie,* Vitale. *Mille grazie.*"

"*Prego,* Julietta." He nuzzled his mouth and nose into her hair. "I think she is still much to celebrate, yes?"

"More than ever."

She scampered off to the bedroom and change into her hiking clothes and flip-flops, and soon, they were racing toward Lerici.

The ferry to Porto Venere was packed with people, but Vitale's unwavering attention made Julia feel like they were the only two around. He stayed in constant touch with her—holding her hand, guiding with a touch to the small of her back, draping an arm around her shoulder. Several times during the boat ride, they shared a kiss.

She'd never been with a guy who was so demonstrative with his affection, and it unsettled her in the most delicious way.

One kiss was particularly long and deep. When they broke apart, the elderly couple sitting across from them smiled broadly and the gentleman nodded approvingly. He said something Julia didn't understand, but she caught the word *amore.*

Vitale nodded. "*Sì.*"

"What did he say?"

"He say the day, she is perfect for the love."

With the sun on her back and the wind in her hair and Vitale at her side, Julia couldn't agree more. "The day, she is perfect for everything."

Vitale kissed her again with a perfect kiss that turned her perfect breathing pattern into a muted mass of imperfect panting.

They got off the boat at Porto Venere and explored the village while they waited for the next boat, which would take them to Riomaggiore, the first of the five towns known as the Cinque Terre and the place where they would board the train.

Vitale had convinced her to leave her cane behind, so she had a good excuse to keep a hand or an arm in contact with him as they moseyed about the village. Her heart sighed at each of the frequent kisses to her fingers and light squeezes to her hand. She was treading in a totally new territory in so many ways. Even the vending machine they happened on confirmed it.

"Pesto!" God, she loved the surprises from this culture. "Can we buy some?"

Vitale laughed, and she realized she'd probably sounded like Melissa used to when the ice cream truck was in the neighborhood. "We do not carry all the day," Vitale reasoned. "We buy when we return. Or we make the fresh at home." The way he said the word *home,* so casually including her in its parameter, caused a delightful flutter in her stomach. "But come now. I show you the special place."

He led her to Byron's Grotto, a quiet cove reputed to be one of the favorite haunts of its namesake poet, according to the plaque affixed to the tall rock wall that separated the cove from the bustle of the village. Stepping through the gate was like stepping into a postcard. Several people swam while others sunned on the rocks, which horseshoed around the crystal blue inlet.

"Do you enjoy to swim, Julietta?" Vitale tucked her arm under his and led her to a large rock where they could enjoy the view.

She breathed the salty air deep into her lungs. "Swimming's one of my favorite summer things. Frank and I used to take most of our vacations at the beach. Melissa actually swam before she walked."

He cocked his head and stroked her hand absently with his thumb. "How long did you marry Frank?"

"Twenty-three years."

His eyebrows shot up. "That is many."

"Yeah, it is." Today it sounded longer than it ever had before.

The breeze caught a strand of her hair and blew it across her mouth. Vitale caught it and tucked it behind her ear. "And you were not happy?"

The way Vitale had just touched her . . . Frank would never have done that, would never have realized how sensual even such a tiny gesture could be. "I thought I was happy. Not deliriously happy, but I was comfortable. I thought our marriage was good."

"To speak of the marriage, she make you unhappy?"

"No, it's okay." That truth surprised her. She was a different person today in more ways than just a hairstyle. It was like she could see things more clearly.

"What make the divorce happen?"

She considered the question for a moment. "I guess my cancer did. Frank had a difficult time accepting the way my . . . um, my body changed."

His dark eyes darkened even more. "He should not do this. Not a man who loves."

The voice of experience echoed in his words, causing Julia to imagine him at the bedside of his dying wife. This man wouldn't have turned away—would never turn away—from someone he loved no matter how scarred and ravaged she was.

"Were you able to be with Luciana when she died?"

He shook his head and his eyes darted away, but not before she saw the dark irises swimming in tears. "She die too quickly. I do not have the opportunity to say the good-bye. To take the care of her. To . . . feex."

The haunting words echoed in her brain. Two small words that told her more about the man than anything else he'd said. He knew who he was.

"The correct way of the life is the opportunity to help the people we love, yes?" He blinked hard several times.

"Yes, to be there for them."

"But not for Frank."

"No, not for Frank." She shook her head. "But I don't need anyone to take care of me."

Vitale didn't say anything. He simply brushed the back of his finger across her breast.

Yesterday, his intimate gesture here in front of God and everybody would've caused her whole body to stiffen with inhibition. Today, she didn't care who saw or what they thought. "I guess none of us knows how we'll react when we're faced with the unknown until we're faced with it. Then we find out what we're truly made of."

Vitale was a man of rock with a heart as soft as spun sugar. Ironically, Frank was the exact opposite.

Vitale's gaze bored into hers, searching. "To not take the care of you . . . to not accept the scars, I think is not all Frank do."

There he was, reading her mind again, which might've been disconcerting on any other day. Today, the uncanny talent piqued her interest. "How can you tell that?"

"I study the face for the art. I know the many looks and the emotion she bring. The pain I see the last night, she was not only from the scars."

Julia sighed. She didn't want this perfect day blemished by conversations of Frank's rejection of her or his infidelity. "Let's just say Frank did a very bad thing."

"Like Francesca, I think. She have the sex with the other man."

So there it was. The bad thing Julia had wondered about. Now she understood Vitale's adamant rejection of the beauty, and the family's clueless reaction. He'd never told them what she did. But, in Vitale's mind, it was the deal-breaker, just as it was to her.

"And Frank had sex with other women. In fact, he left me for one." A little of the old bitterness rose in her throat. And though it burned, it no longer made her want to throw up. "It hurt me a lot, Vitale. I'm sorry you had to experience that same kind of hurt." She breathed deeply, letting her eyes roam to the far side of the cove where a couple lay stretched out on a long rock, engaged in some heavy foreplay, oblivious to everyone else.

Vitale ran a finger along her jaw, drawing her gaze back around to him. He cupped her face in his hands and tilted it up. "Yes, the much hurt. But I do not have the sorrow." His mouth turned up at one corner. "I would not have the sex with Julietta if Francesca she did not do the bad thing."

That was one of the sexiest things anyone had ever said to her. Julia grasped the back of his neck and pulled his mouth down to hers, wanting to reward him with her most perfect kiss.

His playful shudder when she pulled away made her confident she'd succeeded. He cocked his head, and the side of his mouth twitched as he scanned her face. "The music you hear today, she is happy?"

"Soooo happy." She tilted her head to mirror his. "You know, until you mentioned it, I never realized I tapped the rhythm with my finger or toe. And I couldn't believe you noticed it."

"I watch to see if the eye and the finger both say happy. Today, the eye, she is happy . . ." His voice trailed off.

"The music is always happy, Vitale." His eyes squinted in question. "After the cancer and the divorce, I was very sad, so I used music to help me work through the sadness. I put together a group of songs that make me happy." She pulled her phone out of her bag and opened the music app to her *Happy* playlist. "See?"

Vitale's curious eyes scanned her choices. "I listen?"

She touched one of the titles, and "The Tide Is High" by Blondie erupted from the speaker. Vitale's face broke into a broad grin as their bodies swayed together to the beat.

"The song, she make me happy also," he agreed when the last strains died away. "We listen to more later, yes?" He stood and offered his hand to pull her up. "We must go to the ferry now."

Quite a throng had gathered by the pier and the ferry had already arrived when they reached the seaside. Vitale had to muscle his way through the crowd to get them aboard. He kept Julia close, protective of her foot, glaring and growling at anyone who came too close.

There seemed to be no rhyme or reason to the chaos, and Julia said a prayer of thanks she was with Vitale, who not only understood the non-system, but also commanded enough awe that people moved out of his way.

The amount of attention they garnered as a couple wasn't lost on her either. Yesterday, she was invisible. Today, everyone noticed her . . . or rather *them*. Some people actually did double takes from her, to Vitale, and back to her, or vice versa. Overt reactions ran the gamut from obvious envy to disapproval to appreciation.

She'd grown used to invisibility, so the new-found attention pushed her beyond her comfort zone, but today she chose not to care and muted her internal voice. Only four days of her fantasy with Vitale remained, and she intended to milk the time for all it was worth.

The ferry ride to Riomaggiore, the southernmost village of the Cinque Terre, took only a few minutes. Vitale and Julia and half of the ferry passengers disembarked there.

"It's going to be crowded," she said, noting how the mass moved like a herd of cattle in the direction of the ticket booth.

Vitale struck a statuesque pose and pointed at a staircase leading up a cliff. "She is the most popular of all the trail. Via dell'Amore." He sighed dramatically and covered his heart with his hand. "The Path of the Love." When Julia rolled her eyes, he laughed. "You do not do the thing as the other women, Julietta."

She tugged him to the side to wait for the crowd to get in front of them. "I'm not other women, Vitale. I'm just me."

Although the climb took longer with her toe than it would have normally, it was more than worth the effort. The view from the top left her breathless. The wide trail edged along the center of a cliff, and below, nothing but beach and colorful fishing boats and sparkling blue water. Above her lay the almost straight-up hillside, dotted with cedar trees and wildflowers. The noonday sun rode high in a cloudless sky while the cooling breeze brought scents of woody herbs and a touch of moisture from the sea.

The walking was easy—much easier than she imagined. Within fifteen minutes, they reached the small covered hut that marked the halfway point. Vitale indicated the wooden bench with its carved back of two lovers kissing. "We take the photo."

He set the timer on his camera and placed it on the stand. When it started to beep, he made a lunge for the seat by Julia, wrapping his arms around her quickly and snuggling his cheek against hers just as the shutter snapped.

They were both laughing hard, and the picture turned out so cute, she made him promise to e-mail her a copy. They took several more with his camera and with hers. For some, they kissed; for others, they embraced. In one, he dragged her onto his lap at the last instant. All were priceless memories.

She would be able to bank them against the inevitable future times that wouldn't be so pleasant.

"Woohoo!" Julia pumped her fist into the air as the second village came into view. "I made it!"

"I walk this trail the many times." Vitale shook his head and grinned. "But she is the much fun with Julietta."

The short hike brought them into Manarola, where they sauntered around the village for a half hour before catching the train to Corniglia. From there, it was on to Vernazza.

By midafternoon, both of them were ready for a break from the stuffy confines of the crowded trains. Vernazza offered a nice selection of restaurants and snack shops, so they chose to have lunch there before going on to Monterosso.

Julia eyed the sandwiches and pastries as they strolled through a street market filled with vendors hawking a vast array of delectables. The aromas changed with every step, morphing from subtle garlic to pungent rosemary and finishing with toasty vanilla. Her taste buds moved into action, making her mouth water in anticipation. "What are you hungry for, Vitale?"

With his perfected rakish timing, he leaned into her and brushed his lips along the rim of her ear, his voice low. "I hunger for the Julietta."

Did he seriously think he still needed to use those lines with her? She leaned away and shot him a sidelong glance. "Really? 'Cause I was thinking in terms of pizza."

Her answer jarred a laugh from him. "Then we have the pizza now, and I have the Julietta later."

She rolled her eyes but couldn't hold back the grin.

While Vitale went to get the pizza, Julia watched the crowd for a while and then used the opportunity to put in a call to Hettie. Relief darted through her when she heard the perky voice on the receiving end rather than yesterday's desolate tone.

"*Buon giorno,* Hettie. It's Julia."

"Bon Jovi, yourself. I've been going through the telephone book, trying to figure out which tattoo artist to use, and I'm about to flip a coin between Twisted Sister and Angel Eyes. I mean, Angel Eyes sounds like she'd be more gentle. . . ."

Sheesh! Not just perky. Way too much caffeine this morning. Julia made a mental note to talk to the staff about switching her mother-in-law to decaf.

"Course, I could bypass all this trouble if you'd out-and-out tell me you've already won the damn bet."

"Well, tattoo house calls *are* pretty expensive," Julia relented.

"Knew it, knew it, knew it! I thought so last time, but something in your voice told me maybe it didn't go so well. This morning you sound different. Hold on. I need another sip of coffee."

Julia heard the soft thud of the phone being laid down while Hettie took another slurp; then the shuffle and the voice returned. "Okay. I'm back."

"Do you want me to call back after you've finished your coffee?" Having only one useful hand made it difficult for her mother-in-law to handle two things at once.

"Not on your life. I want to hear all about this guy you're falling for."

Falling for? Julia's breath caught on the phrase. "I'm . . . I'm hardly falling for him. I recognize a line when I hear it. Vitale and I, um"—she cleared her throat—"we're just having a good time together."

"That so? When you say his name, it's got a certain dreamy quality about it. You used to sound the same way when you would call Frank 'Franklin.' "

It wasn't fair for Frank to even be in the same thoughts with Vitale today. There was no comparison between the two men, so she redirected this conversation. "I sound different because I'm finally getting to hike the Cinque Terre. Although, truthfully, 'hike' might be pushing it. I got to walk between the first two towns, but we're taking the train the rest of the way."

"How did you walk the distance between two towns with a broken toe?"

"It wasn't far. We took it slow, and I had Vitale to hold on to."

"I'll bet you did." Hettie laughed. "Does he have a fine handle?"

Julia gave a self-conscious laugh and pointedly ignored the question. "We've had a glorious day. Vitale speaks English well and is so easy to talk to. He's interesting . . ." A sheet of wax paper with four large wedges of pizza appeared in front of her along with a bottle of Pellegrino water. "And . . . and here he is now with lunch." How long had he been standing there?

"And you won't talk flippantly about him, which tells me you're not considering him a one-night stand. Hoo-ey! Sounds like you're falling for him, my dear."

Julia cringed at the words and at the thought that Vitale might've heard them. "I have to go now, Hettie. I don't want my pizza to get cold."

"Yeah, you really should eat it up while it's hot."

The parting shot wasn't lost on Julia. "I'll talk to you tomorrow. Bye." She hurried the words as she smiled at Vitale and shook her head. "That Hettie."

He winked and took a gigantic bite from one of the slices.

The toes on Julia's good foot curled as she watched him devour the food. His teeth gripped and tore the crust, and his tongue swept out to capture the sticky cheese from his lips. She'd known him less than a week. And he was fourteen years her junior. Love didn't happen that way. She took a bite of pizza and watched his lips curve into a smile, his gaze warm and inviting.

A delightful twinge tickled the nape of her neck at the thought of what would happen once they got home.

She couldn't be falling in love, but without a doubt, she was hungry for the man.

* * *

After lunch they took the train on to Monterosso, then a boat back to Porto Venere where they caught the ferry back to Lerici and picked up some fresh fish to grill for supper.

While it marinated, and with her *Happy* playlist as accompaniment, they shared a glass of wine in the courtyard and talked about the perfect day they'd shared.

Julia secretly hoped the rest of the week could be like this, but her heart sank when she learned Vitale had a wall-repair job that would take the next two days.

She smiled to camouflage her disappointment.

Vitale saw through the subterfuge, of course. He took her hand and kissed her fingers before reaching deep into his pocket. "For the memory of the day you hike the Cinque Terre." He handed her a small box.

Inside, a sterling silver flip-flop hung from a chain. The symbolism gave her a chuckle, but the thoughtful gesture twanged a bittersweet note that vibrated in her chest. All of this—this house, this day . . . this man—all of it would be a memory soon.

Much too soon.

"And," he continued as he clasped the chain around her neck, "I hope you have the memory of Vitale, also, each time you wear." His fingers moved from her neck into her hair. His thumbs settled in front of her ears while his fingers cupped behind, tilting her face up. He smiled, but his eyes held a hint of something she couldn't read.

"Thank you so much." She fingered the ornament hanging at her throat. "I'll cherish this forever, but I won't need it to remember you or this day, Vitale."

On cue, Matchbox Twenty's "Overjoyed" played in the background.

His kiss closed in on her, fast and furious, but she'd been primed since lunch and was ready. They left a trail of clothing to the bedroom where the sex had an air of urgency about it, both of them aware time was growing short. They wrestled and rolled about the bed in a raucous dance, bodies pounding together with a force of heightened desire and need.

She screamed his name as she climaxed, becoming aware of his warmth inside her a few seconds later. Afterward, they lay exhausted in each other's arms, panting and sweaty.

She finally got her breath under control enough to speak. "I need a shower."

Vitale nodded. "I need the shower also."

She kissed the end of his nose and extricated herself from his embrace. "I called it first." She hurried to the bathroom and jumped into the shower, anxious to rid herself of the grime from the day's travels.

Toweling off, she noticed Vitale was no longer in the bed. She hung the towel on the rack and stepped into the bedroom.

Vitale's angry shout, followed by a string of Italian expletives, echoed from the living room.

CHAPTER 16

Julia flung on a tee and some shorts and hustled toward the next room. The cause of Vitale's eruption wasn't clear, as she'd heard no other voices.

When he came into view, he was running one hand through his hair, the other doubled into a tight fist that pounded the air. He swung around to meet her. The dark scowl on his face brought her up short.

"What's wrong?" she asked, breathless despite the quickened pace of her heartbeat.

He pointed to the computer, mumbling words she didn't understand, but the angry tone was unmistakable.

The screen held an e-mail, official and business in appearance. She could decipher "Dear Mr. de Luca," "sorry," and "thank you." From his reaction, it was obviously bad news, but in regard to what?

She gave an apologetic shrug. "I don't know what it says."

His eyes darted to the screen and back to her, his hand massaging the back of his neck. "From the gallery at Firenze. They do not want the pieces. They say the work, she is, too, um"—his hand made circles in the air as if to wind the word out—"too *commerciale.*"

Julia focused on the sound of the word. "Too commercial?"

"*Sì*. Too commercial." He pronounced the word carefully.

Julia pressed her palm against his chest, where she could feel his heart beating out its frustration. "I'm so sorry, Vitale. I know how much you wanted this."

He moved away, pacing and spewing anger and frustration in batches of phrases and gestures.

She sat on the couch and patted beside her. "Want to sit down and talk about it?"

"No," he grumbled. "I need to make the movement."

Trying to calm him seemed pointless, and besides, he needed the release. She well remembered needing someone to vent to after her cancer diagnosis. Frank accused her of not staying strong and positive, but she'd soon learned that built-up steam had the same effect on people and pressure cookers alike. She'd let Vitale continue as long as he needed.

A glass of wine might be good for him, and she certainly could use one. She kept her movements slow enough to maneuver Vitale toward the kitchen. Once there, she motioned for him to sit while she opened a bottle of wine and poured them both a glass.

When he made eye contact with her, she breathed long, relaxing breaths, which worked for her, but he never caught on to the idea.

What *did* work was the wine. He continued his tirade, broken more and more often by occasional sips, as she rummaged through the refrigerator, creating an antipasti platter of cheese wedges, hunks of sausage, thick slices of crusty bread, olive tapenade, and pickles while the grill heated.

By the time they moved to the patio, his words were spoken in a moderated tone until, at last, they stopped altogether. He popped an olive into his mouth. "Julietta, you are the good listener."

She raised her glass toward him. "Listening to someone who's angry is a lot easier when you know they aren't angry with you— and you can't understand a word they're saying."

His mouth drew up on one side. "Would you like the translation?"

She shook her raised palm. "I don't understand the words, but I'm fluent in tone and body language. No translation necessary.

You're angry and frustrated—and rightly so—and you think your parents will be disappointed in you."

"You understand this from the language of hands?"

"No, the parent part you told me when we were talking Sunday night."

The mirth faded from his expression again as he took a deep, somber breath. "Julietta, if I must spend the rest of the life breaking the rocks, I do not use the hammer to break them." He tapped his temple. "I use the head."

"Have you considered an online business?" She threw out the suggestion that had been hovering in the back of her mind since he'd first told her his dreams for the future. Nibbling a bite of sausage, she watched his reaction.

A deep V formed between his brows. "I do not know how to make the sell on the Internet. I see the many thing on the computer, but I do not have the knowledge to do."

"Neither did Camille and I at first, but it's easy. Really. Find someone to design you a Web site, and display photographs of your pieces with a write-up about each one, something that describes it . . ." He listened, intent on her every word, eyes hooded in doubt.

She described the steps she and Camille went through when they decided to go with a Web site portfolio. "In fact, if you're interested in selling to the US—and I think you should be very interested in that—I have lots of contacts that could help get this up and running. The most time-consuming parts would be working out the ordering and shipping details and getting photographs of everything, but you already have those you sent to the gallery." The muscle in his jaw tightened at the mention. She hurried on, excited by the plan forming in her mind, something she could do to help him out the way he had helped her.

She had four more days. He would be gone for two. "I can spend the next two days taking photographs, making measurements, writing descriptions. This is my business, Vitale. It's what I do. I know what customers like and what dealers want."

He shook his head. "You are the guest. I do not want you to work."

"I would love to do it." The urge to touch him was strong, and she tiptoed her fingers up his arm. "It would make me feel like I had a part in your success."

His hand covered hers. "Do you think I can be the success?"

Julia watched the conflicting emotions flash in his eyes. Hope and doubt, fear and excitement, and something she couldn't name that shot straight through her heart, then fell into orbit around it. "I know you can." Her voice was a tight whisper squeezing its way around the knot that formed in her throat the instant he touched her hand. "Just fix your eyes on the goal."

"Feex the eye?" He shook his head in obvious confusion. "The eye, she see well."

She smiled, but she didn't laugh at her overuse of the word. This conversation meant too much to him. "What I mean is don't let anything—or anyone—stop you from going after something you want. Let it become a part of you. See it with your heart, and I'm sure you'll be a success."

He leaned forward, motioning with his free hand for her to do the same. She leaned in until their foreheads touched. His fingers crept from the back of her neck into her hair. Their breaths mingled. "You make me sure of it also," he whispered, just before he captured her mouth with his and stopped her breath completely. He tasted of wine and olives—sweet and salty and more than appetizing.

He finished the kiss with a slow sweep of his tongue across her lips, then leaned back, stretching out his long legs under the table, totally at ease. And while she was glad to have a calming effect on him, it hardly seemed fair that her heart was now the one beating wildly. With one kiss, he'd transferred all *his* excess energy into *her* system. "Augh! You really have to stop kissing me like that," she scolded. "Those unexpected ones."

The V appeared between his eyebrows. "Why is this?"

"Because." She waved a slice of bread his direction before spreading it with tapenade. "It turns me inside out. I'm not sure my heart can stand the assault."

He smiled smugly. "The heart, she is strong. I feel the beat very hard when we make the love. She can survive the kisses, I think."

His hard gaze aimed straight into her eyes. "And I do not want to stop."

His words stroked her ego, soothed her like a caress. He didn't want to stop. She didn't want him to stop. The best of both worlds, even if the worlds seemed to be governed by laws of nature she didn't fully grasp. "Okay, then," she said, tearing a bite loose. The coarse, flavorful bread required slow chewing. She used the time to redirect her thoughts. "Ahem"—she cleared her throat—"where were we? We'll need something to use as a backdrop to put behind the objects so they'll show up nicely in the photographs. Something soft would be best."

Her memory roamed around the studio, trying to find an appropriate backdrop, but all she visualized were drab tarpaulins. "Do you have any satin sheets?" His surprised expression rendered a giggle from her. "Not to use on the bed. To drape behind in the pictures."

"*Sì*, I have." He gave a sheepish grin as he got up and took the fish off the grill.

"What color?" she prodded, rather enjoying seeing him teetering on the edge of embarrassment.

"*Viola*." He slid a piece of fish onto her plate and another onto his before he sat back down.

"Vee-o-la?" she repeated the sounds, translating them in her mind. "Violet? As in purple? You sleep on purple satin sheets, Your Highness?"

His face turned deep crimson beneath the bronze while his eyes shifted away from her. "Only the one time . . . and I did not sleep."

She snorted. "Of course you didn't." Now she wished she'd let it go as an image of Vitale and Francesca wound up in violet satin sheets plastered itself to her mind's eye.

He read her mind. "I did not have the sex either."

That tidbit erased the image and pulled her upright. "Okay, now you've got me curious." She refilled their glasses and gushed at the delicious flavor of the combined fish, lemon, and thyme. But she wasn't about to let the subject drop. "C'mon. Tell me what happened."

"I slide off."

Julia sat her glass down, thankful she hadn't taken a drink. "You slid off?"

"*Sì.* I jump on the bed and slide off the other side." His look dared her to laugh.

She'd always been a sucker for a dare. She tried to stifle the urge and get by with only a light giggle. But the more she held back, the more vivid the image in her brain became. Vitale naked. Not funny. Hot. Vitale naked, jumping on bed. Playful and fun and hot. Vitale naked, jumping on bed, and momentum taking him off the other side. Not hot. Hilarious. And not just ordinary hilarious. Side-splitting, pee-in-pants, tears-streaming hilarious. The pressure was too much. She had to let it out, and when she did, she couldn't stop. She laughed. Loud.

Her eyes were too teary to see clearly, but Vitale's laugh grew louder and louder until it matched the volume of her own. Then surpassed it.

God, it felt wonderful to be laughing. To be alive. She loved the way her chest heaved, lungs gasping for air. Loved the way this man made her feel. About life. About herself.

About everything.

Coming here . . . staying with him . . . feeling sensual again. Better for her ego than hiking the Cinque Terre. Mission accomplished.

"Julietta?"

Vitale's voice broke through her thoughts. She wiped her eyes and allowed a long sigh to bring her breathing back to normal. "Yes, Vitale?"

"I like to be here with you."

She drew the words in on a sip of wine and let them roll over and around her tongue, savoring the sweet taste of sexual chemistry. "I like being here with you, too." She licked her lips.

Words had never tasted so delicious.

Or so dangerous.

Chapter 17

The smooth material felt exquisite, gliding between the tender skin of her underarm and her breast. Julia gathered a handful of the deep purple satin and tucked it under her chin, catching a whiff of Vitale's clean, earthy scent, which still clung there. She breathed deeply and mentally tagged the scent as her favorite new aromatherapy.

The to-do list for the next two days was long enough to keep her plenty busy during Vitale's absence, but she couldn't shame herself out of bed just yet. The memories of last night were worth a few more minutes of replay in her head.

After dinner, they'd gone to the studio to start sorting the art objects into categories, so she could photograph similar items as a series of shots. Vitale had gone to the house to get the satin sheet backdrop but came back a little later saying he couldn't find it. He sheepishly confessed he'd probably thrown the sheets away after his humiliating experience.

They went into the house and got on the computer where she showed him her Web site and other sites like she envisioned for him. Because there was only room at the desk for one chair, he insisted she sit on his lap, then took advantage of the situation by undressing her, removing an article of her clothing each time she brought up a Web site he liked.

Only Vitale could make surfing interior decorating sites feel like trolling for online porn.

After he'd fondled and teased her to the point of combustion, he'd calmly announced he had a little paperwork he needed to take care of, gathered up her clothes with a wink, and left her alone to answer an assortment of personal e-mails that had cropped up in her absence.

She wrote Melissa and told her all about the toe and the changes in her itinerary, leaving out most of the details—such as Vitale, and the fact that she was answering her e-mail while sitting naked in his living room. If the subject of Vitale ever came up—and it probably would since Hettie had guessed the truth—she'd downplay the whole affair. Until then, the heat in her cheeks coupled with that farther down told her it might be something her daughter was better off not knowing or might not want to know at all. The thought of Melissa's uncomfortable *ewwwww* and accompanying nose wrinkle made her smile.

When Vitale led her into the bedroom sometime later, she found the bed all dolled up in royal fashion, and—mmmmm—he'd certainly made her feel like a queen. The image of Francesca and Vitale tangled in the sheets had been deleted from her memory, replaced by, not simply an image, but a total sensory-heightened experience, a movie in her head she could watch anytime she wanted from now on.

She sat up and smoothed her palms over the luscious fabric of the top sheet. The Italian word for the color had caused her to assume the sheets were a light violet. She hadn't prepared herself for this visually stunning hue that oozed with sensuality. She laughed. Working with this stuff all day was going to keep her in perpetual heat.

Of course, constant thoughts of Vitale were going to keep her in perpetual heat anyway. How long would that last? How long before the feel of his hands and lips dulled to just a vague but plea-

sant memory? Or would the years promote him to legendary status
in her memory—magical and bigger than life?

So little time left here with him . . . The thought threatened to
darken her mood. Refusing to allow anything to spoil this glorious
afterglow, she tossed the cover off and slid out of bed, laughing
aloud as the top sheet glided off the opposite side.

After breakfast and a shower, her first order of business was to
make some contacts about a Web site for Vitale. This would be her
gift to him for all he'd done, as well as an investment in his future.
A way to show him how much she believed in him.

She e-mailed her Web designer, who designed the Web site for
Panache and was reasonable with his cost. She explained what she
wanted to do, the vision she had for the online catalog, and asked
for a price quote.

Next, she burned a CD of her *Happy* playlist. Vitale had a vast
selection of opera CDs he used to enhance his mood while he
worked. If a piece was especially dramatic, he chose a dramatic,
soulful opera. A whimsical piece required a lighthearted, whimsical
opera. But always only opera. Working all day to opera would
numb her brain.

A happy, though nostalgic, tear gathered in the corner of her
eye as she stripped the luscious sheets from the bed and replaced
them with crisp, white ones.

She sighed as she gathered the used sheets into her arms, again
sniffing Vitale's scent among the folds. If only he could join her for
the remainder of her trip. The idea made her heart skip a beat.
Would he consider it? Could she bring herself to ask him?

She nudged the silly notion to the back of her mind where it
belonged—better to leave with perfect memories intact—and got
busy with the task of photographing the art that would make Villa
de Luca a household name.

Now that she had time to touch and hold and study the art
objects closely—now that she knew the man behind the art—
Vitale's talent astounded her even more. His personality, his moods,
his passions were etched indelibly into the angles and curves and
lines of each piece. She replaced her CD with one of his—*I due*

Foscari by Verdi because it said something about Byron on the cover—in order to get the full de Luca effect.

Those creations that followed the styles of the Old Masters begged to have fingertips grazed over them to catch the subtle nuances of the human form. The small, fanciful pieces begged to be placed in unobtrusive spaces where they would stealthily maneuver into nearby conversations, each with a voice of its own. The large, modern sculptures carried a haughty air of defiance, brooding and foreboding . . . and beautiful.

All of them were pure Vitale.

The hours flew while Julia staged and photographed piece after piece, numbering each item and making quick notes that could later be embellished into catchy descriptions. Two o'clock arrived before she noticed the empty grumbling in her stomach. Some of last night's cheese and sausage would make the perfect snack to tide her over until dinner.

She headed out the door, flipping off the switches that controlled the lights and the CD player. The thundering rumble of the drums ebbed away, replaced by an unexpected sound. Women's voices. And they stopped abruptly when the door creaked shut behind her.

Vitale's mother, Angelina, stood up from her kneeling position with a garden trowel in her hand. Her brows knitted in question before her eyes settled into a glare.

"Oh, hello." Julia instinctively braced herself for the angry retort she knew was coming.

Vitale's youngest sister, Orabella, obviously sensed it, too. She sat back on her heels and glanced nervously from her mother to Julia.

"Julietta." Angelina's voice held the expected sharp edge. "Adrianna say you leave."

"I, um . . ." Julia tried to swallow, her mouth having gone suddenly dry. "I decided to stay until Monday." She pointed toward the door she'd exited. "I'm doing some work for Vitale."

Angelina's eyes narrowed in suspicion. "Work?"

"Yes." Julia nodded, hoping the idea she was working might

alleviate some of the disapproval registering from the other woman. "I'm photographing his art pieces and cataloging them for him."

Angelina's eyes darted quickly to Orabella, who translated Julia's explanation.

The older woman gave a derisive snort and launched into an angry rant. After a while, she stopped, flicking a finger from Orabella to Julia.

The young woman's eyes held a deer-in-the-headlights look. "My mother think she is improper for a woman," she hesitated, dropping her gaze to the ground at Julia's feet, "a woman of your age to stay here with Vitale. She say she can lead to nothing good—"

Julia had recognized the gesture of an arm cradling a baby during Angelina's speech, though no baby was mentioned in the translation. She suspected Orabella was rephrasing some of the wording as her version, which didn't carry quite the angry punch conveyed in Angelina's tone.

"She say you should leave Vitale alone." Orabella hesitated again.

"*Sì!*" Angelina punched a finger in Julia's direction, then waved her hand toward the house. "She stay no good." She launched into Italian again.

Various comebacks skimmed across Julia's thoughts ranging from "You're absolutely right" to "Vitale is a man and can make his own decision who to sleep with." But, because Angelina apparently didn't need to stop for breath, Julia didn't get to use any of them, and that was just as well. She wasn't sure what would actually come out of her mouth if she opened it.

Orabella shifted uncomfortably from one foot to another when Angelina motioned her way. "She also say Vitale should use his time to find the wife and have the family. He should not play with the toys." She pointed to the studio. "After the children grow, he play with the clay as he want."

Angelina watched the gesture and started in again while a jolt of anger caused Julia's spine to stiffen. Those were almost the exact words Frank used twenty years ago when she'd wanted to start an interior design company. He convinced her to put her plans on hold until Melissa was in high school. How Julia regretted those years she wasted working for someone else when she could've been following her own life's dream.

"Vitale is a very talented artist with a wonderful future ahead of him." Julia broke into the heated monologue, interrupting Angelina, whose surprised frown registered she wasn't used to being interrupted. "He should be doing what he wants to do rather than trying to please other people—especially people who don't appreciate how exceptional his talent is."

Orabella's eyes widened and she didn't offer a translation until Angelina fixed her with a demanding stare. The girl swallowed hard, then spoke falteringly.

When she finished, Angelina stood quietly for a few seconds. Her gaze swept Julia up and down before she spat out an additional comment.

The trowel in Orabella's hand visibly shook as she took a deep breath. "She say Vitale has only the one talent that interest you."

The words stung as if Julia had been slapped. She opened her mouth and closed it again, trying to relieve the tension caused by clenching her teeth. She was about to speak when Angelina threw one last verbal punch before tossing the trowel to the ground and stomping away.

Orabella gathered the gardening tools with a sigh. "She say, if you are still here Sunday, you are not welcome to the house of Angelina." Her eyes softened apologetically. "I am sorry." She hurried to catch up with her mother.

Stomach in a knot and appetite gone, Julia went back into the studio to fret the afternoon away. How could Angelina not appreciate the depth of Vitale's talent? And how frustrating that must be for him—to be so talented, and not have that talent recognized by the people closest to him. Julia turned an exquisite bronze horse in her hand, marveling at the detailing. What was wrong with these people? Couldn't they see?

A double pang of sorrow and sympathy compressed around her heart like a giant hand had gripped it.

Vitale suffered from his own brand of invisibility, perhaps one just as unfair as her own.

The strange turn of events that brought her into Vitale's life right at this time? It wasn't only Adrianna's scare that gave her purpose here. She was here to help Vitale as well. Just because this fling had a limited engagement didn't mean what came out of it couldn't be lasting.

What was it that Hettie said?

"That stone didn't just fall on your toe. Fate pushed it there, so be ready."

The compression around her heart returned.

By the time Vitale returned home around eight, Julia greeted him with a genuine smile and a controlled tongue, her anger at his mother, the rest of his family, and anyone who couldn't appreciate his talent subdued, thanks to several hours of hard work and a switch of CDs from his opera back to her *Happy* music.

Much talking on her part wasn't required this night anyway. Vitale had gone immediately into action on the online business. He went on and on, sharing details of his meeting with his brother-in-law, Giovanni, an attorney. They'd talked in-depth about sole proprietorships and business registration requirements, which he'd been advised could take a few days. But Giovanni had assured him things would go quickly after the business was registered, provided Vitale had start-up capital, which he apparently did.

"I have the more money than the family she think. I build the home. I do not use the much money since Luciana die. I have the no one to spend the money to, and I need the very little." Although his voice was full of enthusiasm, Julia could tell he was bone-weary by his sluggish movements. He'd put in a very long day.

"Julietta, you very quiet tonight." They sipped their wine in the courtyard after a light supper she'd put together.

She smiled and shrugged. "Just tired, too, I guess." She wouldn't mention Angelina and Orabella's visit. If they wanted to tell him they could, but she wasn't going to mar her stay with any more unpleasantness.

"You work very much today. Too much. You should not spend the holiday in the studio."

"I'm spending my holiday the way I want to," she assured him, and his answering smile warmed her like a deep drink from her wineglass. "You're the one who's done too much today." She smoothed a finger down the tired lines in his face.

Turning his face to kiss her finger, he closed his eyes and sighed. "I do much work today," he agreed. "And I think, if I do much tomorrow, I finish so Vitale and Julietta have the Saturday and the Sunday together."

"That sounds heavenly." She would have to beg off from Sunday dinner somehow. Maybe feign a headache or too much packing to get done.

Vitale's eyes opened and his gaze locked with hers for a moment. He started to say something, thought better of it, and took another sip instead.

Something about his look, and maybe the heady effect of the wine, made her bold. She took a deep breath and threw caution to the wind. "Vitale, would you like to go with me to Florence? I'll be working some. That's the part of my trip where I'm scheduled to be looking for lines for the business. But, since I've found your pieces, some of what I came here for is already taken care of, so I won't mind taking additional personal time—" She stopped when he started shaking his head.

"I cannot, Julietta. I would enjoy, but I must work much when the weather she is good. The winter, she does not allow for the stonework then. That is when I spend the time in the studio."

Julia swallowed her disappointment. "I understand." She hadn't really expected him to accept her offer, but hearing the finality in his voice made her wonder if she'd overstayed her welcome after all. Was he anxious to be rid of her so his life could get back to normal? She enjoyed having houseguests, but she was always relieved when they left.

Bedtime a couple of hours later compounded her angst.

"Julietta." Vitale pulled her close as they settled in for the night. "I think I am too tired to make the love tonight."

"I understand." That damn word again. "You've put in a long day." And she did understand, or at least her brain did. Her body was a different matter. It surged out of neutral merely at the thought of him. The sound of his voice, his touch, his breath on her neck sent her into high gear in record time.

His eagerness night after night had suggested she had the same effect on him, but she should've known better. Reality had a knack for showing up when it was least welcome.

Angelina's fears were ungrounded. The expiration date on this fling had now been set.

Julia could only hope the remaining time would somehow pass slowly.

CHAPTER 18

Julia awoke the next morning with an emptiness that was more than hunger. Vitale was already gone. She'd wanted to start the day with at least a glimpse of him, a chance to read his mood to see if he really was simply exhausted last night or if his ardor for her had started to cool after a week.

A week. Was it possible she'd met him only a week ago? She was as comfortable with him as if she'd known him for years. *Her* desire hadn't cooled a bit. But she couldn't let it consume her either. She forced herself out of bed.

Concentrating on the photographs and descriptions kept her focus off the limited time remaining with Vitale, although as soon as she stopped for a break, it sprang to mind.

Around two o'clock, she called Hettie, hoping the distraction would be good for them both. She waited patiently as the phone rang. It sometimes took Hettie a few rings to maneuver the phone into place, especially in the morning when she claimed her good arm wasn't awake yet. But Julia's patience turned to anxiety as the ringing continued long past what should've been acceptable.

Her breath left her in a whoosh when the familiar voice finally answered. "Hello?"

"Hettie, it's Julia. Is everything okay?"

"Everything's fine. You just woke me."

Julia checked her watch. "I woke you up? You've usually had breakfast by now."

"I wasn't hungry." That seemed odd. Alarms started going off in Julia's head until Hettie added, "Camille brought the chocolates, and I did have a couple of them with some coffee, though."

"Now, now. You shouldn't let chocolates take the place of breakfast.

"Now, now." Hettie mimicked her tone. "You shouldn't try to tell me what to do. I've earned the right to eat chocolate for breakfast if I want."

There was the spark Julia had been waiting for. She relaxed. "Duly noted. So, how are you feeling?"

"I'm tired. We had a pianist who came in and gave a concert last night. He could play anything, and he took requests, so we ended up staying up until after nine listening to him. I haven't been up past nine o'clock in years."

"That sounds like you had a great time."

Hettie chuckled. "Yeah, it was fun. So, anything keeping you up at night?" She sounded like her old self again.

"Well, I do have this project I'm completing for Vitale," Julia answered.

"I'd have bet on it."

Julia ignored the insinuation and proceeded to explain how she'd been spending her daylight hours. Halfway through her story, Hettie yawned loudly. "Are you sure you're okay?" Julia asked.

"I'm fine. Just sleepy."

If Julia had hoped for a rousing exchange, it definitely wasn't going to happen this morning. Hettie simply wasn't up to it. "Well, shall I let you get back to your nap?"

"Yeah, and you get back to playing with your Italian."

Julia laughed. "Okay, but only because you told me to."

"Love you, dear."

"Love you, too. I'll call you Sunday."

"I'll be here. Bye."

So staying up until nine had exhausted Hettie. That was probably to be expected. Hard as it was to admit, her beloved mother-in-law was slipping.

The thought churned Julia's belly as she went back to the job at hand.

Time was such a frustrating entity. Sometimes it moved too fast, like her time left with Hettie . . . and Vitale. Other times moved too slowly, like these hours away from him.

The thought had no more surfaced in her brain than Vitale came bursting through the door of the studio. One look at his dark features told her this was not a "Honey-I'm-home" moment.

"Julietta." He stalked to where she stood and loomed over her, hands fisted and resting on his hips.

What had she done that had angered him so? "What's wrong?"

"You do not tell me Orabella and Mama come yesterday."

Oh, that. "No." She shrugged and started rearranging the purple sheet for the next shot.

His hands grasped her shoulders and swung her around to face him again. "Orabella say Mama not nice to you. Is this true?"

"She's worried about you. She wants you to be with a woman nearer your age. Get married. Have children." She shrugged again.

His bottom lip protruded as his brows lifted. "But Mama should not say the not nice thing. We go now, and I tell her this. She apologize."

"No, Vitale." Julia mirrored his raised eyebrows. "You can't go around trying to fix everything for everybody."

"I do not feex the everything for all the people." His angry tone confirmed she'd hit a nerve. "But I feex this." His finger poked the air, punctuating his words.

"There's nothing to fix here." Julia grabbed his hand. "Your mother is caring for you because that's what mothers do. She's trying to keep you from making a mistake with me. That's all."

He cupped her chin in his hand and raised it slightly. "Mama is not Vitale. Do you think the time, she has been the mistake?" His eyes searched hers as if he would find the answer there rather than in her words.

She licked her lips as she pondered his question. Yesterday, she'd been so sure she had a purpose here. But last night and this morning she'd been wondering if she'd stayed too long. So now it came down to this—if she had the time to do over, would she do it again? Yes. Unequivocally yes. But how did he feel about it? "No," she answered. "I've had a great time, and I don't think it has been a mistake. Do you?"

"No, no the mistake." His lips swooped down and met hers with such force she stiffened, preparing for pain, but there was none. His lips were demanding, yet tender. His heat flowed into her, and she met his demand and added some of her own.

"I would make the mistake if I do not make the love to you now." His voice was husky against her cheek. "But I need the shower. You join me?"

She nodded and he kissed her hand and pulled her toward the door.

"Vitale, did Orabella come see you on the job?" she asked as they made their way inside. "How did you know they were here yesterday?" Not that it really mattered, but she was curious.

"Yes, and then I hurry to finish and to come the home early."

He wasn't in a hurry for her to leave. He was in a hurry to finish . . . to get back to her. She pulled him to a halt. "Vitale?"

He looked down at her, surprised.

She took his face in her hands, raised up on the tiptoes of her good foot, and kissed him again.

He smiled. "Tonight we make the love and relax, yes? I plan another surprise tomorrow."

Julia wasn't sure what he had in mind for tomorrow, but she suspected nothing was going to top the next few hours.

CHAPTER 19

Julia hadn't spent a day on the beach in years. Not since their last family vacation in Destin, Florida. Melissa's last summer at home. Five years ago.

And Destin never looked like this.

Vitale led her through a stand of cypress trees so thick they gave no hint of what lay beyond. Stepping out on the other side was like stepping into another world. Before her lay a horseshoe-shaped cove rimmed by a narrow beach of small, cream-colored pebbles. Turquoise water deepened to sapphire and then midnight blue as her eyes scanned away from the shore. Even her large sunglasses couldn't tame the brilliance of the sunlight sparkling across the crest of each wave.

"Is beautiful, yes?" Vitale's arm hung casually across her shoulder.

She slipped her arm around his waist and gave him a squeeze. "I've never seen a more beautiful beach."

"I have the hope we would be alone." His wave indicated the three other couples who dotted the coastline. One was elderly, the other two twenty-somethings. They all had one thing in common.

"The women are topless." Julia fought to keep the shock out of her voice. She'd seen topless sunbathers during the boat tour, but those had been on lone yachts out on the water, away from every-thing else. These women were within spitting distance. She glanced up at Vitale, whose attention was focused on a sailboat out at sea.

He shrugged. "*Sì*. Is common on the some beaches in Italy." A cloud of concern dropped over his face, and he turned to her. "Oh, Julietta, *mi dispiace*. The many beaches are not. We go to the dif-ferent one." He grabbed her hand and started retreating toward the line of cypress trees.

She pulled back. "No, Vitale. Please stop feeling that you have to protect me."

"But I tell you before, I feex the things it is possible to feex, yes?" His hand pushed through his hair in frustration.

"It's fine. Really. This is a perfect place. I want to stay." She gave a sheepish laugh. "It's not the issue with my breasts so much as my prudish, American upbringing reaction."

His eyes searched her face. "You are sure of this?"

She flashed him a smile and nodded. "Positive. C'mon." She dragged him back toward the water, trying not to stare, but the sunglasses afforded her some glances that satisfied her curiosity.

None of the women had telltale swimsuit lines. They obviously did this often. The elderly woman's large belly swayed as she moved from the surf toward her towel. Her biscuit-brown suntan stretched from forehead to toes, broken only by the swath of red swimsuit bottom and the dozen gold chains hanging between her pendulous breasts.

The young women chatted, flanked by their male companions, both of whom appeared to be asleep. She wasn't surprised to see the chatting stop and all three of the women gawking at Vitale.

Julia nudged him playfully. "I could take my top off and they wouldn't even notice."

"This is true, *bella mia*. For the woman to be without the top on the beach is very common in Italy. They would not notice the breasts. Only how beautiful you are."

But they would notice her scars. She couldn't show those in public . . . could she? As he shook the towels out to lie on, she shook the notion from her head. It was silly to even toy with the idea.

She turned her attention to Vitale and watched with awe as he pulled his shirt over his head, leaving him in only his swimsuit. Even after a week of seeing him naked, the perfection of his physique still made her breath stop.

She stepped reluctantly out of her shorts, feeling like a Volkswagen next to a Ferrari. "Want to swim first?" The water called to her—and it would be the perfect cover.

Vitale nodded enthusiastically. "I am ready to swim at all the time."

"I'd race you to the water"—she gave a dramatic sigh—"but I have this toe thing going on."

Like a gigantic bird of prey, Vitale scooped her up. "I have the Julietta thing going on." His announcement came just before he took off toward the water. Julia's laugh became a shriek, and she clung to his neck, heart pounding as fast as his feet on the pebbles. He plunged in at full speed.

The water engulfed them before she had a chance to dread the cold, which turned out not to be cold at all but more like bath water.

Letting go of his neck, she took a deep breath and pushed out of his arms and under the incoming wave. After a week of hobbling about on foot, the freedom was exhilarating. She remained underwater until her breath ran out, then surfaced to find Vitale right beside her.

"You are the very good swimmer."

The awe in his voice sent her ego soaring. "That's been part of my workout, swimming laps several times a week." She pointed to a log floating fifty yards away. "Wanna race?"

The side of Vitale's mouth quirked. "Do the champion win the prize?"

She thought for a moment, searching for something appropriate with other people present, and at last came up with, "How about a backrub?" Vitale's eyes hooded in question. "A massage. On the back." She gave him a quick demonstration.

"*Va bene.*" He gave a curt nod.

"That's settled, then. On your mark. Get set. Go!" Julia shot off as soon as she finished the last word. She gave it all she had, keeping her head down as much as possible, pulling with her arms, pushing with her legs. She skimmed along, the tepid water giving her buoyancy and freedom, leaving Vitale in her wake. She wasn't swimming, she was flying. Soaring. Winning.

Soon, her fingertips scraped across the rough wood. She grasped it and turned to find him several lengths behind her, his graceful form cutting elegantly through the water.

He straightened up and ran his hands up his face and through his hair, flinging water in all directions. "You win the backarubba, *bella mia*." He held her by the elbows and nibbled playfully on her neck, teeth grazing the outside of her ear. "I give it here?"

Still reveling in her victory, the hot sun warming her back and a hot Greek god warming her front, she was Aphrodite, emerging from the sea in all her glory. She had won the first challenge. The second was within reach...and this chance might never come again. Besides, no one but Vitale could see her out here.

She pulled at the neckbands of her swimsuit until they dropped to the side and her breasts fell free.

Vitale's eyebrows shot up in surprise before his mouth settled into an approving smile.

"When in Rome..." She unhooked the back of her top and flung it away along with her inhibitions.

Vitale gave a wild whoop and caught up with it, holding it up in one hand like a victor's trophy before slinging it around his head and letting go.

For the better part of an hour, they played catch and raced and frolicked until they were both exhausted. The time had come for a nice, relaxing float on the air mattresses, which were still folded up in the bag on the beach. They swam to where the water was shallow enough to walk out but still chest high.

Julia hesitated, clutching the swimsuit top like a lifeline. Could she actually walk out of the water with her breasts bare, scars exposed? The saltwater stung where she'd chewed her bottom lip too vigorously.

Vitale's stride had taken him a couple of yards ahead. He stopped and turned to look at her, not saying anything, but the tender expression in his eyes shouted, "You can do this." He held out his hand.

She moved forward and took it, still covered but gathering strength and courage from his willingness to be her escort. His hand around hers was warm and large and, when he touched his lips to her hand, she knew she could probably face anything.

They walked out of the surf together.

The other beachgoers did turn and look, but no one stared. At least not at her. The men smiled, but the smiles were friendly, not mocking.

The women had no clue Vitale was in the company of anyone.

When Julia and Vitale got to the towels and the air mattresses, it was Vitale who had to blow them up. Julia's heart was still racing too much, demanding all of her extra air. She talked herself through the hyperventilation, assuring herself this was merely a new experience, she was a survivor, and she simply needed to get through the first fifteen minutes. After that, everything would be fine.

And it was.

Within a quarter hour, she was relaxing back on her elbows, face turned up in homage to the sun, chest thrust out to catch the rays as if, like these other women, she'd done it all her life.

Julia heard Vitale move and sensed he'd left her. When he didn't return after a couple of minutes, she squinted one eye against the sun.

He squatted a few feet away, his camera aimed directly at her.

She shot up into a sitting position, hands molding to her breasts in a reflexive move that shielded them from the lens. "Vitale! No!"

"*Sì*, Julietta. Do not cover." His tone was that of a father correcting an errant child. He stood up and moved a few feet to the left. "You have the need to see how beautiful you are." He tilted his head and raised his eyebrows impatiently. "I feex if you do not like. Yes?"

She glared at him, hands defiantly gripping the skin that stayed perpetually cool with only liquid sacs beneath.

One side of his mouth rose. "When in Roma . . ."

Her shoulders slumped in surrender and her hands fell away. Sheesh! One twitch of his mouth and she was exposing naked breasts to a camera. Thank God he hadn't given her one of his smiles. . . . She rested back again on her elbows, trying to ignore the sounds of the camera as he caught her from every angle. But she only truly relaxed again when she felt Vitale settle onto the towel next to her. His lips laid a path of kisses up the back of her arm from elbow to shoulder, and her body shuddered a responsive hurrah to this newly found erogenous zone.

"The photographs, they are not only to see how beautiful you are." Vitale's voice was right beside her ear, and his breath shimmied across the lobe and down her neck. She smiled at the double pleasure of the feeling and his words. "They are for Vitale also. I want to remember you in this way."

His voice was drenched in the sensual huskiness she'd grown used to—the one that preceded the descriptions of delicious things he wanted to do to her body in bed, sometimes murmured in Italian, but easily translated.

When he didn't follow up, curiosity got the best of her, and she turned to him in question—one that froze on her lips as soon as she saw the look in his eyes. The passion was there, as expected. But something unexpected lingered also. Something she recognized, knew, feared, lived for, loathed, grasped with her heart, flung aside with her mind.

It had only been a week, and they had only one more day. She couldn't let this happen.

She surged to her feet so fast her head swam. "Hey, I thought we were going to make use of these floats you worked so hard to blow up."

Carefully avoiding Vitale's confused frown, she grabbed up the green float and limped toward the sea.

Vitale stayed onshore and watched her for a while, as stunning from a distance as he was up close with the sun deepening the bronze luster of his skin. Eventually he followed, paddling out to her on the yellow float, chiseled features set with determination.

She had to gain control of the conversation, and she had to do it fast before he started talking about things that would only make her distraught to think about.

"Teach me some Italian, Vitale," she said as soon as he reached her. "I've been here a week, and you've been speaking English the whole time. What's the word for sea? Like the water, not 'see' with the eyes."

"*Mare.*" He cupped his hand and let a stream of water flow through his fingers onto her stomach.

"*Mare,*" she repeated, trying to mimic the inflection he placed on the first syllable, making the last one sound like an afterthought. She practiced it a few more times as he floated behind her and dribbled water onto her hair. The water crawled along her scalp, making her tingle. "What about swim? What's the verb for 'to swim'?"

"*Nuotare.*"

"*Nuotare. Nuotare.*" She flung out an arm dramatically and gave it her best Italian effort. "*Nuotare.* Mmm. I love the Italian language. It makes even the most mundane things sound glorious."

"The *americana,* she love everything."

She heard the splash as he rolled off his float. A wave of motion flowed under her; then he popped out of the water at her feet.

"You say you love to swim. You love the food. You love the flower. You love the daughter. Everything. Always 'love' . . . or 'feex.' "

He made a good point . . . sarcastic, but good. "You're right," she acquiesced. "We do tend to overuse the words. They're just expressions." She sat up and shrugged. "So, how would *you* say, 'I love to swim'?"

"*Mi piace nuotare.* It please me to swim."

Sitting up made the mattress a little wobbly. She hooked her knees around the edge and dangled her legs in the water.

Vitale took immediate advantage of her position and claimed the bottom half she'd just freed up. Somehow he managed to get astride without tipping them over. They floated face-to-face. The sudden close proximity caused Julia's breath to hitch, and the air around them rose several degrees.

"We do not use the word *love* for everything," Vitale said. "Only the special thing. The special people." Using his hands as paddles, he moved the two of them smoothly across the water. "I love Mama, Papà. To them I say, *Ti voglio bene.*"

Julia nodded, remembering the words he'd spoken to Angelina at lunch last Sunday. "*Ti voglio bene,*" she repeated.

He dropped his gaze as his hands left the water. He began to trace the indentation of the muscle on the outside of her thigh with his fingertips. "When the man love the woman, he say to her, *Ti amo.*"

Julia swallowed several times, trying to force her heart back down into her chest where it belonged. She didn't repeat his phrase. Her spine stiffened with dread of what she feared would come next. *Don't say it. Don't hand me a line now.*

His eyes drifted up slowly until they locked with hers. "Julietta. *Mi. Sono. Innamorata. Di. Te.*" He spoke slowly, pronouncing each word precisely.

She'd expected *ti amo,* so this threw her off, but the breath that left her in a rush was fringed with relief. She managed to find her voice, though it still fell to a whisper from the lack of air behind it. "What does that mean?"

A calm stillness settled over his face. No blinking. No twitch at the side of his mouth. "I fall in love with you."

For a split second, unbridled joy zinged from synapse to synapse throughout her body until his words got tangled in the logic center of her brain. "Don't say that." Her frustration was chased with anger. She eased off on her tone. "I'm not one of those younger woman you have to make bedroom promises to in order to keep having sex with. I don't expect anything from this." She wagged a finger between them. "Certainly not love."

The frustration she'd felt now bloomed on Vitale's face. "You think I say this to have the sex with you? Why would I do this? We have the sex now." He leaned forward and leveled his eyes with hers. "I say this because I say the truth."

Okay, so he was forcing her to be the adult . . . *of course.* "You can't. We can't." She sighed, and forced herself to say the words. "I'm too old for you."

He rolled his eyes and then focused intently on hers again. "I know you will say this. The age, she is the too much for you. I say, too old? No." He took her hand and leaned closer, and her breathing started to come in uneven spurts. "I do not care you are older. I care how you make me feel."

An unseen hand gripped at her insides and twisted. "How *do* I make you feel, Vitale? I mean, look at us. Look at you. Look at me. What could possibly make you think you could fall in love with a woman my age?"

"This I will tell you." He studied her face for a long moment. "When we meet, you do not look at me with only the sex in your eyes as the most woman."

"You read me wrong if you thought that." She snorted. "When you introduced yourself to me, I was filled with lust, which felt totally inappropriate, so then I got so flustered, I ran into that pile of stones."

"*Sì.* But when we meet at the beginning—when you arrive—you look at me with the some sex but the more anger. You are tired. You do not ... do not ... *flirti.*" He flipped his hand in circles under his chin, trying to come up with the word.

"Flirt."

"*Sì,* flirt." He punctuated the word with a nod. "You do not flirt. You act angry with me, though I do not know you and do nothing to anger you."

She chuckled, thinking how her reaction must have looked to him that first day. "I *was* tired ... and frustrated and hardly in any mood to flirt."

His bottom lip protruded as he continued. "At the dinner, you are still angry even after the rest, but you tap the happy music. The next day at the pool, you act as though I am not there. And when I want to talk with you at the bar, you are gone. All through the night, I see the face and the finger, and I wonder how the anger and the happy together can be? And why you do not like me?" His eyes grew wider as a small smile brightened his dark face. "Then, the next day, I see you, and you are not angry, and you like the fountain, and I think to talk to you. You are friendly. Maybe a little sex in the eye ..." He held his thumb and index finger about an inch apart between their faces. "Some flirt. But then you hurt the toe, and you are angry again. To me. And you scream and try to hit."

"I didn't try to hit you," she huffed. "I was just lashing out. You happened to be standing there."

He laughed. "But I know then you are the different because you show me not only the outside but the inside emotion also." He brushed his knuckles down her cheek. "You do not treat me as the one of the sculptures I create. The something only to be looked upon. The something without the brain or the intelligence to see the emotion inside. You treat me as the person, Julietta, and you make me feel like the man." He leaned in closer, his face so close her eyes lost their focus. She lowered her lids and breathed in a deep breath.

His mouth caught her exhale, and her lips trembled when his pressed softly against them.

"It is not the sex," he whispered, and trailed his fingers down her neck and across her breast to rest on her thigh. "The sex, she is good. Very good. But the sex, she is *you. You* are good, and it is you I want. You believe inside I can be the artist I dream. You make me believe it inside as well."

His honesty was a sledgehammer, working hard to break down her defenses, but she had that age of wisdom thing going for her, *damn it.* She laid her hand against his chest, her eyes blurring as she started speaking. "You are very special, Vitale, and yes, I probably put too much emphasis on our age differences." Her voice vibrated with emotion as she relinquished that point, and hope flashed in his eyes. "But the fact remains that I'm leaving the day after tomorrow and we live far apart. We can't stop time, and it takes time together for love to grow. Time together we don't have."

A brooding darkness covered his face. "I know of the time." The words poured from his heart. "I learn the difficult lesson of the time with Luciana."

"Yeah," she agreed. "You learned the hard way there's never enough time with someone we . . . care for."

"Never the time to . . . feex."

The dissonant chord of life's unfairness rang in Julia's ears. Vitale longed for more time to care for Luciana while Frank bailed at the first opportunity.

Vitale's eyes shifted away from hers, to the water, and then fastened on to something in the distance. He squinted and a slow grin spread across his face.

Julia turned to see what he was looking at. Caught up in their deep discussion, they'd forgotten about Vitale's air mattress. It had made its escape, bobbing playfully on the waves forty or fifty yards away.

Vitale turned to her and raised an eyebrow in challenge. "We race, eh? The champion choose the prize?"

His timing was perfect. Their talk had her muscles needing an activity that would rid them of some tension and break the tension that had accumulated between her and Vitale. And she would certainly enjoy an additional massage. "You're on, bud!"

She dove in without saying "Go."

About halfway to the goal, she felt a rush of wave against her side. Vitale had passed her. She stole a quick look and saw him cutting through the water at an unbelievable speed. His stroke was smooth and powerful, making little disturbance in the water.

Try as hard as she might to catch up, he pulled away from her easily. Without a doubt, she'd been had. He'd thrown the first race to salve her ego. This time, he was out to win.

When she finally reached the float, a good fifteen lengths behind him, a smug smile stretched across his face. "Julietta, I wait for you."

She sent a huge splash into his face. "This was a fixed race, de Luca."

He cocked his head, looking unsure he'd heard right. "Feexed the race?"

"Yep." She laughed, hardly believing how many times she'd used the same word in so many different ways. "Another definition for fix. If a sports event is fixed, it means the winner was determined before the event took place." She could see the question still in his eyes. "You let me win the first time."

"*Sì,* I do not want the backarubba. But the prize I want? That I swim very fast for. I feex."

The glimmer in his eyes didn't have the serious look from

before, so it seemed safe to ask. "So, what do you want, Vitale? What's your prize?"

"Get on." He patted the air mattress.

With his help, she managed to get on the float without too much awkwardness. As he pushed her toward shore, a thrill pulsated through her. This was the first time she'd lain on her stomach since the surgery. She'd always been afraid the implants would burst, though the plastic surgeon assured her they wouldn't. Now, here she was, lying on her stomach, topless on a public beach with a kind and handsome Italian hunk pushing her to shore.

If she ranked her life's most memorable moments—at least the good ones—this would certainly be near the top.

He floated her by the mattress they had abandoned, and she latched on to it. "You want this one?" she asked.

"No, I want this one." He laughed and kissed the bottom of her foot.

"It hardly seems fair that I have a massage waiting for me, and your prize is to convey me around like Cleopatra on her barge."

Vitale chuckled but made no comment.

When her belly dragged the sand, she stood up. No reservations this time, though it wasn't much of a challenge. The two young couples had left, and the elderly couple appeared to be sleeping. She was confident that even if the beach had been packed with people, she still could've walked out calmly.

They'd worked up quite an appetite and, with a vengeance, attacked the sandwiches they'd brought. Salty prosciutto. Pungent chèvre. Sticky sweet apricot marmalade. All piled together on crusty baguettes. The concoction had been Julia's creation. Vitale's lusty groan of approval told her she'd scored.

When they stretched out on the towels in the hot sun, his arm draped across her stomach, she felt a complete fullness. Body and soul.

"Julietta?" Vitale's whisper caught on the rim of her ear and stirred her insides out of their tranquility.

"Hmmm?"

"I win the race, yes?"

She smiled. "Yes, Vitale. You won the race."

"I wish to claim the prize now."

His thumb brushed across her navel, and her eyes flew open in surprise. Going topless on the beach was one thing, but sex? In public? That was going too far. She gave him a startled glance and started to protest.

He cut her off. "Stay with me, Julietta."

"What?" Was he saying what she thought he was saying?

"She is the prize I desire. You to stay with me."

"Oh, Vitale, I'm not sure that's—"

"I say I think I love you. You say you have the need of the time for me to show you this is the truth. You have the more time in Italy. You stay with me for the time."

"But I have work to do. This isn't just a pleasure trip. It's a business trip, too."

"*Capisco.* You have the need to find the artists and the pieces for the business. You find Vitale. I know the many good artists. I introduce you. Adrianna has the automobile. The day, she take you to meet them. The night, you come home to me. We have the time together to allow me to prove the love. The love she bloom like the flower, yes?"

Two more weeks with Vitale?

The earnest look in his eyes held her like a vise and set her heart to hammering in her chest. Even taking the bedroom promise out of the equation, this was not an offer to be taken lightly. He'd made the offer. He *wanted* her to stay. The idea ping-ponged between the emotional and logical areas of her brain. What she felt for Vitale was certainly more than a mere physical attraction, but staying with him was dangerous.

It flew in the face of who she was...or, at least, who she'd always *thought* she was.

On the other hand, it would give them more time to get Villa de Luca up and running. More time to help Vitale gain some visibility with his family.

His hand crept up her stomach until his palm lay flat between her breasts, his thumb picking up the beat beneath it. When she brushed her knuckles across the stubble of his jawline, he turned his face just enough to kiss her fingers. Logic and emotion started

to merge, fusing into a muddled mass. But the question remained—
did she want to stay . . . or did she want to walk away knowing
she'd never have a chance like this again?

She watched Vitale's eyes soften around the edges and knew
that he knew what her answer would be though she hadn't spoken
yet.

She felt the smile break onto her lips, saw it reflected in his expression. He leaned forward until his face hovered close to hers.
"You stay. *Sì?*"

Her breath caught at his nearness, and she nodded. But this
decision rated higher than a mute answer. She pushed through the
emotion and found the air she needed. "*Sì*, I'll stay. I want to stay."

His hand slid up to cup the side of her face, and he pressed his
lips to hers in more of a caress than a kiss. It was unlike anything
she'd ever experienced, and she realized with a tremor that she was
no longer relating to this man with her mind.

She may have only known him for a week, but he was getting a
grip on her heart.

If she wasn't careful, those lines he fed her would start to sound
like truths.

"Now, Benigno and Oria are the ones who live together, and
they both paint." Julia wanted to make sure she had the three
people she'd met at the restaurant tonight straight in her mind. She
turned on the water in the shower to allow it to heat up.

"*Sì*, and Damiano is the brother, and he carve the wood."

Vitale had rid himself of his shirt and was stepping out of his
shorts. It appeared he intended to shower with her, which made it
even more difficult to think about the schedule he had arranged for
her for Monday.

"You're sure Adrianna won't mind? I'll pay her for
chauffeuring me around."

He slid the shower door open wider and adjusted some cold
water into the spray. "I talk to Adrianna. She want to do." Taking
her hand, he stepped inside and pulled her in with him. His arms
circled her, holding her tightly as the warm water cascaded down
their backs. She snuggled her head against his chest.

For a while, they just stood. She was vaguely aware the earth was still turning and an outside world existed beyond their small space, but for the moment that seemed inconsequential. They were untouchable from the outside. The only touch that mattered was Vitale's.

She felt his arms reach out behind her; then his hands were in her hair, massaging shampoo into a rich lather. It was heavenly, the alternating of his strong fingers gripping and releasing. Her scalp wasn't the only thing enjoying the sensation. His erection grew taut against her stomach.

She was about to stroke him when he turned her around and directed the spray to rinse her hair. As quickly as that was done, his soapy hands caught her shoulders and began a massage. She groaned in pleasure as his thumbs kneaded the muscles above and between her shoulder blades and then made their way slowly down each side of her spine.

When she let out a particularly lusty moan, he laughed and slid his hands around to lather her breasts and stomach. "You make the same sound when we make the love." His hands slid lower for a few sensual strokes. His lips caressed her rear as he stooped to reach her calves and feet.

Removing the showerhead from its cradle, he ran the water over her slowly, rinsing her thoroughly and strategically aiming the spray to keep arousal just ahead of relaxation.

After the shower, he dried her off with brisk strokes that left a nice, healthy glow to her skin. The biggest surprise, though, came when he turned on the hair dryer and blew her tresses dry as he combed his fingers through them. The result was a strange-looking coif that bore no resemblance to the cute do Adrianna had fixed.

"Do not worry about how the hair look, Julietta." His mouth turned up at the corner. "We make the mess soon, yes?"

He led her to the bed and immediately started to make good on his promise.

She'd left the last remnants of her inhibitions back at the beach apparently. Before the afternoon had played out, she'd not only gone topless, but had stripped off totally naked to change into the clothes for the restaurant. By that time, they'd had the beach to themselves, but the possibility that someone else might show up at any minute had only made it more exciting. They even swam naked for a while, something she'd never done except by moonlight. There was something immensely freeing about being naked in sunlight—like she'd absorbed the light and now could feel it emanating from her.

She brought all of that vibrant, new energy to bed, trying everything that came to her mind to tease and tantalize. She soon had Vitale wide-eyed and panting and giving her looks that begged for more despite the teeth marks she left on his shoulder.

From the foot of the bed, he inched toward her slowly on his hands and knees, eyes full of lust, an animal in heat. She leaned against the headboard, poised for, longing for his attack.

"*Ti amo,* Julietta." His voice was ragged with emotion. More words poured out, words she didn't understand, but the sensual growl of the tone made each pulse throb with need throughout her body. "I say to you the truth."

"Show me."

With a strangled cry, he caught her around the waist and dragged her beneath him. She wrapped her legs around his hips and guided him into her.

His whispered endearments and kisses fell softly on her ear, even more provocative and cajoling than before. He was meeting her challenge and upping the stakes, taking full advantage of the overtime he'd moved this game into by forcing her hand. And here she was, still at the table. Accepting his offer to stay—wasn't that simply feeding his line back to him? Making him believe she actually thought this fairytale could end with a happily-ever-after? The darkness of fear began to eclipse her light. Panic rose in her chest, cutting off her air. In a matter of seconds, she plunged from the peak to the valley, bringing her climax to a deathly standstill.

Vitale was too far gone to stop or even to notice. With only a few more thrusts, he erupted inside her, calling her name amidst beautiful, erotic words of passion.

She held him close as he caught his breath, feathering her fingers down his back and through his hair, hoping he hadn't noticed her faltering enthusiasm.

He noticed.

Hoisting himself up, he looked her squarely in the eye. "You did not finish."

She shook her head. "I started thinking too much. Staying with you. Us." She waggled a finger between them. "This might be a mistake."

He shifted his weight off of her to lean on his elbow, propping his head on his fist. His free hand cupped her face, turning it toward him. "To stay she does not make you happy?"

"To act like I believe you love me is the mistake."

"You do not act in this way. You say the love she is not true." He slid a finger around her ear and stroked softly. "I say she is true. We wait and we see who is the winner, like in the race, yes?"

"No fixed winner this time," she whispered the warning.

His bottom lip puckered. "I tell you before, the prize I want I work very hard to win. I feex." He proceeded to use that lip and the rest of his mouth to its full advantage until he had her writhing under his tender assault. And when her body rocked with the glorious contractions it craved, the hazards of losing anything to Vitale seemed entirely inconsequential.

They fell asleep, tangled in the sheets and each other's embrace. Nothing was more important than the feel of his touch and the sound of his breathing.

Nothing . . . until the outer world broke into her reality once again, interrupting her life with a phone call at 2:17.

CHAPTER 20

Julia grabbed for the phone, knocking it off the table. She quickly rolled out of bed and dropped onto her hands and knees, groping for the square of light. Only a few people had her cell phone number. They all knew she was in Italy. None of them would call her in the middle of the night without a good reason. Something was wrong. Terribly wrong. Her heart thudded with dread as she hit the button to answer the call. "Hello?"

"Julia, it's Frank."

And then her heart screeched to a halt as only a mother's could. "Oh God. Is Melissa okay?"

"Melissa's fine. I just spoke with her to get your number." Emotion held his voice tight, his words jerky. "It's Mom. She's had another stroke. She's in a coma. They don't think she's going to make it."

Not Melissa, thank God. But Hettie. Julia's heart fluttered back and then kicked into a double-time beat. "Oh God. Oh, Frank."

"Evidently, the nursing home tried to call your house first."

The irritation in his voice put her on the defensive. If she'd stayed at home, Hettie wouldn't have been alone. Maybe she could've done something preemptive. "I'm in Italy." Her voice shook. How she hated when it did that. "But they have my—"

"Yeah, Melissa told me."

"I'll have to get a flight out." She started to tremble uncontrollably as the news sank in, odd sounds wobbling from her mouth. "That may take me a while." Vitale lowered himself onto the floor beside her and pulled her close, cradling her head against his chest. "I'll get there as quickly as I can."

Frank's breath shuddered across the line. "Me too. I'll have to get to Oahu and take what I can from there. I hope to God we're both not too late."

The line went dead. He'd hung up. "Hettie's had another stroke." Julia battled to hold herself in check. The words sounded flat and dull. "She's dying." Her composure broke, and the sob she'd been holding back broke free with it.

Vitale pried the phone from her hand and pulled her onto his lap. As she sobbed uncontrollably, he rocked her gently, stroking her hair and arms, whispering kind, soothing words.

Once the flood of tears washed away the initial shock, her brain began to function in a somewhat normal mode. "I've got to get home."

Vitale's hold tightened around her, his chin resting on the top of her head. "Give the information for the travel to me. I make the arrangements more fast than you, yes?"

She nodded but didn't get up. When she moved out of his arms this time, the world was going to be different . . . tilted to an uncertain degree off the axis she'd grown accustomed to. She wanted to hold on to her former world for a moment longer.

He seemed to sense what she was thinking and didn't prod. He gave her the time, gave *them* the time. He kissed her eyelids, the slight pressure squeezing out the last of her tears.

Taking a deep, fortifying breath, she pressed her forehead to one of his cheeks as she stroked the other. "Taking care of things would help a lot. I could use the time to get packed." If he kissed her, she'd fall apart, so she twisted out of his embrace and stood up.

She located her flight information in her bag as Vitale got her luggage out and placed it on the bed. She gave him the papers, and he took off with her phone to the other room and the computer while she emptied the drawers and closet of her things.

A glimpse in the mirror showed her that her hair was a mess. Vitale's styling after their shower had deteriorated even more during the short night. She hurriedly showered again and washed and dried her hair. By the time she finished, Vitale met her back in the bedroom.

"*Il treno da Genova a Milano parte alle sei.*"

He spoke quickly, but she thought she understood. "The train from Genoa to Milan leaves at six?" Could she make it to Genoa by six?

"*Sì,* and *l'aeroplano,* she leave *Milano undici a venti.*"

"Eleven twenty?"

"*Sì,* I borrow *l'automobile* from Adrianna, and then we must hurry."

"I'll call for a car or something, Vitale. I don't want you to wake Adrianna at three in the morning."

He took her hands and pressed them to his lips. "I want to drive Julietta. Adrianna, she understand."

Tears blurred her eyes again as the awful pain of leaving him so abruptly tore at her heart. Vitale brushed away a hot one burning a path down her cheek. "Do not cry, *bella mia.* I return quickly."

"Be careful."

He nodded and, with a kiss to her forehead, was gone. The roar of his Benelli echoed through the house. She listened until it faded away in the distance, reluctantly acknowledging it would be the last time she heard it. An image of Hettie ran through her mind then, and she remembered their last conversation the day before yesterday. Sobs built in her chest, compounding into a pressure that stifled her breathing.

She hobbled into the kitchen, determined to stay focused on some mindless task so she could make it through the next half hour without falling apart. There would be time to fall apart later. At home.

Muscle spasms twisted her stomach into a mass of hard knots and trying to eat would be futile. But Vitale would be hungry. She toasted some bread and fried some eggs and slices of pancetta, putting together a couple of breakfast sandwiches. She heated

Vitale's thermos and filled it with coffee, and had everything ready and packed in his lunch bag when he returned with Adrianna's car.

He loaded her bags into the back and held the passenger door open for her. With a last look around, she climbed in, clutching the cane he'd carved for her like a lifeline. If she let it go, she might lose her grip on everything.

With no traffic to impede them, Vitale took the road at a fast clip—not that traffic would've made any difference. How calm she was with his driving now. What a difference a week had made. Had it only been a week since he'd terrified her on the way to his parents' . . . since he'd first kissed her?

How was that possible?

They stayed quiet for a long time. He held her hand when he didn't need to shift, and when he did, he'd drop her hand, shift, and then grab it again. He kissed her knuckles, ran the back of his fingers against her cheek, small gestures bearing voluminous messages that caused her thoughts to volley back and forth between him and Hettie.

Either direction brought her closer to a good-bye she didn't want to say.

She turned her mind to the passing cedar trees looming dark against the hillside. A margin of silver outlined them in the moonlight against the rocky backdrop. Any other time they would be hauntingly beautiful. Tonight, they were skeletal fingers, dark and ominous.

She trembled and closed her eyes against the sight.

"You are cold, *bella mia?*"

Julia shook her head. "Just frightened."

They took the ramp that swept them onto the deserted highway, but gaining distance from the dark hills didn't lessen the icy grip that held her in its foreboding clutch.

With a gentle finger, Vitale eased her face toward him, looking away from the road long enough to indicate he had something important to say. "Hettie, she know you love her the much. She wait for you to say the good-bye." His words ripped the unspoken fear right from her heart as if he'd seen directly into its depths.

She started to sob again, voicing the guilt she'd been restraining. "Oh, Vitale, it breaks my heart to think she might die alone, without me or Frank there." Anguish flooded her, clogging her eyes, and nose, and lungs. She fought to get some air into her lungs, but it shuddered on its way in and out, never quite giving her as much as she needed. Her head spun.

She wasn't aware they'd pulled over until Vitale's arms tightened around her. Her sobbing was loud and beyond her control. "Breathe, Julietta." He took long, deep breaths. "You are strong, but you do not have to do this thing alone. I hold you. You hold Hettie with your love, and I hold Julietta with mine."

Somehow, his comforting whispers reached through her despair, taking hold and reining it in. Without any conscious decision on her part, her breathing slowed to match his. The dizziness subsided, allowing her eyes to focus again. She found a handkerchief in her hand. When she blew her nose, her head started to clear and the ringing in her ears faded away. Vitale allowed her to slump back into her seat.

She wiped the tears from her eyes and cheeks. "*Mille grazie,* Vitale."

He nodded. "*Prego,* Julietta."

Back out on the highway, she remembered the sandwiches. "Are you hungry?" she asked, knowing the answer. Vitale was always hungry.

"*Sì,*" he answered, which made her smile a little. She unwrapped one of the sandwiches for him. He eyed it as if some new creature had appeared before his eyes, but a smile replaced the wariness as soon as he took a bite.

She poured him a cup of coffee, then opened the second sandwich and tore off a fourth of it. She stared at it, trying to conjure up an appetite, but even that small amount was too much to force into her tightened stomach. Vitale made quick work of the remainder when it became evident she wasn't going to eat it.

The rest of the trip consisted of talk about his new Web site, what was being done, what else needed to be done. They both pointedly avoided any subject that might send her into a tailspin.

It seemed much too soon when they pulled into the parking lot of the train station. As she got out of the car, her legs and her heart both felt like they'd been encased in lead. Or maybe bronze.

By the time they got her tickets, passengers had started to board. They both got on and found her a seat, storing her luggage away; then she got back off with Vitale for a proper good-bye, determined not to make them both miserable with a dramatic show of emotion.

They held each other for a long while until finally he pushed away and rested his arms on her shoulders, his forehead against hers.

"I'm sorry it had to be like this." She broke the silence. "So fast. Not the way I would've chosen if I'd had my choice. But I want you to know how wonderful this week has been, and I want to thank you again. For everything."

He raised his head to look into her eyes. "We e-mail, yes?"

"Yes, when I can," she promised. "Things at home are going to be hectic."

"This I know." He nodded and paused. "When do you return?"

Emotion closed her throat. She didn't have an answer, hadn't been able to think that far ahead. "I don't know, Vitale. I have a lot of things going on, and . . ." She bit her lip to stop it from quivering.

He ran his fingers from her temples through the ends of her hair. She closed her eyes, breathing in his scent, wishing she could stand there with him touching her like this forever. But an announcement came over the loud speaker, and she knew enough of the words to know they were calling for final boarding.

Vitale's mouth came against hers. Their lips parted and their tongues met, her arms clasping his neck, his tight around her waist. In the back of her brain somewhere it registered that they were making a spectacle, but she didn't care. She kissed him more fiercely, trying with one last touch to convey all she was unable to say.

The kiss softened, and they slowly, reluctantly broke away.

"*Ti amo,*" he said, and she sucked his words in on a shaky breath.

She started to board, had one foot on the step, when he caught her hand and pulled her back around to him.

He smiled and touched her fingers to his lips. "*Ritorna da me.* Return to me, Julietta."

The train gave a forward lurch. There was time for one last kiss blown in his direction, but nothing more.

As the train picked up speed, she settled in her seat, only then realizing she hadn't given him an answer.

CHAPTER 21

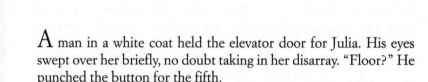

A man in a white coat held the elevator door for Julia. His eyes swept over her briefly, no doubt taking in her disarray. "Floor?" He punched the button for the fifth.

"Four," she answered.

He punched that one also, then directed his eyes toward the closing doors. They rode in silence without any further eye contact.

Welcome home . . . and back to invisibility.

After a three-hour train ride, an eight-hour flight followed by a two-hour layover, another two-hour flight, then a three-hour drive, she couldn't care less that she looked a mess. She'd purchased a snack box on the plane, but her stomach began to lurch after a couple of bites of cheese and crackers, so she'd given the rest to the young woman who shared her row.

Sleep had proven to be a good escape, though it only came in short spurts. Her brain numbed out somewhere over the Atlantic. She needed to go home and rest—her body ached for it.

But more than anything, she needed to see Hettie, who, according to Frank's last phone call, was still alive, unconscious but breathing on her own.

The elevator doors opened and somehow Julia managed to propel her weight toward the double doors that marked the ICU.

She was leaning more on the cane Vitale made, not because her toe hurt—it was hardly noticeable—but because it made her feel she was leaning on him, that a part of him was there with her, holding her. Just as he'd promised.

The visitation times were posted on the door. 8 to 9 a.m. Noon to 2 p.m. 4 to 6 p.m. 8 to 9 p.m. She'd made it in time for the second afternoon visit. She gripped the cane tighter and pushed her way through the door.

The temperature dropped dramatically on the other side. Or perhaps the sterile, medicinal scent that perfumed the air made it seem colder.

The ICU was dully lit. An assortment of clicks and swishes filled in as the only background noise, music to loved ones' ears, no doubt. A quiet serenity pervaded the area in juxtaposition to the monumental battles taking place within those walls. A nurses' station sat in the middle, surrounded by rooms with glass fronts.

As Julia approached the station, one of the nurses looked up. The quiet in her eyes echoed in her voice. "Can I help you?"

"I'm looking for Hettie Berkwith." She paused to clear her throat of the fear clogging it. "I'm Julia Berkwith, her daughter-in-law."

"She's in this room." The nurse came from behind the desk to show the way.

"Her son, Franklin, has he gotten here yet?" Frank was hop-scotching his way home, taking any available flights that got him closer. At last account, he was held up in Dallas by weather and the battery on his phone was almost gone.

The woman's eyebrows drew together in concern. "No, you're the only one who's been here besides the doctor."

Julia took the nurse's body language as a warning and tried to prepare for what she was about to encounter. She envisioned Hettie hooked up to various sinister-looking machines by miles of tubing, face and limbs drawn or hideously distorted.

The scene that greeted her was nothing like that.

Hettie lay sleeping, breathing peacefully with only an IV in one arm and a tube protruding from her nose.

Julia walked over to the bed and rubbed her arm, expecting her to wake up and smile.

She didn't.

The nurse checked the laptop on the stand at the end of the bed before she spoke. "She's been unconscious since they brought her in yesterday. The tests show that she suffered a severe hemorrhagic stroke, which means that a blood vessel ruptured and bled into her brain." The nurse seemed to be anticipating Julia's questions, answering them before she asked. "She's breathing on her own, but that's a feeding tube that runs directly into her small intestine."

Julia cringed. "A feeding tube?" And then a flare of hope sparked. "Does that mean she might be able to recover?"

The nurse's eyes softened. *C'mon, Julia. You know the answer to that one,* they seemed to say. She shook her head. "Recovery isn't likely with the extent of brain damage she suffered, but she can't swallow on her own, so a feeding tube is the only way of keeping her body nourished."

"She wouldn't want that keeping her alive."

"Maybe not." The woman raised her eyebrows and gave a resigned sigh. "But whoever has the health care power of attorney made the decision. Her son, I suppose."

Guilt thumped at Julia's heart. How many times had she and Hettie talked about getting a living will drawn up? Changing the health care power of attorney to Julia? They always thought they'd have more time.

That song seemed to be stuck on replay from the playlist of her life.

An alarm went off somewhere, and the nurse made for the door. "Talk to her," she said over her shoulder. "It'll comfort you both."

Julia scooted the lone chair close to the bed so she could hold Hettie's hand while she talked. The cool skin was very white, as if the heart had decided the hand was too great a distance for the blood to travel. Julia grasped it, willing her own body heat to stir the hand awake. It lay limply in her grip but effectively tore at her heart nonetheless.

"I'm sorry, Hettie." Julia brushed back a wisp of her mother-in-law's hair from the smooth, serene forehead. "I'm sorry you had to go through this alone, but I'm here now." She took a deep breath, relaxing her blocked throat, allowing her to cry. Her sorrow no longer required deep, bone-shaking sobs. Now there were only tears, and she let them flow freely as she talked her way through the shattering upheaval.

She was convinced that, at some level, Hettie heard her and understood what she was saying. She started her one-sided conversation with details of her arrival in Italy. That's where Hettie would've insisted she start even though they'd spoken often and had already talked about those things before.

In her mind, Julia heard the questions and comments Hettie should be making if life had any fairness to it. They should've had one more chance to say the things that held true meaning. She should've had one more chance to tell Hettie of the fun she'd shared with Vitale . . . and how he'd *seen* her.

She was in mid-sentence, about to confide her topless beach escapade, when the soft chime sounded the end to visiting hours.

"I'll be back at eight o'clock and tell you the rest then." She kissed Hettie's cheek, catching a faint whiff of the Blue Grass perfume that had always been her signature scent. Julia closed her eyes and breathed it in, finding peace in Hettie's slow and steady breath.

The serenity lasted only through the ten-minute drive from the hospital to her house. As soon as she walked through the door of her home, Julia began to doubt if she could make the 8:00 p.m. visit. Her body felt triple its weight, rebelling against the lack of food and sleep, crumbling beneath the emotional and physical strain. She couldn't even consider dragging her luggage up the stairs to the bedroom.

Three more hours, she promised herself. *Then you can collapse.*

The house didn't produce the soothing effect she expected either. It seemed big and empty and lonely, and she wondered again if she'd made the right choice keeping it after the divorce. So many things needed repair—the screen door in the back, the leak in the basement, the rain gutters that seemed perpetually clogged. Finding a reliable handyman was harder than finding a plastic surgeon. A small house, one like Vitale's, would fit her current lifestyle much better.

But times of crisis weren't the best times to make life-changing decisions, and the last two years had been one long, continuous crisis.

The week in Italy made those problems seem so remote. But she was home again now, and her real life had run to greet her with open arms.

She would get through the ordeal of Hettie's death—a shudder ran through her as she realized she'd faced the inevitable and now was only waiting for the final good-bye—give herself time to grieve, and then make a decision about what to do with this place. She dragged her tired feet up the staircase, noticing how loose the banister was now that she needed it to lean on.

A warm shower revived her somewhat, her blood stirring as she remembered the details of her last shower with Vitale. His fingers massaging her scalp. His lips nibbling her ear. Her chest heaved with loneliness, and she hurried through blowing her hair dry and changing clothes, in a near frenzy to check her e-mail.

Her fingernails drummed on the desk impatiently as she waited for the computer to boot up and download the 682 messages accumulated since she'd last checked.

She scanned the list, only interested in one, and her heart leaped when she found it. With a shaky finger against the mouse pad, she tapped it to life.

> Bella mia,
> My family pray for you, for the strength to face this sad occurrence that find the path into your life. Write the news when you are able. I miss to hold you. Ti amo.
> Vitale

She hit the reply button.

> Vitale,
> Thank you and your family for your prayers. I am
> going to need them over the next few days. Hettie is
> very bad. She breathes on her own but is
> unconscious and not likely to recover. They are
> feeding her with a machine, which I'm sure she
> would not want, but my ex-husband has the
> guardianship over her health care and it is his
> decision.
> I miss you, too.
> Julietta

Typing the last word pinged her heart, bringing her back to the space she occupied in the real world.

Her name was Julia, not Julietta. She was Julietta only during her time in Italy. Julietta was a fantasy. But as long as she didn't get carried away by this little diversion from the real world—and she wouldn't... she was much too pragmatic to allow that to happen—what was the harm of hanging on to it just a little while longer?

Several other e-mails now drew her attention, and before she knew the time had passed, it was after 8:00. She kicked herself mentally for not being at the hospital already.

During the drive and then the long walk from the parking lot to Hettie's room, she had to shake out of the threatening zombie state several times.

But at Hettie's door, every muscle tightened to full awareness. A man hovered over Hettie with her hand pulled to his chest, his body jerking under the pressure of silent sobs.

"Frank."

He straightened and turned toward her, his face contorting in a look that moved from recognition to doubt, then back to recognition before settling into surprise. "Jules?" He wiped his red, swollen eyes before stuffing his handkerchief into his back pocket. "You, uh, you look different."

"Well, it's been a while." She wondered at the lack of sarcasm in her voice, which would've been so easy to apply to that comment. Not only was it absent, but there wasn't the slightest regret for not using it. Whether the result of jet lag or emotional healing, she couldn't be sure. Time would tell.

Frank seized her hand when she moved to stand by the bed. Her first reaction was to pull it away, but he started to cry, so she accepted that he could use a friend at the moment, and she was the nearest thing to that available.

"She looks so beautiful, doesn't she?" He laid his hand on his mother's head, his grasp on Julia's hand tightening. "Like she could wake up any minute and ask for some chocolate truffles."

"Yeah, she does." The unspoken *but* hung in the air around them, making it heavy, making their breathing difficult and loud. "How long have you been here?"

"I came straight from the airport. Got here a little before eight. In time to talk to the doctor." His chin quivered, and Julia felt the weight of his sorrow merging with what was already pressing on her heart. "He says she's in a vegetative state. No hope." His voice broke into a moan as he crumbled in a miserable heap against the bedrail.

"I'm so sorry, Frank."

His hand pulled hers around him as he shifted his stance and clasped her hard against him. He wept uncontrollably, his face buried against the side of her head, his body shuddering with convulsive sobs.

Julia held him, trying to find the right words of comfort. "It's okay. Let it all out," she urged. And he did.

The nurse came to the door and shot Julia a look that asked if there was anything she could do to help.

Julia waved her away. He just needed time.

Everyone always needed more time.

Eventually the sobs started to ebb away, and his breathing became more rhythmic, almost, but not quite, matching Hettie's. He continued to hold Julia and she determined to stay rooted until he decided he could let go and stand on his own. She refused to acknowledge the irony of that thought when it started forming in her mind.

202 • *Pamela Hearon*

He squeezed her tightly and then let her go with a sigh. "I'm sorry," he mumbled, turning back toward Hettie.

"It's okay. A normal reaction."

They stood for a long time, not saying anything, the sound of Hettie's breathing acting as the timepiece.

Julia watched him, trying to carefully time her next indelicate question so it wouldn't send him off. She had to do it for Hettie. "Frank." She took a deep breath. "She wouldn't want to be kept alive like this. You know that, don't you?"

His face jerked toward her, his eyes wide and lit by agony. Fear flickered in the background. "I can't, Jules. I can't do it yet. Not tonight." He shook his head, his gaze darting between her and his mother. "I'm too tired to make the right decision, to know what's right for her. Tomorrow. After I've rested. Not tonight."

Okay, that was fair. They *were* both exhausted and in dire need of sleep. Tomorrow would be better for everyone—maybe even for Hettie now they were both here and could say good-bye properly.

The chime sounded the end of visiting hours, and they left the ICU along with the family members of other patients. Varying degrees of fear, sadness, and hope reflected in the surrounding faces.

She waited until they were alone in the parking garage to ask. "Where are you staying?"

"I wanted to get the keys from you." Fatigue saturated Frank's voice. "Thought I'd stay at Mom's. I don't think I can face a hotel room."

Julia's insides twisted at the realization that Hettie hadn't told him. "Frank, your mom's house is empty. Well, almost empty. She had me sell all of the big pieces. The bedroom suites, living room and dining room furniture..." Her voice trailed off in an apologetic whisper.

"Oh." He closed his eyes and gave a defeated sigh, squeezing the bridge of his nose between his thumb and forefinger.

She felt the eyes of the universe watching for her reaction. Vitale had shown her every kindness. Now she was faced with the challenge of paying that kindness forward.

Frank may be her ex and he may be a pathetic scoundrel, but he was hurting, and if he were a wounded, stray dog there was no doubt what she would do.

Nonetheless, a little voice in her head screamed *No!* even as her mouth opened to speak. "I've got plenty of room. You can stay at my house."

CHAPTER 22

"We can make this hotel the crown jewel of Lerici, Mario. Perhaps of all Liguria." With a dramatic flair, Vitale unrolled the sketch he had made last night of the hotel grounds with his artistic rendition of how it *could* look.

Mario's eyes widened at the sight. He placed his hands at the opposite edges and leaned over to peer closely, not wanting to miss a single detail.

Vitale kept quiet, letting his friend take it all in. The idea had come to him right after he'd read the e-mail from Julietta. He smiled. Today, he would write her and tell her how she was still inspiring him, even though they weren't physically together.

Mario's finger traced a path to each of the art pieces. "You have all of these finished already?"

Vitale nodded. "All except this one." He pointed to the large space at the north end of the pool. "But I have something in mind for there. I'll show you the sketches, and you can decide if you want to commission the work. I will warn you, Mario. This will be an expensive undertaking, but one your father would approve of, I think."

Mario grimaced at the mention of "expensive," but it was well-known in Lerici that the hotel owner was much more well-off than he pretended to be. For years, under his father's management, the Lord Byron Hotel had been Lerici's premiere place to stay. The elder Moretti had been wise enough to know money attracted money. If his son didn't learn the same lesson quickly, the Lord Byron would lose its tenuous four-star ranking soon.

"Of course, if you're not interested, it's fine." Vitale shrugged. "I wanted to give you the first chance. I'll go to Nicolina next."

"You would work for Nicolina?" Mario sneered. "I don't think she would allow you to get much work done."

Vitale shrugged. When he was sixteen, Nicolina had been the older woman who'd taught him the art of making love. And though he hadn't warmed her bed since the day he met Luciana, her attempts at seducing him back never wavered—another well-known fact around Lerici. "The Hotel Fiori needs it even more than this one. And time doesn't have to be a factor. Whenever it gets done, it gets done." Admittedly, he didn't relish the idea of approaching Nicolina with the launch of his new business, but he would do whatever he had to do to make it a success. And if kissing Nicolina's ass was what it called for, he would do it . . . as long as he didn't have to kiss her mouth also.

"Can we start with these four smaller pieces first?" Mario indicated the three adjacent to the parking lot and the one at the edge of the breakfast patio.

"Absolutely." Vitale kept his tone even while his heart did a joyful dance. "Orabella and Cesare can start tomorrow, if you want." His sister and brother-in-law had been short on money since Cesare's layoff. They wouldn't take a handout from anyone—not even family. But a chance to use their landscaping talents to help Vitale launch Villa de Luca had left all three of them breathless when he'd approached them this morning with his idea.

Mario straightened and thrust his hands into his deep pockets. "Let's start small." He tapped the spot by the pool. "I'll have to let you know later about this one."

Vitale's heart sank a little. The poolside piece had kept him awake most of the night. It was a large piece he couldn't afford to create on speculation. It would have to wait for a commission.

Good things took time.

He could wait.

What was that delicious scent? Mmm. It smelled like . . . bacon? Remembering her capricious offer the night before, Julia shot into a sitting position in the middle of the bed. Frank must be preparing breakfast. She threw a glance at the clock, then did a double take. 12:36. Daylight at 12:36? "Afternoon! Oh. My. God." Was it possible she'd slept over fourteen hours?

She threw on the clothes she'd worn to the hospital, ran a quick brush through her hair, and hurried down the stairs as quickly as her toe would allow. She'd already missed part of the visitation times with Hettie for today. Missing more was out of the question.

Frank's face spread into a huge grin when she hustled into the kitchen. "So Sleeping Beauty can awaken by herself after all." His eyes swept over her appreciatively, hovering just a fraction of a second too long on her braless breasts.

She glanced down and realized too late that her fake nipples were protruding gaudily through the knit top. Damn him. She squelched the flash of anger that swept through her, refusing to allow Frank to put her on the defensive in her own home. But she couldn't stop the heat that rose into her face.

She slid onto the nearest barstool. "Prince Charming could've had all the women he wanted with a side of pepper bacon."

"Well, maybe he only wanted one."

She ignored the comment and the raised eyebrow that accompanied it. "Why are you frying bacon? And why didn't you wake me earlier?"

The toaster popped up two pieces of toast. He took those, added two more, and pressed the lever down. "BLTs. Do you know how long it's been since I had a real BLT with a western Kentucky acid-so-high-it-bites-you-back tomato?"

She knew exactly how long it had been, give or take a couple of weeks, but she bit her tongue.

"I didn't wake you," he continued, "because you obviously needed the rest. And it wasn't like Mom's going anywhere. Not today anyway." His tone had a finality that told her he'd made a decision not to decide. "I woke up early enough to visit her this morning."

"Any change?"

He gave a disconcerted shrug. "The doctor was there, and we talked again. I wasn't so emotional this time." His glance darted away, then back. "He says even with the feeding tube, she probably won't last long. Maybe a few days. A couple of weeks. There'll be signs when she's letting go. We can call Melissa to come home then."

"I see." Julia wasn't sure how to take the news. There was certainly no surge of joy. It wasn't like Hettie was still living. She was just sort of hanging on. Good-bye wasn't imminent, but it would almost be easier if it were.

"I appreciate your letting me stay here, Jules." The message in his eyes—the unspoken "I don't deserve it"—palpated the air between them.

Julia gave him a stern look and set her voice to a tone that would match. "It's *only* for a few days. We'll make it work."

He nodded his understanding. "I don't want to be a burden, so I took the liberty of going by the grocery to pick up a few things. I also hit the farmers' market. Look at this yellow squash." The basket he indicated was filled to the brim with at least a dozen of the unblemished, creamy summer vegetables.

Looking them over, she had to agree. "That's indeed some fine-looking squash, but when did you start cooking? And shopping for groceries? And hitting the farmers' market? I used to have to draw you a map to the kitchen."

He laughed and lay open the avocado he'd halved. "I started watching the Cooking Channel." With a quick action, he popped the knife into the middle of the pit, twisted, and pulled the pit free of the flesh in one fluid motion. "Got interested and found out I'm pretty good at it."

Between the scent of the bacon and the sight of the avocado, Julia's hunger attacked with surprising force, taking the edge off her discomfort with the temporary living arrangements. She swallowed to keep from drooling on the bar.

"You look fabulous, Jules." Frank's glance roamed over the part of her visible above the bar, pausing to study her hair. "Never pictured you as a redhead, but I gotta say . . . wow!"

She ran her fingers through her hair, feeling a bit self-conscious with all the attention from him. Vitale's attention kept her teetering of the edge of excitement. Frank's just set her on edge. Thankfully, the toaster released two more pieces and his attention turned to slathering them with mayonnaise. It was on the tip of her tongue to tell him she'd given up mayo, but she let it go.

"Spinach, avocado, pepper bacon, and the world's best tomatoes on German rye. I could probably market these and make a million." He slid a plate in front of her loaded with sandwich.

She hesitated, waiting for him to finish preparing his.

"Go on," he coaxed her. "I'll catch up."

Hunger won out. Her first bite drew a groan of approval that came out sounding much more sensuous than she intended. "Sorry." She gave a self-conscious laugh. "I haven't eaten in a while."

Frank closed his eyes and gave a leer that could almost pass for a grin. "I can name that song in one note." He opened his eyes and winked at her, then took a couple of diet sodas from the fridge and indicated the table with a nod.

Julia moved her plate to the seat adjacent to his at the table. The second bite grew larger in her mouth as she realized they were sitting in exactly the same position they habitually sat in for twenty-three years. She chewed slowly, eyeing Frank covertly as he dug into his sandwich.

Fit and tan. Just like Melissa described him. "Life in paradise seems to be agreeing with you," she said.

"In some ways, I guess. Hawaii's beautiful, but way too expensive." He started to say something, hesitated, took a drink of soda.

Julia took another bite and waited.

"I'm moving back to Paducah, Jules." He set down his sandwich and leaned back, resting his arms on the table, watching her intently.

Would that mean he'd be back in her social circle? She still ran around with quite a few of their old friends. She checked her own reaction, careful not to show anything that might give her emotions away. Her pulse had kicked up a notch—nothing major. Mouth a little dry. A sip of her drink took care of that. A year ago, this news would have rocked her world—in a bad way. She was better with it now. "Oh, yeah?" She kept her voice casual. "What brought this on?"

Frank gave a sheepish grin. "Turning fifty mostly. Missing our friends. Missing home. This is where I want to be." His index finger tapped the table as if it were pointing to that exact spot.

Julia felt her mouth draw downward at the corners, trying not to take his finger literally. "I see."

"And that brings me to something I wanted to talk to you about. God knows it's difficult to talk about this right now." When he pinched the bridge of his nose, Julia went on alert and laid down the sandwich she had partway to her mouth. "I'm assuming Mom hasn't changed her will?" he asked.

"I'm pretty sure it hasn't changed since she redid it after your dad's death." Pretty sure was an understatement. She knew. Frank wouldn't have health care power of attorney if it had changed. "Everything will be left to the two of us." Talking about Hettie as if she were in the past tense already plunged the sandwich into the lowest depth of Julia's stomach.

Frank evidently felt the same way. His eyes misted over. "See, I was born and raised in that house and I'd hate to let it get away to somebody else. I was thinking I would buy out your part and move in there myself if you'd be okay with that."

His sentimentality toward the house shocked her even while it touched her heart. Despite the hurt and disappointment his actions had caused the past couple of years, Hettie still loved her only child very much. Oh, she ranted and raved and called him names, but her mood was always brighter after he phoned. Julia was sure that, deep down, Hettie would've been pleased he wanted the house. "I'd be more than okay with it, Frank. I think it's a great solution. Your mom would love it."

"Yeah, I wish I could've talked to her about it." He cleared his throat. "Would you consider letting me pay rent and stay here until—"

"No, not a good idea."

"I figured you'd say that, but we'll have to work out the agreement on the house. That will take time. If I'm going to be paying rent to someone, why not you?"

"Because I don't want you living here. I only offered last night because you were distraught." She winced. That was pretty harsh. He was grieving, after all. She sighed and tried for a softer tone. "Look, Frank, it's just not a good idea for either of us. Melissa said you had a new girlfriend. She probably wouldn't be too keen on the idea of your cohabitating with your ex."

"Dawn and I broke up."

"Oh. Sorry." The sarcasm that would've normally intoned her words had been tempered by her recent parting from Vitale.

Frank gave an indifferent shrug. "She was too young. We're a different generation from those guys, you know? They have a whole different set of values."

Julia wasn't hungry anymore. She pushed the rest of the sandwich away.

"I'm gonna be honest with you, Jules." Frank clasped his hands in front of his plate. "The company's floundering in the bad economy. Laying people off left and right. I'm taking unpaid time to be here with Mom, and a pay cut to move back here. Nobody will want to rent to me for only a month. At least, no place I'd want to live. And a hotel room for however long I need it will be pricey."

Julia's mind raced to find a reason that sounded less selfish than "I don't want you here." Suggesting he go ahead and move into Hettie's seemed like the best solution, but she'd learned not to make hasty moves until she talked to her attorney.

Frank must've read her expression and sensed she was weakening. "I can be a help around here, Jules. I noticed a loose rail in the banister. The screen in the back door needs fixing."

The word and its reminder of Vitale almost brought a smile to her lips, but too many other pressing things booted it away.

She held her hand up to stop Frank, not needing any reminders of the things she'd let go. What she needed was legal advice. "Let me think about it. You've hit me cold with this."

"I know. It just came to me this morning when I woke up in the guest bedroom. It felt good, you know?" He dove back into his sandwich with gusto, finishing it in a couple more bites.

Julia pulled a slice of bacon off of hers and munched on it as Frank stood up and began clearing his place.

"I want to hire you and Camille to redo Mom and Dad's house, too. If it's empty, I guess you'll have to start from scratch. I know that won't be cheap, but you always talked about what a showplace it could be." He put the dishes in the dishwasher and came back to stand by the table like he was waiting for an answer already.

But his comments had churned up questions. "You ask if you can stay here, using the hard economic times as your reason, yet with the next breath you talk about this expensive project."

He grimaced, and the pain she saw flash in his eyes was real. She knew him well enough to recognize it. "Just trying to come to terms with the inevitable, Jules." He lowered his voice. "Mom's dying. I know that. I wish to God I didn't have to think in terms of an inheritance, but the time has come for me to think about it. And since, by right, Mom should've been able to spend it, I might as well use it on something she would've wanted."

Julia bit her lip, feeling like his words had been plucked from her own heartstrings. She'd always imagined what she could do with Hettie's house given the opportunity. Now she regretted the opportunity. She waved Frank away as he reached for her plate. "I'll get this. I'm not finished yet. And thanks. It's delicious."

"Well." He rubbed his hands together and glanced around the kitchen. "I'm gonna get out of here for a while. The nursing home is needing the room, so I'm going to pick up Mom's stuff."

"Oh." Julia blinked back the tears that seemed to be set at dead ready. "Do you want me to go with you?"

"Naw, I need this time alone."

She gave him the keys to Hettie's house so he could take her personal items home where they belonged.

As soon as he left, she wasted no time phoning Grayson Chapman, her attorney. She caught him between appointments, so she hurried to explain what was going on. Kenneth Chapman, Grayson's dad and law partner, was Hettie's attorney, and Grayson was

212 • *Pamela Hearon*

Julia's attorney during the divorce, so he was enmeshed in the legalities of her private life. He voiced his sorrow about Hettie, asked a few questions, but mostly listened, waiting for Julia to finish.

"Well, you've probably heard that possession is nine-tenths of the law?"

"Yes." Julia could see where this was going.

"So, let me ask you this . . . do you trust him?"

Grayson had a way of cutting straight to the heart of the matter. Julia liked that about him. But this question cut straight through to her heart also. "I—" She had to stop and think it over.

For over twenty years, she'd trusted Frank implicitly. Sharing everything in the good faith that she was receiving the same as she was giving.

He'd taken that trust and shattered it.

She didn't think he'd try to cheat her out of the house, but then she'd never thought he'd cheat on her in their marriage either. She wouldn't give him the chance again. "No, I don't trust him."

"Then you have your answer, Julia. I can't advise you to let him move into Hettie's house until you have a legal agreement drawn up. Furthermore, I would suggest you wait until Hettie has passed and her will has given you possession before you start trying to draw up an agreement, but you know I'll do whatever you decide on."

"That's all I needed to hear. You've made up my mind for me. Send me a bill for the time."

Grayson gave a low chuckle. "We'll work out something."

"Yes, we will. See you soon," Julia answered. She and Camille were almost finished with the nursery they'd designed for the twin girls the attorney and his wife were expecting.

The conversation left her agitated with the situation she'd placed herself in, so she decided to work off her frustration by unpacking. She set to work, leaving the camera out but putting everything else away. Once that task was completed, she finally set to downloading the pictures from her camera into her computer.

Vitale in his workshop. Vitale sitting at the table in his garden. A shirtless Vitale, dark stubble thick around his mouth and chin, standing in the doorway the morning she'd made up her mind to leave him. Her breath caught and she brushed a finger down the screen.

Did she dare?

Oh, why not?

A few strokes on the keyboard gave the photo the prime setting as wallpaper on her monitor.

It was a silly thing to do, maybe. But it would serve as a reminder that this home was hers alone as she spent the next few days trying to not feel weird about the fact that, even if it was in the bedroom down the hall, she once again had her ex sleeping under the same roof.

Why had she let that happen?

Last night, she'd been trying to show kindness, but why had she agreed today? It wasn't for Hettie's sake. Hettie's advice would be to let him find his own way. And it certainly wouldn't earn any brownie points with her friends, who referred to Frank as "Public Enema #1." She didn't need—or want—his money, and not even a dispute over the inheritance of Hettie's house could make her do something this foolish.

So what was her true motive?

She'd told Grayson she didn't trust Frank. While that was true, it wasn't the whole truth.

Frank had hurt her beyond pain. Ignored her. Cheated on her. Discounted her value as a person. Those things should make it easy to hate him.

But she didn't.

Why?

She'd been through hell. She'd come through the fire and emerged on the other side. What burned away and what had been hardened by the flame?

She was learning new things about herself almost on a daily basis, it seemed. The trip to Italy had shown her that her subconscious was often way out ahead of her decision making, laying groundwork.

She owed it to herself to find out why she'd deliberately added another hurdle to jump over in her life.

* * *

"You would've been proud of me. I just decided what the hell and went ahead and ordered some fabulous pieces from Vitale and some of the other artists I met in Italy. They should be here pretty soon, and I wish you could see them, Hettie—they're so different from anything I've ever bought before. I'm spending money like crazy, but Camille doesn't seem to mind."

Julia had been keeping up these one-sided conversations with Hettie for a week now, trying to follow the nurse's advice. But it was getting harder, and she was running out of things to say. Mostly, it was anything that popped into her head—even if she'd said it before. She put a rubber band around the bottom of the braid she'd just finished and laid it carefully over her mother-in-law's shoulder.

"There. You look beautiful. I'll check and see if it's okay first, but if it is, I'll bring some polish and do your nails tomorrow." She didn't think the hospital staff would mind. They were all being so kind, encouraging her and Frank to interact with Hettie as much as they wanted—even allowing the unconventional. Frank had brought his ukulele and serenaded her yesterday. It seemed that ukulele lessons were something else he'd taken up in Hawaii. Turned out he wasn't half-bad.

"Camille has been preoccupied since I got back. I was afraid maybe she and James were having problems, but he came in yesterday to pick her up for lunch and everything seemed fine. Of course, everybody thought Frank and I were fine, too. We always managed to put on a good front. Even when things were falling apart." She placed the brush in the drawer of the bedside table. "I'm sure there's speculation among the neighbors that we're getting back together. We've probably got everyone wondering what in the world's going on."

She moseyed over to the window and looked out at nothing in particular. "And, to be honest, I'm still wondering that myself." The reflection in the glass shook its head. "I don't mean to sound like I want to reconcile, because I don't. I don't have any desire for that. This actually has nothing to do with Frank, except that his presence in the house makes me...I don't know...fidgety? It's like..." How to verbalize this so it made sense? "I feel like I'm standing at the edge of something. I don't know what it is because I can't see. It's hidden behind . . . darkness. And I want to step through the darkness and explore what's on the other side, but . . . what if it's a void? What if I step off into nothingness and just disappear?"

She wandered back to the bed and sat down next to Hettie. "Yet the little voice in my head keeps telling me to do it, but I'm confused, and the confusion makes me restless and edgy. I know I want action. Change. At the same time, I want . . . peace."

The revelation her words jarred free stilled her breath. She leaned over and rested her cheek to her mother-in-law's shoulder, missing the hug that always used to accompany the gesture. "You're going through exactly the same thing, aren't you?"

She sat back up and searched the placid face for any movement . . . the slightest tremor of an eyelid or the tiniest tic of a cheek muscle. Nothing moved.

But she didn't need physical proof.

"If Frank had been able to understand and empathize with me the way you've always done, we'd probably still be married."

As she brushed the backs of her fingers across the smooth forehead, Hettie's response echoed in her heart as surely as if the words had been spoken aloud.

"But he didn't, sweetheart. And he never will."

The insistent knock on the patio door jarred Vitale from his light sleep. He'd awakened a couple of hours earlier at dawn to a light drizzle and had rolled over and allowed the patter of the raindrops to lull him back to sleep.

Now the sun was shining brightly, making him ashamed he wasn't already stirring. He quickly donned yesterday's shorts and rushed to open the door for his youngest sister and brother-in-law.

"We woke you?" The chastisement in Orabella's tone was overshadowed by her excitement.

He knew he should be excited, too—and he was. But Mama's unrelenting skepticism still caused anger to burn slowly in the pit of his stomach, and the resulting irritation kept him awake far into the night.

Cesare had asked him a question, but he had no idea what it dealt with. "What?" He stretched, hoping his inattentiveness would be attributed to having just woken up.

"I asked if you need me to help load the art pieces. The truck bed is almost full, but we left room for one large piece or maybe two small ones."

Vitale already had the large metal abstract wrapped for transport. He'd chosen the piece not because it was the most expensive but because it drew the eye quickly. As soon as the other hotel owners learned of the Lord Byron project, they would come see for themselves, so he wanted something that would grab them as soon as they stepped onto the property.

He and Cesare loaded the heavy piece gingerly into the truck bed, bolstering it on each side so it couldn't slide on the bumpy roads between here and town.

Orabella gave him an apologetic look. "There's no room for you."

He gave her a peck on her forehead. "You two go on and start unloading the plants. I have to wait for Adrianna anyway." His other sister would be there shortly to work on the online facet of his new business. This was becoming quite a family venture. He only hoped it paid off.

Orabella and Cesare were obviously anxious to be on their way, turning down his offer of coffee.

He made himself a cup and went to check his computer for another e-mail from Julietta, but there was none. He took a drink and let the hot liquid burn away the frustration while he reminded himself that everything—their love, his business and his family's part in it—would be okay if he could only keep the faith.

"Fix your eyes on the goal," Julietta had told him. *"See it with your heart, and I'm sure you'll be a success."*

Julietta was a shrewd businesswoman. He hoped her advice worked on other facets of life as well.

Chapter 23

"It's been two-and-a-half weeks. You need to throw his selfish, good-for-nothing, lying-and-cheating ass out." Camille fished a prune out of the cardboard canister and popped it in her mouth. She shivered as she chewed, and her mouth pulled down so far at the corners she resembled a lizard.

"Why are you eating prunes?" Julia dodged the intended conversation. She'd heard the same line, or something akin to it, every day since she'd returned to work and informed Camille of her and Frank's temporary living arrangement.

"Constipated." Camille made a dramatic show of swallowing.

"Why don't you take a laxative?"

"This is better for me and—" Camille paused, seeming to contemplate the wisdom of another prune. "Quit changing the subject." She closed the canister. "When's he going to find somewhere else to stay? He's using you and you know it."

"It's a trade-off," Julia corrected her. "We're using each other. We're both saving money. He's been repairing all those things I would've hired done. He's been buying all the groceries, doing all the cooking and the cleaning. There's no way I could've come back to work and made Hettie's visits without hiring somebody to keep up with the household stuff."

Once she'd laid down the law to Frank that she wouldn't put up with all the sexual comments—had actually told him to either shut up or get out and reminded him she'd never been completely honest with Melissa about the reason for the divorce—he'd cooled his heels and had been the perfect houseguest.

Camille brushed her fingertips absently over the brocade swatches lying on the counter. "Well, you could at least give him some real shit jobs. Stop up the garbage disposal or the toilet."

"Eat another prune and I'll invite you over."

Camille snorted, but she didn't laugh, which Julia found odd. "Are you okay?" Julia asked. "You seem a little distracted."

Camille flashed her a smile. "I'm great. Relatively speaking, of course." She pointed to the prunes.

Julia held up her hand. "No more details, please." Camille wasn't ready to talk about it yet. They knew each other well enough to know talk would come when the time was right.

The time had never been right to confide the details about what really happened in Italy, though. Dealing with Hettie and Frank and the business had her life in a strange flux right now.

Camille drummed a beat on the prune carton before moving to her desk. Soon, she appeared absorbed with reading and answering their e-mails.

The door chime sounded, and Julia looked up to see their UPS driver carrying a package in one arm and his electronic tablet under the other. "Hey, Douglas," she called.

"Morning, Julia. Camille. Got several boxes for you today. Want them here or around back?"

Julia looked at the small showroom, already crowded from wall to wall. "Bring them around back," she told him as she signed the electronic ledger. "We'll move the items in here once we clear out a space."

Julia unlocked the double doors that opened onto the alley and propped them back. Douglas made four trips, his dolly loaded down each time.

"One more." He grinned, wiping away the sweat on his brow with his handkerchief.

When Julia saw the large, heavy box he unloaded on his last

trip, her heart skipped a beat. They'd ordered only one thing lately that would come in a box that size. The return address confirmed her suspicion.

Vitale.

In spite of her promise to keep in touch, she'd only e-mailed him once—her first night home. And that had been in answer to his message. Instead, she moved through her days on automatic pilot and fell into bed exhausted at the end of each one. She'd even started checking her phone each morning as soon as she woke to remind her what day it was.

He hadn't written her any more either, which probably meant she'd faded from his memory as quickly as she'd appeared in his life.

She said a hasty good-bye to Douglas and grabbed the box cutters, holding her breath in anticipation as she slashed away at the cardboard and tape. A mountain of Styrofoam peanuts gathered around her feet as the box broke open. Then there was cording and bubble wrap to deal with.

She felt like one of the bubbles crawled into her throat when Vitale's sculpture emerged, a twisted mass of wood, steel, copper tubing, and gold leaf.

"Wow!"

Camille's whispered exclamation right beside her caused her to jump. "Amazing, isn't it?" she whispered back, not trusting her full voice.

Camille nodded mutely.

A small black card dangled from a black string attached to one of the wood pieces.

Camille stilled it. A gray etching of Vitale's studio stood out against the black. "Villa de Luca," she read. She opened the card, sounding out the Italian inscription, handwritten in silver ink. "Ses-pug-leo in fy-am-me."

"The Burning Bush," Julia translated. "*Cespuglio in Fiamme.*" Her heart vaulted to her throat as she remembered the sultry way Vitale uttered those words when he gave her the name of the piece.

Camille flipped the card over, and Julia's heart stopped briefly before bounding into double time.

Vitale stared back at her, not smiling. Serious. Brooding. Sexy. She closed her eyes as a surge of heat flashed through her body. *Julietta in fiamme.*

"He's . . . wow, he's . . ." It wasn't like Camille to stammer. "You didn't tell me he was *this* hot."

"I told you he was gorgeous."

"This isn't gorgeous. This is hubba-hubba-momma-mia-damn!" Camille punctuated her words with a few pelvic thrusts. "How could you stay with him for a week and not be all over him?"

"He's more than *just* gorgeous. He's funny and gentle and kind, and—"

"You totally have to fix him up with Melissa."

Julia's praise for the artist froze on her tongue. "Melissa?" Her daughter's name fell from her lips, sounding like it belonged to a stranger.

Still gawking at the picture, Camille didn't seem to notice. "I mean, just think of the two of them together."

Julia waved a hand in front of her face, trying hard not to conjure the image Camille had suggested.

"Can you imagine the grandkids they'd give you?"

Geez!! Now Camille was picturing her as a grandmother. She was only forty-eight, damn it. Her admission of their fling bungeed from Julia's heart to her mouth several times. As she fought to get the timing right between the two, Camille looked up and her eyes filled with concern. "Oh, Julia, don't look so mortified. I'm sure she could talk him into moving to the States. And if not, wouldn't you like to have a good reason to go back to Italy?"

An exclamation she *had* an excellent reason to go back to Italy—and it had nothing remotely to do with mothering or grandmothering—clawed at her throat, but she couldn't force it out. Camille would think she'd lost her mind.

Had she?

She'd certainly made a lot of odd choices lately. Three weeks ago, she'd gone topless on a beach.

Camille took her hand and squeezed it. "I guess grandbabies are on my mind right now." The expression on her face softened in a smile, but tears welled in her eyes. "I'm pregnant again."

The words engaged the emergency brake in Julia's thoughts and shifted her attention to Camille. She understood the strange mood her friend was in now. After two miscarriages in two years, Camille and James feared children might not be in their future. "Oh, Camille. That's wonderful news." She pulled her friend into a hug.

"Yeah, it is." Camille sniffed and dabbed at her eye. "But I'm afraid to get too excited yet. I found out for sure yesterday, but I've been suspecting for a couple of weeks. We haven't told anybody."

"Your secret's safe with me."

"I know. I'm not worried about that." Camille chewed her bottom lip and a ragged breath escaped. "I know now isn't the best time to hit you with this, but I'm worried I might have to quit work. All the heavy lifting and ladder climbing and stretching we do." She indicated the boxes surrounding them, still waiting to be opened. "I don't want to take any chances this time. And I think I might want to stay home after the baby's born, too."

Julia kept her body from reacting to the cringe she felt inside. With everything else going on in her life, she didn't need the loss of her business partner added to the list.

Still . . . "I don't blame you a bit." She brushed a tear from her friend's cheek. "I want you to do what's best for you and the baby. Don't worry about the business. You were here during my cancer ordeal. I'll be here for you. We'll make it work, whatever you need to do."

Camille looked her in the eye. "You're more than just a business partner to me. You know that? You're a second mom."

Julia smiled, taking the statement for the compliment it was meant to be, and then pulled Camille back into her arms for her best mom-type hug.

Vitale didn't expect to see Adrianna's auto still at his house, but his smile grew even wider at the sight of it. Except for Julietta, there was no one he'd rather share his news with.

"He did it!" he announced as soon as he walked through the door.

Startled, Adrianna looked up from the computer, eyes wide and curious. The next instant, his words sank in and she jumped up. "Mario commissioned the piece?"

Vitale proudly waved the signed contract and the sizable check for the down payment.

Adrianna ran to meet him halfway, flinging her arms around his neck and letting out a squeal loud enough to be from one of the children . . . or two or three.

"I can't believe he came around so quickly. Something must have happened to change his mind. Do you have ideas for the piece yet? Have you made sketches?" The words tumbled from Adrianna's mouth on one breath. When she sucked in some air, Vitale jumped in with his answers.

"Several other owners have been up to see the work we've done. In fact, Mario caught Bastani sneaking around last night taking pictures."

Adrianna gaped at that news, and Vitale chuckled at the image in his mind of the two men in confrontation. It was well-known how fiercely they took the business competition, so for Bastani to go at all was astounding. To be caught sneaking in? Priceless. But Bastani's interest was no doubt the final push Mario needed, and Vitale made a mental note to thank Bastani with one of his small pieces.

"And, yes, of course I know what I am going to do." He continued answering her questions. "I've been planning this piece for several weeks, and yes, I have sketches."

"Will you show me?"

Adrianna's enthusiasm was delightful, but he wasn't sure he wanted to share his design with anyone yet. What he had in mind was controversial, to say the least. It had been a hard sell, even to Mario.

"I will show you sometime after I get started," he promised. "But I would like to keep it a secret for now."

Adrianna's pout didn't last long. Of all the siblings, they were the closest. She had to know she was the first he would share with when the time came—which, of course, still caused a sting because it reminded him of how she'd turned to Julietta in her time of need rather than him.

"Come look at this." She pulled him to the computer desk where she'd been working all day and picked up a small stack of paper. "We have more orders!"

Vitale thumbed through invoices, astonished at the addresses of so many faraway places. Brazil. Japan. New Zealand. The wonder of seeing international destinations where his art would find new homes caused his head to spin, and he sat down hard on the chair. How had Julietta known this was possible? His heart ached with the frustration of not being able to share this news with her in person.

He wiped his hand down his face, and it came away wet with perspiration.

"Are you okay?" Adrianna's touch to his shoulder was as gentle as her voice.

"I'm fine." His throat tightened. "It is just that . . . everything is happening so quickly."

"And you wish Julietta was here to share this time with you."

"Yes." He shrugged. "Exactly."

"But she is where she needs to be right now." Her earnest look begged him to agree. "With her family."

He certainly wasn't the one who needed to be reminded of the importance of family. His vexation flared again, a little higher this time. "I know that."

His tone came out gruffer than the conversation warranted, and her head tilted in question. "What, Vitale? What is it that you've been holding in since Julietta left?"

"It isn't about Julietta."

"Then what is it? Are you still angry with me because I was going to take her to the hotel? Because I really didn't have any say in the matter—and I *was* returning a favor."

"It's not about your agreement to take her to the hotel." Although he still *would* be aggravated about that disloyalty if the evening had turned out differently. "It's that . . . when you had the lump in your breast, you should not have turned to Julietta." Her brown eyes flashed at the mention of the delicate matter. "If you didn't want Antonio to know—and that was your first mistake because you should have gone to him. It's a husband's job to be there for you. But if not him, then you should have come to me. I'm the one who should take care of you in his absence. Not someone like Julietta, whom you hardly knew."

"I'm not twelve anymore, Vitale." She tapped her chest. "I decide who goes with me to the doctor, and it's none of your concern. I needed a woman, and Julietta was the perfect companion. She knew exactly what to say to make me feel better."

"But if the outcome had been different, you would have wished for family."

"The outcome wasn't different." She glared hard at him, her mouth opening and closing. It opened again and she sucked in a deep breath. When she blew it out, her eyes softened. "I'm not Luciana. None of us are, and neither is Julietta. But if you continue this quest to try to save everyone because you couldn't save Luciana, you're going to drive yourself crazy. And you're going to push Julietta away for good."

"That's not what I'm doing."

He thrust his finger toward her face and she grabbed it and held on. "It's exactly what you're doing. It's fine to take care of the people you love when they need it, but a strong woman doesn't want to be treated like one of your fragile pieces of art. She wants you to recognize that strength and admire that about her. Don't make her feel like you want some kind of dependent weakling—unless that *is* who you want. But I don't think it is, and I know you well."

"I want Julietta," he answered simply. But the small piece he'd carved for her and tucked away in the large package . . . had it been the wrong thing to do? Would she think he saw her as weak? God, this was all so frustrating! He was a master at body language and reading people's faces. E-mails—and the lack of them—gave him no clue. He needed to *see* her.

One thing he knew for certain, though—Julietta's words echoed in his brain. "And she does not need to be fixed."

Adrianna rolled her eyes and laughed. "Your favorite new word. But, no, you're right. She does not need to be fixed. And neither do you." She put her arms around his waist and squeezed. "Even with all your faults—your quick temper, your stubbornness, your conceit." She swatted his rear. "You're still the most perfect brother a girl could be blessed with and tonight, you will come to our house for dinner. You need to be with family also during this celebration."

He cupped his hand behind Adrianna's head and gave her a kiss on the forehead, thankful to have his family to turn to.

Perhaps someday in the not-too-distant future, this forced separation would be over, and he would have the opportunity to find out if his sister's perception of Julietta was accurate. There was still so much about the woman that he wanted to learn.

That day could not come soon enough.

The conversation with Camille kept Julia preoccupied and jittery, making the day drag on and on. Having Camille as a partner had worked out so perfectly. Thoughts of losing her and what it would mean to the business made Julia's head throb. She tried to busy herself with projects that kept her out of the office, but each time she returned, Camille loomed large in her sight along with Hettie in her thoughts, reminders of voids or soon-to-be voids in her life.

By 5:00, all she wanted was to go home, which made her feel guilty, and added to her mental self-flagellation. She tried to think of some jokes she could tell Hettie to cover up the fact she really didn't want to be at the hospital.

She stopped in the hospital gift shop and picked up a *Cosmo*. If all else failed, she would read her mother-in-law a sexy story. That had been one of Hettie's favorite pastimes in the nursing home.

Frank's face lit up when she entered the room. "Hey. How was your day?" He closed the book he'd been reading.

"Tiring." She left it at that.

Hettie was propped on her side with the aid of some bolster pillows. The bedsores on the back of her left arm looked some improved, but the sight of them still made Julia wince.

"Well, I'll have dinner ready when you get home." Frank leaned over the bed and gave Hettie a good-bye peck. "See you at eight, Mom."

Julia plopped into the chair he'd vacated by the bed, a little disconcerted at the routine they'd settled into.

Frank had breakfast ready each morning when she got out of bed. They both went to the hospital for the 8:00 visit; then she went on to work while he went home and took care of things around the house. She ate her brownbag lunch at the hospital from 12:00 to 1:00; Frank stayed from 1:00 to 2:00. He came back from 4:00 to 5:00; she came after work, staying from 5:00 to 6:00. Dinner was usually waiting for her when she got home. They ate and then returned to the hospital together for the last visitation.

The schedule left her exhausted and moody—like perpetual PMS.

She sat for a while in the quiet, listening to Hettie's breathing, counting the number of breaths in one minute. Fewer than yesterday. The muscles in the back of her neck tightened at the implication. She started talking about everything that came to mind, anything to keep her from thinking about the fact that Hettie was going to be gone soon. She was too weary to shoulder that right now, too.

She talked in a stream, sharing about Camille's pregnancy, confident the secret would never leave that room. She described the sculpture that had arrived in vivid detail, hoping Hettie was picturing it in her mind. She vented some frustration by turning the subject to Frank and the living arrangement they had going on, confessing that it probably should be bothering her more than it did.

She didn't take the time to analyze why it was working—only that it was, for the time being.

"You've picked a helluva time to leave me," she whispered to Hettie when the chime rang the end to the visiting hour.

The sound was just a rattle from Hettie's lungs, but to Julia, it sounded like a chuckle.

True to his word, Frank had dinner on the table when she got home. Meatloaf, mashed potatoes, green beans, fried okra, and Blackhawk Bakery rolls.

Her favorites.

She picked around at her food, although it was all delicious. She could tell Frank was disappointed she didn't show more enthusiasm, but she refused to put on an act for his benefit.

He poured a glass of wine and handed it to her. "You seem really tired tonight."

"Yeah, it's been a long day." She took a sip. The dry red brought back memories of evenings with Vitale. She closed her eyes and let the memory infuse her as she swallowed.

When she opened her eyes, Frank was staring at her, an open look of desire on his face. She cut her eyes away quickly, not wanting to see that look.

"Jules." He leaned toward her, his voice was soft, his tone husky.

She knew that tone well. *So help me, if he makes one seductive move, I'll throw his ass out of here tonight.* She brought her eyes back up to meet his, letting them flash her warning.

He leaned back in his chair, his face tightened with strain. "Um, why don't you stay home tonight?"

She would've bet money that was not what he'd been prepared to say, but at least he'd taken her warning seriously.

"You've been hitting it pretty hard. You need some time to relax. Mom would, um, will, understand."

That was perceptive of him. She did need some time at home to just do nothing. It seemed like forever since she'd done nothing.

"I think you're right," she finally agreed. "I'm worn out, and I think I'll stay home tonight."

Frank nodded, followed by an awkward moment of silence that hung like a curtain in the air. "Hey, Earl Stone called today." The look on his face showed his relief that he'd thought of a conversation starter.

Earl was an old friend from high school, now a Paducah policeman. "How's he doing?" She frowned, trying to remember how long it had been since she'd done something with the Stones. "I need to give them a call. He and Martha were so kind to me right after our divorce. They invited me to their house and out to do things with them."

Frank shifted uncomfortably in his seat.

Just like a man. Get anywhere near the subject of his infidelity and he becomes aware of the uncomfortable position his balls are in.

"He'd heard about Mom." Frank didn't respond to her comment. "Wanted to see how she was. We got to talking about the time he and Sully Winters and I got arrested for cutting cane on Henry Wortham's land to make fishing poles."

Frank's guffaw jolted a laugh out of Julia. It was unexpected, but it felt good to have a break from the intensity for a while.

He went on, telling the story, which she knew by heart. She let him tell it, though, and it led to another, which led to another.

They reminisced about high school high jinks through the rest of supper, while they cleaned up the kitchen, and up until the time Frank left to return to the hospital.

The light conversation took the edge off—not completely, but some. She changed into her swimsuit, poured herself another glass of wine, and relaxed in the hot tub on the back deck for a while.

The combination of the wine and the pounding hot jets of water soon relieved the tension in her back and shoulders. She got out and went upstairs to her computer with the intention of sending a quick e-mail to Vitale to let him know the sculpture had arrived safely.

She started to type.

> Vitale, "Cespuglio in Fiamme" arrived today. It is such a beautiful piece of sculpture. My partner—

A ping indicated a new e-mail had come in. She brought up her in-box. A message from Vitale had just arrived! He was online.

She hit Show and opened his message.

> Julietta, I do not know how it happen so fast but I receive the seven more orders.

Not surprised by the information, she felt the smug smile break across her face. The interior decorating forum she frequented had been abuzz about Villa de Luca ever since she raved about the new catalog she'd "discovered" online.

> It make me very happy.

She didn't take the time to read the rest but hurried to reply so she could catch him before he got off.

> Vitale, what are you doing awake at this time of night?

It was in the early hours of the morning in Italy.
Ping. A reply from him.

> I could not stay to sleep. I think I write to my Julietta.

Oh! Her fingers flew to type another reply.

> I know I should have written before, but I have so little free time. Hettie is still in a coma, but I know she can't hold out much longer and that makes me so sad. How are you? How is your family?

Send and wait. While she waited, she went back to the original message.

> Mario commission me (I use the new word you teach me yes?) to create the sculpture for the pool at the hotel. He want the large piece. She to be expensive.

The *ping* had her scrambling to open the new message.

> I am sorry for this. The grief make you the much tired also. This I know. The family she is fine. Mama she ask how is Julietta? And the others she do the same.

That brought a chuckle. If Angelina was asking how she was, it was probably with the secret hope that she'd been hit by a train.

Another *ping.*

> The e-mail is not so good as to hold you and make
> the love to you. When do you return to me?

Her heart stuttered at his words. He couldn't honestly still be
expecting her to return when this was over, so why continue with
the cajoling? Her fingers hovered over the keys, waiting for her
brain to send the command to type what she was thinking. But
sitting there, within the fantasy again, felt so good after such a
trying day.

A sharp rap at her door startled her. "Jules?"

"It's open," she called.

The grim look on Frank's face shouted the news before his voice
caught up. "The doctor says we need to call Melissa. Tonight. Now."

"Oh." The wind rushed out of her on that one word. The screen
blurred to the point she couldn't see what she was typing.

> I have to go now, Vitale. Frank has just told me
> that Hettie is leaving us soon. Maybe tonight. I will
> e-mail again when I can.

She hit send and didn't wait for a reply.

CHAPTER 24

Each time he awoke during the remainder of the night, Vitale's thoughts sprang to Julietta, wondering what she was going through at that moment. Had Hettie left them during the hours since their last e-mail? Most of the time, a shadow of sadness would descend on him. Not a *true* sadness because he didn't know Hettie personally, so he experienced no acute sense of loss. But a sadness filtered through his Julietta's pain.

At other times, a different emotion would absorb his rest and leave him punching the pillow that flattened under the weight of his head, which constantly flipped from side to side, trying to find a comfortable position. One that would relax him back to sleep and take away the image of his Julietta seeking consolation in the arms of another man.

Perhaps her ex-husband who must be there with her. *Frank has just told me,* she wrote.

Vitale did not believe any attraction for Frank remained within her. But it did not take attraction to seek solace in someone's arms—or bed—when you were grieving.

He knew that firsthand.

He was glad, at last, to greet the dawn with purpose, even if that purpose was to check for the message he hoped Julietta had not had to post.

Nothing from her, and for a moment he was relieved, but then he thought of the anguish she must be going through, and the early sun cast the shadow upon him once more.

Which was worse—having the loved one snatched away by a galloping tide that allowed no time for good-bye, or watching them drift away slowly on a tide that stole them inch by inch?

He prepared some breakfast and took it out to the patio to enjoy in the cool of the morning. A breeze shimmied through the leaves of the small tree nearest him. The sound always reminded him of an intimate whisper, and he always attributed it to Luciana speaking to him now in the only way she could.

"Yes, my love, I hear you." He sipped his *caffe latte*. "I'm glad you have come to visit this morning. I have a favor to ask." The leaves stirred in response. "The woman I spoke with you about— Julietta. Someone she loves will be making her way to your home very soon. Would you go to meet her when she arrives? I know how frightening it must be—taking that first step into a world unknown, and I cannot but think your warm smile would help vanquish her fear. Her name is Hettie Berkwith." He said the strange name slowly. It didn't roll off the tongue easily. "And . . ." He paused, but there was no need for pretense. Luciana had always seen through him, like Julietta. "Perhaps you could put in a good word for me with her? Her opinion matters a great deal to Julietta."

A warm breeze touched his cheek in reply.

Satisfied, he finished his *caffe latte* in silence.

With a more cheerful heart than the one he woke up with, he took his dishes back to the kitchen and made one more stop at the computer to check his e-mail.

Still no word from Julietta.

On his way to the studio, a burst of stronger wind whipped about him. He stopped and closed his eye until it passed, wondering if perhaps it was the rush of a spirit to greet a new friend.

* * *

"I can't get over how good she looks." Melissa repeated the words she'd murmured several times since she'd arrived at the hospital. "I keep expecting her to open her eyes and ask me when I'm going to quit sticking my finger in that socket."

Julia smiled at the reference to the ongoing feud between Melissa and her grandmother concerning Melissa's short, spiky hairstyle.

"From what I'm hearing about the winters in Alaska, Gram"— Melissa pulled Hettie's hand to rest against her cheek—"I may want to let it grow back out."

"Or move to Hawaii," Frank quipped. His arm tightened around Melissa's shoulder and he kissed her temple.

The bone structure of the two faces side by side was strikingly similar, and regardless of Hettie's opinion, Julia thought the blond fringe encircling Melissa's face gave her a soft, angelic appearance. Dark brows and lashes emphasized the translucent green irises. As she had so often before, she marveled she and Frank had produced such a beautiful child who had grown into such a breathtaking young woman.

That their daughter made it back to Paducah in time to say good-bye to her grandmother put Julia in a mood of peaceful gratitude and made her wonder if Hettie had enough of a foothold in heaven already to be pulling some strings. For once, the difference in time zones had worked in their favor. Melissa had gotten on a flight from Anchorage to LA where she spent the night. A morning flight from Los Angeles to Nashville had meshed seamlessly with a commuter flight from Nashville to Paducah, and there the four of them were, together at last.

The hospital staff had suspended the visitation hours for them, so they were at liberty to come and go from Hettie's room as need be.

As alarming as it should've been, even the labored rattle from Hettie's lungs rang as a welcomed relief, proof that life still hovered, however precariously.

Melissa's gaze drifted down the length of the figure in the bed. The concerned crease between her eyebrows softened. "She doesn't seem to be in any pain."

"No," Julia agreed. "I don't think she's hurting. Her breathing's too peaceful. I think she's drifting into a deep sleep."

Like it had done all afternoon, the conversation shifted back and forth from Hettie to catching up on tidbits in their lives. "I think she'd be pleased you're moving back to Paducah, Dad, and back into the house."

"Yeah, it feels right to me, too," Frank said. "I think whoever said 'You can't go home again' was wrong. Home feels pretty good."

Melissa smiled wryly and shook her head as her eyes darted from Frank to Julia and back. "I was blown away when you told me you were staying with Mom at our house. I would've bet my last three paychecks that would never happen."

"Let that be a lesson to you, young lady." Frank wagged his finger in her face. "Never bet against the home team."

Melissa arched an eyebrow. "Especially when *you're* pitching, huh?"

Frank gave a quick nod. "You know it."

Melissa turned to her mom, obviously expecting a remark, and Julia bit back a retort about it being Frank's last inning. No use breaking the peace for a cheap shot. But it wouldn't be right to give Melissa any hopes their broken family was mended either. "He can pitch it till he's blue in the face," she said, sending the banter in a different direction. "I'll just keep shoveling it out."

Melissa laughed and made a mark in the air with her finger. "Score one for Mom."

"Actually"—Julia nodded toward the sleeping figure in the bed—"I'll give that point to Hettie. She would've come out with it first."

"Yeah, but you've been around her so long you've picked up a lot of her sassiness, Mom. Even more than the last time I was home." Melissa eyed Julia thoughtfully. "I mean, look at your hair. When did you change it?"

The comment took Julia by surprise. She pulled the top strands through her fingers and shook her head so it fell back into place.

"I woke up one morning in Italy with this wild idea I wanted a change."

She had to force the memory of the specific morning and the true impetus for the change from her mind before her facial expression gave her away. "A young woman in Lerici did it while I was there, and Darlene's been able to copy the cut and match the color."

"Well, you look beautiful. Doesn't she, Dad?" Melissa nudged Frank for an answer.

"Yeah, she looks fantastic."

Melissa laid Hettie's hand gently on the bed and moved restlessly over to the window. "I can see the river from up here." Her wistful tone was punctuated with a sigh. "Besides y'all and my friends, that's one of the things I miss most about this place. I miss sitting at the river on summer nights and picnics at Kentucky Lake. I would never have admitted it to Grandpa, but I even miss that old bass boat he used to take me fishing in."

"All part of growing up, Issy." Frank used the nickname he'd pinned on the child at birth. "Figuring out the things most important to us."

Julia caught the brief, sidelong glance he cast her way.

Melissa spun from the window, eyes wide with expression darting around the room. "Do you think Grandpa's here? Waiting for her?"

"I hope so." Frank's eyes shifted from his mother's face again to settle on Julia's. "They had a lot of happy years together. I'm sure he's anxious to be with her again."

Julia picked up on the subtle message, though she tried to ignore it. She hoped Melissa did the same. Still, she couldn't keep her eyes from misting up as a memory washed over her. "The night he died, she told him to walk slow and she'd catch up to him soon."

Melissa moved back to the bed, and they stood quietly for a long moment, each lost in personal reminiscence.

Recognition broke slowly as Julia realized she was listening for a sound that wasn't forthcoming.

And never would be again.

Her eyes moved slowly up to meet Frank's . . . Melissa's . . . back to Frank's.

A sharp breath shuddered his chest, and she watched his Adam's apple bob as if in slow motion.

"I think she just caught up," he said.

CHAPTER 25

Vitale gently pushed his thumb into the plasticine, making a delicate indentation below the ankle. Although he often worked straight from imagination, the piece he'd been commissioned by Mario to create was too costly for there to be any mistakes. He'd chosen to first create a small clay model to scale. When the model was completed, which meant it had to be perfect in every detail, then and only then would he allow himself to move on to begin the actual piece.

It would take time. Time during which Mario would become impatient. Vitale closed his eyes and drew in a satisfied breath. But time he now had.

His days were his own at last. Or rather four days a week were his own to work in his studio to his heart's content. Two days he still spent on projects he had promised, working on walkways, walls, and patios. And Sunday he kept reserved for family.

Adrianna did a fine job of taking care of the business end of Villa de Luca, but some nights he had to work also on that mundane end of things.

All in all, he was satisfied with the turn his life had taken. Making a living doing what he wanted to do, never again looking forward to retirement. This *was* retirement. Happily, this was the way he would spend the rest of his time on earth.

The CD Julietta had left was in the player rather than one of his operas. The songs usually brought joy and comfort—a piece of Julietta from across the miles. But today, they brought thoughts not only of her, but also of Hettie, whose funeral would be today. And with that came sadness. Julietta had described Hettie as someone with such energy and zest for life. Someday, he would create a sculpture of his vision of Hettie for Julietta, capturing that energy.

But first, he needed to concentrate on the task at hand. Plucking another piece of the oil-based clay, he kneaded it between his fingers until it was soft and pliable, then pressed it onto the model.

This day would not be an easy one for Julietta, although, after what she'd been through the last few weeks, there surely would be relief the ordeal was finally over. Perhaps in a few weeks or a couple of months, Julietta would be able to come back to Italy, and they could pick up where they left off.

He smiled, thinking of the changes she would see in the studio, in the way he spent his time . . . in him. And he had her to thank.

An image of precisely the way he would thank her in person spread across his brain, causing his thumb to tighten on the plasticine and make an indentation where one should not be.

"*Porca vacca!*" He ground out the expletive through clenched teeth.

"Vitale! You should be ashamed. Using such language in front of your mother."

"Mama! This is a surprise." He grabbed a nearby towel to wipe the clay from his hands and deposited it on top of his sketches to obscure them from view.

"Obviously," she answered wryly, closing the door behind her. "Those ugly words would not have come from your mouth had you known I was here."

He met her with a kiss halfway across the studio, preferring to keep her as far away as possible from the project. "That was the first time I've ever said those words." He couldn't hold back the telltale grin.

She patted his face a little harder than a proper love pat should be.

"Let's go in the house"—he tilted his head toward the door—"where it's more comfortable. What brings you here?" With a hand to the small of her back, he managed to move her in the right direction without being too pushy . . . or suspicious.

"Adrianna tells me you work all day and often skip lunch now you're working here at home. So I decided we would have lunch together today. I brought minestrone and that parmesan-rosemary bread you like so much." Her eyebrow arched slightly, daring him to decline her offer.

Instead, he raised his arm to rest across her shoulders and hugged her to him as they walked. "Thank you. That sounds delicious."

Adrianna was at the stove, stirring the soup, when they walked in. "I hope you are hungry." She gave him a contrite look of apology she hadn't been able to warn him of Mama's surprise visit.

"Starved." He smiled and winked to let her know everything was cool.

The scent of his mother's minestrone made his mouth water, and he found he was indeed happy for the disruption of his day.

They chatted about how well the business was going as Mama sliced the bread and he prepared drinks. She seemed genuinely pleased and perhaps a little awed one could make money by selling wares off the computer, which was not something she'd taken the time to learn much about.

Adrianna dished up the soup into large bowls, and when they sat down to eat, Mama recited a quick blessing. Vitale said a silent prayer for Julietta, that she would have the strength and courage sufficient for what she would face this day.

As if she'd heard him, or maybe the years had somehow taught her to read his thoughts by the look on his face, Mama asked, "The funeral is today, then?"

"Yes." He dipped a piece of the warm bread into the broth and watched how quickly the red color infused through the coarse texture.

"You have contact with her often?"

"We e-mail." He filled his mouth with a spoonful of soup and swallowed. "Mmmm. This is delicious, Mama." His eyes met Adrianna's, sending a verbal cue it was her turn.

She took the hint. "My bread is never this light, Mama. I don't think I inherited any of your bread-making skills."

Mama ignored the comment. "So, how is Julietta holding up through all of this?" The woman was obviously not going to be deterred from her chosen conversation.

"She is doing as well as can be expected. She is sad. Her mother-in-law was more like a mother to her, and Julietta loved her very much."

Mama cast him a sidelong glance. "And what will Julietta do now she is gone?"

Vitale wished to hell he knew the answer to that. "She will continue working in her business. This is really a pleasant surprise—it's rare for it to just be the three of us." He eased the subject away from Julietta again and this time Mama didn't press.

She filled them in on various things she had heard around town, mostly things and people he didn't care to know much about. But it gave him a chance to eat his soup without requiring too much exchange.

"I had a pleasant surprise yesterday," Mama said, and the timbre of her voice shifted. He looked up to see her smile, but it was forced, and his grip on his spoon tightened reflexively. "Francesca stopped by."

Adrianna shot him a wary look, but he continued to eat his soup.

"She says everyone in town is talking about your new business. Apparently Mario is quite excited about a large piece you are creating for the area beside his pool."

Vitale kept his eyes on his soup and shrugged. "News travels fast in Lerici."

"I told her I didn't know anything about the work you are doing for Mario. I'm only your mother, I told her, so I am usually not included in discussions about your business."

After all these years, the guilt-inflicting tone she used shouldn't have an effect on him, but it did. He laid down his spoon and stretched his hand out to cover hers and pat it gently. "I never want to worry you with bland business details. They might drop into the delicious soup and ruin the taste."

Adrianna's lips twitched and she rolled her eyes. "If it's any consolation, Mama, I work with him, and I have yet to be told exactly what this mysterious new piece is."

Vitale grinned at them both. "I will show it when the time comes. Until then, everyone will have to wait." He finished up the last few bites of his soup but helped himself to another piece of bread, which he dipped into the shallow bowl of olive oil.

"Speaking of waiting..." Mama finished her soup also and rested her clasped hands on the table in front of her. "Francesca wanted to know how long it would be until Julietta returns to Lerici. I told her—" She paused, weighing her comment.

Francesca again. The name caused a bitter taste to come into Vitale's mouth and he let the bread drop onto his plate. "What, Mama? What did you tell her? I hope you told her it was none of her business."

Mama swallowed a sip of water. "I told her you did not know."

He doubted that was all Mama told her, but she didn't elaborate, and he didn't want to know. He pushed away from the table, no longer hungry for the piece of bread he'd taken.

"The flowers Orabella and Cesare planted in the beds at Lord Byron's are certainly beautiful," Adrianna gushed. "I can't believe they've rooted and started to fill in the bare areas so quickly."

"I taught her well," Mama answered. Her eyes cut to Vitale, and she added, "She was a fast learner. She listened to me and took to heart everything I told her."

The dig scratched at Vitale's composure. Mama could compare Francesca and Julietta only on the surface. She had not yet seen their hearts. If she had, she would realize she was championing the wrong woman. But until Julietta returned and Mama got to know her better, arguing the point was futile.

He wiped his mouth and set his napkin aside. "Well, I need to get back to work." He stood and reached for his dishes, but Adrianna waved him away.

"Mama and I will get those. Go." She gave him a conspiratorial wink.

He gathered them anyway and placed them beside the sink. Then he went back and bent down to wrap his arms around Mama from the back and kiss her cheek. "Thank you for lunch. And if you leave the rest of the soup, I'll make good use of it."

She chuckled and patted his face.

He left them, knowing only too well Adrianna was about to be cross-examined to determine everything she knew about his new business. That didn't worry him much. Of all his sisters, Adrianna knew best how to dodge Mama's personal questions.

But the question of when Julietta would return burned in his stomach.

He looked forward to the time when he could prove to Mama he was a grown man with a keen insight when it came to judging people . . . especially women.

Hettie's funeral was straightforward and simple, a fitting tribute to the woman it honored.

Julia had been both surprised and relieved when the funeral director informed her and Frank that Hettie had called him to the nursing home a few days before her last stroke and had planned the entire thing.

Hettie's decision not to have a wake *didn't* surprise her. "I don't want people standing around, gawking at me, saying how good I look. I'll be dead and I hope to God I don't look better than I do now." Hettie's tone would get wrathy when she brought up the subject.

The pastor had commended the sweet soul into God's hands during the final prayer and the people who attended the graveside service had started to disperse from under the blue tent.

Julia stood beside the vault, aware of the open grave below even though it had been camouflaged with artificial turf carpeting. Too fully aware that her precious mother-in-law would be lowered into the ground as soon as the mourners were out of sight.

Her heart hung heavy in her chest, taking up double its normal space, barely allowing any room for air in her lungs. So many things needed to be said, but the muscles in her neck tightened into steel bands. She wasn't sure she could push enough air through the constriction to make a sound.

She laid a hand on the coffin and closed her eyes, imagining Hettie's smiling face, full of animation and life. "You're the finest person I've ever known," she said, finding her voice at last. "You've been a mother . . . friend, and you've taught me so much." A deep breath loosened the muscles a bit. "I'm so thankful you've been a part of my life." Another deep breath, and she knew she could say it. "I'll miss you."

She placed a pink rose and a box of Godiva truffles on the casket and then moved out from under the tent into the bright sunshine.

Frank and Melissa were talking with friends when another stab of regret caught Julia. None of Hettie's friends were there. She'd outlived almost all of them, and the ones who remained were too feeble to come.

Camille's arm sliding around her waist broke her reverie. "I know how tough this is for you, Julia. I'm sorry."

Julia drew a long breath to steady her voice. "We had so long to prepare, I thought I'd handle it better than this." She wiped a tear, amazed her eyes could produce any more.

Camille's husband, James, patted her arm. "We're here if you need anything."

"Thanks."

As Camille and James moved away, Grayson Chapman took their place, holding the hand of his wife, Olivia, who looked like she was going to pop at any minute, though the happy glow on her face negated the apparent discomfort of her swollen tummy.

Grayson clasped Julia's hand with his free one, and Olivia did the same. The love in their touch moved through the circle, filling Julia with comfort. "We're sorry for your loss, Julia." Olivia's eyes misted as she spoke.

Grayson squeezed Julia's hand gently. "Give me a call when you're ready for me to draw up that agreement we spoke about."

"Maybe the first part of next week?" That was only four days away. Anxious as she was to settle things with Frank, Julia wanted the rest of the time with Melissa worry-free.

"Whenever you're ready," Grayson answered.

Grayson's father, Kenneth, walked up beside them. Olivia let go of Julia's hand and he took it. "You have my deepest condolences, Julia. Hettie was a wonderful woman."

"Yes, she was."

As the three of them moved away, Grayson still held Olivia's hand and Kenneth got a firm hold on her opposite elbow. Big as she was, movement was difficult and the uneven ground could be a hazard.

Someone said something, and Julia squinted into the sunlight at the tall figure standing beside her. "I'm sorry. What did you say?"

"I'm Joe Proctor, the administrator of the nursing home Mrs. Berkwith was in."

"Oh yes." Julia shook his hand. "We've, uh . . ." Heat moved from her neck into her cheeks as she remembered their first encounter. "We met once before."

A puzzled dent appeared between his heavy eyebrows. "Have we?"

Of course, he wouldn't remember. She'd been invisible. Maybe still was. She'd found herself wondering more and more of late what had happened to that woman she'd glimpsed in Italy.

But relief Joe *didn't* remember her stamped down the flicker of indignation starting to flare. "Well, it was very briefly." She pulled her hand from his grasp and waved it dismissively. "I want to thank you for all you did for Hettie. We couldn't have asked for better care for her."

"I appreciate that. People like Mrs. Berkwith make my job worthwhile." He smiled a genuine smile and the warmth from her cheeks seeped downward into her chest. Joe Proctor was a nice man. That Hettie had been in his care during her last days of consciousness was a comforting thought.

"And thank you for coming today."

"It was my pleasure." His features contorted. "Well, not pleasure." A flush bloomed on his forehead and cheeks. "I mean, I was glad to be here . . . not that I enjoy funerals." His face was crimson by then.

Julia laughed. "It's okay. I know what you mean."

He laughed, too. "Whew! I'd better get out of here while I've only got one foot in my mouth." Shaking his head, he moved away.

Julia smiled as she watched him go.

"Jules? You ready?" Frank's hand came to rest lightly on the small of her back.

She glanced around, noting most everyone was gone. A few people still stood by their cars talking, but most of the small crowd had dissipated.

Her gaze turned back toward the tent. The workers from the funeral home would want to finish up and get on with their day.

And she needed to start putting the pieces of her life back together . . . without Hettie.

She turned to face her ex-husband and her daughter, who waited patiently. "I'm ready."

As they moved toward the car, she turned and blew a final kiss toward the tent.

CHAPTER 26

Earl and Martha Stone were the last to leave.

"I really want you to consider getting a security system put in here." Earl paced up and down the porch of Julia's house, scrutinizing the doors and windows as only an officer of the law would. "Lotsa mean bastards out there, you know? A woman living alone needs protection."

Julia dodged a June bug that couldn't resist the lure of the porch light. "Maybe I should move to one of those gated retirement communities with the old folks." She landed a soft punch on Earl's bicep, surprised to find it as rock solid as it had been when he was a football star in high school.

Earl grinned. "Maybe you should. Or maybe you just need to be finding yourself a man."

Julia raised an eyebrow. "I could turn an alarm system off and on whenever I want."

Earl's laugh shook the paunch around his middle. "You got a point there."

"Earl, c'mon, and leave Julia be," Martha called from the car. "I'm burning up out here."

Earl gave Julia a quick hug. "Call me if you need me, Julia May."

Julia smiled. Nobody except her mom and Earl had ever called her Julia May. "I will," she promised. "And don't worry about me. I'm fine."

Halfway to the car, Earl turned and shook a finger at her. "Lotsa bastards out there."

"Duly noted," she called back with a wave good-bye to Martha. She watched until their taillights were out of sight before she went back into the house.

Melissa and Frank were in the kitchen, trying to make room in the refrigerator for the leftovers. For two days, friends and neighbors had been dropping things by in a constant stream. There was still plenty, even after feeding seventeen friends and family members after the funeral.

"I've never seen so much food." Melissa blew a strand of hair out of her eyes. "I wish I could take some of it back with me."

"I wish you could take all of it," Julia agreed. "It's certainly more than I need."

Frank pulled a piece of foil off the roll big enough to cover the enormous pan of lasagna. "At least now people use plastic or throwaways that don't have to be returned. Used to, we'd have to sort out and take back all those casserole dishes to their owners."

"And there would always be a stack of orphans who'd lost the masking tape with their owner's name on it," Julia added.

Frank handed the last pan to Melissa, who slid it into the fridge on top of Mamie Trimble's blue-ribbon recipe blackberry cobbler.

Melissa stood for a moment, chewing her lip, looking the same as she did when she was four and about to get into mischief. She set the lasagna back out and removed the cobbler. "I think I want some of this."

"Me too." Frank seconded her idea.

It did seem like a shame to refrigerate the cobbler just yet. "Get three bowls," Julia instructed. She ducked into the mudroom and raided the freezer for the tub of vanilla ice cream Mamie had brought as accompaniment for her still-warm-out-of-the-oven cobbler.

They heaped their bowls and made for the Florida room to enjoy the evening breeze, which brought not only respite from the heat but also the quintessential sound of the summer cicadas and bull frogs.

"We've been so distracted by Gram, I haven't heard much about Italy yet, Mom." Melissa pinched off a piece of crust and dragged it through her ice cream as if it were chip and dip. "Did you have a good time, or did the broken toe manage to spoil the whole thing?"

Frank set his cobbler aside and propped his elbows on his knees, all ears. He suspected something happened in Italy, she could tell.

Julia thought back to how unabashedly relieved Melissa had been when she learned Dawn and Frank had broken up. Julia wasn't sure if it was the woman, the age difference between her dad and the woman, or simply one of her parents in a relationship that made their daughter react that way.

She finished the bite she'd taken, using the time to gather her wits and choose her words. "Well, I was pretty bummed at first, but I met a wonderful Italian family. The son is an artist and he kind of took me in and helped me get around. To pay him back, I photographed his work for a Web catalog and he's starting to make sales, so everything worked out well for everybody. The country's even more beautiful than I had pictured." She hurried on, diving into an extended monologue about the colors and the terrain.

She talked until Frank became interested in his cobbler again, and she could almost see the glaze of boredom dropping across his eyes. At that point, she passed the conversation to Melissa. "But enough about Italy. Now that I can see your expressions, I want to hear in person what it's like living so far north. You know, the stuff you don't tell me over the phone."

Melissa snorted. "Where do I even begin?" But she found her start with how different it was from what she expected and let her zeal for the new experience carry her on for a long time.

Frank joined in, adding his two cents about Hawaii, and the conversation turned lively, reminiscent of past conversations around the dinner table.

One subject segued into another with the easy verbal sparring that had always characterized their family discussions.

Time passed quickly, and before Julia knew it, Frank was looking at his watch, exclaiming, "My God, it's after eleven!" As if
brought on by the acknowledgment, a wide yawn contorted his
face.

Melissa's girlish giggle faded into a long sigh. "This has been
nice. Tonight. The three of us here, together again."

Their daughter had been away at college during the divorce and
had kept a stoic attitude about it anytime she'd been home, ever
the trooper. Her wistful tone displayed the truth behind her cool
façade, and it squeezed Julia's heart.

"Yeah, it has," Frank said. He cut his gaze to Julia and allowed
it to linger a shade too long.

She shifted in her seat, not wanting to spoil the moment, but not
wanting to let it develop into something it wasn't. "Hettie would be
pleased," she said. Maybe reminding them of the occasion that
brought about this reunion would squelch any false hopes.

It seemed to work. "Well, I don't know about y'all, but I'm going to bed." Frank stood and began gathering up the dishes.

Julia stayed put, waiting to see if her daughter would want to
stay up and talk more. Her emotions volleyed between disappointment and relief when Melissa agreed it was probably time for bed.

The three of them made quick work of washing and drying
these last dishes by hand and putting them away.

They went up the stairs together, dropping Frank off at the
guest bedroom.

Julia's room was next, and Melissa gave her a long hug. When
she stepped away, her bottom lip drew up in a thoughtful pout.
"Are you sleepy, Mom?"

"No," Julia answered honestly. "I'm probably going to read for
a while."

A big smile brightened her daughter's face. "I'd love to see your
pictures of Italy."

Ack! The Italy pictures were all in one file. One big file, which
consisted primarily of Vitale. Julia had been meaning to create a
separate file with pictures of the scenery—pictures she could share
when someone asked—but had never gotten around to doing it.

"Oh, honey, they're all in one file with lots of duplicates. I, um, I haven't deleted any yet. Let's wait until I sort them out. You won't want to wade through all of them."

Melissa slid past her and bounced onto her bed, grinning and looking thirteen again. "It's only after nine by my time, so I'm not sleepy. C'mon, Mom. I want to see all of them."

Busted, Julia thought. *I'm soooo screwed.*

Julia took a deep breath and tapped the computer key. The monitor came to life, the image of Vitale filling the screen.

Melissa giggled. "You go to Italy for a week, come back, and put an Italian model as your screensaver?"

"That's not an Italian model. That's Vitale, the guy I stayed with."

That certainly got her daughter's attention. Melissa shot into an upright position and leaned closer to the screen. Her eyes widened. "This is the guy who took care of you?"

Julia nodded and wished her mouth had not gone so suddenly dry.

"You stayed at his house?"

"Uh-huh." Julia tried for a nonchalant tone as she clicked on the file that brought up the rest of the photos.

"Just the two of you?"

Julia shrugged. "We're adults." She pointed at the screen. "This is the hotel in Lerici."

"He's hot, Mom." Melissa's voice held the same wonder it had when she was six and Julia gave her a cherished gold locket.

"Yeah, he's nice looking, and a little conceited. But he's very pleasant . . . and talented." She clicked through the next group of pictures she had taken on the first sightseeing cruise. "This is the town. And these are other villages. Look at all the colors."

"These almost look like they've been enhanced."

Julia breathed easier as Melissa became absorbed in the scenery photos. But her finger trembled against the mouse pad when the first shot of Vitale's house came up. "This is Vitale's home. He built it himself along with almost all of the furniture." She tried to steer attention away from the man in the picture and onto the house or garden or whatever piece of art was showing.

Close-ups of flowers gave her a respite, but then the screensaver photo came up and her breath caught as it always did. She cleared her throat. "I was out in the garden taking pictures one morning, and I couldn't resist this shot."

"I don't think I could have resisted *him*."

Julia tapped the mouse pad absently. "This is the Cinque Terre, which I didn't get to hike, but I did get to walk for a bit." Her finger froze as an image hit the screen. She and Vitale kissing on the Via dell'Amore. She took a fortifying breath and met Melissa's stunned look head-on.

"You hooked up." Melissa's eyes darted from the monitor to her mother and back several times.

"No," Julia protested. "We didn't 'hook up.' "

Melissa's eyebrows disappeared under her bangs and her grin stretched across her face. "Yes, you did! I can see it on your face. You totally hooked up with an Italian hottie!"

"It wasn't a hookup. It was . . . it was more than that. We . . . enjoyed each other's company." She tapped through the photos of embraces, looking for safer ones. "This is the market where we had lunch."

Melissa gave it a quick glance. "Pretty." But she obviously wouldn't be deterred from the other line of conversation. "Omigod, my mom had a fling! Tell me about it." She held her palm up. "No embarrassing details, just the cool stuff."

Cool stuff. "Well, he doesn't have a car, so we traveled around on a Benelli motorcycle."

Melissa smacked her hand across her eyes. "Oh, man, I can't see my mother riding around on the back of a motorcycle! With an Italian stallion!"

The word choice vibrated a disconcerting thrum through Julia. "It wasn't just a fun fling," she blurted, sounding defensive. She bit her tongue to slow it down. "I mean, not that I really believe it, but he says he loves me . . ." Her stomach tightened around the cobbler she'd eaten.

Melissa's sarcastic snort spoke volumes. "Don't they always?"

The warning in the words put a blip on Julia's mom-radar. "Why do you say that?"

Melissa's lips pressed together in a thin line before she spoke. "I mean, what is it with guys that they can use the L-word without batting an eye, and fools that we are, we lap it up and believe everything they tell us?" She grabbed a throw pillow and hugged it to her chest. "If he really loved you, he'd be here with you, right? But he's not. And it's one of your worst times."

"Well, like I said, I didn't really fall for his line. But in his defense . . ." Not quite sure *why* was she feeling a need to defend him, she pressed on. "He is, after all, in Italy."

"*Where* doesn't make any difference. He's not *here*. He's in Italy or Alaska, or . . . or Kamchatka." Melissa's inflection on the last word made it sound like she was cursing.

What? Julia's mouth dropped the words it had prepared. "Kamchatka?" She had the feeling *he* no longer referred to Vitale.

"It's a Russian peninsula, not far from Alaska but very remote." Tears welled up in Melissa's big green eyes. "Michael left five days ago on an expedition to study the brown bears there."

"Oh, baby, I noticed you'd hardly mentioned him since you got home, but I didn't want to pry." Julia scooted over onto the bed and pulled her close. "Why didn't you say something sooner?"

"I don't know. Y'all had Gram to worry about. And honestly? I felt stupid, I guess." Melissa buried her face against Julia's chest. "I followed him to Alaska and within a few months he takes off and goes to Kamchatka. What does that say about our relationship?"

"I don't know. Maybe that he thinks it's strong enough to survive a separation?"

"Nine months, maybe a year, with little to no contact?" She smacked the pillow and tossed it away. "That's not separation— that's divorce."

Wow. That was perceptive. The gelled hair spikes on the back of Melissa's head tickled as Julia's palm smoothed across them.

"I want him to follow his dream," Melissa continued. "Really, I do. I guess I just wanted that dream to include being with me."

"You're young, sweetie. You have lots of time."

"I know. These are the best years of my life, which is why I wanted to spend them with Michael. I moved to Alaska so we could be together. And now we're not."

The misery in Melissa's tone broke Julia's heart. "If you're unhappy up there, you can come home."

Melissa shook her head. "Oh, I like it. It's exciting getting to experience a different part of the world. And I love my job." She sniffed. "I'm afraid his leaving says something about our relationship he couldn't admit consciously yet. I'm beginning to wonder if I can count on him. I mean, I knew Gram was dying and I was prepared for that. But what if it'd been something else? Something unexpected and horrible? What if something happened to you or Dad? He wouldn't have been there for that either."

Julia's heart ached that her precious baby was having to learn one of life's hard lessons so early—that you couldn't always depend on other people. She cupped Melissa's chin and raised it so she could look her directly in the eye. "You would face it like the strong woman you are, and you would deal with it."

The chin in her hand wobbled in protest. "But it's okay to lean on other people sometimes, too. That's what love's all about, isn't it? Being there for each other? I mean, I'm not strong like you are, Mom. The things you've been through. Taking care of Gram. Cancer. Dad." She stopped abruptly, catching her bottom lip between her teeth. So she *did* know—or suspected. "You handle everything by yourself. You're so solid and so . . . logical."

"Most of that comes with age, sweetheart. You'll learn. And you know your dad and I will always be here for you."

Melissa's lips pursed, and her eyes closed briefly before opening and locking back on Julia's. "Mom?" She hesitated as her eyes cut back toward the computer monitor. "Do you think you and Dad are ever going to get back together?"

Julia's spine stiffened at the question, but before she could answer, Melissa went on.

"I've been watching the two of you since I got home. It's plain as day Dad's still crazy in love with you. It's all over him when he looks at you. You're more guarded, but there still seems to be something there. . . ."

Julia could hear the wistfulness, knew what her child wanted the answer to be, and she hated to disappoint her, but this was something she couldn't fix any more than she could whatever was going on with Michael. "There will always be 'something there,' baby. It's *you*. You unite us." She shook her head. "But, no, we won't ever be together again as a couple. I'm sorry."

Tears started to slide down Melissa's face, and each one of them burned Julia's heart like drops of acid. She reached for a tissue and dabbed them away.

"Love sucks," Melissa whispered.

Julia shook her head again. "No, love doesn't suck. Love's wonderful when it's right."

"Can we finish your pictures tomorrow?" Melissa drew a jagged breath. "I think I want to go to bed after all."

"Sure. There were only a few left anyway." *Of the beach, which I wouldn't show you.* "Frank called about Hettie shortly after that last one."

Melissa stood up and grabbed another tissue. "Sorry I've been weepy. Everything hit me at once." She smiled a sad smile, tight and forced.

"Don't ever apologize for your feelings." Julia kissed her daughter's forehead. "You'll get them sorted out and you'll do the right thing about Michael. I'm sure of it." The logical, prophetic words landed heavy in her chest.

Melissa gave her a long hug, then slipped out, closing the door behind her.

Julia moved back to the chair in front of the computer and sat down hard. She tapped the mouse pad through the photos of Vitale's work until she came to the pictures of her on the beach.

She stared at herself. Topless. Carefree. Exposed to the world. She didn't even know the woman she was looking at. That woman had vanished sometime during the stress of the last few weeks.

Julietta was indeed fantasy. Not life. Not logical.

She didn't even exist except in photos.

The real Julia had a home to take care of and a business to run. Responsibilities.

She fingered the silver flip-flop that had lain at the base of her throat since Vitale placed it there. A memento of a beautiful summer . . . *fling*. Her arms felt leaden as she reached behind her neck and undid the clasp.

Then she pulled out the drawer of her jewelry chest and dropped it in.

CHAPTER 27

Camille glanced up from the box she was opening when Julia entered the office. Her face creased in concern. "You shouldn't be here. You should take off at least until Monday."

"I'm only going to stay until Melissa and Frank finish their golf round." Julia frowned when she saw the large box Camille had been cutting into and all the others scattered around her desk. "And you shouldn't be doing that. I thought we agreed I would take care of the heavy stuff."

"I didn't touch any of it except with this." Camille held up the box cutter. "Promise." She crossed her heart with her other hand. "James is taking excellent care of me. He came in with me yesterday after we left your house, and he moved everything right here so it would be handy."

"How are you feeling?" The question was rhetorical. Camille already had that pregnant woman glow about her, which people chalked up to the vitamins, but Julia suspected was more from happiness. "You look wonderful," she added.

Camille patted her tummy and a smile spread across her face. "Fine. So far so good."

"Well, I have an idea, which is why I came in."

Camille narrowed her eyes. "It's not gonna involve the two of us posing naked for a calendar or anything, is it? 'Cause my body's not gonna be at its best for the next few months."

Narrowing her eyes in response, Julia chuckled. "Are you channeling Hettie?"

Camille gave a fake evil laugh and patted her tummy again. "I hope so."

"Me too." Julia grinned and gave her a wink. Snatching the phone book off the counter, she flipped through it as she answered Camille's original question. "I know in the next couple of months I'm going to have to decide on some major changes here, but last night, I came up with a small one that I think will get us by for now. I'm going to call Tanya Fields at the Placement Office at the college. Students are always looking for part-time work. We'll hire a stout young man to come in a couple of hours a day to move this stuff and help around here."

"Oh, great idea." Camille gave her a high five. "And tell her we want our money's worth, so she should send a good-looking one that'll take his shirt off and strut around showing off his six-pack." She reached into an opened box and pulled out the Villa de Luca label and pointed at Vitale's picture. "One that looks like this."

Julia's forced laugh came out on a staccato beat. "Nobody else looks like that."

Camille eyed the photo and grunted. "Mmmm! That is one fine specimen of human masculinity." She licked her lips appreciatively.

Julia searched for the Placement Office number, and once she found it she lost no time making the call. She'd been spinning her wheels around here for a few weeks and it was time to do something productive.

As soon as Tanya Fields heard Julia's request, she came up with a name. "Bryan Thomas. Great kid. IT major. Big guy and he's looking for work. When shall I send him by?"

"Hold on." Julia moved the phone away from her ear. "Tanya has somebody. Is next Monday good?"

Camille gave her a thumbs-up.

"How about Monday afternoon?" Julia said.

"Okay, then. I'll give him a call and tell him he has an interview next Monday at two. If that doesn't work for him, I'll give you a call back."

Julia thanked her and hung up. "He'll be here Monday at two."

"That should work out fine." Camille looked at her watch. "I'm going to Lucinda Sherril's house now. I told her I'd drop those blind samples by and measure the windows today." She shook a finger at Julia. "And you need to go on home."

"I won't stay long," Julia promised.

Camille gave her hand a sympathetic pat. "I'll put the BE BACK LATER sign on the door."

"Thanks."

Camille left and Julia started to examine the boxes. Five were from Italy, and two of them bore the Villa de Luca emblem on the return address.

She grasped Camille's abandoned box cutter and slit the largest box. The bubble wrap and Styrofoam pulled away to reveal one of Vitale's ornately carved washstands.

Julia's breath caught in her throat. She forced air through the constricted muscles as she smoothed her hands across the delicate scrolls.

Assuming the small box held the knobs and handles for the washstand, she sat it on top, determined to deal with it when she could breathe easier. But her eyes scanned the address label and her breath came to a complete halt this time. The small package was addressed to her personally, not the firm.

With shaky hands, she sliced through the cardboard to find a mass of bubble wrap. She took it out and examined it closely. A small box hung suspended by all the protective layers around it. Hardware shouldn't require that much cushioning. Besides, the package was much too light.

As she carefully unwrapped it, the plastic fell away to reveal a carved wooden box. On the top, a small white card had been attached. And on that card, one handwritten word—*Julietta*. A gift from Vitale? She didn't know whether to be happy or sad.

She used a fingernail to cut through the tape at the sides, not trusting the box cutter on the beautiful wood. More bubble wrap inside. She plucked at the tape that held it, but her fingers shook and made it difficult to get a grip. At last she did, and the plastic dropped away to reveal a circle carved of wood and another small card.

Examining the circle closely, she could see it was a bracelet, hinged in back. The design was two arms—two strong arms with muscles intricately detailed by the passion of the artist—with hands that closed together to form the clasp. The wood was stained a deep brown and polished to a high luster. She gasped as she recognized the color as Vitale's skin tone.

She unfolded the card. Vitale's bold scrawl filled the inside. *I hold you.*

The wood warmed against her skin when she slipped it around her wrist, and she closed her eyes and imagined herself wrapped in Vitale's arms. She glided her fingertips across the bracelet, marveling again at its beauty, its intricacy . . . the love that had gone into the details.

I hold you. He was doing his best to "fix" things for her—to make her feel better and to be with her in the only way he could.

With the force of a knockout punch, understanding shook her. Vitale was a man of his word. Hadn't he told her that repeatedly?

He loved her.

He hadn't been feeding her lines just to get a hookup. It was more than that. Her heart had known all along it was more than that. The bracelet was Vitale's way of showing his love in the most intimate way he could across the miles.

And . . . *oh God!* She loved him, too. Her heart had known that as well.

She stood still, allowing the joy to consume her heart for one long, blissful moment.

And then her brain came out of *sleep* mode.

She and Vitale loved each other. What did that change? They still belonged to different generations. She still couldn't give him children. An ocean still separated them. If she wrote him and told him how she truly felt, which of their major stumbling blocks would change?

None.

So what was the use of putting either one of them through that? There wasn't any.

The double loss of what she'd had with Hettie and what she might have had with Vitale if things had been different gushed out on a sob then, followed by another and another, making her thankful Camille had locked the door.

Her conscience told her she should send the bracelet back, but for once, she refused to let her conscience goad her into giving up something she wanted to have for purely selfish reasons.

But there was something she had to do immediately. She went straight for her computer and pulled up her personal e-mail, dashing off a message.

> Vitale,
> I want you to know how grateful I am for everything—the hospitality, the encouragement, the gift. You are a good friend, and I cherish that friendship. But your words of love make me uncomfortable. We both know that kind of relationship between us isn't possible, and there is no use pretending. We're separated by age and distance—two things we're unable to do anything about.

She stopped. The muscles at the back of her neck tightened to the point of pain, and she pressed her fingertips into them, trying to massage away the tension.

She forced her fingers onto the keys again.

> I don't want to lose you out of my life, but can we stop the talk of love and just be friends?
> Please believe I care for you very much,
> Julietta

As she pressed the send button, she knew she was saying their final good-bye. No way would Vitale accept her offer of friendship. He had too much pride.

The hot flash started in her chest and crept up her neck, perspiration breaking out above her lip and then on her forehead, mixing with the tears that streaked her face. She imagined the fluids as a cleansing force, purging Vitale from her system.

It wouldn't happen instantly. Unlike the cancer, there wasn't an operation that could remove him from her heart.

She grimaced as she realized the biggest difference between healing from cancer and healing from love. When she was diagnosed, she wasn't even aware the cancer was there.

No pain.

On the other hand, letting go of Vitale felt like a huge chunk of her heart and soul had been carved out of her with a dull knife.

"You're right, Melissa," she said aloud. "Love sucks."

CHAPTER 28

"Let me check my e-mail first." Vitale caught Adrianna before she sat down. "And then you can have the computer again."

He was eager to get to the studio...eager to check out the model he'd completed during the wee hours of the morning. He'd been pleased with his work at two a.m., but whether he would still be pleased at ten remained to be seen. Sometimes, a few hours made a huge difference in the visual acuity of his critical eye.

Adrianna nodded and wandered off. He was vaguely aware of the sound of the bathroom door closing.

He typed in the address of his personal account, scanning the few headings until his eyes locked onto the one he was looking for.

His finger rested on the mouse button for a moment, his gut tightening instinctively. This would be the sad one, probably filled with details of Hettie's funeral. In her last post, Julietta hadn't mentioned the special gift he'd sent, and he regretted his timing had been off.

Hopefully she would find comfort in it whenever it arrived and wouldn't take it as a sign that he thought she was weak.

He continued to stall, gathering the strength to deal with his Julietta's unhappiness. Perhaps, after this message, the healing would start, and it wouldn't be too long until she was herself again. Smiling and happy, ready to take on the world . . . and him.

He pressed the mouse button, opening the message.

> Vitale,
> I want you to know how grateful I am for everything—the hospitality, the encouragement, the gift.

She had received it after all. That she was thanking him was a good sign, was it not? So why would his jaw muscles not relax?

He read on.

> You are a good friend, and I cherish that friendship. But your words of love make me uncomfortable.

Uncomfortable? His caring . . . his love made her uncomfortable? His whole body followed the way of his jaws, tightening into hard knots.

He read the rest and then started at the beginning again, reading each sentence slowly, feeling the weight of each additional word in his heart, which, by the end of the message, dangled somewhere between his feet. He could tell that because he stepped all over it as he surged out of the chair.

No, it wasn't he who'd stepped all over it.

Julietta had walked all over it and all over him in the process.

She wanted to just be friends after all they'd meant to each other?

The anger roared from him and he slammed his fist into the opposite palm.

"Vitale?"

He swung around to find Adrianna's eyes wide with concern. "What's wrong?"

Anger stifled his breath, blocked his voice. "Julietta" was the only thing that escaped his snarled lips, and it came out on a growl.

"What about Julietta? Is she okay?"

"I do not want to be only her friend." He jabbed a finger toward the computer. "Stop the messages from her. Fix it so there can be no more messages from her. Ever."

"Vitale." Adrianna's tone begged him to be reasonable as her eyes softened with understanding and—*Damn it!*—pity.

He couldn't stand that look. For too many years he'd seen that look in everyone's eyes. Enough years to fill a lifetime. And he wouldn't stand for it anymore.

"No more messages from her, Adrianna." He ground the words out through a still tightly clamped jaw. "Ever."

He stormed out of the house, heading for his cycle. A ride was what he needed. Wind in his face and his hair, clearing his head of the fairy dust Julietta Berkwith had used to desensitize him from the real world.

Yes, a ride would be good. But he needed to do something else first.

He turned with a purposeful stride that took him into the studio. Once there, he went straight for the model he'd worked so diligently on. He snatched it up, prepared to fling it against the wall. The plasticine was pliable and wouldn't break, but it would smash and flatten. Then he would place it on the shelf as a reminder of how his heart felt at that moment.

He raised it over his head just as a warm breeze came through the window, catching him in the face, startling him.

He lowered the model and looked at it. Really looked at it. This was *his* creation. Something he had worked hard on. A goal he saw with his heart.

For too long, he'd allowed others to destroy what he believed in. In the process, he'd almost allowed them to destroy him.

He was a different man now.

This piece was beautiful, and on a greater scale, it was perfect for Mario's pool. Why should he allow someone else to destroy that vision?

He took a deep breath. Because it wasn't someone else who was about to destroy the vision. He was the one holding it in his hands.

He placed it back on the table, looking at it with his artist's eye rather his emotion.

Without a second thought he started to clear his large work table.

He had hours ... days ... perhaps even months of hard work before him.

But first, he changed the damn CD from Julietta's happy music to Wagner's *Tristan und Isolde.*

A strange feeling of déjà vu passed over Julia, causing an involuntary shudder to run up her spine.

She and Frank were seated in Grayson Chapman's office—in the same chairs, the same position even—signing their names to the legal documents placed in front of them. It was like a rerun of the day they signed their divorce papers.

"One more." Grayson placed the agreement he'd drawn up in front of them—the one that passed ownership of Julia's half of Hettie's house to Frank.

One more. The words chased away the anxious tingle, replaced it with calm resolve.

The two weeks since Hettie's death had passed quickly. Much too soon, Melissa had gone back to her life in Alaska, still fretting about her relationship with Michael, but showing a strength and a resilience Julia knew would lead her to the correct decision.

A couple of days before she left, Julia showed her the bracelet and told her the truth about her feelings for Vitale. Once she'd gotten past her mortification that Julia had broken things off by e-mail, she'd shown a true woman-to-woman sympathy.

"I want you to fall in love again, Mom," she'd said. "I may not've come across that way the other night, but that was my selfishness talking. I really do want you to find someone. And it needs to be somebody really different from Dad. You're ..." She'd paused, and given a grin that looked so much like Hettie's, Julia's breath had stopped. "Different now."

The sincerity in her daughter's eyes opened a lock on Julia's heart. She'd never realized she was waiting for Melissa's permission to move on.

Bryan, the young man from the college, was working out well, allowing both Julia and Camille more time to spend directly with customers. That pleasant side effect had given Julia time to start on the remodeling plans for Hettie's house, which would officially be Frank's house as soon as she finished signing her name.

She hurried to date the form, set the pen down, and leaned back in the chair with a smile. As of this afternoon, Frank had his own place and wouldn't be under her roof anymore.

Ever.

Grayson handed the papers to his secretary with instructions to copy them for Julia and Franklin. "We'll keep the originals here in our files," he explained. "But we'll give you copies to put in your lockboxes or safes." He picked up the tennis ball that sat on his desk and squeezed it absently. "While we're waiting, do you have any more questions I can answer?"

Julia didn't have any. Everything had come together seamlessly, thanks to Hettie's will. The sizable amount they each inherited had allowed Frank to buy out Julia's half of the house and would allow him to redo it to his taste and still have some leftover.

She shook her head in answer to Grayson's question, so he turned to Frank.

"I'm satisfied," Frank answered. "You, Jules?"

"I'm good with everything," she said, though the word *good* hardly seemed adequate. She would now have enough cushion in her savings accounts to live comfortably, provided she didn't make any major investment blunders.

Grayson chuckled. "I wish all my clients were as easy as you two."

"You earned your pay with us the last time around." She regretted the flippant comment when Frank's mouth drew down at the corners. She'd wanted to get through this with as little discomfort as possible.

She turned the conversation to the twins, who were due any day now, and Grayson dove in. It was fun to see a man absolutely giddy about parenthood. Frank had been that way, too, and she couldn't keep from sharing a knowing smile with her ex as they listened to the attorney going on and on.

Grayson talked until his secretary returned with the copies

placed in light blue, legal-looking leather folders—one for each of them. He flipped through them quickly, then folded them over and closed them with a tab that snapped. He handed the documents over. "And that's that."

Julia stood and took hers, ready to leave, pausing to shake the attorney's hand. "Thanks so much. I hope I don't need to see you for a long time. Except socially, of course."

"Well, you know where I am if you need me." He shook hands with Frank, and they made a hasty exit.

"Want to grab a bite?" Frank pointed toward Market Square as they walked to the car. "It's almost lunch."

Although Julia was hungry, she was more anxious to get Frank on his way to his new home and get back the life she'd made for herself. "I'm not very hungry," she lied.

They made small talk on the way back to the house. Once there, Julia went straight to her room to change clothes and then went to the kitchen for a bottle of water.

She'd just gotten one from the fridge when she heard Frank shuffle down the steps with his luggage and drop it by the door. He came into the kitchen empty-handed.

"I guess that's it." The tightness around his eyes told her he wasn't as pleased about his leaving as she was. He walked over to where she stood, stopping only a foot from her. "But it doesn't have to be."

She sat her water on the island. "Yeah, it does."

He moved so quickly, she didn't have time to react. His arms came around her and his lips pressed against hers in a kiss that belied both passion and desperation. Her bent arms were caught between them, giving her little leverage to push, but push she did. He clutched her tighter, leaning her back. The edge of the granite countertop dug annoyingly into the small of her back.

She tore her mouth from his. "Frank! Stop it!" With all the strength she could muster in the awkward position, she pushed against him until he finally stepped back away from her. She gasped and pressed the back of her hand against her mouth. "What in the hell was that about? Get out." She pointed toward the door.

"No." He planted his feet and clasped his arms across his chest in a defiant stance. "Not until you hear what I have to say. I've been happier here with you the past month than I've been the past ten years of my life. I love you, Jules. You know I do. I love you, and I don't want to leave. I want to be with you."

Julia closed her eyes and raised her hand to stop him, blocking off the reality for a split second in order to regain her composure. "Don't do this," she whispered.

He grabbed the hand she held up, not hurting it, but holding too tightly for her to pull loose. "I have to do this. I refuse to walk out of here without knowing I tried everything. Maybe I won't have to walk out of here at all."

Julia's eyes flew open. "You didn't have trouble walking out the last time." The words spewed out as blood pumped harder through her veins.

"I know." Frank nodded and gave a long blink. "I was horrible... such a coward. I couldn't stand to watch what you were going through. It scared the hell out of me. And I didn't want you to know how scared I was." He dropped her hand, making a sweeping motion with his arm. "I tried to run away from it all. Sickness. Aging. The inevitable." His finger traced down her arm lightly, and she brushed it away. "Ludicrous as that sounds, it's true," he continued. "But the past two years have been like a spiritual awakening for me. I've learned to be happy with where I am in life... learned what's truly important. Most of all, I've learned what a treasure I had in you, and how stupid I was to ever let you go." He stepped toward her again.

She jammed a finger into his chest and gritted her teeth. "Get out of my space."

He gave her a smirk but backed a step away just the same. "Look. I don't care that you fell in love in Italy—"

Julia gasped. "Melissa told you?"

"She didn't have to tell me. It was written all over you when I saw you at the hospital." His mouth drooped into a frown. "Your face, the new hair, the new attitude..."

"It's none of your business," she snapped, hating she was letting him get under her skin. She thought she was beyond the anger, *wanted* to be beyond the anger.

"I'm just saying, I don't care. It's obviously over. I can tell that, too." He reached to touch her again, but the warning look she shot him sent his hand to rub the back of his neck instead. "I know you, Jules . . . better than anybody. You're the most loyal person I've ever known. When you love, you give it all you've got. So you didn't really love him or you'd still be trying."

"You're deluding yourself, Frank. You may have known me at the beginning, but you didn't keep up with the refresher courses." She kept her expression impassive, trying not to let him know he'd found the chink in her armor. "If you want to talk about us, then I'm ready. But I refuse to be goaded into talking with you about anything personal."

"We had too many years, Jules. Your love for me wouldn't simply evaporate."

"You're right about that," she admitted, able to think straight again. "My love for you didn't 'simply evaporate' in a matter of days or weeks or months. It took a long time and a lot of tears. And maybe it didn't go away. Maybe the tears carved it into a different shape, or maybe the pain sculp . . . sculpted it." She stammered, immediately regretting her word choices. "All I know is it evolved into something else." A settling calmness stole over her as the words rang true in her soul. She cleared her throat, wanting her voice to be strong and sure so there would be no mistaking what she said. "I don't love you, Frank. Not that way. Not anymore."

His face contorted with pain. "Yes, you do. You're only saying that to hurt me the same way I hurt you."

She searched her heart, and it told her he was wrong. "No, I have no desire to hurt you. I used to, but it's gone now." Her reasons seemed so logical to her now—crystal clear, as though she were viewing them under a magnifying glass. "That's why I could let you stay here. That's why I've been careful about what I said about my personal life around you." Her voice vibrated with growing emotion. "I don't *need* to hurt you. There was no threat of any old feelings reappearing because those feelings have vanished."

He shook his head more vehemently. "You can get the feelings back. They're there."

"You're not hearing me, Frank, and you *need* to hear me. I still have feelings for you, but they're not the same kind of feelings I used to have. You're like an old friend. Like Earl." Her eyes pleaded with him to understand. "I don't want to hurt you, but I also don't *want* you. The desire I felt for you is gone. I want you to be happy, yes, but I want me to be happy more. I wouldn't be happy with you. I'm sorry." She could feel his pain, but it was only that—*his pain.*

Frank's eyes clouded. He dropped his gaze before letting out a sigh that shook his core. "You have nothing to be sorry for. You gave me everything. Melissa. Your love. Your loyalty. I'm the one who's sorry." His eyes found hers again. "I'm sorry for leaving you when you needed me most. Sorry for distracting your attention when you should've been concentrating on your health. Can you forgive me?"

Her heart twisted. She wasn't to that point. "Someday, maybe. But not yet."

His chin quivered, but he nodded. "Jules, I'm sorry for making you feel like anything less than the beautiful person you are."

"You never even saw me before." Emotion strangled her words to a whisper. "I was invisible to you."

Frank's eyes remained locked on hers. "Well, you're not invisible to me now. I see you clearly, and you're beautiful. Inside and out."

"I don't know about beautiful." She shrugged. "But I'm interesting. I'll always be a work-in-progress, I think."

Frank gave her a tender smile. "A masterpiece." His voice was husky with emotion. He cleared his throat and clapped his hands together. "Well, I'd best be getting out of here." He took her hand, clasping it between his. "Thanks for taking me in."

She nodded. "You earned your keep. Thanks for all the cooking and handiwork you did around here."

He patted her hand and gave a long, dramatic sigh. "Well, like I said before, that's it."

She watched him leave, scanning her heart for any sign of disappointment or remorse, but there was none.

Only a sense of profound relief.

* * *

"The molds are loaded...so whenever you're ready." Vitale walked up behind Adrianna, who was hunched over the computer. He laid his hands on her shoulders, pressing his thumbs into the tight muscles and massaging them. She winced at even the small amount of pressure he applied, which made him wince inwardly at how hard he'd been driving her lately. "And take tomorrow off. You're going to be bent over like an old woman if you keep this up."

She rolled her shoulders forward and back a few times and leaned her head to both sides to stretch her neck. "I have seen computer desks that will raise and lower so you can stand or sit. Maybe we should get one? And I think I'll bring one of those stability balls to sit on. I have read doing that will keep your core muscles engaged."

The image of his sister sitting on a ball to work brought a chuckle. "Whatever you want to buy is fine with me. I want to keep my assistant happy."

Not having to worry about the cost, as long as it was within reason, was fabulously freeing. They were making a good living. Not getting rich by any means. But he was comfortable, and he was keeping his family comfortable. Even Papà's attitude had shifted and he'd started to show an interest in the business, which was causing Vitale to think in terms of how to use his father's carpentry skills in his designs. Structures to provide shade...benches or different types of seating...platforms that could place sculptures at different heights for optimum viewing—Papà would be a master at that type of work. And it would allow him to move away from the backbreaking work taking its toll on his aging body.

"Are you sure you don't want to go with me?" Adrianna stood and stretched her arms over her head. "It would do you good to get out...away from here for a while."

Much as he'd like to go, the trip to the foundry near Pisa would take the entire day, and Vitale didn't have the time to spare.

He shook his head and pointed to the spreadsheet she'd been working on. "The orders are pouring in too quickly for me to keep up with production now. Orabella and Cesare are coming by for training this afternoon. And Papà and I are going to work on their greenhouses tomorrow." The fact his father had asked him when he would be available rather than scheduling the work and telling Vitale after the fact spoke volumes.

With autumn in the air, the young couple's landscaping business had started to wane. Papà had come up with the idea to build them greenhouses so they could save money by starting their own plants from seed. And Vitale had decided to employ them through the winter months to help him with finishing his artwork. He always hand-sanded the small bronze pieces. It was delicate work, but until now he had the time—something he found in short supply these days.

But that was fine. Staying busy kept his mind off Julietta. Until he went to bed. Even with his body exhausted and begging for sleep, memories often kept him awake.

What plagued him the most was not knowing whether or not she'd gone back to Frank.

It was difficult to imagine her doing that, considering the way her ex had devastated her, and Vitale hoped she had not. Hoped she had seen herself worthy of better treatment than that.

And so, when he pictured her in his head at night, she was sleeping alone . . . fitfully. Dreaming of him and the time they shared.

It kept his heart softened toward her enough that he could do what needed to be done, although it fell just short of forgiveness.

He had never been good at that—Luciana's only complaint about his character.

"Learn to forgive, Vitale," she would whisper against his pouting lips. "Not for the other person. For you."

Like his art, he was still a work-in-progress, as evidenced by the envelope addressed to Julietta Adrianna held up.

"Are you sure you want to do this?" Her eyes flashed the message she was giving him one last chance to reconsider, and the angry edge to her tone caused his jaw muscles to tighten. Adrianna was the one sibling he seldom argued with, but the discussion over this particular decision had been as heated as any he could recall.

"Yes." He hoped his tone brokered no more discussion.

"With nothing from you directly. No note. No kiss-my-ass. No anything."

"Yes." He kept his answers to one word and his tongue caged firmly behind his teeth.

"There is an old saying about burning bridges, you know." She slapped the stack of envelopes against his chest, and the *smack* echoed in his heart.

"But the bridge from Italy to America is too far, yes? A bridge that can never be crossed is of no use to anyone."

She glared at him for a moment longer, then, with a final disgusted huff, she turned and left.

He stared at the spreadsheet on the screen but didn't really see it.

Perhaps he had been too hasty in his actions, but Julietta had made it clear that the type of relationship he wanted was over.

It was she who set fire to the bridge.

He just hoped to hell the fire in his heart would burn itself out quickly.

Eleven days had passed since Frank had moved out, and this morning was the first time Julia had woken without sniffing for the scent of bacon. She'd read somewhere that it took eleven times to make something a habit. Perhaps it was true after all.

She'd gotten up with one goal in mind—to get her life back to normal and to start making firm plans about the business. The events of the summer had taken their toll on her both emotionally and physically. She went to the office, prepared to do battle with the pile of paperwork threatening to take control of her desk. And she was determined to go to the gym after work or go for a run.

The self-pity wallow had gone on long enough.

Camille was fabric shopping for dining room chair covers with Madge Poindexter, and Bryan was obviously overjoyed to be tinkering with Camille's computer in her absence. He was a pleasant kid, eager to please, and his computer skills were proving to be an additional boon.

Already, he'd made suggestions and installed software that improved their bookkeeping system. Now, in his spare time, he was designing spreadsheets for their inventory.

With the trashcan at her side, Julia sorted through the pile of mail Camille had left on her desk. There was very little of interest, mostly advertisements and credit card offers, until her eyes fell on the return address of Lerici, Italy.

The handwriting on the envelope wasn't Vitale's, but the address was. In one quick movement, the letter opener sliced through the heavy paper. Inside, she found a sheet of paper and a check, and her eyes flew to the signature first. Adrianna. Not Vitale.

> *Dear Julietta,*
> *Thank you very much for the monetary investment you were willing to make in Villa de Luca. As the company is doing well at this time, Vitale would like to repay his debt to you. Please accept this check with his sincere appreciation.*

Ouch! He couldn't write her himself? That stung.

The check was for more than she paid for the development of the Web site. The itemization showed that he'd also paid her for the hours she spent photographing his pieces.

She didn't want payment for those things. Didn't want this money. Putting a monetary value on what they'd had together only cheapened it. She crumpled the check in her fist as anger flashed through her.

But why should this surprise her? She was the one who essentially broke things off—sending that e-mail, all the while knowing how he would take it. Of course, he wouldn't want her investment hanging over his head—a reminder of unrequited love that she'd never bothered to tell him wasn't unrequited at all.

She laid the check on her desk and smoothed it with her palm, the anger cooled now. She didn't want the money, but he needed to settle up with her for closure.

His way of *fixing* the situation and keeping his pride intact.

She could allow him that . . . sort of.

A few keystrokes on her computer brought up the online catalog for Villa de Luca. She clicked through the items until she found one whose price was almost a perfect match for the amount of the check.

Available for pre-order.

It was a piece she hadn't photographed, but one she was familiar with. Apparently, he'd kept the mold. Her eyes blurred, but she blinked away the nostalgia and went through the ordering process.

Having a de Luca piece of her own would invest the money back in his company and be a lovely memento of the most remarkable time of her life.

And a constant reminder of what might have been . . .

She clicked the button to finalize the order before she could change her mind.

CHAPTER 29

The void left by the loss of Hettie was difficult to fill. It was the circle of life, after all, Julia told herself, and she tried to keep her focus on the many, many ways Hettie had enriched her life and not dwell on the hole left in her heart.

She went back to the gym with a new commitment to stay healthy and fit and to accept her scars as proof of a life reclaimed, and she threw herself into her work with zeal, determined to find the perfect answer to the question of how the business needed to evolve over the next few months in regards to Camille's departure.

She went about her work with more confidence now, making bold suggestions where she'd always played it safe before. Camille had referred to one of Julia's latest purchases—a female figure sculpted in opal and covered in wax, which brought out exquisite colors and details—as "eerily beautiful and collector worthy."

She'd even had the house painted inside and out. For the first time since she and Frank bought it, she stepped away from the white exterior, opting for gray with white trim, and had gone so far as choosing a romantic pink for her bedroom.

She seldom listened to her *Happy* playlist anymore. Instead, she'd traded it for the *Calm* list in an attempt to quiet her mind enough to sleep at night.

As proof that time was moving on, the heat of August eventually gave way to the cooler days of September, followed by the frosts of October.

Too often Julia found herself flipping through professional journals or scanning their ads for employment, searching for the missing link in her quest to find what she wanted most to be when she grew up.

So it came as no big surprise when Frank's voice startled her from her daydream as she raked the leaves into large, crispy piles on her front lawn. "Jules, you okay?"

"Oh, sorry. Yeah, I'm fine." She hadn't noticed how hot she was until she stopped moving. She unbuttoned the barn coat she was wearing.

Frank's eyes dropped to her chest and widened in surprise.

A flash of irritation shot through her, but it dissolved when she followed his gaze. Perspiration had soaked her red T-shirt, making a giant target on her chest that would be difficult to ignore. "Guess I've worked up quite a sweat," she admitted.

Frank looked around at the piles. "You need some help?"

They'd been seeing each other almost daily as work on his new home progressed, and Julia found it easier to be around him. Not a true friendship, by any means. She still battled daily with forgiveness. But she also knew hate destroyed the vessel that carried it, and she didn't want any more erosion to her heart.

The two of them had come a long way from where they started, but they still had a long way to go.

"No, but thanks," she answered. "I'm enjoying it. I'm thirsty, though. You want a soda or a cup of coffee?" She motioned to the house.

"No." Frank reached into his jacket pocket and pulled out a pink envelope. "I wanted to drop this by."

The envelope he held out had Julia's name written across the front. She recognized Hettie's handwriting. "What's this?" She held the rake in the crook of her elbow and took the envelope, running her fingertips across the dark rose-colored ink.

"I don't know." Frank shrugged. "I finally got around to going through Mom's things that I brought home from the nursing home. This was in a side pocket of her purse."

Julia held it up. Against the sunlight, she could see writing. "I, um..." Emotion swelled in her throat. She tried ineffectually to swallow it away. "I think it's a letter."

"Yeah, that's what I thought, too."

Julia was too overcome to speak. A letter. From Hettie. She gripped it at both ends, afraid if she loosened her hold, it might dissolve into thin air.

Frank shifted uncomfortably, seemingly caught between curiosity and sensing she wanted to be alone when she read it. Thankfully, his best instincts prevailed this time. Maybe he was growing as well. "Well, I gotta be going." He threw a thumb over his shoulder toward his car. "I've got raking that needs to be done, too."

Julia clutched the letter to her heart, feeling the accelerated pounding against her knuckles. "Thanks, Frank."

He waved. "Sorry I didn't find it sooner."

As his car pulled away, Julia marveled again at the precious object she held in her hand. She dropped the rake onto the leaf pile and hurried into the house.

Her finger trembled as she started to ease it under the glued flap. *This is a treasure. Don't rip it.*

She flew into the kitchen where she kept the odds-and-ends basket containing the letter opener. It sliced through the flap easily, despite her shaky hand.

Her knees buckled when she pulled the paper out and read the first line.

Dearest Julia, Daughter of my Heart.

The words were written in Hettie's labored hand—uneven henscratching that zigzagged above and below the imaginary line—and it was one of the most beautiful sights Julia had ever seen.

She fought the urge to let her eyes roam any farther down the page until she felt the solid oak chair beneath her. A deep breath stabilized her, and she continued.

If you're reading this, I'm probably not physically with you anymore; otherwise, you shouldn't have gone snooping through an old woman's purse.

You just left here, headed for Italy, and from the way I feel, I'm not sure I'll see you return. There are a few motherly things I need you to know. I write them rather than tell them because you'll listen better this way.

First of all, thank you for your love and care. You are everything I ever wanted in a daughter and then some. God blessed my life with you.

Second, I lied. I never made love with an Italian, but I always wanted to. It's time for a new man in your life. Not all of them are like Franklin. I hope you meet someone in Italy who stirs you enough to get your blood pumping again.

Julia laughed and pulled a paper napkin from the holder to wipe the wetness from her cheeks. Hettie could always make her laugh, even through her tears.

That brings me to point number three, my last one. You always say you're invisible. You're not. The world didn't stop seeing you. You stopped seeing the world. Instead of focusing your efforts toward gaining visibility, you need to focus on gaining vision. Big difference. Big gains.

I'm with you. Now open your eyes, put yourself out there, and have some fun.

With more love than I could ever show,
Hettie

Julia read the letter again and again, running her fingertips across the words, trying to touch Hettie in some metaphysical way.

The world didn't stop seeing you. You stopped seeing the world.

Had her perspective changed somewhere along the way? Starting the business had absorbed so much of her time. Then Melissa went away to college and she retreated more into her work, tried to take up the slack of time that loomed so large over her. Hettie became the focus of her attention, a surrogate child of a sort who fulfilled her nurturing need. She grinned at the thought. Some women adopted pets; she adopted a mother-in-law.

She'd certainly withdrawn when the cancer was diagnosed. The shock and fear had utterly devastated any sense of the self she thought she knew so well, left behind an empty shell that needed more than silicone to fill it up.

Looking back now, it appeared Hettie was right. *As always,* she thought wryly.

She reread the last part of the letter. *Now open your eyes, put yourself out there, and have some fun.*

"Your advice is as sound as ever, Hettie. I *do* need to put myself out there and have some fun." She folded the letter carefully and slid it back into the envelope. "The question is *how?*"

Julia's answer came a couple of weeks later during the final round of *Wheel of Fortune.* She took a bite of her glazed chicken Lean Cuisine and studied the visible letters in the Places puzzle.

"Piccadilly Square," she called out, while Pat Sajak warned the audience to stay silent.

Her telephone rang as if confirming she was the winner.

She frowned at the Unknown Caller ID that appeared on the TV screen. If this was a telemarketer, she was going to let him have it between the ears. What good was being on the No Call List if they were going to keep calling anyway?

She snatched up the phone, her voice loaded for bear. "Hello?"

There was a hesitation on the other end and then a man's voice sounding apologetic and vaguely familiar. "Um, hello. I was calling to speak with Julia Berkwith. Is she available?"

It could be a customer, so she trimmed her tone to businessy curt rather than out-and-out rude, allowing for an easy shift either way. "Yes, this is she."

"Oh, hello, Julia. This is Joe Proctor, the administrator at Manor Hill Convalescent Center."

"Hi, Joe." She quickly inserted a smile into her voice. "I remember speaking to you at Hettie's funeral. How are you?"

"I'm fine, thank you. And you? Are you doing okay?" His voice was full of genuine-sounding concern. "I know you and Mrs. Berkwith were very close."

A follow-up PR call? Not standard procedure for most nursing homes, she would bet, but a nice touch. "It's been hard, but I'm doing all right. It's nice of you to call and check."

His chuckle had an embarrassed ring to it. "Well, I did want to know you were doing okay, but that's not the only reason for my call."

Ah, some unfinished business with Hettie's account, then. "Well, then, what can I do for you?"

"Actually..." He cleared his throat. "I was hoping you would consider having dinner with me."

"Dinner?" Julia cringed. Her intonation made it sound like she was unfamiliar with the word. "You mean, like a date?"

"That's... yes, that's what I had in mind."

A date. The man was asking her on a date. Her mind whirled. Did she want to have dinner with a man? With *this* man? She didn't really know him, but he seemed very nice. "I, uh..." She stalled, trying to give her brain time to catch up to her mouth. Why not? She couldn't come up with an answer, and Hettie's advice pinged in her brain. *Now open your eyes, put yourself out there, and have some fun.*

She could do this. For Hettie. For herself. "I think I'd like that." She managed to keep the emphasis off the word *think,* although the emphasis screamed in her brain.

"Great."

Was that a sigh of relief that reverberated across the line? Julia breathed one of her own.

"I was afraid maybe you were seeing someone."

"No," she answered. "I'm not."

"I'm glad to hear that. I've been trying to work up the courage to call you for a couple of weeks." The embarrassed chuckle made a reprise. "Would Friday night work for you? I was thinking maybe Max's Bistro."

"Friday would be fine." She tried to pump some enthusiasm into her voice. "And I love Max's. It's my favorite restaurant."

"How does seven sound?"

"Perfect."

"Okay, then. I'll be at your house around seven o'clock Friday evening, and I'll make reservations for seven thirty."

"I'll be looking forward to it, Joe." Not exactly the truth, but not an out-and-out lie either.

After they said their good-byes, she set the phone down slowly. A date. A groan escaped as she slumped back into the chair. "I have a date. Dinner. *Ghah!* Three hours of making conversation while I try to keep broccoli from getting stuck between my teeth." She squeezed her eyes shut. *Why am I doing this? Why put myself through this?*

She took a hefty gulp from her wineglass.

Because it's part of putting myself out there. Changing my perspective.

She sucked in a breath and blew it out in a *whoosh*. "Okay. This is not an insurmountable task." Her chest tightened as the glazed chicken started to tap dance in her stomach.

"This is the next step, old girl." She spoke aloud again, needing the physical sound of a voice to ground her. "Change your vision of the world. You can't see what's around the corner until you make the turn."

But I hope to God when I get there, I'm not going the wrong way down a one-way street.

Vitale left the Hotel Fiori in a mild state of wonder. Minutes ago, Nicolina Egidi had agreed to hire Villa de Luca to redesign the area around the pool of her hotel. The two of them had talked as adults, keeping the conversation business casual with none of her usual sexual innuendo. It had been pleasant. He smiled. Most of all, it had been profitable.

The work wouldn't begin until late February, and it wouldn't be on such a grand scale as the Lord Byron project. But it would keep him, Orabella and Cesare, Papà, and, of course, Adrianna busy for the better part of March.

Luciana's advice to forgive had served him well in this instance. Perhaps he would give it another try . . . sometime.

He'd left his new auto parked behind the gallery after making his delivery this morning. With the happiness currently coursing through his veins, he would have preferred to have the freedom of his motorcycle on the ride home. But the auto had become a necessity with the business.

Such a good problem to have.

He rounded the corner and felt the smile break onto his face at the first sight of the small, but shiny, silver auto. His steps slowed as he recognized the form leaning against it, dressed in a tight red dress that clung to every curve and high heels that accentuated her shapely legs.

Francesca.

She pushed her sunglasses to the top of her head and took a few steps in his direction. "Hello, Vitale."

His spine stiffened as she neared. "Francesca."

"I heard you bought an auto. It's very nice." Her smile was friendly and matched her tone flawlessly.

"Thank you." He shrugged, loosening the muscles that had tightened in his shoulders at the sight of her. "Having to borrow a vehicle every day was becoming too much of a problem."

One of her eyebrows arched in question. "From what I hear, your business is doing very well, yes?"

"Yes, it's keeping me busy."

"I think it's wonderful . . . that you're sharing your success with your family. You're a good man, Vitale." A long-forgotten sincerity rang in her words, touching his heart and softening some of the edges that had grown so hard against her.

Still, he found her compliment a bit unsettling. "Yes, well . . . I should get back to work now."

She ran her fingertips along the back door and then leaned her hip against it. Crossing her arms, she looked up at him. "I miss you, Vitale. I know we won't ever again be"—she paused, choosing her words—"what we were. But I would love to be friends again."

A snort escaped him. What was with all these ex-lovers wanting to be friends? "I don't think that's possible."

He reached for the door handle, but she uncrossed her arms and laid a palm against the window edge. "You're a successful businessman. People are snatching up your art." She gave him a friendly grin. "Anything is possible."

Perhaps it was the sunshine beating down on him, or the wonder leftover from the morning's dealings with Nicolina . . . he wasn't sure. But something warmed him to the idea of reclaiming another lost friendship.

He leaned his forearms against the edge of the roof and felt the heat from it absorb into his body. Is that what forgiveness felt like? Sunshine and warmth permeating the soul?

He relaxed, leaning his head back and stretching his mouth open to release the tension in his jaws. "Maybe you're right." He dropped his eyes to meet hers. "Maybe it's time to become friends again."

Her grin stretched into a radiant smile. "That makes me so happy." She threw an arm around his neck in a quick hug. "Let's celebrate, can we? Take me for a ride."

He couldn't keep from laughing at her childlike exuberance. Nothing about Francesca had ever seemed childlike to him before. "I'm sorry, but I can't. I really do have work to do." He'd blocked off this afternoon and the next two days to work on the large piece for Mario. He was so close to completing the model for the mold, he begrudged having to take time away from it.

Her lips thrust out in a pout, but only momentarily. Then her eyes grew large. "Let's go out to dinner. It doesn't have to be any-place fancy . . . or romantic. Someplace friendly."

Dinner with Francesca could be dangerous. He hadn't had sex since Julietta left over three months ago, and one slip could put him right back into the shallow rut he'd wallowed in for so long.

But things had gone well with Nicolina and here was Francesca, so perhaps today was the day to mend broken friendships . . . the day he was to learn about the power of forgiveness.

Francesca seemed to sense the battle raging in his mind and she prudently kept quiet.

"I can't go until . . . Saturday." He eased his way into the suggestion.

Her eyes grew even wider. "Saturday is perfect. Pick me up around seven thirty. We'll go to Simba." She slipped her glasses back on, but not before he caught the gleam of pleasure shining in her eyes.

Simba was an odd choice. The music was loud and the crowd a bit rowdy, but it was casual, and the food was good for the price.

"All right," he agreed, but suddenly doubt about this being a good idea gripped his insides. He pushed the apprehension away as he pulled open the door. "Saturday. Seven thirty. Simba."

"Fabulous!" Francesca threw a kiss on a wave and dashed away . . . before he could change his mind?

The confines of the auto were warm from the sun, but it turned hot as flashes of Francesca's unfaithfulness tumbled through his mind. Anger boiled up inside him, and he felt the burning deep in the pit of his stomach.

What a fool he was. Why in the hell had he agreed to go to dinner with her?

He lowered the window to let the heat escape, taking deep breaths of the cooler outside air.

This was all about forgiveness, and this would be the most difficult one of all.

How would he know if he'd grown in that direction if he never accepted the challenge?

He kept the window lowered all the way back home to his studio, needing the constant reminder it was time for him to cool down.

CHAPTER 30

Julia and Camille both went uncharacteristically silent as the last piece of bubble wrap fell away from the iridescent orb and Julia placed it carefully in the opening of the sculpture that resembled a clamshell . . . or a sunburst folded in half.

"So, what do you think?" Julia gave the ball a nudge to set it in motion, watching it glide to the end of the curve and then back to the other end.

"It's . . ." Camille spread a hand over her chest. "It's exquisite."

"I think it'll be pretty in my front flower bed. Vitale had one set up as a fountain at his house with the orb floating back and forth. But the first one I saw was at the hotel in Lerici. As a matter of fact, it was what I was looking at when the stone fell on my toe."

Camille gave a snort and elbowed her. "You're sure you want a constant reminder of *that*?"

The tears stinging the backs of Julia's eyes agreed with Camille, though not for the same reason. Buying this particular piece—living every day with the memories it conjured—might've been a mistake after all. She gave some hard blinks and Camille looked up in time to catch them.

"Hey. You okay?"

Opening the sculpture—her own personal Villa de Luca purchase—had unexpectedly exposed a raw spot on Julia's heart. She didn't want to take the chance of making it worse by talking about it . . . about him. "I . . . um . . . have a date Friday night," she said instead. She'd planned on announcing the news as soon as she got to work, but Bryan had placed the box right beside her desk after she'd left yesterday, too conspicuous to ignore, so she'd put it off until now.

Camille's eyes grew saucer-wide. "You do? Who is it? Is it somebody I know?" Suddenly her eyes narrowed to slits. "It's not Frank, is it, because if it is—"

"It's not Frank," Julia interrupted before her friend's pregnancy-charged hormones sent her off. "It's with Joe Proctor, the administrator at Hettie's nursing home. Did you meet him at the funeral?"

With the swiftness of the mood swings that had become commonplace lately, Camille's eyes widened again. "Tall guy? Good-looking . . . fiftyish?"

Julia nodded. "That's him."

"No, I didn't meet him. But . . . yay!" Camille grabbed Julia's hands and danced a little jig in place. "This is so exciting! Did he call you or did you run into him somewhere? Tell me how it all happened."

"He called last night, and at first I thought it was just PR stuff, but then he asked if I'd like to have dinner with him—"

The door chime rang, and they turned to see Sybil Lancaster bustling through the door in her usual hurried manner. "Hey, y'all, I know I'm early, but I've got ten jillion things to get done before noon, and I thought maybe you'd have those samples already pulled together for me?"

"I do, but I've got them spread out on the table in the back." Camille was already moving in that direction. "Give me a minute, and I'll pack them up."

"You need me to do that?" Julia called, but Camille waved her back. Julia turned back to Sybil. "We've got hot, spiced tea."

Sybil dropped into the chair at Julia's desk. "Only half a cup. I'm having a hot flash." She grabbed a piece of cardboard and fanned madly toward her face.

Julia moved to the table by the door, purposely placed to surround customers with the homey, cinnamon fragrance as soon as they entered. "Any good prospects on the house yet?" She poured Sybil a generous half cup.

"Not really, and I'm running myself ragged trying to do all this staging stuff myself. Thanks." Sybil accepted the cup and took a sip. "Mmmm. This is delicious."

Julia smiled. Hettie's recipe was always a hit.

"The realtor insists the staging will help it sell, but we don't have enough furniture to fill the old house and the new house, too. So I'm running my legs off, begging friends for things they have in storage and trying to find things to rent at a reasonable price to make the old house look fabulous and trying to get the new house livable at the same time. There's a huge need here for staging specialists like they have in big cities. Y'all could make a mint doing that." Sybil stopped for a breath and took a gulp of tea.

Julia's breath simply stopped.

Staging specialist.

The air in her lungs released on a gasp. "There *is* a dearth here!" How many times had she and Camille loaned pieces to help people out? Or made suggestions about what was needed? But no one around here took on all the leg work for the homeowner for the entire project.

Sybil didn't seem to notice the stir she'd created. She lifted the hair off her neck and fanned wildly again. "Furniture stores in the cities are competitive about being used for staging projects. People like the way the house is furnished and sometimes just buy everything exactly the way it's set up. It's a win-win for everybody, if you ask me."

Sybil's hot flash must have been contagious because Julia had one of her own as she looked around. No need for a warehouse or up-front costs—she could work from home. All she needed was a trustworthy reputation and an eye for detailed perfection.

She was blessed with both.

Camille appeared from the back with a plastic crate. Julia started toward her, but she shook her head. "Not heavy. Just bulky."

Sybil finished her drink with a huge gulp and jumped up to grab the container. "Thanks so much. You're a doll for getting these done so quickly. See y'all soon." She was off in a whoosh.

Camille grinned at Julia and shook her head. "Woman's always on a mission." Then she shrugged her eyebrows. "But I'm glad she was in a hurry 'cause I'm dying to hear the rest of what happened between you and Joe Proctor when he called."

Julia nodded, trying to still her breath enough to speak cohesively. "I'll finish that in a minute." She pointed to the chair. "Sit down, though. I've got something really important I need to discuss with you first. Sybil just gave me an idea for what I can do with the business when you leave. . . ."

She laughed as she took Camille's hands and repeated her friend's jig steps from a few minutes earlier.

Her heart did a jig all its own.

Although Camille's first reaction to Julia's announcement of her upcoming date was teenage excitement, as the week progressed, her business partner had taken on the personal project of preparing Julia for what Camille assumed to be her first sexual encounter since the divorce.

Julia didn't bother to correct her. Oh, in the beginning she protested sex on the first date was unthinkable. But Camille had countered with "Why not?" and a list of reasons why one should always be prepared for the unexpected.

Eventually, Julia had listened politely and glanced studiously over the numerous Internet articles Camille referred her to each day revolving around sex after breast cancer, sex after bilateral mastectomy, sex after breast reconstruction, sex after menopause, ad nauseam. Some of those people in the help groups had way too much time on their hands.

Bless her heart, Camille meant well. And when Julia protested, Camille had patiently explained, "When you care for someone, you take care of them when they need it. That's what the term means."

As Julia sat enjoying the shiatsu chair and the foot massage that was part of the mani-pedi Camille paid for and arranged for Friday afternoon, she had to admit being cared for and pampered felt pretty good—another lesson she would've learned from Hettie if she hadn't allowed her stubborn self-sufficiency to blind her.

But not anymore. Her eyes were wide open now and she was determined to view the world with a broader scope. The new business would require it.

Staging specialist—she'd been trying the title on for several days now and had decided it was a custom fit. She could see herself happy in that role for the rest of her life.

When her phone rang, she actually groaned at the intrusion and considered not answering until she saw Melissa's number. A call from her daughter on Friday afternoon was unusual. She answered with a wary "Hello?"

"Mom!" Melissa's voice was breathless. "Michael's home!"

Julia took her cue from Melissa's obviously excited tone. "That's wonderful, sweetheart. When did this happen?"

"He called me about an hour ago. Some famous Russian scientist requested a chance to be on the research team. They didn't want to turn him down, but their provisions didn't allow for anyone else to be added. They asked for volunteers to leave the team and Michael volunteered!"

She was talking fast. Julia waited for a chance to get a question in, but Melissa came up for only a quick breath before plunging in again. "He said he'd been miserable the entire time without me. Being away from me had been pure hell, and he never wanted to be away from me again."

The voice on the other line shook and Julia felt the vibration in her own heart. "How do you feel about that?"

"I love him, Mom," Melissa whispered. "I mean, I knew I loved him, but I didn't know how much until I heard him saying those things. I've taken the afternoon off, and I'm headed to his place now. I can't wait to get there."

Michael left the project. Melissa was leaving work. "Then that's where you need to be." She caught her bottom lip between her teeth to stop it from trembling as a wave of emotion engulfed her.

Melissa agreed. "Yeah, it is." A moment of silence was cut short by the sound of a car honking and then "Damn it!" exploded in Julia's ear, followed quickly by "Sorry, Mom. I better hang up before I cause an accident."

"Melissa, are you okay?"

"I'm fine. Just too excited to be talking and driving at the same time. I cut off a guy in a Hummer."

"Hang up the phone this instant, young lady."

"Okay. Love you. Bye."

Julia sank back into the massage chair and tried to allow the expert hands on her feet to lull her back into relaxed oblivion again after Melissa's call had caused her blood pressure to spike. She was on the verge of calling up her *Calm* playlist when a thought made her pause. This was exactly what Hettie had warned her about—she needed to embrace life's experience, not cut it off.

Melissa was in love. Camille was pregnant with a healthy child. She herself had an eye on the future . . . and a date tonight.

Her heart pounded faster and she did nothing to slow it—just enjoyed the feeling and let it do its own thing until it ran out of steam and slowed to its normal rhythm.

It was the simple solution to her problem—and Julia hoped Joe liked the idea as much as she did. She had a feeling he would.

Joe Proctor was a delight.

The perfect gentleman, he'd complimented her on her outfit and her hair as soon as she'd invited him in, and the past five minutes had been filled with easy conversation about Hettie, which gave a perfect time for this transition.

"Joe, before we go to dinner, I'd like to show you something and see what you think."

He gave her a quizzical look and nodded. "Sure."

She led him to the foyer, and after taking a deep breath, lifted the box and set it to the side.

Buying the Villa de Luca sculpture had been a mistake. She knew that now. She'd brought it home, thinking—hoping—she would grow used to it and her insides wouldn't throb with need every time she looked at it. So far, that hadn't happened, and she was beginning to doubt that it ever would. So, there it had sat for three days. In her foyer where she'd dropped the box over it to keep her eyes from being drawn to it.

"I would like to have this fountain set up in the garden at the nursing home in Hettie's memory if you think it would be okay."

A smile split Joe's handsome face from ear to ear. "Be okay? I think it's a wonderful idea, and so generous of you." He stooped down and ran his hand across the fine detailing, set the ball to rolling—and Julia's stomach, in turn. She swallowed repeatedly, fighting the emotions that were suddenly causing an upheaval. "Hettie loved that garden," he went on. "This will be a fitting memorial."

"I'll get all the arrangements made, then. As soon as possible." Julia pretended to look at her watch, although her eyes were too blurred to make out the time. "We probably need to be going."

Joe patted her shoulder, obviously seeing her tears and thinking they were because of Hettie.

Julia dropped the box back over the sculpture, but it was an action that was too little and too late.

She'd already been infected with a bad case of the Vitales.

Joe didn't seem to notice anything was amiss, or if he did, he accredited it to first-date jitters. He asked polite, innocuous questions about her business and the interior decorating work in general, none of which was remotely related to Vitale, but nonetheless didn't keep him from constantly flashing to Julia's frontal lobe.

She told herself the attack of the Vitales would pass soon, but she had the same feeling she always had when she talked to someone with a bit of food on his face. The more she concentrated on not seeing it, the larger it loomed. And Vitale was huge.

Once cocktails had Joe and her relaxed—or as relaxed as she was going to be—conversation moved smoothly into the "What's your favorite . . . ?" phase. She chose the topic of favorite authors carefully because she and Vitale had never talked much about books.

The eggplant spread appetizer made a perfect prop for the discussion. Not having to use utensils lent an informal air, and Joe animated his defense of Thomas Hardy by showing how a whole pita point could cut smoothly through the thick concoction with no waste of energy. Julia countered by demonstrating how a torn pita with jagged edges, symbolic of William Faulkner's stream of consciousness, grasped and held on to more of the substance. It required more work to get through, but the payoff was greater.

She tried to be absorbed by the repartee, but Joe's hand gestures reminded her so much of Vitale's animated way of speaking, even the silky texture of the eggplant spread was difficult to swallow.

When the salads arrived, she shifted the conversation to "What's your favorite type of music?" and Joe launched into a persuasive argument that would've made Grayson Chapman proud on the cross-generational timelessness of the Beatles.

Julia only half-listened as one bite of the balsamic vinaigrette dressing propelled her imagination to Vitale's dinner table . . . and how much more delicious the same mixture had tasted on his tongue when he kissed her.

"How about you?" Joe asked, and her mind tried to zip through a replay to know for sure what he was referring to, but came back fuzzy.

She settled for a coy "What about me?" and took a sip of her wine.

"What kind of music do you like?"

"I'm more of an eighties fan when I listen to rock, but most of the time I keep my dial tuned to country."

Joe's forehead wrinkled as his eyebrows shot up. "That's a surprise. I pegged you for classical."

"Because . . . ?"

He gestured toward the strand of pearls around her neck. "You have a refined quality about you. Cultured. Sophisticated."

Julia grimaced. "Stuffy?"

"Not at all." His eyes strayed ever-so-briefly to the bit of cleavage displayed by her scoop-neck tunic before meeting hers once again. "Lovely."

The warmth in his look warned Julia they'd moved into a more serious phase of flirtation, which she wasn't at all comfortable with but could come up with no reason why—except that Joe wasn't

Vitale. "Thank you," she acknowledged the compliment, and, for a moment, old insecurities knocked on her chest wall, reminding her of scars and dead nerve endings stretched across silicone sacs. A memory of Vitale's fingertip tracing the surgical lines followed quickly, bringing with it a surge of heat so strong she reached for the glass of ice water and took a gulp.

This wouldn't do. She had to stop thinking about Vitale. It wasn't fair to her or to Joe, who might misinterpret the rosy hue imbuing her face.

She pushed her salad away, unwilling to let another bite freshen her already too-strong image of the Italian.

Joe's dark brows furrowed. "Is something wrong with your salad?"

Yeah, too much de Luca undressing. "No, no," she assured him. "It's delicious. I just don't want to get filled up before the entrée gets here."

Concentrate on Joe. She flashed him a smile. *See how the silver turtleneck and black sport coat set off his hair so nicely? Ask him something. Anything.*

"Where are you originally from, Joe? Your accent doesn't sound like Kentucky." *Good girl. Now, lose yourself in his pleasant voice and pray he doesn't answer "Italy."*

Joe finished his bite. "Originally Erie, Pennsylvania. That's where my mom was from. But we moved to Dearborn, Michigan, when I was ten. My dad took a job in the Ford factory."

Julia's smile grew broader in relief. Nothing Vitale-ish there. She took a sip of wine.

"But he didn't like that. So then we moved to New Madrid, Missouri, where Dad was from, and he went into business with my grandpa building houses."

Damn! Father and son carpenters! Mayday! Julia swallowed the mouthful of wine to keep from spewing it, doubting the possibility of finding anything to talk about—or eat or drink or smell or touch or taste or hear—that wouldn't remind her of Vitale. Even the pulse swishing in her ears seemed to be whispering his name.

When the grilled salmon arrived with its sides of wilted spinach and Italian roasted potatoes, she was pretty sure she had her answer. But the dessert choices of homemade gelato and tiramisu convinced her the universe was indeed laughing its ass off at her.

The tension in the back of her neck was going to manifest into a whopper of a headache if she didn't do something fast. She excused herself to the bathroom. Within the privacy of its locked confines, she leaned against the wall, closing her eyes, wobbling her head from side to side to lessen the strain. "Vitale's not here and never will be," she whispered. Her body tensed, bracing for the pain those words never failed to elicit. The quick punch tightened her chest. "Joe *is* here, and he's a great guy." Her inhale stopped halfway down, then came back up of its own accord. She pressed on. "Interesting. Handsome." Opening her eyes, she gave herself a serious look in the mirror as she said the words slowly. "And. Close. To. Your. Age." The next breath sank deeply into her lungs, her body finally accepting the message her brain was sending.

She unlocked the door and hurried back to the table before her heart could demand time for a rebuttal.

Joe suggested an after-dinner stroll to enjoy the murals painted on the floodwall, and she readily agreed. A walk along the river in the fresh night air could make any problem seem fixable. The Ohio wove its spell, and she even allowed Joe to hold her hand as they walked.

She flinched only slightly when he asked about her trip to Italy, and *that* she explained away as the memory of the broken toe.

The light at the end of the tunnel came in the form of the lamp she'd left on in her foyer. Never had home looked so good—her safety zone. But the thought had hardly formed before the damned little voice in her head started preaching she had to invite Joe in. It was doubtful he would ask for a second date if she didn't, which satisfied her heart completely but did nothing toward silencing the little voice. It argued that a second date was required as the next step in her endeavor to get on with her life. She invited Joe in and forced a delighted smile when he accepted.

They sat at the bar and talked over another bottle of wine. She dared not move to any room with a couch that might put them so close they would touch, and the box still stood in the foyer, which expressly vetoed the living room Still, Joe seemed at ease and comfortable, and by the time she walked him to the door, she knew he was going to kiss her good night. She thought she was ready, the chaperoning sculpture notwithstanding.

They stood by the door, her hand on the knob, and Joe said he'd "like to do this again."

She lied and said it would be nice, although the words *less grueling* were shaped on the tip of her tongue. He leaned toward her and she closed her eyes and his lips pressed against hers, softly, carefully, and thankfully briefly.

A bubble of emotion swelled in her chest, pausing her breath as she closed the door behind him and watched his car pull out of the driveway, never allowing her eyes to drift to the box, which was screaming for attention through its silence. The emotion grew heavier with every step as she turned out the lights and made her way up the stairs. She flipped on the bedroom lamp and sat on the edge of the bed as the bubble grew until it squeezed the air out of her lungs, expanded until it filled her inside and no room remained. She ached from the pressure.

Fireworks exploded in her brain, sending out a volley of concussions, booming the same message repeatedly.

It wasn't the sculpture that haunted her. It was the man.

Joe Proctor was delightful . . . but he wasn't Vitale and never would be.

And neither would anyone else.

Her heartbeat accelerated.

What good was all she'd been through—all the changes—if she never tried anything new? What purpose were these new wings she'd grown if she never allowed herself to fly?

She could stand up to Frank, but not to her own feelings? She could listen to her daughter's joy, but not to the song from her own heart? She could accept Camille's care for her, but not Vitale's?

She'd been hung up on their age difference, letting her prejudice blind her. But logic argued that she couldn't make herself love someone like Joe because he was labeled with a correct number just as she couldn't not love Vitale for the same reason.

Vitale. His parents aptly named him. Life. He brought life to everything he touched. Wood. Marble. Clay. People. She'd never felt more alive than when she was yelling out her very real anger and frustration, or laughing at his funny antics and his petulant manner . . . or loving him with a passion she'd kept hidden for far too long.

Julietta wasn't a fantasy. Julietta was alive and well and her heart was beating wildly in her chest at that very moment.

And she loved a man fourteen years younger than she was.

Love transcended age and race and nationality and religion and politics.

Love filled all the gaps. Her breath came to a standstill. *All the gaps except the ones from the children Vitale won't have if he's with me.*

She forced air in and allowed the breath to clear her head.

That was his choice to make—not hers to make for him.

Another bubble swelled in her chest. This one was filled with love for the man, and it was followed by one of hope. They combined and multiplied until she felt like a human bottle of champagne.

And there was only one way to release her cork.

She flew to her computer and sent off a quick e-mail.

> Vitale,
> I've been such a fool. I love you and I'm asking for another chance to make things work between us.
> Will you forgive me?
> Julietta

Her breathing became ragged as she waited and tore from her lungs when the message returned with a Permanent Delivery Failure notice.

"It's time to put your pride and my prejudice aside, Mr. de Luca. The happy ending's there if we don't close the book too soon."

With hardly a blink, she called up the Web site for her contingency plan.

* * *

Camille was like a kid at Christmas when Julia rushed in the door the next morning. She actually bounced up and down on her toes. "How did it go?"

"Great," Julia answered. "How do you feel?"

"Great," Camille echoed.

Camille didn't lie well, and Julia searched her face for any signs of strain. "Well enough to handle the office for a week without me?"

"Absolutely." Camille's forehead wrinkled. "But why would I need to do that?"

"Because I've got some unfinished business I have to take care of in Italy."

"What?" Camille's tone implied she hadn't heard; then she repeated the word as though she had. "What?"

"I'm in love with Vitale de Luca, Camille. I've got to know if he still feels the same way." Julia was at her desk now, pulling out the files she needed to take with her to work on.

"If he *still* feels the same way? What in the hell happened the las—"

"I don't have time to explain." Julia stuffed the files in her briefcase. "My plane leaves St. Louis in six hours and that's a three-hour drive." She gave her friend a hug and headed toward the door. "I'll call you when I get on the road and explain everything."

She was taking a huge risk, flying all the way to Italy, not sure if Vitale would speak to her or even see her when she got there. But Mr. Moretti, the hotel owner, had assured her Vitale was in town—he'd seen him that morning.

So Vitale might not speak to her, but he would hear her.

And, one way or another, he would see her.

She refused to ever again be invisible.

To anyone.

Chapter 31

Coming to Italy might not be the stupidest thing she'd ever done, but it was the most impetuous.

Julia was convinced now that the stupidest thing she'd ever done was letting Mr. Moretti talk her into allowing his son to drive her to Vitale's. When he said he'd arrange for a car, she'd assumed a rental. What she'd gotten was an eighteen-year-old Jeff Gordon wannabe whose primary goal in life was to waste as much gasoline as possible.

After throwing on the brakes to creep around a curve, he once again slammed the accelerator down. His driving made that first ride with Vitale seem like gliding across ice.

Julia held the dashboard in a death grip and spoke through gritted teeth. "Slow down!"

Lino grinned and shook his head. "My father says I should drive very fast to get to Vitale's before he leaves."

A flair of apprehension shot through Julia's system. Did Mr. Moretti know something he didn't tell her? He hadn't been very forthcoming with any details about Vitale. Only that he saw Vitale often because he'd commissioned another sculpture for the pool area of the hotel and Vitale had been hard at work on it for some time. "Why would he leave? Does he know I'm coming?"

"I do not know, signora. But he always has lunch with his family on Sunday."

"Oh geez! Sunday family lunch," she whined, pounding her head against the seatback a few times. "I was in such a hurry to get here, I didn't think about the hazards of arriving on Sunday morning." But if they caught Vitale before he left his house, it would certainly make things easier. "Can't you go any faster?" she snapped.

Lino laughed and stomped the accelerator to the floor. "Vitale teach me to drive. I go very fast."

Julia snorted as she braced herself. "Well, that explains it."

Her body eventually adapted to the movement to the point where she felt like she could let go. Between lurches, she attempted to freshen her makeup and hair again. On the train, she'd had a chance to tidy up a little and change clothes, but the dark circles under her eyes required a new coat of concealer and powder. Another coat of mascara was out of the question with Lino's driving, though. She wanted to arrive with both eyes intact.

They pulled into the long, winding drive that led to Vitale's house. Her pulse quickened as she watched a whisper of smoke rising over the trees.

Lino must have noticed it, too. His dark eyes danced with merriment. "A fire in the fireplace? That is a good sign, yes?"

"I hope so," Julia muttered.

The house came into view. How could such a tranquil scene cause such trepidation in her soul?

Before Lino brought the car to a complete stop, she was already getting out.

"I wait," Lino called after her.

She strode to the door and knocked, then stepped back and waited, holding her breath.

This was taking a chance. It had been three months. He might be with someone else. Maybe in bed with her right then. Maybe Francesca.

Julia blinked away the image and pounded on the door so hard her knuckles hurt.

She'd prepared herself for Vitale with someone else. She'd gone over and over the scenario a thousand times in her mind on the plane. If it came to a choice and he chose someone else, that would be okay. It would hurt like hell, but it would be okay. She was a survivor.

Never having the choice was the option she couldn't live with the rest of her life.

When no answer came, she hurried around to the back door and peered through the glass.

The kitchen area was empty.

She could see the door to the bedroom slightly ajar and beyond it to the bed. Her eyes misted over and a small cry erupted from her lips.

The bed was empty. Already made.

She pounded on the glass, but there was no movement anywhere to answer her knock.

Vitale wasn't there. He must have left the embers smoldering so they'd be easy to stir back up.

Now she had a decision. She could wait for him to come home. Wait for hours probably. She could go back to the hotel and come back later. Her heart was pounding so fast and so hard, she wasn't sure it could take hours of this. She needed to do this and get it over with. As quickly as possible.

She retraced her steps back to the car and got in. "He's not here."

Without waiting for further instruction, Lino shrugged and threw the car into gear. "I have been to Piero and Angelina's house many times, signora. I know the way."

Vitale was three bites into his gnocchi when the question came. He'd been waiting for it . . . making wagers in his mind on who would be brave enough to bring up a subject sure to incite his anger. It was Giada's husband, Michele, who took the dare.

"How did you get the big dent across the hood of your new car, Vitale?"

All talking at the table ceased. If Vitale wasn't mistaken, someone even dropped his or her fork.

"A limb hit it as I left Francesca's last night," he answered, and took another bite to keep from smiling.

"Oh, that's right. You and Francesca were at Simba together last night." Michele grinned around the glass he held poised at his lips. "You were eating and dancing. And the word in town is a reconciliation is in the works."

"Is this true, Vitale?" Mama's voice held an excited, hopeful note. "Have you and Francesca gotten back together?"

Vitale took his time answering, first wiping his mouth on his napkin, then replacing it in his lap and smoothing it out. He wanted his answer to be slow and deliberate and heard by everyone so it couldn't be misconstrued. "Yes, Francesca and I were at Simba together last night. Yes, we ate and danced. No." He spread his eye contact around the table. "We are not getting back together. We were finished long ago."

"But why, Vitale?" Mama again, this time with a much more impatient tone. "Francesca is a beautiful woman. Such beautiful children you would have."

"Francesca is not the type of woman I see myself marrying and having a family with." Vitale took another bite of his food, hoping he had put an end to the conversation for good.

"I cannot imagine why not." Obviously Mama was not going to let it go so easily today. "What more could you want? She is beautiful and nice, and she gets along with our family well. . . ."

Vitale had grown weary of this same conversation, week after week. Month after month. There was only one way to put a stop to it. Mama had left him with no alternative. "Nice women do not see other men behind my back. She is unfaithful."

This time, there was no doubt whose fork fell. Vitale watched Mama's clatter to the table as her mouth dropped open in surprise—not only at the information about Francesca, but also that he would announce such news at the Sunday family gathering.

Her eyes fixed on him, wide and horror-stricken, and he watched as they softened in sympathy toward him and hatred toward Francesca all at the same time. He wouldn't want to be Francesca the next time she ran into Angelina.

He turned his attention back to his gnocchi, remembering the events as they'd played out last night—how quickly things on the ride home had shifted when Francesca informed him he needed to get a phone.

"I do not like phones," he'd said. "They disturb my work."

She ran a finger around the outside of his ear. "But you could call me, and I could say all kinds of hot things to you when we're not together."

He'd realized Francesca was seeing this hookup as the beginning of something more permanent rather than what it actually was.

Casual sex.

No promise of tomorrow.

His conscience had niggled that he wasn't being honest . . . but she hadn't been honest with him about her intentions for the night either.

"You're so old-school." She'd laughed, and he had to admit to himself she was right.

And then she said something else. "I was afraid that old woman you were with . . . what was her name? Julietta?"

Old woman? Julietta? His foot involuntarily pressed the gas pedal.

"I was afraid she'd make you even worse, but apparently I was wrong."

"Yes, you were wrong. Julietta was very good for me." The words punched him in the chest even now. She *had* been good for him . . . in so many ways. He'd been a different man when he was with Julietta.

A better man.

Francesca's hand had smoothed down his side and between his legs, where she'd stroked him again. "I'm glad to see some things haven't changed, though."

Again, her words burned into him.

Some things hadn't changed. That much was true. He *was* still old-school about many matters in his life. Having a telephone was only one.

But he was also still old-school in his belief that faithfulness was the foundation in a relationship. That once trust had left, it was gone for good. That sex without love was an empty and meaningless act.

That forgiveness was no good unless it could be followed by forgetting.

His feelings for the woman in the seat beside him had taken shape with one blow of the hammer. He didn't love her and never would. He wasn't even sure he liked her.

They'd pulled into her drive. He stopped the car, got out, went around and opened her door.

She got out and pushed herself against him, clasping her arms around his neck.

He reached up and loosened her hands, and said, "Thank you for dinner, Francesca. I had a nice time."

She'd stepped back and looked at him, confusion evident in her eyes. "Aren't you coming in?"

"No," he answered. "Not tonight and not ever. We're finished."

He'd gone back around to the driver's side, hearing the strangled frustration when it left her throat. And as he started the engine, she rushed over to a fallen limb lying on the ground and snatched it up.

He backed up quickly, but not before the limb came smashing down across the shiny silver hood.

He probably should be angry—the old Vitale would be—but instead, he couldn't hold back the laugh at the bizarre scene.

He'd waved as he pulled away, seeing her reflection in his rearview mirror, still holding the limb over her head, prepared to inflict another blow. Even in the darkness he could make out the dent across the hood, marring the newness.

The image settled in his chest.

His auto wasn't new anymore. It was old-school like him. And the dent Francesca left on it was a small price to pay considering the one she would have left on his heart.

The rest of the table was quiet, and Vitale was so caught up in the memory, he didn't bother to look at the sound of the auto coming to a stop in front of the house.

It wouldn't dare be Francesca . . . and no one else's presence could throw his world into chaos.

"Vitale." Adrianna touched him softly on the arm.

He looked up and followed her gaze to the window.

"Julietta!" The name exploded from his mouth as the world around him lost all of its defining parameters.

He stood up with such force his chair creaked as it slid across the wooden floor.

Breathing slowly in and pushing out each breath, he made his way to the front door.

Lino slammed on the brakes, bringing the car to a screeching halt in front of the home of Vitale's parents.

Julia scanned the yard. Autumn had brought little change to the cedar trees and rosemary bushes. A prickle of déjà vu raised goose bumps on her arms, but she pushed away the memory of her first visit here.

No more dwelling in the past, She'd reached the point of no return. If Vitale rejected her—and he had every right to do that— she would leave and not look back.

No regrets.

She pulled the handle of the door, felt the latch loosen. Pushing it open took all her strength, and she stood on wobbly legs.

She turned back and leaned down to meet Lino's wide-eyed stare. "Wait for me," she instructed.

He nodded solemnly.

Her legs moved faster than her mind thought prudent with the uneven paving stones beneath her feet. She ordered her legs to slow down, but the adrenaline pumping into her system insisted on an outlet. Halfway up the walkway, she saw the great front door swing open, and Vitale stepped out.

Everything—breath, strength, logic—left in a rush as the jolt of seeing him again slammed into her. She became aware she'd stopped moving after the fact. Their eyes locked, and she watched his darken and narrow in unspoken question, saw his bottom lip droop into that brooding pout.

"Hello, Vitale."

"*Buon giorno,* Julietta."

The actual sound of his voice after so many months vibrated through her, shaking her center of gravity. She waited for him to say something else, show his surprise, order her away.

He remained silent. Stoic.

Not the welcome she'd imagined in her fantasy world, but he was here in the flesh, so it wasn't her nightmare either. Nevertheless, perspiration broke out across her upper lip. She faked a cough and dabbed it away. "I know this is crazy ... the craziest thing I've ever done ... coming all this way and surprising you like this, but you don't have a phone and you keep bouncing my e-mails, and I had to know if you still love me, and if you still want to try to make things work for us as a couple."

She was aware of talking much too fast, but she'd wrestled control from her brain and given it to her heart, and she wouldn't stop now.

"I know I wrote you that I want to be friends. But I lied. I was letting my perspective of the world dictate my life. I don't want to just be your friend. I want to be the person you love. And I know it might be over between us, but I can't love anyone else unless I know for sure that it is." He moved forward, and her chest seized. Her speech stopped on a ragged intake of breath.

Taking only the few steps that brought him from the surround of rosemary into the open, he planted his feet and crossed his arms in front of him.

Julia was determined not to mirror his defensive gesture. She forced her hands to let go of each other and dropped her arms loosely to her side, palms out and open in invitation.

She waited, watching for any sign of acceptance or rejection, but his face remained impassive, chiseled in stone.

"I was foolish to let the difference in our ages be a factor," she said. "A number can't determine who I love. It took me a while to figure that out, but I've figured it out now and I'm hoping you can understand...."

Vitale's hand shot out in a stop gesture, cutting off her air from ten feet away. He moved toward her slowly.

This was it. She tried to read his expression, but found nothing that hinted at either acceptance or rejection. Locking her knees was a mistake, but she did it anyway, determined to stay strong and face whatever was coming. She fought the urge to glance back and make sure Lino was still there, offering quick escape.

Vitale advanced until he stood only a foot away, invading her space, invading her senses. The temperature rose slightly as a result of his close proximity. His breathing echoed in her ears. She inhaled, letting his familiar scent permeate her nostrils and lungs, lingering with subtlety on her tongue.

He filled her vision until she saw nothing but him.

"Julietta." He spoke low and the darkness of his tone haunted his eyes. "I do not accept the e-mail because the message, she tear my heart. I suffer much."

He was so close now. She longed to touch him, but that would be a mistake. One touch and her self-composure would evaporate. She clasped her hands together and held on tightly. "I'm sorry I hurt you. I thought I was doing you a favor. Setting you free to love someone else closer to your age, someone you can have children with. But then I realized how good we were for each other. We brought out the best in each other, and that's what love should do. And the decision to have children or not is yours. Not one I should make for you."

"Julietta, you speak too quickly. I do not understand all you say." He inched closer. "I think you return to me, yes?"

"Yes." Her voice drifted into a whisper.

"You return to me and stay with me forever?"

"If you want me to, yes." Her mouth formed the word, but the lack of breath behind it nullified any sound. She nodded for emphasis, trying to make him understand.

The dawn of understanding broke through the darkness in his eyes.

The touch of his large, warm hands was agonizingly tender when he cupped her face, and her bottom lip quivered in response. He stilled it with a brush of his lips.

His hands dropped away from her face, replaced by his arms enfolding her, pulling her to him. She felt gloriously pinned against the stone wall of his body as his mouth closed down on hers with more intensity. Vibrant heat coursed through her veins, and she threw her arms around his neck, meeting his grip with the strength and certainty of her own.

Their mouths met. Their tongues danced. Their bodies melted together in the heat of the embrace. Their hearts fused.

The world faded completely and Vitale became all the world right then.

She could have—maybe would have—stood there kissing him forever, had the sound of giggles not developed into laughter and then noisy chatter all about them.

She forced her reluctant mouth to let go of Vitale's and let her eyes focus on the outside world again.

"Ah!" A surprised gasp tore from her kiss-swollen lips. The world was full of people. Vitale's family. She'd expected them to stay in the house, but they obviously wanted to be a part of this happy scene, and that warm thought filled her heart to bursting.

Adrianna was the first to squeal and rush to them, joining their embrace, and then Julia was in the middle of a group hug, arms embracing her from every angle including around her knees.

She laughed and Vitale laughed with her, his eyes gleaming as he kissed her again.

But as quickly as they'd appeared, the embraces from his family evaporated as everyone got quiet and stepped away.

Glancing around for the cause of the sudden abandonment, Julia's gaze ran headlong into Angelina's. She stood ready to meet the challenge in his mother's eyes.

"Angelina, I know you don't approve of my relationship with Vitale." Her voice remained calm, drawing strength from Vitale's arm resting around her shoulder. "And, as a mother, I know you want what's best for your child." She looked up at Vitale's face, and the love in his eyes propelled her forward, out of his hold.

She walked over to stand in front of his mother, meeting her woman-to-woman. "I may be older than he is, but what's best for Vitale is what makes Vitale happy. And I intend to make Vitale very, very happy. I can't give him children, so he has a decision to make. But I'll accept whatever he decides. I love him that much."

Someone, one of Vitale's sisters, translated. Julia dared not break eye contact long enough to acknowledge who was speaking.

And so it was Angelina who broke the eye contact, shifting her gaze up and beyond Julia. She asked a question, and Julia heard Vitale's strong, "*Sì,* Mama." Her scrutiny turned again to Julia.

The tightness around Angelina's eyes softened, but only minutely. When she spoke, Julia listened intently to try and comprehend, but came up blank except for the words *Adrianna* and *Vitale.*

Vitale's voice came from close beside her. "She say you help Adrianna the very much when she fear the cancer and you love the mother-in-law. You are the good woman."

A smile budded on Julia's lips despite the tears that blurred her vision.

Angelina said something else, and pointed to Vitale and then to Julia.

Vitale took a deep breath. "She say she do not think you stay with Vitale, but she hope to be wrong."

Julia nodded, holding Angelina's gaze. "That's fair. Time is the test for all things. . . . I'll take as long as I need to prove myself."

Vitale repeated her words in Italian.

Angelina's eyebrow rose in a "we'll see" gesture that Julia returned. A half smile told Julia the message had been received. Then Angelina motioned toward the house. "Come. We eat."

As she allowed herself to be towed toward the house, Julia remembered Lino. She needed to tell him it was okay to leave and threw a quick glance over her shoulder. To her surprise, Vitale was already loading her luggage into a different car while Lino walked up the walkway accompanied on one side by Celeste and Orabella on the other.

Angelina scurried to set two more places at the table as everyone settled back down to their half-finished meal.

Vitale leaned over and whispered to Julia, his warm breath a sensuous caress around her ear, "We do not stay long, *bella mia.*"

She reached for his hand and gave it a squeeze. "*Ti amo,* Vitale."

In response, he kissed her softly on the cheek.

"I have the need to speak with her." Vitale watched Julietta's reaction, unsure what to expect but breathing easier when she showed no anger or animosity and merely nodded.

"I understand. Take as long as you need. You and I need to talk, too."

He kissed her fingers, a gesture he hoped conveyed he could love her for that statement alone.

Excusing himself, he went in search of Mama, who'd remained conspicuously absent from the gathering since the meal and clean-up duties were finished. Despite her welcome to Julietta, her demeanor had grown more sullen with any reference to his and Julietta's future . . . and the references had been many. So by the end of the meal, Mama's tight-faced scowl looked like a clay mask that had been pushed in on the sides.

She thought he was making a mistake, and he knew in his heart he wasn't—a regretful impasse, sure to go on for years. Perhaps to the end of her days. But he couldn't let it begin in earnest without first trying to soothe away as much of the pain as possible.

He found her the first place he looked—in the olive grove. "Mama."

She turned to him with weepy eyes that said she knew he'd come—had, in fact, been waiting for him. He held out his hand and tucked her arm in close to his side. "Walk with me."

They made their way slowly along the path, deeper into the surround of trees, out of view from the house. She leaned into him as she walked, sniffing and wiping her eyes. When it became evident she wasn't going to start the conversation, he did, leading with, "I told you she would come back."

"And I told you she will not stay," came the matter-of-fact retort.

He gave her a sidelong glance and shook his head. "You do not really believe that. You cry because you know she *will* stay." Her grip on his bicep tightened, indicating he'd hit a nerve. "And, therefore, because of the grandchildren you will never have."

Her voice exploded from her chest on a sob. "I cry because you obviously have not thought this through. Not like I have, Vitale." When her chin quivered, his chest tightened in response. "Since the day you were born, I have thought of little else. Thirty-four years I have imagined the handsome line of sons you would produce." She halted midstep and tugged his arm to turn him toward her, stretching up to take his face in her hands. "Sons like yourself, who would carry on the proud name of de Luca. Am I to toss those dreams away as if they never existed?"

The callused palms caressing his cheeks twisted his insides. Hard and rough, they were living evidence of how hard his parents had worked to give him and his sisters a good life. How could one possibly repay such a debt? Despite her dramatic posturing, Mama asked little in return.

But what she asked, he was unwilling to give. He needed to make her understand.

"I grieve for the children I will not have, Mama. I will not deny that. That grief was especially strong after Luciana died and burdened me a great deal in the years that followed. I would lie awake at night and think, *If only we had had a child together. If only a part of her remained that I could physically hold and watch grow.*" The poignant memory sliced his heart wide open, and he didn't try to hold back the tear that slid down his cheek. "I even thought of getting someone pregnant—someone I didn't love—just to have a child. But that would be wrong, would it not?"

Mama brushed his tear away and nodded. "Yes, Vitale, that would be wrong."

"But now, the person I love cannot have children. Do I stop loving her because of this? If Luciana could not have had children, would it have been right to stop loving her?"

"No, of course not." She patted his cheeks, and he turned his head to place a reverent kiss on each of her palms.

"You and I agree on this." He took her hands and cradled them against his chest, so she could feel his heart as well. "But there is more that I need to speak from my heart, Mama, and I pray that yours will listen. I do not ask you to toss the dreams away—only that you modify them to accept the path my life has chosen." He drew a long breath. "I have, in fact, produced a line of sons that carry on the proud name of de Luca."

The way her eyes went suddenly wide with dismay caused him to smile. "My work," he said. "The pieces I create—each one is my child that I breathe life into . . . that I nurture and grow into a form I am pleased to present to the world bearing the de Luca name.

These—my creations . . . my children—will be around for many generations, I think. Probably long after you and I have left this world. They will remain, and the name will remain. This is the life I have chosen, and Julietta is the woman I have chosen to share that life with if all goes as I hope."

A tear slid down Mama's cheek. "But those children cannot fill the seats around your table when you are old," she whispered, her voice heavy with emotion and what he realized was selfless concern. "Cannot hold your hand when you lie dying in your bed."

He shook his head. "No, you are right about this. But Julietta has a daughter who will perhaps fill the seats around our table with grandchildren. And when I lie dying in my bed, I hope it is Julietta's hand that I still hold in mine. I love her, Mama. She makes me happy. A parent cannot wish a better life for a child than to see him happy and fulfilled, surrounded by love."

Mama looked at him long and hard, scanning every inch of his face. Finally, she drew a long breath and shook her head. "Such talk, Vitale." The corners of her mouth drew up slightly, but not all the way into a smile. "You are too much like your father."

He tilted his head and gave her a grin. "With the perfect amount of Mama mixed in."

She chuckled as he tucked her hand once again against his side and started to walk, though he wanted to run.

This time, they headed in the direction of the house.

Where Julietta waited . . . holding out her heart to him.

Exactly the way he had seen it with his own.

Julia woke, lying on her side with Vitale's arm curled protectively around her waist. She blinked, allowing her eyes to become accustomed to the darkness.

They'd been so preoccupied with each other when they arrived at Vitale's, she hadn't looked around much. From what she could see now in the dim moonlight, the bedroom looked the same as it did the morning she left in such a hurry. Nothing had changed . . . nothing discernible by vision.

In reality, many changes had occurred on the ride home and in the quiet times in between their lovemaking.

Vitale now owned a car, the one he'd moved her luggage to. But he still had his Benelli, thank God. She would've been terribly disappointed if that had been gone for good. But he explained he was in constant need of a bigger vehicle to move his pieces, and he couldn't keep borrowing Adrianna's. He was making a living full time as an artist now, the change he was most proud of.

He'd asked her to move to Italy to be with him and she'd agreed. She'd asked him to come to the US and be with her while she took care of settling the changes in the business and putting her house on the market, and he'd agreed.

Lots of changes. Exciting changes.

But for now, they had a week to relax together and map out the future. She smiled, and her cheeks ached slightly. She realized she'd been smiling for hours, even in her dreams.

She snuggled back against his naked body, so warm and firm even at rest. His arm adjusted to her move, pulling her closer.

"You are awake, Julietta?"

"Yeah, the time change has my system screwed up." She shifted around to relax her cheek against his, noting the bit of telltale soreness between her legs as she moved. While their second round of making love last evening had been slow and gentle, the first had been wild and rough with pent-up passion.

She did have something on her mind, though—something they needed to talk about and now seemed as good a time as any. They'd discussed it . . . sort of, but she had to know he understood without question. She tilted her head back a few inches, meeting his eyes in the soft light. "Vitale, we said many things in the heat of passion the past few hours."

His mouth slid into a lazy grin. "*Sì,* Julietta."

"You understand I'm through menopause, right? I'm unable to have any more children."

His grin disappeared, replaced by a somber look of reflection. "I know this, Julietta. I have thought on this the much since I know you and love you." His palm smoothed down her arm, warming her where it touched. "Is not for me to have the children if I must give you up. She make me the sad, yes. But not the sad I would feel if I could not have my Julietta. I cannot exchange the Julietta I know for the children I do not. But my work, she is my children—my creation that I give to the world that will continue the name. And I pray that Melissa, she fill our life with the children also, yes? Someday?"

He was thinking of Melissa's children as his grandchildren already? Julia thought her heart might explode with joy any minute now. "Oh, I hope so, Vitale."

There was something else, though . . . something she needed him to understand. "And, Vitale, I can't be your penance for losing Luciana. You can't spend your life trying to fix me—can't live in fear of losing me."

He sighed. "Adrianna, she say I do this. And so I try to not do this. But when I love, she is difficult."

She could tell he had more to say, so she stayed quiet and listened.

"I think to feex my Julietta."

The words caused her to stiffen, but he shook his head. "Not the body. I feex the heart. Not the feex, *riparato.* The feex, *preparato.* I prepare Julietta's heart to love, yes."

His hands slid around her back as she wrapped him in a hug. In the quiet of the night, she breathed an unspoken word of thanks for this man and the circumstances that brought him into her life.

"Do you mind to leave the bed for some time? I have the something in the studio I want to show you." The excitement in his voice caused the hair on her neck to rise in anticipation.

She located yesterday's trousers and sweater, flung in opposite directions of the room, and slipped into them while Vitale pulled on some jeans and a heavy sweatshirt. He tossed an additional sweatshirt her way. "You need. She is cold this time of the morning before the sunrise."

The fleece-lined garment was as long on her as a coat, and just as toasty. Vitale's chuckle at the sight warmed her to the point she thought she would have to come out of it to keep from overheating. She was glad she didn't, though, when she stepped through the sliding door onto the patio and the brisk air whirled around her.

Millions of stars danced in the clear sky overhead, making her want to break out into a joyful rendition of "Sh-Boom." She stopped for a moment to take in the beauty of it all. Millions of worlds to be explored. Millions of wishes to be granted. Millions of dreams to come true.

She had only one. That Hettie could see her and know she was happy.

A warm air stirred around her as Vitale pulled her close. She could swear a voice in the breeze whispered her wish had been granted.

Vitale's heartbeat thumped hard against her ear. "Come," he said. "You see." He led her to the back of the yard toward his studio. "Do you remember I tell you Mario commission the sculpture for the pool?" His eyes glittered in the starlight.

Julia nodded. "Yeah, and he mentioned yesterday you'd been working on it. Is that what you want to show me?"

"*Sì.*" The stars dancing in his eyes disappeared when he flung open the door and blinded her by flipping on the bright light.

She blinked away the blindness and then blinked in confusion. Astonishment caused her to blink one more time.

She wasn't only standing in Vitale's studio with both feet planted firmly on the ground. Another Julia lay right in front of her on a table, resting on her elbows with her legs bent, face upturned to catch the rays of the sun, bare breasts thrust out proudly.

She swallowed, too stunned to speak.

Every detail was perfect, right down to the thin lines etched across the middle of both breasts. *My God, he's even included my scars.* She pressed a shaky hand to her mouth.

"You like, yes?" Vitale asked, hope and pride mixing in his voice. "She to be perfect by the pool, I think."

"I . . . I don't know what to say." This was something so far out of her world of experience, she had nothing to weigh it against for like or dislike.

Vitale's arms came around her waist from behind, and he rested his chin on her head. "From the day on the beach, I dream of capturing you in the moment forever. The photograph, she is the not enough"—he paused and gestured toward the clay model—"the not enough Julietta."

Worded in such a manner, how could she not love it?

She laughed, giddy with excitement. "I love it, Vitale. I think it's fabulous."

He hugged her close, leaning down to kiss the smile she turned up toward him. When he straightened, she saw his eyes scan the sculpture, watched his bottom lip droop into that pout that signaled his displeasure. "One imperfection I feex, though."

Her eyes settled on the scars across the sculpted breasts. While it was a lovely gesture for him to include them, he would surely smooth them out before the clay mold went for its casting in bronze. "The scars," she said. "You'll take them out?"

Vitale's look suggested she'd grown a second nose. "Remove the scars? No, I work very hard to make the scars. I tell you I do not feex my Julietta, yes? She is perfect." He grabbed her hand and pulled her to the head of the table, pointing at one of the ears, and shaking his head disgustedly. "The imperfection, she is the earlobe. I attach to the side of the face." He flipped her lobe lightly with his finger. "She is not attach."

Julia laughed, and when Vitale's eyebrows drew together in a dark frown, she laughed even harder. "She is not funny, Julietta. She is the serious mistake. I must feex."

Julia took Vitale's face in her hands and smoothed away his frown lines with her thumbs. "*Ti amo*, Vitale."

His mouth curved into a smile, and the heat in his look warmed her to her toes. "*Ti amo, bella mia,*" he whispered before he captured her detached earlobe between his parted lips.

Julia's head spun with happiness, with the changes the past few years had wrought in her life—the losses and gains. The loss of her breasts, the gain of new confidence. The loss of Frank, the gain of new love. The loss of Hettie, the gain of a new perspective. The loss of Camille, the gain of an opportunity for a new business venture. For every action there was a reaction, for every push a pull. The laws of nature gave balance to an ever-shifting world.

She'd wanted visibility? Well, Vitale had certainly fixed that. She smiled as her eyes shifted again to her uncanny likeness on the table beside them. He'd captured her perfectly—a lovely work of art—but only for that snapshot in time.

Julia was changing . . . would always be changing . . . a perpetual work-in-progress.

But, like Hettie, she'd finally summoned her courage and stepped through the darkness into the unknown. A world of light and beauty had been there all along, waiting for her on the other side.

And perhaps a taste of immortality as well.

Keep reading for more from Pamela Hearon,
including a behind-the-book essay
and a Reading Group Guide.

THE STORY BEHIND THE STORY

As a writer, I've had one question asked of me in almost every interview I've ever done: *Do you pull material from your real-life experiences?* And, of course, my answer is, "Yes." I'm not sure it would be possible to write situations and characters who draw readers into stories if I didn't tap into my own gut reactions and instincts. Even the villains are filtered through my perceptions of what their thoughts and actions would be.

Now, I realize when that question comes around, most people are referring subtly (and sometimes not so subtly) to the more intimate scenes, and to those people I also happily reply, "Yes," and boast that I'm making my husband a legend in his own time. He gets plenty of ribbing from his friends around the breakfast table at the restaurant where they meet every day to solve the world's problems.

To be honest, I'll tell you up front that my husband, Dick, was upset when he first read *Gaining Visibility,* terrified readers would think I'd modeled the antagonist after him, though nothing could be further from the truth. He was my rock throughout the ordeal: supportive, loving—everything a caring person should be and the exact opposite of the character I wrote.

Which brings me to the story behind the story.

In 2007, I was diagnosed with breast cancer. We live in a very small town where my husband had a very successful furniture store and for fifteen years I was *the* eighth-grade Language Arts teacher at the only middle school. Between us, we knew everybody. So when word of my diagnosis got out (did I mention how quickly news travels in a small town?), friends and neighbors immediately began calling and dropping by to offer their love, prayers, and support to see me through the next two difficult years.

One elderly gentleman who was especially close to Dick stopped by one day and during the course of his visit, he told me how, when he was a child, his mother had also been diagnosed with breast cancer. Radical mastectomy was the only option available to her at the time, and she faced the inevitable with a strength and dignity that stayed with him these many years after.

He also confided that, after his mother's surgery, his father never touched her again.

His story broke my heart and, to this day, still brings tears to my eyes. To think that this woman fought the physical and mental battle placed before her, only to be shunned at the end by the very person who had vowed to stay by her side through everything, haunted me.

His story brought pangs of guilt that I got off so easily . . . that I had so much support . . . that I had never felt so loved by so many, but especially the man I shared my life with.

I didn't write much during those two years. Other things were more important, and life always takes precedence. But as soon as I started writing again, my fingers flew across the keys with a determination to right the wrong done to this woman and all those like her.

My purpose? To let them know they are not invisible. They are not alone.

And, in the only way I know how, to give each of them the happy ending she deserves.

GAINING VISIBILITY

Pamela Hearon

About This Guide

The suggested questions are included
to enhance your group's reading of
Pamela Hearon's *Gaining Visibility*.

DISCUSSION QUESTIONS

1. Julia Berkwith feels invisible to the world after her bout with breast cancer and her divorce. Have you ever felt "invisible"—as if no one could see the real you? What did you do or what could you have done to remedy the situation?

2. Julia goes to Italy to hike the Cinque Terre in celebration of her health and her victory over cancer. Share a time when you did something special for yourself in celebration of a personal victory.

3. The word *visibility* has two different meanings. It can refer to how well something can be seen (Her book's visibility at the front of the bookstore thrilled the author's family.), or it can refer to the range of view from the perspective of the viewer (The pilot's visibility increased by twenty miles when he dropped below the clouds.). In what ways does the author focus on each of these definitions during the course of the story?

4. The main theme of a book can be thought of as the most important life lesson learned by the main character over the course of the story. What do you consider to be the main theme of *Gaining Visibility*? What other themes presented themselves to you as you read?

5. Julia and Vitale both deal with issues of "invisibility." In what ways are their issues similar? In what ways are they different?

6. Individually, what do you consider to be Julia's and Vitale's greatest strengths? How do these strengths work to bring them together?

7. Individually, what do you consider to be Julia's and Vitale's greatest weaknesses? How do these weaknesses work to push them apart?

8. At the end of the book, Julia and Vitale's mother, Angelina, have not quite made peace. How do you see their relationship progressing in the future?

9. Hettie adds both comic relief and seriousness to the story. Share a story about someone who has played those same roles in your life.

10. Hettie is Julia's mentor. Do you have, or have you had, someone you consider to be your mentor? In what ways did your mentor lead you to discover new things about yourself?

11. Julia is prejudiced against a relationship with Vitale because of the difference in their ages. What are your thoughts about their age difference?

12. Frank and Vitale are written as very different characters, yet they both love Julia, which would indicate at least some similarities in their personalities. Did you find similarities between the two? Share your thoughts.

Connect with U S